Acknowledge

Firstly, a huge thank you to my small bu
anyone who has read one of my books.
review, to anyone who has spread the word and shared their
enthusiasm. Thank you so very much.

A special mention must go to my core beta reader Hannah Gallyon.
You were a massive help and support with this book, and in fact with
all my books. I don't know what I'd do without your brutally honest
advice!

Thank you also to Justine Pateman for the artwork on the front cover
and the illustration at the back of the book and to Luke Fielding for
creating a finished front cover for me. To Shalaena Medford for
formatting the ebook and for Steph Gravell for formatting the
paperback; thank you lovely ladies!

For this book, I must also thank those early readers on Wattpad. To
those who read the book in the very first draft, as it was being written,
and kindly left comments and feedback.

Finally, I must thank my four beautiful children. This book was
written for you for two reasons. One, I wanted to write a book that
would be suitable for you all to read! And two, because this story was
inspired by our love of Nature and our hopes for a better world.

For Daisy, Ruby, Dylan and Johnny.

The Tree of Rebels

Chantelle Atkins

'They tried to bury us…

They didn't know we were seeds…'

(Mexican Proverb)

'Until they become conscious

They will never rebel.'

(George Orwell)

Before

'We never thought that the bombs would come for us...because we lived here...You never think about bombs coming for you in a country like this...You think that bombs are for other children in other countries.

Until suddenly they are not.

Until suddenly your house is dust and you are running for your life.

Until people are screaming and burning and dying all around you.

Until everything the crazy people said has come true and no one even knows who is fighting who anymore, or why, because the whole world has gone crazy.

And then, it's just about who survives...'

Elizabeth Wakefield, 2075

Chantelle Atkins

1: I Am Lissie Turner

'For no more war and no more fear...we thank you all, we thank you all...'

I was thinking about what Grandma said when I saw the dog that was not supposed to exist. The dog that changed my life.

I was thinking and singing as I walked along the dusty path towards home. I looked up to a soundless, grey sky, and then down to the clouds of brown dust that circled around my ankles as my sandals moved through them.

'For food to eat and clothes to wear...we thank you all, we thank you all...'

I was singing the song and thinking about what she told me last night;

'It happened while we were all online.'

What a thing to say! She spoke these words through her parched and toothless mouth, while her claw like hands gripped mine. I didn't know what they meant, of course. We hardly ever knew what Grandma Elizabeth was talking about.

'That's how it started, Lissie...while we were all online so much, that we didn't notice, or we didn't care...'

And then she fell asleep. That was so typical of Grandma. My mother and father often said that she was not long for this world. Grandma often said that we didn't have much time, but that time was all we had.

The Tree of Rebels

The Song Of Thanks was mixing and sloshing about with her words inside my head, as I walked slowly towards home. I'd been thinking about it all so much that my temples ached with it. I had a lot on my mind, to be honest. Not just Grandma and the strange things she tried to tell me when my parents weren't listening, but the fact that I was soon to turn fourteen and become an adult. That meant leaving school and childhood behind me. I was not entirely sure I was ready for this change, but there was nothing I could do about it. My mother and father didn't think I had it in me yet, and they were probably right.

'*You have your head in the clouds, Lissie,*' they would have said to me if they'd seen me walking home from school in a daze while I murmured the lyrics to everyone's favourite song. '*She's in another dream.*' Sometimes they said it in this soft and smiling sort of way, as if dreams were worthwhile, and then other times they said it whilst rolling their eyes at each other. They sounded sort of clipped and huffed, and they made me feel like I had missed something but I was never sure what. Mum sometimes said that Grandma Elizabeth had a strange effect on me. She said that we met inside each others minds.

With my parents' words invading my thoughts, I remembered to stop when I saw something that did not belong. Curled, green leaves pushing up through the cracks of the dry, brown earth. I stooped down, swung my satchel around and pulled out a piece of chalk. It felt like my mother and father were watching me with their breath held, as I did what I was supposed to do, and drew a neat, white circle around the unknown, unwanted plant. Dusting my hands off on my dress, I sighed, put the chalk away and carried on.

It was just me on the tramped and worn path that ran alongside the fence. The words inside my head were turning into daydreams and the dreams had got me stuck, and the last lyrics to the song escaped me.

'I am Lissie Turner,' I said out loud to break the silence. The silence stood though. The path was as silent as the sky above me and as grave as the tall pine trees that led me home. They towered above me; dry, dusty and decorated with the ragged plastic bunting of the Old World. If the plastic was close enough, we would use stones or sticks to knock it down. Collecting enough to trade at the main store was always a worthwhile pursuit.

What usually happened was I floated on aimlessly and everything always stayed the same, and it was always just me and the words and the dreams and then nothing. But this day was different. Sometimes you get a day like that, don't you? A day when everything changes forever. On this day, my dream, my trance-like state was broken into and vandalised. On this day, something unexpected happened. On this day, I saw a dog...

2: The Dog

I had no idea where it came from. I mean, it didn't belong to anyone because no one had dogs. Dogs were not allowed. Ned said they didn't even exist anymore, but now I knew that he was wrong. We'd seen pictures of them in books. There were three books about dogs in the museum. One was small, hard backed and called 'Guide To Dog Breeds.' Some of the pages were missing or burnt, but it was still a pretty good read. The other two books had been put together by people over the years. One was just a load of photos and drawings cut out and pasted onto loose pages. The long-dead author titled it simply; 'Pictures of Dogs.' The third book was another cut and paste job. It was called 'Extinct Animals' and had four pictures of dogs stuck inside. You couldn't take these books out of the museum, because they were so old and precious. The books and the other things in the museum were salvaged by the scavengers beyond the fence. They brought things back. Anything from the Old World that might interest us. They didn't scavenge so much these days though because we had everything we needed.

When I was little they used to call out that a scavenger had been sighted, and we'd run to the fence and watch out for them. They'd be in their wagon, driving the horses back home. It was exciting wondering what they had found for us. Mum used to hope for more pots and pans for cooking. Dad wanted a new banjo, or at least another instrument he could take strings from. What they nearly always had was plastic. There was a really nice scavenger once called Jonas. He was pretty old, and people used to say; don't go out again Jonas, you're getting too old for this now, let a young one take over. They made him stop in the end. There were rumours that he went a little bit

8

crazy. I remember once I got a doll. He'd found a load of things like that. Bricks and dolls and a stuffed bear with one ear burnt off. The children would chase after his wagon squealing with delight.

I tried to remember the pictures in the books. Grandma was the only person left who could remember dogs, because she was the oldest person in Province 5. She told me once about a black dog named Henry. Dog stories were our fairy tales. But this one was real. I wondered for a moment if I was wrong. Was it really a dog? Maybe it was something else. It was over by the fence that I had never been beyond. It was sniffing the ground, nose down, tail up. I examined its physical properties from a safe distance. Furry brown coat, long tail, four legs and four paws. Its ears were twitching as it sniffed about noisily.

I was frozen to the spot. Mesmerised with this mythical beast. I wished Ned was there to see it. Then it started doing something else. It started digging. I moved closer. I didn't even know I was doing it at first. The dog was using its front feet to tear up the earth next to the fence. Dirt and stones flew over its head. It seemed to be in a hurry. I was so close to it now that I could have reached out and touched its scraggy, brown fur. The fur was curled and knotted and hanging off in clumps. It had bald patches close to the base of its tail. The tail swung from side to side which I seemed to recall being told was a good thing, like it was happy. Did they have lots of teeth? I tried to remember. Ned would have known!

Suddenly, it noticed me. It stopped digging and glanced over its shoulder. I saw big brown eyes and a face full of dirt. Then it pushed itself through the hole and reappeared on the other side of the fence. Damn!

The Tree of Rebels

'Wait!' I called out. The dog looked back at me once more. Then it ran off through the long grass with its tail held high. It didn't seem to care that I was meant to tell someone I had seen something that did not belong. I looked around wildly, not knowing what to do, and the dog bounded off.

I was losing sight of it! I couldn't lose it! No one would ever believe me! They would say I was dreaming again, making up stories... I had to tell Ned and I had to tell Grandma that dogs were not extinct! I looked around. No one was here. No one came this way. Why would they? There was nothing here apart from the lonely drab path that led to our hut. There were over three hundred huts, spread out across the Province, sometimes a mile or more of land between them.

So, I went after the dog; and that changed everything. Looking back, I'd have to say it was a momentous decision. But at the time I barely gave it any thought at all. I was just suddenly crawling through the hole after it. I was just suddenly on the wrong side, in the wrong place, going after a creature that should not be there...

I went after the dog, pushing all of this aside. I just somehow knew that it was important to see it again, to touch it, to *know* that it was real. I ran after the dog and I followed it, and that was how I got a little bit lost, and that was how something else unexpected happened. That was how I found the tree that should not have existed either.

3: Beyond The Fence

I was not supposed to be on this side.

I was breaking the rules.

For a small moment, I stopped running after the dog and stood still. I stopped and considered these things that I knew. I looked back over my shoulder at the fence, as if giving myself one last chance to forget this crazy stuff and go back. I mean, I had that chance, I *gave* myself that chance. I could have trudged back and squeezed back under and no one would ever have known... The fence stared back at me accusingly, as if it knew what I was thinking. All the way around the Province, the rusty metal swayed and groaned. Fifteen feet tall, and, if it had eyes, they would have been scowling at me right then. But it didn't have eyes and it couldn't see me, and neither could anyone else. I didn't know what would happen if anyone found out. No one had ever said. Because people in the Province didn't break the rules. Why would they? The rules were there to protect us. My dad said this all the time. The rules kept us all safe.

But the dog didn't know any of this. No one had told it to stay on the right side of the fence because people had stopped believing that it existed. So, I convinced myself that I was only on the wrong side because of the dog. My father worked in Animal Control and he would need to know about this creature. I took a moment to imagine how proud he would be if I managed to catch it. I imagined myself drawing a white chalk circle around it, and stifled a giggle. I knew I was lying to myself, but that didn't stop me either. I ran on after the dog. Close to the fence, the ground was just like ours. Hard, flat and brown. Grass peeped up cautiously here and there like it did on our side; always appearing shy and afraid, expecting to be dug up or hacked down at any moment.

But the further I ran from the fence, the thicker and longer the grass became. Eventually the spiky stalks were whipping at my ankles. I only thought briefly of the chalk in my bag, and the unknown things we were supposed to circle. There was no undergrowth, no shelter, only grass and more grass.

But then something changed. The grass started to slope downwards, and I went down too, after the dog. Was it running from me? Or was it running towards something? I was breathless by now, even though I was a very fast runner, probably the best in my class. I was faster than all the other kids, all except Saul Lancaster, and Ned said that one day, when I grew even taller I would be faster than Saul too. My forehead was sweating and the warmth was clinging to my spine beneath my school dress. I wondered how long I had been running for, and how far?

It was nice running downhill though, so I kept going. My arms were spinning and my knees shook from the impact of my feet smacking against the hard earth. The faster I ran, the faster the air whipped through my hair. I ran and I gulped the air, and I was thinking; I should be afraid, I should be feeling guilty. I was on the wrong side of the fence. I was not old enough. I was not a scavenger, or a guard or a dome worker. But the grass was the same. The sky was the same. The only thing that was different was me, running down a hill on the wrong side of the fence after a dog that should not exist.

The dog looked like it was slowing down. The land had flattened out again, so I caught my breath and hurried on. Up ahead I could see nothing but land, but then suddenly the dog vanished. Just

12

like that, it vanished from view. It looked for a moment like it had simply dropped off the surface of the world. But as I got closer I could see what had happened. The land had dropped again, steeper this time. Grey rocks jutted out from the ground, and I stopped, breathing fast with my hands on my hips. Where had it gone?

Then I saw it again. It was scrabbling down the hill, running along a sort of pathway. I followed slowly, cautiously, planting my hands out to either side of me to touch and test the rocks. My head, so full of so many words I could hardly breathe.

'I am Lissie Turner,' I told the strange looking land, introducing myself, but it had nothing to say back.

I didn't know this was here. Why did the land keep going down? Was it a mountain? I didn't know we had mountains in Province 5. I couldn't wait to tell Ned. And Grandma! I would have to ask her if she remembered any mountains from before the wars. Was this place on the maps they showed us at school? No, because the maps at school didn't show the land on the wrong side of the fence because there was no need to. Because we didn't need to go there. Or anywhere.

At the bottom of the path my feet grew cold. I looked down to see why. Water. Trickling gently across where the land had gone flat again. I looked up. The rocks and the grass climbed upwards again on the other side of the water. I was standing in a narrow unknown crevice. Where did the water come from? I thought about the water at home. It was brought to us every week in litres. Pumped from the reservoir out by the domes. The dog must have wanted a drink. It was right there, just about a metre away from me, lapping greedily at the water. I gazed up, past the dog, and my eyes took it all in, the dense, wet, greenness, and my nostrils were twitching violently with the scent of something damp and pulsing and alive. It was all so strange that I had to sit down.

'I shouldn't be here,' I told the water as it chilled the bones of my backside and soaked into my dress. But my eyes kept going, following the greens, all the many, many shades of green that I never knew existed, and the smell was filling me up, and it was breathing, alive inside of me, and the green was lush and thick and fat and shining and beyond it, among it, standing proudly yet unwittingly in the centre of it all, was a tree.

And not just any tree. Not just a dry old pine or spruce.

A tree filled with fruit.

A tree filled with apples.

4: The Tree

A *tree*.

An apple tree.

Out here. Alone. Where it was not supposed to be.

Me and the dog and the tree, on the wrong side of the fence. Breaking the rules.

'I didn't mean to,' I blurted out, and the dog stopped drinking and stared at me properly for the first time. I made myself get up, and I walked stiffly to the tree. I could feel the water running down my legs and into my sandals. 'Oh my goodness,' I said, because I didn't know what else to say. Then I covered my mouth with my hands and stood before the tree. It was only a little bit taller than me, and it was nothing grand, not really. Still growing. It was spindly and wiry like me. It looked fragile, and yet defiant. 'You shouldn't be here,' I told it in a whisper. 'You're only meant to grow inside the domes where they can look after you.'

I reached out slowly and my fingers met the bark of the slim trunk, and I rubbed the tips of my fingers against its lumps and bumps. It felt cold and lonely. It was possibly the loneliest thing I had ever seen. Yet it was triumphant.

I ran my fingers along one of the thin, trembling branches. I touched its leaves. I inhaled its smell. And then the apples...I counted them first. One, two, three, four, five, six, seven, eight and nine. Not yet fully grown. I cupped my hand around the biggest one.

I'd had an apple at school last week.

The people who worked in our domes brought the food to

school every week on a Monday. It was off-loaded from the wagon in wooden crates, and stashed away in the cool room. It had to last the week, so it was all divided up by Mrs. Temple. She prepared the trays of fruit for each class every day. And last Monday we had apples. Big, green apples. They were almost too big to hold in your hands. Mrs. Temple said that the people from the domes were very proud of these apples. They were vivid green. Not a blemish, not a scuff or a bruise. Your teeth had to press hard before the skin yielded and sometimes my gums bled onto the crisp white flesh.

These apples were different. Small and red and green, and as I caressed their skin with my fingertips, I could feel bumps and dips and scars. I let go and covered my mouth again. The dog was sniffing my feet and a little noise escaped me.

'You got out,' I said behind my hands, and I meant both of them; the tree and the dog. 'You shouldn't be here.' I pointed at the dog. '*You*! You don't exist, and *you*!' I pointed at the tree. 'You aren't supposed to be out here like this!'

It was then that I started getting scared. I didn't mean to and I didn't want to. I was Lissie Turner, taller than most, faster than most, and I didn't want to be scared, because I was almost fourteen. I was almost fully grown and that meant you had to leave childish things behind you. But being on the wrong side of the fence with a dog and an apple tree did scare me. I was scared of where I was, and what I had found, and what I didn't know, and how lost I might be. Tears pricked my eyes but I wouldn't give in to them. I would be an adult in three months. No time for tears then. No time for daydreams, my mother always said.

The dog laid down under the tree as if it belonged there. It

16

seemed content now it had drunk from the stream. I wondered what time it was. I wondered if I had been missed yet. I wondered what they would say if they knew...I turned and ran.

5: Grandma Elizabeth

On the way back I got lost and I panicked. In reality, I was probably only lost for about ten minutes, but believe me when I say it felt like ten hours. I scrambled back up to the top of the slope and expected to know which direction to run in, but it all looked the same. My throat constricted with instant, crawling panic. I looked around for the fence but could not see it anywhere. I couldn't see anything that would tell me which way to go, so I did the next best thing I could think of. I just ran. The faster I ran, the more panicked I started to feel, and then it was like my feet forgot how to work, and they kept tripping me up and finally sent me flying. It was only then, with my hands and knees on the ground, that the glint of the sun rebounding from one of the domes way off to my left, caught my eye, and I relaxed.

By the time I found the hole under the fence and re-emerged, my throat was tight and dry and the tears of frustration were hitched up there, strangling me. My mother served dinner at five o'clock on the dot, and I got back to our hut at twenty past. My father was out the front chopping wood.

'You're late,' he said without looking up. 'Where have you been?'

'With Ned,' I replied, without thinking. 'Doing school work. I thought I told Mum?'

Dad looked up and made a face that let me know he thought this was unlikely. Then he went back to chopping the wood. The ration was delivered on the first day of every month. My mother was inside, stood at the stove, still in her hospital apron.

The huts of the Province were all basically the same. Each one was divided into four simple quarters. Through the front door, the centre made up the main living area. It contained the stove which burned the wood to heat the entire hut, a table and a bench, shelves, and two rocking chairs. A simple rug covered the floor, which like the hut itself, was made of hard baked mud. To the right of the living area were two bedrooms. Mum and Dad shared one, and me and Grandma Elizabeth shared the other. To the left of the living area was the wash room. The walls of our hut were carefully constructed out of sapling poles, and wet clay and grass, by my Great-Grandfather back in 2087. The Turners were among the very first settlers to make Province 5 their home; a fact my father was particularly proud of. He was the last of them, except for me of course. He often made jokes about the next Coupling Dance and how I would be old enough for it soon. Looking back, I suppose he was hinting at the excitement of a grandchild one day, but at the time, I just found it embarrassing. I wasn't interested in being a couple. Not one little bit.

'I was getting worried!' my mother scolded me when I came in. I bit my lip, offered a smile and hoped like hell the guilt and the fear were not stamped all over my face. She turned and handed me two bowls of steaming hot soup. It looked and smelled like potatoes.

'I thought I told you I was going to Ned's?'

'Nope,' Mum shook her head at me and frowned. 'You didn't.'

My mother frowned a lot. She was sombre and serious, while my father liked to make light of things. She looked a lot like me. We had the same strawberry blonde hair, thick and wild and hard to contain. We had the same spray of freckles across our nose and cheeks. She looked at me now the way she always did. As if she couldn't quite understand me, and couldn't stop worrying that she had missed something important.

'Oh I'm sorry! I really thought I did!'

'Take that through to Grandma, and get your head out of the clouds!' She ruffled up my hair with one hand, and I scuttled off to see Grandma Elizabeth before she could question me any further.

Grandma and I often ate our meals together. She was bedridden, and it didn't seem fair to me to leave her on her own all the time. Her bed was next to the window and she liked to sit propped up by pillows so that she could see outside. She said that she could not breathe properly if she laid flat, but I had a sneaking suspicion that she was also afraid of the dark. She insisted on the curtains remaining wide open all night long.

'Are you awake, Gran? I've got your dinner.'

I closed the door behind me, and instantly her eyes were open and gleaming. I smiled back. Sometimes I thought that Grandma only showed life for me. Mother was convinced that every day was going to be her last. But somehow she kept on fooling them.

'You look excited, Lissie,' she rasped at me from her bed.

I went to her and passed over the bowl. Her hands shook when she took the weight of it, and some of the soup spilled onto her blankets. We ignored it. I took up my usual place on the stool beside her bed and we were both silent for a few moments, watching each other and spooning soup into our mouths.

'So, spill it then, Lissie,' she said eventually with a wink. 'Tell me what's put that fire in your eyes.' She licked her lips and waited.

'Grandma, I've got a secret.'

'For who?'

'For us. For me and you. And maybe Ned.'

Grandma's hand continued to shake as she lifted the spoon to her mouth. Her teeth were all gone now. Her lips had a mind of their own. She had sparse white hair which sat on her head like puffs of clouds. When the sunlight poured through the window you could see her yellow skull under the hair. I was shaking my head now. I guess it was all tumbling through me; shock and adrenalin and something more. Something like pins and needles coming to life inside of me. Something that made me want to scratch at my skin. Her eyes scanned my face, narrowing down to pale grey slits. I couldn't lie to her; not in a million years.

'You have to promise not to tell anyone,' I whispered, and she instantly crossed her heart.

'And hope to die,' she said with a wink.

I brought my face close to hers and I could smell the tea tree oil hospital soap my mother washed her with.

'I was walking home from school alone, along the fence, and I saw a dog.' Her eyes shot wide open and her hand clutched at mine. I got the rest of the words out before anything could stop me. 'It went under the fence, and I didn't want to lose it, so I followed it. I ran after it. Down two hills, and into this strange place where there was water and a tree. An *apple* tree, Grandma.'

Her hand tightened on mine. It looked and felt like the claw of a bird curling around my skin. Her other hand left the soup bowl half eaten on her lap, and fluttered up to her throat, where the skin was paper thin.

'Can you draw it, Lissie?' she asked breathlessly. 'Can you draw me a picture of it?'

I scraped back the stool, dashed over to my bed and fetched the slate and chalk from under my pillow. I sat back down and concentrated hard. I drew the tree exactly as I remembered it. Nine apples. Grandma took it from me and held it up to her eyes. They seemed so full suddenly, shiny and moist and burning up.

'You're not making up silly tales, Lissie? You really found this?'

'On the wrong side of the fence. Will I be in trouble if anyone finds out?' This part worried me the most. Finding the tree was huge, but not exactly my fault. I mean, I didn't break the rules and plant it there, did I? I didn't put the dog there either, and had anyone ever said that seeing or following a dog was against the rules? It was being on the wrong side of the fence that worried me. *That*, I had done, willingly.

'No one must find out,' I heard her say, her voice hoarse and strangled. 'No one must know it's there.'

'Why not Gran? How did it get there? All the food grows in the domes, doesn't it?'

'Since they took it away from us, yes. But not this one. This tree is a rebel, Lissie.'

'What do you mean they took it away?' I asked her, because my head was spinning with it all. My throat felt like it was swelling with words and questions. 'They didn't take it away. They just protected it. Like they taught us in school. To protect it from disease. To end the famine.'

'It was not as simple as that, Lissie Turner. It didn't happen exactly like that.'

'I don't understand, Grandma.'

'Lissie, when I was your age, a great war raged. An endless war.'

'I know about that Gran. War after war after war. Dad says that's what sent us all back in time.'

Grandma chuckled at me, but her eyes looked misty and far away. 'Your father has an interesting way of looking at it, child. Back in time...makes sense I suppose. But you remember I told you when I was your age my father grew his own food? He had an apple tree too. And a pear. He grew carrots and potatoes and peas and tomatoes. So many plants. I used to help him.'

'You told me this before.'

'This tree you found is very special. It might even be the very last of its kind. Natural and free. Is it hurting anyone? Being there? No. But if you tell, the guards will put a patrol out there and destroy it.'

'What about the dog?'

'The same. They will destroy it in a heartbeat.'

I was shaking my head slowly. My hand was still inside hers but her grip loosened. Her whole body went slack. She seemed to slip down the pillows as if the air had whooshed out of her body.

The Tree of Rebels

'But why?'

'There is so much you don't understand, child. Maybe you are still too young.'

'I'm not Gran, I'm not!' My voice rose slightly. How dare she say that? It was me who followed the dog who should not have existed, and it was me who crawled under the fence after it. 'I followed the dog and found the tree!'

'Maybe you were supposed to.' She looked at me and her eyes half closed. 'I'm tired, Lissie...'

'You are the oldest person in Province 5,' I decided to remind her. 'Maybe in the whole world! You know more than anyone. You can tell me. I'm not a baby. I'm nearly fourteen.'

'Yes...and knowledge is dangerous...But that's not what they used to say.'

'Gran?'

'They used to say that knowledge was power.'

'You're not making sense Gran. What should I do about the tree? What does it mean?'

'You have to decide for yourself,' she told me, and her hand left mine and slipped back under the blanket. 'I'm too old now. I can't leave this bed. This view is the last thing I will ever see. But I wish you to know that there is more...*so* much more. There *was* so much more. Maybe it's still there if people are brave enough to find it.'

I shook my head again.

'Gran?' Her eyes closed for a moment and her breathing slowed right down. She did that a lot. She would get me going with her memories and her cryptic sayings I was somehow supposed to just understand, and then she would fade away, drift off, leaving me in total confusion. I would sit there waiting for more; desperate to hear her strange tales of the machines that once connected people all across the world. And then she would fall asleep on me, just like she was doing again now. I reached out and shook her shoulder, gently, but firmly enough to shake her eyes open. 'Gran?'

'There will always be those who say no, Lissie. There will always be those who do not believe what they are told.' She closed her eyes again. 'There will always be those who rebel.'

6: Dreams

After Grandma Elizabeth fell asleep I lay on my bed and stared at the ceiling. My head was in a mess. My mind kept drifting off. As darkness fell, my mother called me to the wash room to get cleaned up. The washing water was lined up neatly against the wall in bottles. She had half-filled the metal tub for me and was pouring in the hot water she had boiled in the gallon bucket that hung above the stove. I eyed the variety of waiting bottles with vague disinterest. Plastic bottles, in fact any kind of plastic discovery earned you a token at the store. When we were younger Ned and I used to spend a lot of time looking for plastic to trade in. Melted down, there were so many new things you could turn it into.

'I saw Ned's mother out in the square today,' she said, not looking at me as she swirled her hand around in the bath, mixing the hot water with the cold. I stopped breathing and just stared at her back. 'She said Ned had to be home right from school today because he had agreed to help his father with some cleaning duties. Earned himself some tokens apparently.'

I was silent, barely breathing. I wanted my mind to come up with a solution, an answer, but it flat point refused to. It just went blank and numb and I was in a mess all right, a big fat lying mess of trouble, because lying to your parents was breaking the rules as well.

'So were you lying to me earlier, Lissie?' My mum finally turned to face me. She had changed out of her hospital apron into her plain house dress.

'I got lost,' I said, and a sigh of relief escaped me. Words, at last. Words that almost made sense and weren't entirely lies. 'I was in a dream...making up stories...I just got lost. I'm sorry Mum. I was embarrassed.'

'Embarrassed?'

'Yes. At my age. Getting lost.' I shrugged my shoulders and stared at her miserably. She frowned, but I think she believed me.

'Well, you are right about one thing, young lady,' she said with a click of her tongue. 'You *are* too old to be getting into daydreams and getting lost!' She rolled her eyes at me and squeezed past to get to the door. 'Honestly Lissie, I do wonder when you will grow up. You've only got three months! What are we going to do with you? I think I need you to start acting more responsibly. Which is why I have taken a leaf out of Hilda Fleck's book and organised some duties for you. We need to get you started. You can earn some tokens like Ned.'

She stood in the doorway. One foot tapped the floor. Her eyes waited for me to argue or complain, but I just forced a weak smile across my face and nodded.

'Okay Mum, in the hospital with you?'

'No, actually. They need help at the Governor's offices, Hilda said, so I went and asked and they said they'd happily take you.'

'Oh.' This was unexpected. The normal route into employment was to shadow one of your parents for your duties. 'To do what?'

'Paperwork. Cleaning duties. I'm not entirely sure, but if you go along tomorrow after school you'll find out, and you'll have to be gracious and take what you're offered. I wouldn't expect Level 2 or anything. But you'll earn and you'll keep yourself out of trouble.' My mother nodded curtly at my frozen smile. A slight frown remained on her forehead. 'It will do you good,' she added, as an afterthought. I wanted to ask her why I couldn't just do duties at the hospital with her, but I didn't dare annoy her again, so I kept quiet.

When she had gone, I closed the door, pulled my dress over my head and climbed into my bath. The light outside was dying. Mum had left me a candle in case it grew dark before I finished, but unlike Grandma I did not mind the dark. I slipped under the water and closed my eyes. Through the door I could hear my mother trying to wake Gran properly to give her a wash. Their voices mixed and murmured beyond the wash room. Grandma started coughing and Mum soothed her gently.

I opened my eyes with a sense of urgency. I started thinking about what my parents said all the time; that Grandma Elizabeth was not long for this world. She was one hundred and three years old, the oldest person in our Province. On her one hundredth birthday, the Governor came to see her in person. Soren Lancaster was Saul's father; a tall, thick chested man who wore a wide, white hat upon his head. He was a pleasant and orderly man. People were always saying how lucky we were to have him. How he had filled his father's shoes so effortlessly after his death ten years previously. I wondered what it would be like working in his offices and my heart clutched at me suddenly, like it didn't want me to breathe. I couldn't think about that now. I couldn't think about working for Saul's father to keep my head out of the clouds. I couldn't let my mother know that it was not clouds my head was stuck in, but other things, more important things, like the truth.

Grandma Elizabeth, I thought, the oldest person here and not long for this world. Every day could be her last, and she has so much

28

to tell me, doesn't she? What if she dies before she gets the chance? What if I never know what she meant about anything? I had the strongest feeling that she had been trying to tell me something dreadfully important, maybe for the longest time. Maybe that was what spurred me to crawl under the fence. Maybe she had been inside my head right then.

After my bath, I got dried and dressed and went into the living area to say goodnight to my parents.

'Did you finish your school work?' Dad asked me when I planted a kiss on his whiskered cheek. He looked tired and grubby from chopping the wood. He was smoking his pipe with the window slightly open. I nodded at him obediently and he looked sceptical. 'History?' he asked.

'Yes Dad. All done.'

'Year the Great Famine began?'

'2075 Dad, but we did that last year!'

He grinned and tipped me a wink. 'Okay then, the year Peace was declared?'

I groaned at him. '2085, Dad.' It was easy because everyone knew that date. They drummed it into you from the moment you were born. My dad smiled his end of the day smile. It always transformed his work weary face. He took my hand and kissed it.

'And Peace lasted forever more...' he said, and I couldn't help smiling back, because the way he said it was so soft and dreamy. He sounded like a child, tucked up in bed, repeating back the words of a comforting bedtime story. I felt the urge to crawl onto his lap like I used to do when I was small, but I was drawn helplessly back to my room, back to Grandma Elizabeth. I kissed both my parents goodnight and left them alone in the dwindling light.

Grandma was asleep. I could hear her gentle snores as each one rippled through her tiny body. I got into my own bed, but sleep didn't come easily. My stomach churned painfully with the lies and the breaking of rules, and my chest tightened with the thought of Soren Lancaster and duties for tokens...I couldn't help thinking maybe he knew somehow, about me on the wrong side of the fence, about me and the dog, and the tree. My heart beat hard and fast under my nightdress. I thought about my father sat out there in the candlelight, smoking his pipe, weary from his day on Animal Control. The dog was still out there. If anyone needed to be told about the dog, it was him. But I couldn't do it. I was in deep; one lie after the other, and it hurt inside my chest with them all stacked up on top of each other.

I only knew I had finally slept when I was awoken again. It was disorientating at first. One moment I was lying there with my eyes wide open, sweating about the trouble I was in, and the next moment I was jerking away, torn from a deep dream where I was running through the grass and the water...

Grandma Elizabeth was talking in her sleep. Talking and moaning and twisting under her blankets. I got up quickly and ran to her side. I put my hand across her forehead and felt her fever. I thought about calling my mother but Grandma's hand shot out to find mine, and her fingers clawed at me again, holding me tight. Her eyes were closed and her mouth stretched open with another terrible moan.

'Gran? Wake up. What is it? Gran? It's okay.'

'Lawrence, we have to go...' she muttered, not seeing me. 'They

30

know it's you. Lawrence! Lawrence! Don't let them find you...'

'Who's Lawrence?' I asked her, but she barely knew I was there.

'Fight back...' she whimpered in the dark. 'They're waiting for you...'

'Grandma,' I was begging her now. 'You're not well...you're making no sense!'

Her eyes finally opened and she saw me. Her hand was damp with sweat upon mine. Her eyes glowed. Her fragile chest was rising and falling scarily fast. I put both my hands over hers.

'Lissie? Is that you? Where's Lawrence?'

'I don't know who Lawrence is...There is no Lawrence. You're scaring me Gran.'

'He's gone...They are all gone...I'm the only one left...but you can't tell...'

'Tell who what? I don't understand.'

My Grandma licked her lips. I watched her tiny tongue whip back and forth, as she moistened her mouth, and her eyes locked onto mine the entire time and she seemed to be building up to something.

'The book, Lissie,' she said when she was ready. 'You can have the book. You can have it if you want it. Maybe you are old enough.'

'What book?'

'Under the mattress. They know it's there. But they don't know what it really is.'

31

I didn't say anything. I just slid my hand underneath her and found it with my fingers. I watched her face as I pulled it out. There was indeed a book, a hardback notebook. It was wrapped in paper and bound with string. It smelled of dust. I showed it to her and she nodded weakly.

'I wrote it all in there,' she said, and closed her eyes again. 'You can read it Lissie, if you like. It will help you decide what to do about the tree.'

I wanted to tell her that she was really scaring me now. That I had no intention of doing *anything* about the tree, or the dog. That mother was sending me to earn tokens from working at the Governor's office, and what if he knew I'd broken the rules? What happened to people if they broke the rules? I didn't know, and nobody knew, because nobody ever broke them, and why was that? My mother knew why. Because things were perfect, that's why. Because things were better than human life had ever known before. My father knew why too. Because Peace was declared in 2085 and Peace had been Everlasting Forever More and that was why people did not break the rules, because why would they? Why would anyone want to do that when there was no need to? When we all had everything we needed?

Grandma Elizabeth responded to my fear with snores. She had gone again. She was far away. But I had the book. I took it back to my bed and climbed under the covers with it held against my chest. It felt like she had somehow read my mind while I bathed and worried about her dying.

I unwound the string and pulled off the paper. How could I not? All the time my heart was going crazy, and my throat felt like it was stripped raw, and my head was pounding like a warning. The light from the moon was just enough, and as I lifted away the paper, I traced my fingers across the words written in my Grandma's handwriting on the very first page. *The diary of Elizabeth Wakefield aged 12 and a half. 2074*

7: *Province 5*

Our hut was about a mile from Ned's. Ned Fleck was my best friend. Kids were not exactly spoiled for choice when it came to finding friends. Province 5 was home to three hundred and eighty-seven people, and only eighty three of those were children under the age of fourteen. I lucked out with Ned though. He was solid. I called for him every morning on our way to school.

The school was situated in the square. It was one of the first buildings the settlers put up, along with the hospital. Some of the buildings in the square were built from scratch, with mud and dirt and straw and anything else the first settlers could scavenge. But some of them were rescued and rebuilt from the Old World, from what was left still standing. The Governor's office was one such building, three storeys high and repainted a startling white. Apparently, all they had to do was put a new roof on it. The hospital was also rebuilt, but our school was created from nothing. It had a mismatched, patched up look to it. They were always adding new parts on, and repairing old bits. The main hall was built with bricks and covered in mud. Three of the five classrooms resembled our own simple huts, with straw thatched roofs. There were two new brick classrooms that had been added over the years. They said that one day the whole school would be rebuilt, better than ever.

'We are still recovering,' our teacher Miss Branksome told us often enough. 'As a human race, we still have a lot of ground to cover, a lot of rebuilding to do. But just look what progress we have made!'

Miss Branksome was younger than my mother, with eyes that seemed to be forever smiling. They disappeared in her face when her lips curved upwards, and she had a habit of nodding her head politely every time someone spoke. She had soft brown hair that skimmed her shoulders and everyone always said what a great teacher she was.

You could tell the triumph of Peace was her favourite subject. My dad was the same. He said it was fascinating how the human race started again after so much death and destruction. He said that humans were unstoppable, and that there was always hope, because the human spirit would always prevail. The survival instinct, he called it. That was what those early settlers had plenty of. He had good reason to be proud; his ancestors, the Turners, had arrived in the Province close to death. Skeletal, hairless, yet still walking. Blood trails following behind them. They had seen unspeakable horrors, and yet they had kept walking, kept moving, kept hoping that somewhere they would find life and hope.

They found it in Province 5, although back then it would not have had a name. It would have been mostly dust and human bones, inhabited by a few wretched and desperate people who had started to put up a fence to keep them safe. Everything that had been before was blown to pieces during the wars.

'2085 was the most important year in human history,' my father often said, echoing the refrain that was repeated to us at school. 'We must be thankful that the people who survived finally learned that war is not the answer. War after war brought the human race to its knees. To the brink of extinction. And then finally Peace was declared by the survivors. They said *no more*. They stood up for peace. Things were rebuilt. People are different now, Lissie. People no longer treat each other like animals.' He said we had a lot to be thankful for.

My mother looked forward. While he looked back with

gratitude and pride, my mother carried with her a sense of anxiety, although I was never exactly sure why. She never spoke of the past, and had nothing to say about her own ancestry, or how they survived. I only knew that her mother died when she was just two years old, and her father not long after that. After the wars, illness and disease swept the land, and many people who had survived the bombs, were killed off by germs instead. Grandma Elizabeth survived, and brought my mother up as her own. My mother kept her ears and eyes on the future.

'Things are getting better all the time,' she would often wring her hands and say to my father at the end of their working day. 'They say that, don't they? That's what I hear. That's what everyone is saying. More food, and *better* food. New things all the time. People are beginning to relearn so many new skills. Why, there is plenty now for everyone. They'll change the rules on children soon, I'm sure. That's what they say, Harlan. That's what people are waiting for.'

When the world started again, the resources were scarcer than ever. One of the first rules the new Central Government put in place was a one child per family rule. There was no point in bringing babies into the world who would simply starve to death. While the world recovered, piece by piece, the resources were rationed. The story was the same in every Province of the New World. One child per couple. Enough to begin to replenish the devastated population, but not too much of a drain on the little there was to go around. If anyone ever questioned the rule they were reminded that overpopulation was to be avoided at all costs. In the Old World it had been a contributing factor to the wars. Too many people and too few resources.

'But times are changing,' my mother said this a lot. 'Everything is improving all the time. We can support more children now. The Province *needs* more children.' My father would smile nervously, his

36

expression doing enough to placate her anxieties, while his silence doing nothing to suggest he disagreed with the one child rule.

I thought about this on the way to meet Ned, and I thought about the very first paragraph of Grandma Elizabeth's diary, and how they seemed to echo my mother's words, yet in a frighteningly different way.

'Times are changing. Everything is getting harder, especially if you don't have the right amount of money. Food prices are all anyone can talk about these days. Everywhere you go you hear the same conversations and hear the same fear in people's voices. What will we eat next week? How can I afford this now? My dad is raging on and on about it, and he has started this online protest group called OUR SEEDS. Mum writes a shopping list and then goes through it and crosses half of the things off because we can't afford them. My dad spends all his time on the computer. We have to share the information, he tells me. We have to tell people because they are not listening. Because they don't understand, or they don't care. He says they won't care about food or oil while they still have their free web time. They won't care until it is too late.'

I didn't know what any of it meant. It was like reading words from a different language, from a different world. It was impossible to understand. I had seen books at school from the Old World; pictures of people sat down at these electric screens whilst tapping away with their fingers. They had some of those machines in the museum. Some were larger, like flat hard bags you could carry around, and then flip open. Some of them were small and rectangular, small enough to slip into a pocket. They kept them all locked up in a wooden box as if they were dangerous.

The Tree of Rebels

On our yearly visit to the museum, we would traipse around wordlessly while the curator Mr. Harman explained what the various artefacts used to do. There was always a sense of foreboding when we paused beside the wooden box. Children would gasp softly as the great lid was thrown back. The adults would shudder and shake their heads. It wasn't that anyone ever described these old, useless things as dangerous. It was just that we all somehow felt it.

Well maybe they were, if my grandma's words were anything to go by. Maybe they had something to do with all the wars and death and the humans nearly dying out. I needed to read more, but I was scared. Scared of being caught with it, and scared of what I would find out. One thing I did know; there was nothing about this in the history books at school.

I needed to tell Ned about the tree. I needed to find the dog again.

8: Duties

The day stretched out ahead of me like the longest day of all time. I had no idea how I would endure school followed by duties, when all I could think about was the tree. Ned was waiting for me, with his school bag at his feet.

'I'm sorry about landing you in it,' he said right away.

I sighed into his freckled face. He was shorter than me, with soft red hair that curled around his ears and along his neck. His face was thoughtful, his eyes considering. He was one of the smartest people I knew.

'What do you mean?'

'You know. You lied about being with me? Now we've both been signed up for *duties*.' He said the word with a further grimace and a shiver, as if the very thought offended him. 'I was hoping to get away with it for a bit longer.'

'Oh well,' I shrugged, as we set off together. 'We have to get used to it at some point. Only three more months and then we'll be looking for jobs, Ned. Duties prepare you for that.'

'Don't remind me,' he groaned. 'So depressing. Unless you get given a jammy Level 2 or 1 like bloody Saul Lancaster.'

'We'll get the same as our parents, Ned.' He looked at me and we both nodded and rolled our eyes.

'Well, where were you then? That's the burning question, Lissie Turner. Why did you lie?'

'Massive, massive secret, Ned.' I stopped walking, and pulled him back by his elbow. I stared deep into his green eyes with all the seriousness I could muster. I feared he would laugh at me or think I was messing around, but there must have been something in my face that alarmed him. He went sort of pale. Maybe I did too. I certainly felt sick enough. 'I'll tell you...I'll show you after school, and *damn it*, after duties. But you'll have to swear on your life you won't tell anyone. I *mean* it.'

'Easy,' he said softly, with a weak shrug. 'No problem.'

We walked on. Another half mile over dry dead fields of nothing. Every now and then I caught a glimpse of the fence between the trees, and I shivered. Ned kept stealing sideways glances at me.

'You're different, Lissie,' he announced when we arrived in front of the school building. 'Something's changed in you.'

How is it that I hoped he was wrong, and yet hoped that he was right?

I couldn't answer because someone was watching and listening. Saul Lancaster, leaning in the door frame, all six foot of him and his big meaty face gloating my way. I knew what he was going to say before he even opened his mouth.

'Don't get too excited about duties later,' he told me, as we walked past. 'You'll be on Level 4. Cleaning *my* bedroom!'

I ignored him. You just had to. He was just smug because, despite the fact he was not that bright at school, he knew he would be signed up for at least Level 2 employment when he turned fourteen.

'You can't complain,' my dad warned me once. 'His family have done so much for this place.'

'*He* hasn't done a thing!' I had been quick to point out, but my dad was not having any of it. It was unfair. But you were not allowed to say it.

I was bristling all day; all the way through, I felt wired under my skin. It was a day just like any other, and yet somehow it was as if I were brand new, seeing it all for the first time. We had assembly first. We sang the Song of Thanks.

For no more war, and no more fear, we thank you all, we thank you all...For food to eat and clothes to wear, we thank you all, we thank you all.

As I mouthed the words, my head pounded and my guts groaned.

At the end of assembly, Saul Lancaster and Penny Harvest went up to receive their certificates of duty. It was all about earning enough credits by performing enough of your assigned tasks. Duties could be carried out for any employer, for any kind of job. You were paid in three ways; credits which earned you certificates at school, tokens which you could spend in the store, and finally, an actual job when you left school at fourteen. As most kids ended up doing duties wherever their parents worked the chances were high that they would end up working there too. It didn't always go that way though. You could be offered duties anywhere, and you would be looked down upon if you didn't accept them, particularly if they were at a higher level than your parent's work.

As an Animal Control worker my father was at Level 3. My mother who helped care for patients in the hospital, was also Level 3.

Level 1 were the top jobs and there were the fewest of these. Being the governor and the deputy governor of a Province were Level 1, for example. Level 2 employment was made up of guards and dome workers. The guards kept the peace, and were answerable to the Governor and Deputy. The dome workers provided for us all. Scavengers were also Level 2, because the work they did was the most dangerous. They left the Province and they went looking for things to bring back. Medical supplies, materials, items of interest, anything that could help us. Level 1 and Level 2 were the only workers who went beyond the fence.

Our Head teacher, Mrs. Batton, shook hands with both Saul and Penny and made them turn to face their classmates. We were ordered to give them a round of applause as they stood there proudly holding onto their certificates. I was not interested. I just wanted to get out of there, get my duties done, and get back to the tree.

'Do you think he was serious?' Ned nudged me and whispered. 'About you cleaning his bedroom?'

I nodded my head regretfully. 'Just you watch. I bet they do.'

It turned out I was wrong.

After school, I arranged to meet Ned back at his hut, and then I slouched off towards the Governor's office to find out what was in store for me. The tall white building overlooked the entire square. I'd only been in there once before, with my dad. Every now and again the workers in Province 5 were rewarded for their services. Usually with extra tokens, or extra rations, and they got to have tea with the Governor himself. He was a very busy man, they said. He was not often in his offices, or even in the Province. He had to do a lot of work with Central Government further North, in Province 1.

I was about ten, the day we went for tea with him. He had been wearing a soft blue suit that he seemed very proud of. He told us a skilled seamstress in Province 1 had made it for him, and he kept brushing unseen dust from the shoulders as he talked to us. He paid special attention to me that day, which I remember I really got a kick out of. He kept winking at me. Stuff like that. His secretary Miss Harper had brought up a tray of tea and cakes for my father and me. I remembered my father that day; his face flushed with pride and excitement. He started working in Animal Control when he was fourteen years old.

'I'll happily do it until the day I die,' he had told the Governor, shaking hands with him before we left. 'There is so much more important work to be done.'

'You are very right about that, Mr Turner,' the Governor had replied. 'Very right.'

I pushed through the double doors at the bottom and entered the lobby. Miss Harper was at her desk, scribbling into a notepad. She looked up and smiled when I walked in. She was very young, maybe only around eighteen. She was small and neat with tight blonde curls and huge blue eyes. She put down her pen and got up from her chair when I walked in.

'Ahh, our very new dutiful young lady,' she exclaimed, and I nodded in reply, smiling shyly. She clapped her hands together.

'Hello, Miss Harper.' I approached her desk. 'My mum sent me.'

'Oh yes. She was in here just yesterday on your behalf. Obviously, we were happy to accommodate her, and you. Follow me!'

Miss Harper left her desk and pushed through a door behind it.

I followed her out into a hallway.

'Excited?' she asked me.

'Oh yes. Very. What am I to be doing, Miss?'

'Oh, you'll be pleased,' she looked over her shoulder and beamed at me. She walked through another door, and into a large plum coloured room which appeared to be some sort of lounge, or sitting area. The room Dad and I had taken tea in was upstairs, with a balcony overlooking the square. 'Follow me!' she trilled, and towards the rear of the room she pushed open some doors and took me outside. I stared around me in wonder.

Who would have known Governor Lancaster had such a beautiful garden? It was small, perfectly square, and surrounded by huge brick walls. In the centre was a neat green lawn, and in the middle of that, a square fish pond. The rest of the garden contained borders of flowers and plants, most of which I had never set eyes on before. The colours were breath-taking. Enough to stop you in your tracks. I mean, I'd seen some pictures in books, but nothing like this! Miss Harper smiled at my face.

'Just gorgeous, isn't it? The Governor is very proud. He's been working on it for years.'

'I've never seen so many colours!'

'I know, I know, it's to die for!'

I wanted to say more, to exclaim my surprise, to ask questions about the flowers, but then I remembered the secret. I remembered the tree, and the bright lush green that surrounded it. Why wasn't the rest of the Province the same? So, I shut my mouth, smiled over my teeth and looked innocently up at Miss Harper.

'I like to take a break out here myself sometimes,' she held a hand to her mouth and half whispered, half giggled to me. 'It's so therapeutic!'

'I can see why,' I continued to smile up at her. 'The Governor must be very clever to grow all this.'

'I know! In these conditions! He studies a lot, you know. He studies everything!' Miss Harper sighed appreciatively and clapped her hands together.

'What is it he wants me to do?' I asked, gazing around at the perfect garden. 'I don't know anything about flowers.' No one does, I wanted to add, but didn't.

'Oh, it's simple really,' she replied. 'There are a few things.' She turned to a wooden bench that was situated to the left of the doors. There were some items upon it and she spread them out for me to see. 'Apron and gloves, of course, for you. Water spray. The flowers must be watered with that. Just spritz them gently, each and every one. And these paper envelopes are for the seeds.' She handed me the apron and gloves and I put them on.

'The seeds, Miss?'

'Yes, you'll find some of the flower heads are dying, you know, coming to the end of their season?' She looked at me expectantly, and I shrugged, because I had no idea, who did? 'You'll see the seeds in the head of some of them,' she went on. 'Look out for seeds, and if you do find any you collect them in the envelopes.'

'Separately or all together?'

'Separately, please. Do try not to mix them, though if you do, no need to panic. Soren knows how to sort them. He recognises them all by sight.'

'Okay then,' I nodded, apron and gloves on, envelopes at the ready. I just wanted her to go and leave me to it. 'I think I can manage that. Miss? Am I to do this every time I come?'

'Oh do you know, I'm not sure?' she replied, with a quizzical frown. 'Soren just left me instructions for today. Is this enough to keep you busy for your hour? I'll be busy myself, so the Governor told me to leave your tokens for you in advance.' Miss Harper plucked another envelope from the pocket of her skirt and passed it to me. I took it and smiled. She looked so happy, I thought, as if it was impossible to stop smiling. She even reached out and stroked my cheek.

'Oh, aren't you lucky? Getting a position like this for your duties? The Governor must think a lot of your family, Lissie!'

Miss Harper left me to it and strutted back inside, still smiling. I was left alone, just me and the flowers. I stood and stared at them for a few more moments, just taking them in, the colours and the textures. Just breathing in the heavy scent of them all. How long had he been growing them, and what was the point? You couldn't eat flowers, could you? They had no purpose as far as I could see. Why did they matter so much to him? And if they did matter, why didn't they grow them in the domes? They could grow them there and pass them out to people, just like they did with flour and wheat and sugar, couldn't they?

'I need to get on,' I told myself and the garden. I was thinking of the tree again. The tree and the apples on the wrong side of the fence. I took the water spray and approached the flowers tentatively. I had no idea why those beautiful bright sweet smelling flowers of unknown names made me feel so uneasy, yet when I pictured the spindly outlawed tree with the lumpy bumpy apples, I felt just the opposite. Every fibre of my physical body was crying out to me then, pulling and yanking and urging me to get away from the flowers and back to the tree.

9: Broken Rules

When I finished my duties, I thanked Miss Harper, tucked my tokens inside my school bag and left. I didn't want to alert anyone's suspicions in the square so I just hopped and skipped and hurried a bit, as if I was late home, afraid of being scolded. But once the square was behind me, and only the arid fields stretched out between there and Ned's hut, I took flight and ran like I had never run before. By the time I reached him, I felt like I was on fire. I felt like it was all happening, inside of me and all around me, although I had no idea what. Only that it was like spinning in chaos and I sort of liked it.

Ned was sat on his backside a little way away from his hut with his arms wrapped around his legs. He got up when he saw me coming and we met halfway, exchanged nervous smiles and kept going at a fast pace.

'I told my mum we're running,' he said to me, with a nervous half grimace upon his face. 'You know, to practice? For sports day, next month?'

I nearly laughed in his face. 'She believed you? Bloody hell, Ned!'

'She believed me about *you*. She knows how fast you are, and how much you want to beat Saul. She told *me* to be careful.'

I laughed. I couldn't help it. 'Oh Ned!'

'Oh well, I couldn't think of anything else. She thinks I'm rubbish at everything anyway.'

'She does not,' I said, but this was a lie. Ned's mother *did* think

48

he was rubbish at everything. Everything that mattered to her, anyway.

'What did you tell your mum?'

'Oh it's okay. I just had duties, didn't I? She'll think I'm still there. Anyway, we won't be long. Not if we hurry.'

'Should I be scared? You're not going to get us into trouble are you, Lissie?'

I stopped and looked into his face, biting my lip. It was on the tip of my tongue to tell him about my duties, and the impossibly bright flowers. I could still smell them in my nose. There was so much to tell him, too much. So, I decided to take it one step at a time. To give him a chance to keep up. I nodded at him.

'Probably, yes. So, it's up to you, Ned. Come with me and break some rules. Maybe get caught. I don't know. Or you can go home now.'

'I can't do that!' he exclaimed almost angrily. 'Not now you've led me on! I want to know what's going on with you, Lissie. I've never seen you like this.'

I scratched my neck and looked around us. I felt nervy and on edge. How could I be sure we were not being watched?

'Okay then,' I told him. 'You had your chance. Let's go.'

I turned and ran on, desperate now, feeling like I couldn't get there soon enough. I was starting to fear I'd dreamed it all. Maybe I would find nothing there. Maybe I'd imagined it all, or made it up. I couldn't talk; my mouth was too dry, my throat too tight, so I just hurried on, running like the day before. Ned was silent too. I could just hear him puffing along behind me.

The Tree of Rebels

When we got to the fence, I stopped and checked around again. As usual there was nothing and no one. Just dry, hard land. I licked my lips and leaned on the fence. Ned waited, panting, his hands on his hips. I nudged the ground with my foot and nodded towards the spot. Ned looked and his eyes grew rounder. I nodded again, and then I ducked down and squeezed myself under the fence. I popped up on the other side to see Ned staring at me in disbelief.

'Come on then,' I hissed at him. 'If you're gonna'!'

He didn't hesitate again. He squatted down and shoved himself through, head first. On the wrong side of the fence, we looked at each other one more time, nodded, and ran on. Ned followed me. Through the grass, running and running, my school bag swinging from side to side on my back. I was scared of getting it wrong, and getting us lost. I didn't have the dog to follow this time. How would I remember the way? But somehow I did. Maybe I could smell the water now too, just like the dog had.

Suddenly the land dipped away, and we ran down the slope, and then the next one. When I looked back at Ned he was smiling in amazement, his red curls bouncing about on his head. When the next hill, the steeper one arrived, I plunged on down, and he followed, his arms circling at his sides, and suddenly he hooted and whooped and when I looked at him he was laughing. His mouth hung open and his eyes shone.

'I know!' I yelled back, and I kept taking him down.

The further we went down, the better the air smelled. I couldn't believe I hadn't notice it before. It seemed to open up to us. It welcomed us in. It fizzed inside our nostrils, danced on our tongues, and seeped down into our lungs. There was a breeze in our hair. A coolness on our skin. I wanted to open my mouth wider and wider, and inhale it all deep inside. It felt so good. And although Ned had no idea where I was taking him, when I looked at him I could tell he felt the same. He was licking his lips and closing his eyes and letting his open mouth suck it all up.

Before we knew it, we had reached the bottom. The ground was wet beneath our feet. We could hear the water trickling.

'I can't believe this,' Ned was saying, his eyes huge, his hands clasped beneath his chin. 'I can't believe this is here. I can't believe we are doing this.'

He hadn't even seen the tree yet. I took his hands in mine and kept him still.

'You want to know why I came here yesterday?' Ned nodded desperately. 'Because I saw a dog and I followed it. I followed it here.'

'A dog? A *dog*?'

'Yes, yes! A real dog!'

'But how...I thought they were...how...?' Ned gave up, spluttering over his words, shaking his head. He tore his gaze from my face and stared around, mouth hanging open. 'I didn't even know this was here,' he said softly. 'How is this even here? Where are we, Lissie?'

'We're nowhere.'

'We shouldn't be here, Lissie,' he looked back at me and his hands trembled inside mine.

'You're right. And I wonder why?'

Ned frowned. 'What do you mean?'

'Because there are things they don't want us to see. Places they don't want us to know about.'

'I don't know what you mean...'

'Neither do I,' I admitted, letting go of his hands and turning him gently by the shoulder towards the tree. 'Nothing makes sense Ned.'

He fell silent when he saw the apple tree. I felt his shoulders drop weakly under my hands, like all the air had left his body. I heard him gasp. I think I gasped too. Because it was still there, and I hadn't dreamt it or made it up, it was still there, the spindly, wiry, magnificent rebel tree. I smiled at it triumphantly. I wanted to run up and wrap my arms around it. I felt dizzy with it all. Like I was floating. Like nothing was real any more.

'What the hell?' Ned whispered. 'What *is* that?'

'An apple tree,' I said, pushing him towards it. 'Come on.'

He stumbled over his feet, went down to his knees and cursed. I grabbed his elbow and tried to haul him back up, but he wouldn't move. His hands were in the stream and his fingers were moving and clawing at the earth under the water. He was staring down into the water, watching his own hands grasping.

'It's beautiful,' I heard him say, and he was right. It was. 'I didn't know this was here,' he said again.

'Because no one told us,' I said, pulling him again. 'No one talks about what is on the other side of the fence, do they, Ned?'

'The scavengers don't say much,' he murmured, still staring at the water, and his splayed fingers. 'There's only Drake now that goes out. My dad says they have less and less work to do, because the Province has everything we need. Because it's growing and improving all the time.' He looked up then, looked me right in the eye. 'That's what our parents say, Lissie. All the time.'

I nodded, picturing Drake Cole in my head. He was about my father's age, and like all the scavengers before him, he was tall, broad and muscular.

'I know it. Come on, Ned. You have to get up.'

He did, pushing up with his hands, getting to his feet and then staring at the grit and the sand on his fingers, as the water trickled down his wrists.

'What happens if we're caught here?' he asked.

'I have no idea. What happens if people break the rules?'

'Sometimes they go to prison. My uncle got locked up once, remember? For fighting.'

'Didn't that old guy Jonas get locked up once or twice?' I wondered as I shepherded him towards the tree. His body was heavy and unwilling, and the greenery was dazzling and frightening and consuming us as we approached. It was like being eaten alive by lies. 'Remember him?'

Ned nodded firmly. 'Yeah, they said he was crazy though. My mum used to tell me to stay away from him towards the end.'

'Mine did too. He used to write things in the dust and talk to himself. Then he died, didn't he? But it hasn't happened since then,

53

has it? So, I don't know what this would mean. You see them? You see the apples? I told my gran about it Ned, and she made me draw her a picture. You know what she said? She said this tree was a rebel, and she said the guards would destroy it if they knew it was here.'

'What would they do to us?' he muttered, and we stopped right in front of the tree. I touched his arm and he was still shaking. 'Lock us up like Jonas?'

'Probably nothing,' I tried to reassure him. 'We're only kids.'

'Not for long,' he said back, and he reached out and touched one of the apples. 'Are these even real? Can you eat these? They don't look like the ones we get.'

'I know. I'll ask Gran. If she's able to tell me, she will.'

'So where's the dog then?' Ned dropped his hand and looked around. I saw him ball his hands into tight fists. He was still shaking, but his face had started to change. He looked less shocked, and more determined. 'I want to see it too. I've only seen them in books. They say they were dangerous, in the end. They had to kill them all.'

'Fighting for the same food,' I nodded. 'What was left of it. The humans lived on, the dogs died out.'

'So how did one escape? How can there be a dog? How can this tree be here, and not in the domes?' Ned started shaking his head back and forth. He put one hand to his brow and kept it there as if it hurt. 'Whoa, Lissie. I never knew your secret was gonna' be *this* big. Bloody hell. No wonder you look different. No wonder you *are* different.'

'Sit down,' I told him then. 'Because there's more.'

'Oh,' he said, going pale. 'Oh no.'

I got his arm and pulled him down and there we sat. Wet green grass under our backsides. Water flowing behind us. A rebel tree and its outlawed fruit standing over us. Ned was swallowing. He looked like he was going to be sick. He reached out and patted the grass tenderly with his open palm. I saw him swallow thickly, his mouth slightly open.

'We can't chalk all this,' he said, nodding at the grass. 'My dad…' He sniffed, shook his head and looked back at me for help. I knew he was thinking about his father, who worked in Plant Control.

'Forget about that for a minute. Listen. Gran gave me a book,' I told him before he could faint on me. He did that once, a few years back on sports day. Just turned white and keeled over at the starting line, as if it was all too much for him, and his body quit on him. I remembered looking at his parents and seeing his mother bury her face in her hands. 'It's like a diary. It's made of paper and tied up with string. She's kept it hidden for years and years. I started to read it but I didn't get very far, but it starts when she was a kid. When they had online, and all that stuff?'

'Wow, really? You should bring that to school! Imagine the kid's faces! The teachers would go nuts for material like that!'

I shook my head at him and planted my hand upon his wet knee. 'No way, don't be stupid Ned. We can't tell anyone about it, not about any of it. You have to swear!'

He looked back at the tree and shivered. 'I feel sick Lissie. Sat here, on the wrong side of the fence. I don't know what we're going to do. If my dad knew about all this! All these plants!'

'We can't do anything, Ned, not until I've read more of the

book. Not until I get more out of Gran. So, we do nothing. Do nothing and tell no one.'

'The dog?' he said suddenly, looking around. 'Will it come back?'

'Who knows?' I shrugged. 'I was hoping it would still be here so you could see it too. Maybe it was passing through. I don't know. I'll have to come back another day.'

He looked at me, licking his lips and swallowing repeatedly. His green eyes ran all over my face, while his brow furrowed, and his breath hitched. He was terrified.

'You're really gonna' come back? You'll do this again?'

'Yes,' I said to him, and it was the first time I had admitted this to myself. Yes, I was going to come back again. Not just to show Ned, not just to find the dog either. I didn't really know why I was going to come back, but there was no question about it. I couldn't abandon this place now that I knew about it. How could I just go back to normal life, and pretend I didn't know it existed?

'You'll get in trouble,' Ned told me. 'Who knows what kind of trouble?'

'Well, you have to make a decision then,' I replied and got slowly back to my feet. He reached out, grabbed my arm and used me to pull himself up. He stood facing me, and slowly the colour was returning to his cheeks. We stared at each other. 'We'll go back now,' I said. 'Before we're missed. You think about it tonight Ned. And if you want in, you're in. With me. If you want out, then you're out. I won't mind. I'll understand.'

56

'You'll think I'm a baby,' he said. I shook my head. 'You'll think I'm scared.'

'I'll understand.'

'You'll think I'm weak and useless, like they all do.'

'Ned...'

'I'm in.' He practically shouted it at me. 'I don't need to think about it. I'm in.'

'All right then,' I said, and we turned away from the tree and started slowly back towards the side of the hill.

'You're not any of those things,' I decided to tell him as we went. He was sucking in his breath and letting it out noisily, trying to calm himself down. 'You're way better than they think you are, Ned Fleck. You shouldn't listen to them.'

'I'll never be Woody,' he remarked dully, as we started to climb. 'I'll never be what my brother was to them.'

Ned's brother died of influenza before he was born. If his brother had lived, then Ned would never have had the chance to. If you lose a child, only then are you allowed to have another. But somehow Ned never quite lived up to it. His parents still carried the grief of their loss wherever they went. Their shoulders were low, their backs beaten down by pain. Their eyes never shone with love or gratitude when they looked at Ned. Their eyes were always hollow, as if they couldn't even see him.

'You're Ned Fleck, my best friend,' I told him and I took his hand. It was easier to climb back up that way. We pulled each other on. 'You're the smartest person I know.' He grinned at me. 'And you are also now the bravest.'

'You're Lissie Turner,' he said back. 'The second fastest kid in school, and also the most insane!'

When we got back to the fence, we cowered slightly. It all suddenly felt real, and we were both shivering, despite the solid heat of the day. I went under first, and he followed. Back on the right side, we walked on a little way, checking over our shoulders, while our hearts hammered inside our chests. I remembered then that I hadn't even told him about my duties, or about Governor Lancaster's flower garden. I punched Ned on the shoulder and tried to lighten the atmosphere.

'I didn't tell you about my duties,' I said with a careless laugh. 'But I'll save that one for the morning. I don't wanna' make you sick! I've never seen you so pale.'

'All right then,' Ned nodded, not willing to argue. He looked exhausted. He started off towards his home, and waved a limp hand at me. 'See you in the morning, *rebel*.'

I stared after him, wondering what he meant. And then I knew. He meant breaking the rules. And not just one. I suddenly felt like I did the day before, as I headed towards home. Small and scared and way out of my depth.

When I got back I found my parents sat outside. They had a small fire lit between them, and a pot of water was boiling above it.

'Your dinner is on the stove,' my mother said to me, barely smiling, and I thought how tired she looked, how worn out. 'How were your duties for the Governor?'

'Wonderful,' I said, going to her and kissing her cheek. 'Thank you Mum, you were right. I've got my tokens! Need to think about how to spend them! I was thinking about a new dress maybe.'

'They've got some great new designs in the clothes store,' my mother replied, swapping a surprised look with my father. 'Hilda was telling me. Perhaps we could go together, Lissie, and have a look. I did think the other day you were looking too grown up for those old smock things. We'll take you in and get Hilda to measure you up.'

'Okay,' I nodded, pleased to have made her smile, even if it did mean another lie. Dresses were the last thing on my mind, but somehow I'd known it would please her.

My father laughed and pulled me to his side for a hug. 'That's my girl,' he said. 'Growing up fast! You're going to bag yourself a great position, I just know it, Lissie. No cleaning streets for my girl. And just think, soon you'll be old enough for your first Coupling Dance!'

'That's another good reason to look at dresses,' my mother nodded. I shrugged at them both, still smiling as I eased myself from his side.

'Is Gran awake?'

'Yes,' said Mum. 'But she's had a bad day. I nearly admitted her to the hospital at one point, but you know what she's like, so stubborn. She's determined to live out her last days in that bed, at that window. She would be far more comfortable in hospital, but no.'

'It might not be her last days,' I said, wandering towards the open door. 'She could have a lot left in her, you know.'

My parents did not answer me. They did not argue. They

merely looked at each other and smiled faintly, as if to say, let her dream if she wants to. I went inside, got my dinner of potatoes, carrots and meat from the stove, and took it through to my bedroom. I dropped my school bag to the floor and closed the door behind me. Gran was in her bed, propped up at the window. She looked as if she was waiting for me. Her mouth gaped when she saw me. Her body became animated, wriggling and squirming under her covers.

'Lissie,' she rasped through her toothless mouth. 'Come here child. Please.'

She didn't have to beg me. I loved her so much, and right then I felt so weak and tired and afraid, that all I wanted to do was crawl onto her lap like a small child and have her hold me. But she was too old and frail and broken, and I would be fourteen in three months. I would be grown. I would have to leave school and start contributing to the community. I would have to become useful. I would have to start attending the Coupling Dances so I could find a partner and produce a child. As if she read my fears, Grandma Elizabeth reached out and found my hand. She looked at me with great pity in her eyes. I placed my dinner on the floor because I didn't think I had the stomach for it. I looked into her face and my eyes filled with tears. I put my head down into her lap.

'You are just a child,' I heard her say. 'And yet they ask so much of you. And so do I...'

'I went back Grandma...just now, with Ned.'

Her hand left mine and rested on my head. I could feel her fingers, as light as feathers, stroking slowly at my skull.

'I'm glad,' she croaked. 'I'm glad you took him. You shouldn't

60

have to do this alone.'

'Do what Gran?' I asked, but I didn't really want to know. At that moment, I wanted to turn my back on all of it.

'Did you read the book?'

'No, of course not. I only started it last night.'

'Was that only last night?' She gave a soft little chuckle and then elapsed into a brief coughing fit. I lifted my head and watched her tiny chest rising and falling as she fought for her breath. I was just starting to get scared that Mum would hear her and come in, when she managed to stop. She wiped her mouth of spittle and smiled a wicked little smile. 'I lose track of time,' she said. 'All the days and nights blend together when you're waiting to die. Sometimes I'm not sure when I'm awake and when I'm asleep.'

'You're not just waiting to die,' I hissed her, wiping at my eyes. I was getting so tired of them all talking like that. 'You're alive, aren't you?'

'That's my girl,' she laughed again, ruffling my hair.

'Last night you were talking about someone called Lawrence,' I told her, and immediately her face changed. Her mouth clamped shut like a beak. Her eyes narrowed in on me, and she moved her head forward towards mine. 'Who is he, Grandma? You were calling for him.'

'Someone I used to know,' she nodded at me. 'Someone from the Old World. Before all this.'

'Well, what happened to him?'

'Same thing that happened to lots like him,' she said, and her voice was getting smaller, so that I had to lean even closer to hear her. 'He was destroyed. Sacrificed. Made an example of.'

'I don't understand. By who? Who destroyed him?'

'The powers of course,' she said with an impatient roll of her eyes. 'Who do you think? The powers that be. The powers that were. Always the same. No matter what *they* think.' She jerked her head towards the window, and beyond where my parents were still murmuring around their fire. I frowned at her.

'What about them?'

'Your parents, Lissie, are nothing more than performing monkeys. Like all the others. Brainwashed. Afraid to wake up.'

I was shocked and I glared back at her, moving my hand away when she reached out for it again. 'How can you say that? About your own daughter?'

'*Grand*daughter,' she corrected me, again with a roll of her eyes. 'My daughter died. You know that child. My daughter was not so...soporific. My daughter was more like you, Lissie.'

'Me?'

'She had fire in her eyes. Steel in her gut.'

'You've lost me.'

'Don't lose yourself,' she snapped with a toss of her head, and a brisk smack of my hand. '*That* is more important. Read the book, Lissie. Read it and see what you make of it. See for yourself. Never mind all that they say out there. You found that tree for a reason. I know it. I feel it in my bones. It's like Lawrence is here, all over again.' With those last words, a faint smile settled upon her lips and she closed her eyes and seeped back into her pillows. I nudged her, but she did not respond.

'Who the hell is Lawrence?' I grumbled. But Grandma Elizabeth was asleep. I fumed at how easily she could slip away from me. Like always, she had succeeded in firing me up, stoking up my insides and driving me so crazy I knew I would not be able to sleep. But then I remembered that it was okay. It was okay if I did not sleep. I had the book to keep me company.

10: Hard Times

That night, I read the book under my blankets and when it all became too much, I hid it away under my mattress and closed my eyes, but sleep would not come. She was inside my head, you see. Grandma Elizabeth, when she was only a girl. I'd never seen photos, none survived, but I could imagine what she must have looked like. Small and neat and wiry, her teenage body packed tight with energy and wonder. She was born into hard times. The Endless War began two years before she came into the world, although it still wasn't being called that yet.

'*Dad was arrested again today. I came home from school after mucking about in the park with Lola and Milly. Mum was cooking up a big pot of vegetable stew for everyone and the kitchen was full of the usual bunch. Arrested for handed out his information sheets again, the ones with all the plants you can eat for free. When he got back he was ranting as usual, so I tried to zone him out, put my ear plugs in and went online to chat to Milly. I had about ten minutes before he was telling me to get off so he could do his group stuff! So unfair. The power goes off at 8pm, so I didn't get to go back on. Not important, he reminded me, unless you are talking to your friends about THIS! Whatever THIS is. Mum was crying then, begging him not to get involved. I don't really understand what it's about. It's not the lack of oil or power or the wars that he rants about, not really. It's the seeds. I don't get it, but I do know he has been warned to leave it alone, by the police and by Mum. He is so insistent though. Never stops banging on about it. His online group is getting bigger. He keeps trying to rope my friends into it all. They're not interested though, to be honest. Then he gets mad at me, as if this is my fault!*'

I had to show it to Ned and see if he could help me to make sense of it all. It was mind-blowing; the lives they lived in the Old World, all right there, all stuffed inside a book. In the morning, I woke up foggy and disorientated, with the last words I'd read still ringing in my ears; *'He's taking them on. He says there is nothing to lose. Who would believe it? My dad the rebel!'*

I didn't feel like a rebel today. I didn't feel like anything different or special. I just felt drained and tired, my head aching, my body resistant to movement. I moved the diary from under the mattress and stuffed it under the bed instead. I had decided to hide it somewhere different every day, in case my parents came across it. But then I wondered why bother? What would they care? What harm was there in me reading an old woman's journal?

Grandma Elizabeth remained asleep, so I got dressed and left the room and the diary behind. I sat at the bench and ate the warm porridge Mum had left out for me. She stood at the stove, sipping her coffee and watching me carefully.

'You seem tired, Lissie,' she said eventually. Why did it always sound like there was an accusation in her voice?

'I felt poorly in the night,' I opened my mouth and lied. *So* easily. I lowered my head, and placed a hand on my stomach. 'I feel okay now though. Just tired.'

'I expect your duties tired you out. You'll get used to it though. We all do. So, what did they have you doing?'

I lowered my spoon and paused before replying. I wondered if she knew about the flower garden? If anyone did?

'I was watering his flowers and collecting their seeds,' I told

65

her, watching her face carefully. If anything, she looked pleased. A smile pulled her lips up at either side and she tipped her head slightly.

'Oh? My goodness! I was under the impression they needed people for cleaning or something like that.'

'Me too. I mean, that's what I expected. Weird, eh?'

'Well, not weird. Unexpected. Fortunate! I hope you were polite and showed gratitude?'

'Of course. Mum, did you know the Governor had a flower garden? He grows flowers I never knew existed!'

'No, I didn't know,' she shook her head in wonder. 'Oh Lissie, how lovely for you!'

'But why do you think he has them?'

'Well, who knows? Why not? How lovely!'

'Aren't they pointless?'

'What do you mean, Lissie? Nothing is pointless if it gives you pleasure.'

I wanted to ask what gave her pleasure, but I stopped myself. 'So you think he grows them for fun?'

'Well, how on earth should I know? Why the questions? Lissie, he is a busy man. Hardly gets to see his own son. Too busy trying to improve the Province. Just like his father before him. No one could begrudge the man a nice garden.'

'He could plant more though...I mean, he could share the seeds for everyone. Wouldn't you like flowers here, Mum?'

Her posture stiffened and she watched me quietly, her face frozen. 'I don't like your tone,' she informed me slowly. 'What would I do with flowers here, young lady? Go on, you'll be late for school. You be grateful for such duties!' She put her cup down with a bang, snatched her work apron from the hook and tied it around her waist. 'I would have loved such a chance,' she grumbled on. 'Now go on, get your things.'

I slunk back to my room to fetch my bag.

'He's onto us, Lissie,' Grandma Elizabeth murmured from her bed. But I had no time to question her. I kissed her gently on the cheek and left the hut.

Between our hut and his, Ned was waiting for me with dark circles beneath his eyes. He yawned widely as I approached.

'You didn't sleep well either?'

He shook his head. 'Thinking too much.'

We passed his mother Hilda sweeping the front path.

'Morning Mrs. Fleck,' I called out. She looked up wearily, barely lifting her head. She managed a small wave, waving us on it felt like, waving us away from her and her never-ending despair. I gave Ned a reassuring look and he rolled his eyes in reply.

'Anniversary is coming up. She always gets worse.'

I decided to cheer him up by telling him about my bizarre duties yesterday. 'So, guess what the Governor's secretary had me doing, Ned? You'll never guess!'

Ned rubbed his chin, pretending to be deep in thought. 'Hmm, let's see. Cleaning Saul's pit? Washing his backside? Cleaning his toilet? Spoon feeding him dinner?'

'Nope. None of the above. I was given personal access to the Governor's private flower garden.'

'His *what*?'

'Flower garden Ned. A garden filled with flowers. Beautiful pointless flowers just for him. I had to water them and collect their seeds in an envelope. It was easy.'

Ned slowed down, his forehead furrowed with creases, his top lip curled back. 'Wait a minute. Why does he have a garden?'

'My thoughts exactly,' I replied. 'Miss Harper made me think it was a personal project of his or something. Something he studies at to improve.'

Ned flung his arms out to either side in frustration. 'There must be a point to it! Why does anyone grow flowers? It's not allowed, is it?' He scratched at his head in confusion. 'Unless you *are* allowed and no one ever told us! But flowers, Lissie! What do they even do?'

'They don't do anything. They look pretty. But they smell too much. I mean, they stink!'

Ned just shook his head. 'You get a flower garden, and I get pulling up weeds! How is that fair, Lissie Turner?'

I giggled, and we walked on towards the square. I felt lighter now. Ned had that effect on me. He got more serious, and I felt less burdened. I didn't know why it worked like that, but it did. It was like he soaked up all the worries from me and took them on himself. Not that he needed anything else to worry about. Sometimes I wondered

68

what it could be like for him, living with his parents and their grief. Nearly fourteen years old and they still had not accepted that he replaced his brother Woody. He replaced his brother and did not live up to the job. Poor Ned, I thought, as we ambled past the Governor's offices. If only they could see him the way I did.

At the school building we were greeted with a familiar sight. Saul Lancaster, in usual leering mode; his arms crossed over his barrel chest, with one skinny leg crossed over the other. As smug as ever, and I supposed we knew why.

'Don't know what you're smiling at, Turner,' he sneered at me. I looked up at him and winced at the latest eruption of spots across his face. A small part of me wanted to feel sorry for him, but he soon put an end to that by spitting a ball of phlegm onto the ground between my feet. I stepped back, grimacing in disgust.

'You are way out of line,' Ned told him, scowling darkly. Saul ignored him completely and smiled in triumph at me.

'My father is home,' he said, so I shrugged, so what? 'Don't expect anything quite so cushy today.'

'Of course not,' I responded breezily.

It was my sole aim in life not to let Saul Lancaster get to me. He'd had this superior and snotty attitude for years. I would like to call him a bully, but he didn't even have the guts or the ambition to be that. He'd just got his nose up in the air constantly, and the worst thing was; everyone loved him. I mean, the teachers loved him, the other kids loved him. No one could see through him, except me and Ned.

'I enjoyed it yesterday, though. Really nice of him to let me help in his private garden! Does he let you help too?'

A strange look passed over Saul's face. His eyes were light blue and they narrowed in on me for the briefest of moments, before he smirked again, then sighed in boredom.

'Doesn't interest me. What use have I got for flowers?'

'What use has anyone?'

'Yeah, why does he grow them?' asked Ned, peering closer at Saul. 'What're they for?'

But Saul had no answer for him. He merely looked us up and down as if he were offended by the sight of us, before turning away and walking casually into school.

'He's got something to hide,' Ned had decided with a firm nod. I gave him a grim look, and said nothing. I was beginning to think we all had. Not least of all Grandma Elizabeth.

After school, I found out why Saul was looking so smug. The same look was plastered all over his blemish ridden face as I approached the offices, school bag on shoulder. He was waiting for me at the doors and instead of moving so I could go in, he shook his head and crooked a finger at me, beckoning me to follow.

He slouched around to the back of the building, but it was not the private garden we were heading for. Instead he led me through the back yard and towards the stables. Not everyone in Province 5 owned a horse. Ownership was given on a need to own basis only. So, if you didn't need one for your work, you didn't get one. You walked. Nothing wrong with walking, my Dad liked to say cheerily, when he set off every morning; it keeps you fit and healthy!

Saul stopped at the first stable door and leaned against it, eyeing me coolly. I wanted to ask what my duties were, but I was not going to give him the pleasure. I placed my school bag carefully on the ground and looked at him, waiting. He jerked his head towards the first stable. The door was slightly open, and it appeared to be empty. I looked along the row, and couldn't see any horses peering out. They must have all been working.

'Pitchfork in the corner,' said Saul, raising one lazy eyebrow. I smiled in recognition. I was going to be shoveling horse manure. 'Wheelbarrow there,' he added, nodding to a rusted old barrow propped up against the second stable door. It looked like it had seen better days. Maybe about a hundred years ago.

'All right,' I replied, rubbing my hands together. 'I'll get started. Where do I wheel it to?'

'Wagon,' he said, and I nodded again. Parked next to the exit gate was a large wooden wagon. It also looked as if it had seen better days.

'Okay,' I took in the ramp, trying to work out how much manure to load into the wheelbarrow before it got too heavy to push up the ramp. 'Fine. Where does it all end up, anyway?'

Saul Lancaster moved away from the door, looking incredibly bored. 'It goes to the domes, you idiot. It fertilises the plants, doesn't it?'

'Of course,' I rolled my eyes at my own stupidity. I moved past him, into the cool of the stable and my eyes were met with the biggest pile of horse dung I had ever seen. It looked like they had been storing it up for months.

'Used to be one of my duties,' Saul hung over the door and told

71

me. 'But Dad is preparing me for bigger and better things these days.'

'I'm sure he is,' I responded, with my back to him. 'Lucky you. Hey Saul? Have you even been to our domes?'

'Course I have. I went the other day. I'm learning the ropes, aren't I?'

I wanted to ask him more. I wanted to ask him what it was like inside the domes. I wanted to ask what the guards there would do if they knew an apple seed had escaped long ago and set up its home on the wrong side of the fence. But I didn't, because his presence disturbed me. I grabbed the pitchfork and got stuck in.

He watched me for a while. I knew he would. I ignored him, and threw my back into it; shoveling poo like it was the most exciting duty in the world. I gritted my teeth and bit my tongue and wondered why he had always hated me so much. I mean, what had I ever done to him? Eventually Saul got bored and wandered away.

'Gonna' beat your arse on sports day,' I muttered to the dung when he was out of earshot.

An hour later, and things were bad. There was no way to shovel dung without getting covered in it. I tried as hard as I could to keep my school dress reasonably clean, but it was just not happening. The dung got on my hands, and then in my hair when I tried to push it out of my face. I was sweating, and my back was killing me. I was cross with myself too. I should have asked Saul how long I was meant to do this for. I had no idea how much time had passed. No one had given me any tokens. No one was around to supervise, or tell me to take a break, or that it was time to go home. I wondered what my mother would say when I eventually rolled home, stinking of manure.

I'll tell Gran, I thought viciously. I'll tell her, and see what she has to say!

Some time later, and my frustration was growing. I was starting to think I was being punished, and I was growing increasingly paranoid about the tree, and the fence, and the dog. What if they knew? What if somehow they all knew? Maybe I'd get stuck with this forever! Day after day after day of back breaking work! I seethed, and panicked and chewed at my lip. I longed for Ned and his voice of reason.

I was just wheeling what felt like the hundredth wheelbarrow of dung up and onto the wagon, when I heard a voice call out to me.

'What on earth are you still doing here?'

I turned in surprise. The Governor himself was staring right back at me. He was stood at the gate in a pale grey suit, with the wide brimmed hat upon his head. His hands were on his hips, and his expression was full of wonder. He was a tall man, and barrel chested like his son. He carried with him a calmness though, it had to be said. I felt my shoulders sinking. I felt close to tears but forced them back angrily.

'I saw you through the window,' he said, and opened the gate. I wiped my face on my arm, tipped out the barrow and backed it slowly down the ramp. I was a mess. A complete and utter stinking state. There was straw and dung in my hair. I didn't know what to say to the Governor so I said nothing. I just shrugged my shoulders, trying to work out what I had done wrong.

'You should have gone home hours ago,' he said softly, in concern. I got it then. I thought about Saul Lancaster and his rash of

73

pimples and I wanted to pound my fist right into them. I couldn't say this to his father though, so I just stared in humiliation at my muck covered shoes. The Governor was shaking his head, and rubbing the silver whiskers on his chin.

'My son,' he said then, his voice rising. 'My son was left in charge, and he was to give you your tokens in advance and tell you when the hour was up. My girl, your parents will be getting worried!'

'He didn't say,' I finally spoke up. I bit my lip and looked up into his face. He offered a pained expression.

'Oh my girl, I am sorry. I must apologise. My son...' he shook his head slightly and glared briefly up at the offices. 'I left Saul in charge for the first time. I think, unfortunately, he has played a trick on you.'

I nodded my head glumly. I really did want to cry. 'Oh.'

'Listen. I will pay you double. I will send one of my men around with a horse, and take you home right away. My apologies Miss Turner. I had no idea he would do this.'

'It's okay. I can walk.'

'No, no,' he held up a hand and then turned and beckoned to a short man hovering in the background. 'Martin, fetch a horse. Take Miss Turner back home and apologise *profusely* to her family. She should have been home hours ago.'

The man called Martin nodded and disappeared into another stable. Governor Lancaster looked back at me, his head tipped slightly, his forehead creased under the brow of his hat. I used my hands to wipe down my dress, but it was pointless.

'I told him to let you into the garden again,' he said then. 'I did *not* tell him to assign manure duties.'

'Oh.'

'You did such a fine job yesterday,' he went on, and a grateful smile touched his thin lips.

'Thank you. I enjoyed it.'

'Good,' he said, and the smile stretched. He took a step backwards then. He must have been busy. He always had so many things to do. 'It's very important to me, you know. The garden. I'll have to tell you all about it some day, if I ever get the time!' He laughed a little, and I smiled back, and he touched the brim of his hat. 'Good evening, Miss Turner. Thank you for your hard work. Very loyal. Oh, and please do pass my best wishes onto your grandmother for me. A wonderful lady. Such history! We're very proud of people like her in Province 5.' He left me with a wide and warm smile, a smile that conveyed nothing but pride and gratitude, and then he turned and walked back through the gate.

I stood and stared, and I was a little bit shocked, a little bit awed. But they all said that was the effect he had on you. When the gossip murmured its way around the Province, it was always gentle and smiling, because he was a gentle and smiling man. He just has a way of making you feel better, they all said, my parents included. He really was like that, I thought, watching him go. He didn't assign me to the dung duties, his stupid oaf of a son did. He wanted me to tend the garden again. Lucky you, my mother had said. Lucky me. But why me?

11: The Race

For the next two weeks, I was too busy to go back to the tree. Every day, I finished school, went to the Governor's offices and did whatever had been assigned to me. Saul was not left in charge again. In fact, I barely saw him. Instead I was met in the lobby every afternoon by Miss Harper. She seemed to be very fond of me. I was assigned all sorts of duties, so I didn't get bored. Some days it was cleaning; sweeping the lobby, polishing the glass windows, or dusting in the lounge. But most days, I was assigned to the garden.

The garden work was always the same. I watered the plants gently, being careful not to blast them or their roots. I checked them for seeds and gathered them into the envelopes. I sometimes fed the fish in the pond. I was given my tokens in advance, but I never got time to spend them. After duties, I headed back to school and met Ned on the playing field to practice for sports day. I desperately wanted to beat Saul Lancaster. More than just beat him, I wanted to humiliate him. There were always other kids there too, practicing their sport. Ned sat on the grass, hugged his knees up to his chin and timed my runs in his head. I was getting faster. I was getting faster every time, and that was because every time I ran I thought about horse dung in my hair and on my face, and I thought about Saul Lancaster and his nose stuck up in the air, and him being groomed for bigger and better things, and then I ran. I *had* to beat him.

During this time, Grandma Elizabeth scared us on a near daily basis. My mother begged her to go to hospital, but when she was coherent enough to talk to us, she refused.

'I will die here,' she growled back at my mother every single time. 'You cannot take that away from me.' My mother had no choice

76

but to back off, wringing her hands and muttering under her breath. It felt like she was going downhill fast, and I couldn't bear it.

'You're the only one who understands me round here,' I tried telling her, the night before sports day, but all she responded with were snores. Mum had been struggling to get her to eat, and her body seemed to be vanishing under the blankets. Her skin too, seemed so thin and pale, it was like she was fading away before my very eyes. I sat and held her hand and squeezed it as tight as I dared, willing her to open her eyes and speak to me.

'Think of me tomorrow, Gran,' I told her. 'Stupid sports day. They all make such a big deal of it. Mum and Dad will be there watching. I've got to beat Saul in the sprint. I've just got to. If I don't win, my life will be over!' She just slept on, so I gave up and climbed into my own bed.

The curtains were left open, and the silver moon streamed inside, lighting us up. Me on my side and Gran on hers. I laid on my back with my head on my pillow and I watched her. And then I had an idea. I got back out of bed, pulled the diary out from inside my pillowcase and went back to her side.

'Listen Gran,' I whispered to her. The window was open and a cool breeze tickled my arms as I held the diary over her bed. 'Listen to what you were saying back then. In the Old World. I don't understand most of it Gran. I wish you would wake up and tell me about it.'

I opened the diary and started to read; '...*So Dad is crazy lately. With his group and his online stuff. I know Mum is worried. It used to be different when he had work, but now he has nothing else to occupy his time. There is less and less work for people now they say the oil is running out. I try not to be embarrassed of Dad, but people at school have been talking about it. They see him online and they want to ask me all about it. His group grows bigger all the time. He has this Professor on board, and some scientists too, apparently. They're linking up with other groups across the country too. A load of grubby gardeners and old hippies! Funny bunch, Mum calls them. But secretly I think she likes them, and I think she is on Dad's side. They've got another big protest to go on next month, so he's been making signs and banners. They keep sending off petitions and getting people online to sign them and share them. He does as much as he can until the power shuts off. Then he sits and makes more of those information sheets he keeps getting into trouble for. The power goes out before 8pm now. Gets a little earlier every night. You can almost hear the collective sigh as the millions of bored people get locked out of their online lives. I don't know if anything Dad is doing will make a difference. He wants me to come though. Every time I shovel food into my mouth he waves a finger at me. Won't be much more of that if they get their way, he says. Times are gonna' get harder, he says.'*

I stopped and looked at her face. Her cheeks were loose and sagging into her neck. Her mouth hung open, and she was breathing. Just.

'This is stuff we've never learned about,' I told her, in case she could hear me. 'All our history books start with Peace. That's it. They reckon all the history books got burnt in the wars. Nothing survived, did it Gran? Just you, and a load of plastic and metal. And this.' I tapped the diary and closed it up. 'Maybe Ned's right. Maybe I should take it to school and show it to our teachers. See what they make of it, eh? See if it teaches them a thing or two? I mean, it could change things. Could change what they teach us.'

It was then that she opened her eyes. It looked like a massive effort, as they flickered open, trying to focus, before dropping shut again. Finally, she maintained her gaze with mine. Her breathing was shallow and dry.

'No,' she said. Just one word. No.

'Don't take it to school?' I asked.

'No,' she said it again. Her eyes fell shut. I thought I understood. But she said it again. Softer this time. 'No.'

I sighed, and got up from the stool. I put the diary back inside my pillow and climbed into bed. I needed my sleep if I was going to beat Saul tomorrow. I closed my eyes and met the darkness, and she said it again, and again, and again, all night long; '...no...no...no.'

In the morning, I woke up and ran to her. She was breathing. She lived. I touched her hand, and stroked her face and then I kissed her forehead and left her side. I thought about the diary and my great-great-grandfather going on his protest, and I wondered what had happened next. Did the Government listen to him and his friends? Or did they keep selling off all the seeds like he feared they were going to? What did that even mean? It made me uneasy though, just to think about it. I thought about the food we ate and where it came from and my guts got all hard and tight.

I was going to take the diary and show it to Ned later. He would have something to say about it all, I knew. But for now, there was a race to be run. I had no room for breakfast and left home early.

'We'll see you at one o'clock!' Dad called after me as I set off. 'Got my fingers crossed for you girl!'

The Tree of Rebels

I nodded grimly and kept walking. I felt like a rebel, going off to war. I thought, that is in me, like Gran said, that is inside me too. Great-great-grandfather saying no. No. No to what? And what did it have to do with me? With anything?

When we were lined up for our race, I did not look at Saul Lancaster but I could feel him looking at me. Ned was on the sidelines, clapping and cheering and whistling. Mum and Dad were with the rest of the parents, sat proudly on the long benches we had dragged out of school for them. And right down at the bottom of the field, just beyond the finish line, Governor Lancaster stood under a large fabric gazebo, sheltered from the sun. He was flanked on either side by Mrs. Batton the headteacher, Miss Harper his secretary, and his deputy, Rhys Bradshaw. Deputy Bradshaw wore the same black uniform as the guards, except he had a red stripe on his cap. It matched his red hair, beard and moustache. The women clapped hands and chattered, while the two men looked still and solemn. I thought about Saul running towards his father and his future and I gritted my teeth and lowered my head.

Miss Branksome counted us down.

'Are you ready?' and then; 'on your marks...get set...go!' She blew into a huge silver whistle and off we went. Six boys and six girls. The fastest in the school. The winners of all our heats. They always told us it didn't matter who won. This was not a competition, this was fun. This was fitness. This was well-being. We were all different and we were all special. It didn't matter if you won or lost, or came second or third. It was just for fun. But they were wrong. Because it did matter. It mattered that I was the fastest, because I was Lissie Turner.

I was thinking this as I ran. I am Lissie Turner. I am Lissie

Turner. I am Lissie Turner. I am the fastest. I am the fastest. I am the fastest. I pumped my legs and I pumped my arms and my body was one unified thing, all limbs like pistons, pushing me on, my feet spring-boarding my calves, jolting up into my knees, and then catapulting into my thighs, and my heart pounded and my eyes stared and my head was down, and I was the fastest, I was the fastest.

And I was.

I *was* the fastest.

Because I won.

I won!

I didn't realise it at first. I was over the finish line and I was staring at Governor Lancaster, and he was staring back, and my feet had stopped, and my body fell over them, but I kept my balance and caught my breath and they were all roaring and clapping. I felt someone grab my arm and hold it aloft.

'We have a winner! Lissie Turner!'

I turned in a circle, triumphant and I saw Saul at the other end of the line. He was sat on the ground and he was glaring at me like he wanted to kill me. I glared back. I wanted to go up to him and laugh in his face. I am the winner, I wanted to say. I am the winner because I am Lissie Turner and I am the fastest! And it doesn't matter, Saul, it doesn't matter what happens to us when we get to be fourteen, when we have to leave school and join the rest of them, and earn tokens and be grateful for everything. It doesn't matter if you end up running the town, and I end up cleaning it, because I beat you. I *beat* you.

There were no duties after school. Everyone was allowed to

leave early. Mum and Dad had to go back to work though, so I asked if I could go and hang out with Ned. He didn't win anything at sports day, and his parents trudged off without even saying goodbye. We were told to stay out of trouble and have fun.

The rest of the afternoon was all ours. Our eyes met and we knew exactly where we were going. First, we went back to his hut and left our school things there. Then we packed some bottles of water, and two slices of his mother's ginger cake. Ned looked calm, not beaten down like he usually would after sports day. He had the smallest of smiles upon his face and he said very little. I felt the same. The triumph of beating Saul Lancaster had left me for now. I felt invigorated and yet at peace. We didn't say much as we left his hut and headed across the field and towards the border.

There were no nerves in our bellies, no looks over our shoulders. I didn't know why. Except that maybe, somehow, for some reason, we felt like we deserved to feel calm. We swapped looks, and smiled secret smiles. The breeze chased through our hair, and a large black bird circled in the air above us. You didn't see too many birds in the Province. The ones you saw a lot of were the crows and the magpies. People said they were too clever. They found food anywhere. Just like the rats. But the rest of the birds we knew about were trapped inside picture books, and memories. If the wars and the famines didn't kill them off, then the lack of food afterwards did. The trapping of nature under the domes. Nothing for them to hunt, nothing for them to eat.

When we reached the fence, Ned went under first. I had a brief check of things. The hole was still there. No one had been.

'Do you think the guards ever check the fence?' I asked Ned on the other side as we walked on.

'Don't suppose they have reason to,' he shrugged.

'No one else has ever gone beyond it? Unless they can? Unless they are meant to?'

'Everything is here,' he shrugged again. 'Unless you're a dome worker or a scavenger. You don't need to leave.'

'But why doesn't anyone *want* to leave? Maybe they might find long lost family in another province?'

'Governor Lancaster says Province 5 is one of the most advanced with the best recovery,' Ned said, repeating something we had both heard before. 'Of course number 1 is the biggest and the strongest.'

We fell into silence again and kept walking. We went down the first slope, and then the second, the steeper climb down towards the water. I saw it then. In the distance. Moving around, and moving the water with it. I grabbed Ned by the shoulder and pointed.

'Look!'

'What?'

I pointed again and he squinted down at the water, and then he saw it and he froze.

'Oh my goodness. You were right.'

The dog was back.

It was paddling in the water, sticking its nose under and then shaking out its fur. It looked like it was playing. Having fun. The long tail was sailing back and forth. It was making a noise.

'Oh my goodness,' whispered Ned, and we walked down slowly, carefully. It didn't seem to care though. It saw us and ignored us. It kept playing. Pawing at rocks and sticks under the water, trying to free them. Barking when it couldn't. I stood at the bottom, my feet in the water, and I turned towards the tree. Oh, wasn't it magnificent. It seemed like it had grown and flourished in our absence. The apples looked bigger and juicier. The air smelled like nothing on this earth.

Ned picked up a stick and threw it out across the stream. The dog went after it, making its noise, swinging its tail. I laughed, and so did Ned. The dog found the stick and brought it back. It dropped it with a splash at our feet. Ned stared at it. I could tell he wanted to touch it, but was scared to.

'It wants you to throw it again,' I nudged him. 'It likes it.'

I wondered if it got lonely, all by itself. How long had it been alone? Ned shook himself, grabbed the stick and threw it again. The dog raced off, yapping. I left them to it.

'Still here?' I asked the tree with a grin. 'Still breaking the rules?'

'Crazy thing!' yelled Ned, coming up behind me. 'It keeps bringing it back! Is that what they're supposed to do?'

'They used to do a lot of things,' I told him. 'Gran said they used to help blind people and deaf people and they used to sniff out bombs in the wars, and they could be trained to find lost people, or attack bad people. Loads of things.'

'Why the hell don't we use them now?' he asked, shaking his

head, and grinning. The dog was at his feet, tongue lolling, ears pricked forward, tail swishing. 'Funny crazy thing!' Ned said, delighted. 'Could have fun all day with one of these!'

'I want an apple,' I said to him, and he stared back at me. 'What do you reckon?'

'I don't know.'

'Why not?'

'I don't know Lissie. How do you know if it's safe?'

'How do we know if anything is?'

'I don't get you,' he frowned. 'You've lost me.'

'They don't tell us everything at school,' I decided to remind him as I reached out and cupped my hand under the fattest, roundest apple. It looked ready now. Ready for picking and eating. 'They teach us history from Peace onwards. Not what life was like when Gran was a kid. The stuff in that diary Ned, it's amazing. I asked if I should show it at school and she said no. Just like that. No. And I think I know why.'

'Why?'

'Because they would do the same thing to the diary that they would do to this tree. Destroy it.'

I pulled the apple and it snapped free of the branch. It sat in the palm of my hand. Fat and rosy and covered in bumps and scars. I held it to my nose and sniffed it. The apples at school didn't smell of anything, but this one did. It smelled like I imagined it was going to taste. Crisp and wet and sharp and green. I opened my mouth and closed my teeth around it, and Ned hushed into an awed silence, and the dog waited for the stick, and I was thinking about seeds being owned, and seeds being banned and Gran's father saying no. *No.* And I bit into it, and sweet, sweet juice filled my mouth and dripped down my chin and I closed my eyes because it tasted like a dream, so maybe I was dreaming and then Ned grabbed my arm.

It hurt. I felt him turn to stone beside me. 'Lissie,' he said. 'There's someone watching us.'

12: Stranger

The first thing I did was drop the apple.

It hit the ground and rolled away. The dog immediately gave chase, thinking we had imagined up a new game for it. The second thing I did was curl my hand around Ned's so that we were linked. We were both staring at the same thing. Some strange and tangled bush I did not know the name of. And staring back at us, two dark, penetrating eyes, a nose, and a mouth. We could not tell if it was a woman, or a man, a stranger, or someone we knew. We both started walking backwards together, and the face watched us go. He, or she made no move to come out from the bush. He, or she made no sound either. We kept walking backwards, faster and faster, while the dog dashed about in the water with the apple in its mouth.

'Run,' I heard Ned's voice hissing through his gritted teeth. 'Run.'

He did not need to say it a third time. Holding hands, we turned tail and ran. Through the water, and then back up the way we came, scrabbling and scrambling our way clumsily up the side of the cliff. Our hearts were beating inside our mouths, our throats too full of fear to allow us to scream or breathe. Somehow we just ran.

We kept running until we were back at the fence. Ned let go of my hand and shoved me towards the hole. I went through first, while he stood and looked back over his shoulder. His chest was rising and falling so rapidly he looked like he was going to fall over. Once I was through, he ducked down and followed me. We were back on our side of the fence, and yet somehow it did not feel enough. We grabbed hands without speaking and started running again.

After a while I pulled his hand to slow him down.

'Mum and Dad will be out...' I managed to gasp breathlessly, and Ned nodded in reply. 'Talk to Gran...' I muttered, and he nodded again, understanding. We ran on, across the dry land where nothing ever grew, down the wide flat path, further and further away from the fence, and the tree, and the dog, and the face.

Finally, my hut came into sight, and we stopped running. We were both gasping for breath, our heads hanging, our shoulders heaving and our feet dragging. Then Ned slung an arm around my neck and laughed. I stared at him in bemusement.

'What?'

'I don't know,' he was grinning. 'Your face!'

I turned away from him, as my hut drew nearer and nearer. I could still taste the apple in my mouth, sweet and sharp.

'Whoever it was saw us,' I said, feeling the urge to state the facts and the truth of the situation we were in. 'They saw us. That's it. We're done for.'

'Depends who it was though. No one I know.'

I looked at him sharply. For some reason his words sent a shiver down my spine. 'Who then?'

'I don't know, Lissie. But maybe we scared them, as much as they scared us? Didn't try to follow us, did they?'

'We *hope* they didn't,' I corrected him, twitching and looking back over my shoulder at the nothingness that stretched out behind us.

'How long were they there for? Just watching us? Why? Why would anyone else be there? What are we going to do now?'

'Slow down,' Ned wiped at his sweaty face with both hands. 'Just slow down. Stop firing questions at me. You're hurting my brain.'

But it was too late to slow down. Things had gone too far. I could barely swallow, or breathe. Someone was there! Someone saw us on the wrong side of the fence...and I was eating the apple from the tree. It felt like I had been caught red-handed. I could almost hear the jail cell door slamming behind me. What would my parents say when they found out about this? My mother would be terrified, of everything, terrified that I'd rocked the boat, stirred things up, and for what? And my father, I could just picture his face, I could just hear his sigh. He would be so disappointed in me. *So* disappointed.

We wandered towards my home, and I was shaking my head and staring down at the dusty earth beneath my feet.

'Who was it?' I was mumbling. 'Who the hell *was* that?'

'Someone else on the wrong side of the fence,' said Ned, stating the obvious with a wondering smile. I elbowed him and he yelped.

'You're not helping. Aren't you scared?'

'I think so. I don't know. Isn't being scared very similar to being excited?'

I dropped my shoulders and shook my head. Ned was acting very strangely, I thought. 'We better tell Gran. We better hope she's in a mood to talk. Come on.'

We pushed open the front door and walked into the hut. It was dark and cool and silent. The scent of coffee filled the air. Ned and I headed for the room I shared with Gran. I tapped lightly upon the door before easing it open. I took a lungful of breath and felt Ned closing in behind me.

She was lying in bed with her eyes closed. Barely breathing, it seemed, but I knew her tricks. I knew how she liked to fool us. I crossed the room and took up my position on the stool and I could feel sweat clinging to the bumps of my spine as I placed my shaking hands over hers.

'Gran?' I whispered, gently squeezing her hand. 'Gran?'

'Is she all right?' Ned asked softly, arriving at my side. I glanced up at his face and his skin was pale, and his eyes dark, his forehead creased, his lower lip trembling. He was as desperate to talk to her as I was. 'What is she, just asleep?'

'Course,' I whispered, rubbing at her hand. 'Gran? Wake up, Grandma, it's Lissie and Ned. We need to talk to you, Gran. We *really* need to talk to you.'

She did not stir. I could not tell if she was breathing. I rubbed her hand harder, willing, needing her to wake up. 'Is she ok?' Ned was asking me. 'Is she breathing?'

'Don't Ned!'

'What?'

'Don't scare me.' I pulled the covers back and leaned over her, placing my cheek against her chest. I held up a finger, warning Ned to keep quiet. I closed my eyes and listened. There. I could just hear it. Thump. Thump. Thump. Weak, but still there. She was still with us. I released my relief in a huge breath and rolled my eyes at Ned. 'She's

90

just asleep. Just deeply asleep. Let's read to her.'

Ned looked perplexed while I went over to my bed and fetched out the diary. I didn't look at him. I was wondering how much time we had until my parents got home. I sat back on the stool and opened the diary onto the bed. Ned peered over me.

'Is that it? Is that her book?'

'Yes, this is it. If she doesn't wake up, we might find more out from here.' I cleared my throat, glanced at Grandma Elizabeth one more time, and started to read;

'*September 2074. Last night we heard the news. There will be no more power. Not for us anyway. Not unless we can pay for it. Finally, the free days are over. If you want to live online to escape the hunger of your own life, you will have to find the money to pay for it. It's been coming for years, Mum says, I don't know why people are so shocked. I just sat there thinking about how much things will change. We'll be all right, Mum reassured me, there is the wind turbine and the solar panels. Too little too late Dad told her. It's not enough, not for this many people. Watch them go crazy. Well if anyone is crazy around here it is my father! He got arrested again today at another protest. People are panicking and scared. People are rushing to the shops to buy what is left before the lorries can't bring anymore. My dad just stays up all night in the kitchen talking to the people that gather there with him. They come in with dark worried faces, but they end up bellowing laughter and eating Mum's soup. Some of them have been getting arrested too at protests, for being disorderly. I don't understand, I told him, what were they doing wrong? Instigating, he told me. It would seem my father is turning into a criminal. I am alarmed but also intrigued. I mean, he used to be so straight laced, but*

91

he says to hell with all that, this matters. He is obsessed. Every day he takes me into the garden and shows me what he has growing, and how to take care of it if something happens to him.'

I stopped reading to take a breath and to check on Grandma Elizabeth. She was snoring very, very gently. Ned wiped his hair back with one hand and crouched down beside me.

'It's so weird,' he said. 'Hearing about the Old World like that. You can almost picture it. How old was your Gran when she wrote that bit?'

'About fourteen I think.'

'Hey, same as us.'

'Oh yeah.' I rubbed her hand, ducked my head and read on;

'So now Mum is getting even more annoyed with him. He brings more and more of his rowdyl mates around to the house. Some of them stay the night, or stay for days. You can see Mum is on edge the whole time though, checking out of the window, acting paranoid. I don't get why. What are they doing that is so wrong? I sit in with them sometimes, so I can catch the gossip. There is one big guy called Elias, and he gets them all riled up. He brings his home brewed beer, and he says; that's another thing they're after! That's another thing they want control of! They can keep their hands off my ruddy beer! They all cheer and clap when Elias is ranting. He says they need one final push. They need to keep up momentum. Get more members. Get people involved. Give them no choice. But my dad sits and shakes his head in despair. They didn't care, he says, and he always looks at me when he says it, as if somehow I am responsible for all the other people who didn't listen to him years ago. None of them listened, he shouts when

he has had a few drinks, you didn't listen! You!'

Gran stuttered into life before our eyes and I dropped the diary in fright, as she suddenly lurched forward in bed.

'Gran!' I cried out, reaching for her. She turned her head and looked me right in the eye.

'I did listen!' she moaned at me, before settling back again, sinking back into her pillows. 'Oh he'd say that...he'd accuse me of that!'

'We need to talk to you, Grandma,' I said to her quickly, picking the diary up and closing it on my lap. 'It's urgent!'

She tilted her head at me. And then her eyes took in Ned, and her frown deepened and her hand stole out listlessly, creeping onto mine and settling there.

'What is it?' she croaked.

'The tree,' I told her, tears threatening. I squeezed them away. 'We went back to the tree, Gran, and I tasted the apple and then...then there was someone there...someone watching us!' I looked at Ned and he nodded in grim agreement. I bit my lip, waiting for her to respond. Her eyes were gleaming.

'What did it taste like?'

'What?'

'The apple. What did it taste like Lissie?'

'Grandma, that's not the important part...'

Her hand tightened on mine. 'Yes, it is! What did it taste like,

93

Lissie?'

I ran my tongue around the inside of my mouth. The taste was still there. It made my mouth water just thinking about it.

'It was good Gran...*really* good.'

'We had three apple trees in the garden, you know...'

'Your dad?'

'Yes, he planted them. He planted everything. He planted more and more, even more so when they told him he couldn't.'

'What was going on back then?' Ned piped up. 'What does protest mean?'

'Oh it means so many things,' Grandma chuckled at us, her sweet smile revealing her toothless mouth. She patted my hand and leaned in close as if about to share her deepest, darkest secrets. I was desperate to bring her back on track. How could she not even care about the person watching us? 'It means standing up, making your voice heard. Knowing that you have a voice.'

'Grandma, what about the person who saw us?' I urged her. 'Did you even hear what I said? Ned and I went back to the tree and there was someone there!'

'I wouldn't worry about that,' she said breezily.

'Why not?'

'Did they follow you? Did they chase you? Did they do anything?'

'No, nothing!'

94

'Then what are you scared about?'

I looked at Ned, as if to say, see? This is what I have to deal with! He looked totally perplexed, shaking his head back at me.

'Breaking the rules?' he mumbled wonderingly. 'Getting caught?'

Grandma Elizabeth gave a light little laugh. 'If whoever it was had wanted to catch you, I suspect they would have done. You worry too much. Perhaps you should consider this. Maybe you are not the only ones out there breaking the rules?'

I opened my mouth to say more, but I was stopped by the noise outside. Mum and Dad. Talking and laughing as they approached the front door. Ned and I looked at each other, before dropping our shoulders in defeat. I turned back to Gran, but she had already closed her eyes. I only had time to shove the diary under the mattress before my mother opened the door and poked her head in on us.

'Hello! I knew you couldn't wait to tell your Gran!'

I blinked in surprise. 'Huh? What?'

My dad came up behind her, grinning widely and slipping his hands around her waist. 'About your win of course! You forgotten already?'

They both laughed at this, tipping back their heads and gazing into each others eyes. I glanced nervously back at Gran but she remained perfectly still with her eyes closed. The trickster. I nudged Ned and we shuffled towards the door. My dad winked at Ned.

'Did good didn't she, eh? Fastest girl in town!'

'It was brilliant,' Ned gushed automatically. 'Really something! I knew she could do it.'

Mum smoothed my hair back over my head and guided me out of the bedroom. She looked back at Grandma Elizabeth before softly closing the door behind us.

'Did you get a chance to tell her, Lissie? Before she fell asleep?'

I shrugged in reply. 'I tried to. I don't think she was listening though.'

13: History

The next day I took a big risk. I dragged the diary out from under Gran's mattress and shoved it into my school bag. I suppose I did this for several reasons. Curiosity, obviously. I had duties again after school, and I wanted to grab any spare moment I could to read the diary. Necessity, was another reason. I couldn't explain it any better than that. I *needed* to have the book with me. The thought of leaving it behind seemed absurd. I just had to have it with me. And then there was something else, something I didn't have the words for. Bravery maybe, courage. Stupidity. Something like that. I felt spurred on by Grandma Elizabeth not caring about the stranger in the bushes. I felt spurred on by everything, like I was on some kind of private, crazy mission. I'd never had secrets before, not ever, and it was thrilling and intoxicating, and more than anything, I wanted to run.

I met Ned as usual on the way to school and the look he gave me was both inspiring and intriguing. How was it possible that he looked the way I felt? That I could see it all right there on his face? This was a new Ned too, I couldn't help thinking. He seemed taller and broader and straighter, as he fell in step beside me, his eyes piercing into mine. I was about to tell him my secret, when he told me his;

'Was reading history books last night.'

'Oh yeah? Why?'

He gave me a lazy wink. 'Because they tell a whole other story, Lissie Turner.'

I wanted to laugh at him and at everything. I wondered where my fear had gone. I thought about the face in the bushes and felt nothing but exhilaration.

'What on earth do you mean by that, Ned Fleck?'

He grinned at me, his eyes all fiery and challenging. I wondered if Mrs. Fleck noticed the change in him this morning. How could she not?

'Well, one thing that springs to mind, that I never really thought about before, all our books give us the history from Peace onwards. They're written by survivors, right? Before that, yeah, war, death, destruction, we all know that...but there must have been more. If what your grandma wrote about is true.'

'Hmm.' We were walking fast without meaning to. Hurrying on towards school so that we could hurry on towards what happened next. 'No explanation about who caused the wars or what they were about?'

'No not really. Just that finally people saw sense and stopped and everything has been great ever since,' Ned shrugged at me. 'That's not exactly the feeling I get from your Grandma, what about you?'

I shook my head. 'Far from it. We need to ask more people then. See if anyone else knows.'

'You'd think they would,' Ned reasoned, as we hurried on. 'I mean, the survivors of the last war, they would have passed on the stories, wouldn't they? They would have known why people were fighting?'

I had no idea. In all honesty, I didn't know where to begin. I felt like we'd found a thread hanging. You know, a loose thread in an otherwise perfect piece of cloth or clothing. We'd found the thread and we'd pulled it. And now everything was unravelling. But there might be people with answers. It was possible. Surely Grandma Elizabeth wasn't the only person left alive who knew more than we'd been told?

We didn't get taught history very often at school. I suppose because there was so little left to know. They repeated the same story; war after war after war became the Endless War, and then finally, when there was hardly any people left, Peace was declared in 2085. Today I stuck my hand up in class and posed a question.

Miss Branksome had her hair in a loose ponytail and wore the same patient, soothing look upon her face as usual. She looked mildly surprised at my raised hand but nodded her head at me accordingly.

'Lissie?'

'Didn't *any* books survive the wars, Miss?'

'We've talked about this before, Lissie. Barely anything survived the wars. Let alone literature or books!' She rolled her eyes at me very slightly.

I put my hand up again. 'What happened to it all?'

'It burned,' she told me patiently, whilst coming out from behind her wooden desk and clasping her hands tightly behind her back. 'Fires raged from one corner of the globe to the other. All that was left eventually was a handful of people, Lissie. Our very, very lucky ancestors.'

'So does that mean that no one knows any history from before the wars? I mean, all the years before that, like when my Great-Grandmother was a girl, and when her parents were kids, and so on. Nobody knows what it was really like back then? What happened?'

'Well no, Lissie,' she said with a small laugh. 'That is the point!

Nothing survived.'

'But the people,' I heard myself arguing back as I squirmed uncontrollably in my seat. 'The ones that survived and started again, they must have known things and passed it on? Remembered things?'

'Well like what?' Miss Branksome flapped her hands at me and sighed. 'What is it you think they should have passed on, Lissie?'

I opened my mouth and it fell out unexpectedly. I didn't even know it was there, the sentence that my lips delivered, I didn't even know it was the question I wanted to ask.

'Who started the wars.'

There was a confused silence around me. Saul Lancaster turned very slowly to glare at me over his shoulder, before rolling his lips in disgust and turning back. Ned was watching me from his seat by the window. He looked as if he were holding his breath. I wondered what I had done. Miss Branksome closed her mouth and sucked in her cheeks. She had no idea what to say to me. Suddenly Ned flung up his arm.

'Does anyone know?' he asked, echoing me. 'I've been looking through history books, Miss and it doesn't say anything about who started the wars.'

'Or what they were about,' I threw in.

Flummoxed, our teacher blew out her breath and made a hurummph sound.

'Does it matter what they were about?' she wondered breezily, shrugging her shoulders. She spun to face us and smiled indulgently. I wondered for the first time how she got to be a teacher. How anyone did. I supposed her mother or father must have been one. 'What matters children, is that people survived, and those survivors, those brave souls, decided that enough was enough. There would be no more war, no more pain and suffering and death. Not ever again. What happened in 2085 Saul Lancaster?'

Saul sat up straight and cleared his throat. 'An elected nominee from each land mass with a sizeable surviving population signed the Peace declaration.'

Miss Branksome smiled at us all soothingly, and I could feel myself going with it, as I did when a child, as we all did. It was like a lullaby, you see, a sweet and gentle song meant to sing you to sleep.

'And what did the declaration say? Misty Rochester?'

'That there would never be another war,' Misty piped up from behind me. 'No war, no attacks or takeovers, no guns, no aggression.'

'And everyone signed it,' called out a boy named Trent from the back. 'And then got on with repairing their worlds.'

'And since that day?' our teacher sung to us.

'Everlasting Peace,' we trilled in reply. 'Forever More.'

'And now two generations have been born into that New World,' she reminded us with a toothy grin. 'Isn't that wonderful?'

I couldn't answer her. I knew she was right, and when I glanced at Ned and saw the frown etched across his face, and the way his shoulders seemed to have dropped forward in confused defeat, I knew that I should not need to know more. I remembered everything my father had ever told me. I remembered sitting on his lap and stroking the rough whiskers that grew on his chin. Peace Forever more. And everything we ever needed, brought to us, earned by us, shared by everyone. Simple and perfect.

'Our ancestors started again, going back to a simpler time,' he used to say to me when I was small enough to curl up against his chest. 'Simple ways such as ours...They decided never to repeat the mistakes of the past. The old ways were too dangerous to bring into our new world.'

After school, my head was in a whirl. I didn't want to see or speak to Ned. I needed to be alone. And anyway, we both had our duties. So, he trudged off to find his father, and I wandered over to the Governor's office in the square. There was so much going on inside my head, that I craved peace and silence. A chance to take stock and study the map of my own muddled mind.

Luckily for me I got just that. Miss Harper was there inside the lobby, looking very excited to see me. She had a tray of snacks laid out already.

'The Governor's orders!' she explained, and for a moment I was stunned and confused, but then I remembered Saul, and I understood.

'Wow,' I said, eyes gazing at the thick slice of fruit cake and the bowl of ripe red strawberries. 'He didn't have to!'

'Oh Miss Turner, he's always so happy with your work in the garden. It's just his way of thanking and encouraging you. You'll be out there again today!'

'I'm back out in the garden?'

'Oh yes,' she said excitedly, carrying the tray towards the door for me. 'Of course. The Governor is so impressed with you Miss

Turner. But have your snacks first, won't you? Sit and enjoy the view for a moment!'

Miss Harper left me to my duties and my snacks and scuttled back off to her own work. I sat down carefully on the bench and nibbled at the cake. It tasted divine. It got me thinking about all those carefully selected chickens in the livestock dome. I wondered how they lived under there. I wondered if they were happy. You would think so, I supposed, going by the taste of their eggs. I thought about Misty Rochester at school, and how she would probably end up working in the livestock dome, because both her parents did. She'd be a dome worker; hopping onto one of the wagons bright and early each morning to trundle through the gates and off to work.

When I had eaten the cake and devoured the strawberries, I slipped on the protective gloves and apron, and picked up the water spray and envelope. I had actually been looking forward to this. The last few times I was here I couldn't wait to get away, but this time felt different. This time I felt special and chosen. The Governor was still making things up to me, apologising for his stupid son. And more than that, he trusted me with his special, secret flower garden. It made me wonder if I could perhaps trust him. Perhaps out of everyone in Province 5, *he* would be the one to ask about the past.

I started on the left hand side and worked my way around. Spraying the petals and the stalks, checking for dead heads and brushing any seeds carefully into the envelope. I was thinking about so many things. When I thought about the fence and the apple tree, for the first time I felt guilt. Real guilt, eating away at me inside. It made me want to run to my parents and throw my arms around them. I thought about everything they had ever taught me, everything they believed in. I thought about those last ragged humans, desperate to start again, to not repeat the hellish mistakes of the past. I thought about two generations being born into a truly peaceful world. I thought about everyone in the Province having a job and a purpose that suited them. Everyone having a home and a family. Everyone having enough to eat and drink. No one wanting to break the rules.

Who was I to rock that boat and smash that illusion?

Wasn't that something worth protecting and holding onto?

And then I started thinking about that crooked little old woman resting in her bed by the window, watching us all hurrying about, watching us all scathingly, thinking that we were all performing monkeys. I thought about her words lying in my bag, waiting for me. I thought about the outlawed apple tree and the stranger in the bushes, watching us break the rules.

I thought more and more about breaking the rules.

It ran through my head until I could barely breathe.

And then I plucked a seed from the envelope and I dropped it inside my bag.

14: Charlie

I did not go home. I went back to the fence. It was like it was calling to me all the time and I couldn't escape it. I wished I could just go home. I wished I could forget about the other side of the fence, and the tree and the dog and the stolen seed inside my bag. I wished I could just walk into my hut and hug my mother, and climb onto my father's lap and listen to him talk about his day at work while he strummed lazily at the strings of his banjo. But I couldn't. I wished I could pretend none of this had ever happened, and no questions had ever been asked, but I couldn't. I couldn't un-see what I had seen, and I couldn't un-know what I had learnt.

So here I was again. Crawling under the fence with my heart climbing up into my throat. It felt different, but I had no idea why. I was trembling and I felt weak and drained and alone. I didn't know where Ned was, or why I didn't try to find him. But it was too late now. I was going back. What would I find there this time?

I walked forward unsteadily. My feet did not feel connected to the rest of me. I looked back at the fence as I continued to walk away from it. It seemed to me like there was one world on one side of the fence, and another world on the other. Until the day I chased the dog, I had never even thought about the fence. This seemed strange to me now, but then, why would I? I was happy before. About that, I had no doubts. Happy and safe. The Province was sold to me from the moment I was born. No need for hunger, no need for fear. Enough for everyone. Everyone pulling their weight and rebuilding the human race, Province by Province, everyone being so careful not to repeat the mistakes from the past that had led to so much destruction.

The Tree of Rebels

On the wrong side of the fence, a breeze scuttled across the top of the grass. It seemed to grow longer here, without human feet beating it down. There were not many trees in the Province, as barely any survived the wars. They had been replanting them of course. We learnt in school that they had projects under the domes, where seeds were planted and then transported out to the Provinces for workers to plant. Plant Control workers were Level 3, just like Animal Control. Ned's father was one. While my father went out every day making sure nothing lived inside the Province except us, Ned's went out every day to plant new trees. But that was not all the plant workers did. They also dug up things that were prohibited. If you came across anything that was not allowed, or if you were just not sure, you had to get out your chalk and circle it for them. Which I assume is what Grandma Elizabeth thought they would do to the apple tree, should they ever find it.

I remembered the face then. I remembered that someone else had already found it. But who were they? What did they want?

I walked on, drifting further and further away from the fence, from the Province. I gazed around, thinking where am I now? What is this place called? Why don't the maps at school tell us? Why aren't we allowed over here? What are we scared of? I walked on, feeling the grass scratch at my ankles and I knew that the existence of the apple tree had made one thing inevitable. It was time for questions. And you know what? I could just hear Grandma laughing about it now. *At last,* I imagined hear her chortling at her window, *at last.*

I heard the dog before I saw it. Up ahead, in the grass that was waist high. *Ruff ruff* it was saying over the breeze, *ruff ruff ruff!* I could see it moving about in the grass, twisting and prancing and weaving in and out. I smiled without knowing why.

106

'Hey boy,' I said, announcing my arrival, to which the dog seemed as unimpressed as last time. It looked up at me, tilted its head slightly, and then carried on snuffling about, its tail swishing back and forth in the grass.

Was it even a boy? I crouched down, keeping my eyes on it. It carried on sniffing and weaving for a bit, until it found what it was looking for. A blue ball. It leapt at it, its face shovelling dry dirt as it snapped its jaws excitedly around the object of its desires. The tail wagged even faster, knocking grass down around it, as it seized the ball in its mouth and spun around to show me.

'Am I meant to be impressed? Come here then.'

It bounded over to me and promptly dropped the slobbery ball at my feet. I picked it up with one hand and reached out to the dog with the other. It kept its hazel eyes on the ball, as I dropped my palm onto its head, feeling the soft fluff between its ears. The tail kept wagging like crazy, its back end wagging with it. I smoothed my hand down its neck and onto its body. The fur was rougher there, and knotted with debris it had picked up along the way. I ran my hand back along its spine, and then down its side, feeling the bumps of its ribs. Meanwhile it started squirming and shaking its body from side to side even more.

'Okay, okay, you like this ball, do you?' I bounced it up and down in my hand while the dog looked on, tongue hanging and drool stretching down from between its teeth. 'Where did you even find this? Was that person in the bushes your friend, eh?' I was beginning to think this could be true. It seemed too much of a coincidence otherwise, both the dog and the stranger over on this side.

Before I threw the ball, I ducked my head down low enough to check under its belly. 'Yep, you're a boy,' I laughed, then I stood up and hurled the ball as far as I could. The dog charged after it, yipping in excitement. Had anyone on our side ever heard it, I wondered? How long had it been here? As long as the apple tree? How long did apple trees take to grow anyway?

So many questions. And no one to ask.

I walked on until I reached the part where the land dipped down, gently at first, and then steeply at the mountainside. Again, I thought about us in Province 5. Were we in fact perched on the top of a mountain? In geography they'd taught us about how the seas had crept in to eat up the land, all those years ago. It was something to do with the earth getting hotter because of all the awful things people were doing to it. As it got hotter, the ice caps melted and the sea levels rose. It was just one more nail in the coffin for the doomed human race. So, maybe we were on a mountain? Maybe the land our Province was on had survived due to it being higher ground? It did not seem possible. And yet here I was, going down. Further and further down the cliff, or the mountain, or the hill. Down towards the glistening stream at the bottom, with the dog bouncing along ahead of me with the blue ball between its teeth.

I should have been afraid, striding down towards the unknown yet again. I kept telling myself; whoever was watching us could still be here. But I was not afraid, not really. I just felt strange. Almost like nothing was real anymore, especially me. I felt slightly jaded I suppose, slightly lost, as if suddenly there was a fog surrounding my life, a fog which was growing denser every day.

I reached the bottom and felt the cool of the stream tickling my feet through my sandals. I thought about my parents, born in the

Province, never leaving it, never knowing anything else. Was it really that way for everyone? Apart from the dome workers and the scavengers, did no one ever really leave? I looked at the dog now splashing around with the ball between its feet. He was playing his own game now. Throwing the ball into the air and then pouncing through the water to snatch it up again. Why did you lead me here, I thought, why me? What were the chances?

I sat down on the nearest rock, pulled up my knees and rested my chin on them. I felt washed out and deflated, weighed down by endless, ceaseless questions. I wanted to close my eyes and shake my head and chase them all away. But every time I opened them, every time I even took a breath, there they all were again. Waiting for me. There was nothing to be done but ask them.

The dog stopped playing and lifted his head. I watched his body language curiously. His tail stopped wagging and remained held high and stiff, as if waiting for instruction. His ears pricked upwards and forwards. He was panting noisily, but other than that he was still and listening.

And then I heard it too.

'Charleeeeee...'

I froze. My mouth fell open. My eyes swivelled, my ears strained. How far away? How far?

The dog started wagging his tail again. He knew that voice, he knew!

Again...*'Charleeeee*! Charlie!'

The dog wagged its whole body now, just like he had when I

109

was getting ready to throw the ball for him. He grabbed the ball again, holding it tight in his jaws and wriggling from side to side as if desperate to show the owner of the voice his precious prize.

Instinctively I looked for somewhere to hide. The voice was getting closer.

'Charlie boy!' They called out. Was it a female voice? A girl, like me? I couldn't be sure yet. I left the rock and dashed out across the narrow stretch of water, aiming for the thick tangle of undergrowth on the other side. It was not until I had dived in and crouched down that I realised I was hiding exactly where they had hidden the other day.

'Charleeeee, Charlie boy!'

I was now almost certain the voice belonged to a girl, or a woman. I pressed myself down into the damp cold earth and held my breath. I suddenly felt ridiculously stupid and childish. Why was I hiding? Whoever she was, she already knew about me! But it was too late to change my mind, because I could hear the dog splashing towards her, and then I could hear her feet in the water too. I stayed hidden. Now it was my time to spy. I waited, holding my breath, listening to them beyond the bushes, wading through the stream together.

'Oh good boy, good boy, Charlie,' she was saying to him, while he panted and splashed and yipped around her. She must have thrown the ball for him, because suddenly he was off, and I caught a brief image of his brown fur dashing past my hiding place. He obviously had no intention of sniffing me out to show her. Too busy with that damn ball.

I lifted my head when I heard her coming closer. Through the tangles of leaves and branches and thorns, I could see a shape passing by. A quick glimpse of brown skin, long legs. Nothing more. So, I lay low and waited. She wandered down the stream, paddling aimlessly through the water, while the dog raced back towards her with the ball.

'Good boy, Charlie,' I heard her murmur, and it was too much, I just had to look, I had to see, I *had* to know. I stood up slowly, shakily, thorns catching at my hair and my skin. I stood up and saw the back of her walking away from me. She was tall and thin, with long black hair pulled into a plait down her back. She was wearing shorts and her legs were long, shapely and brown. Her feet were bare and she stared down as she walked, her head bent low, her strides deliberate, considered.

I was lost for a moment, just watching her. This girl, this person, on the other side of the fence in a whole other world next to mine, where it shouldn't be, and where there were dogs and apple trees...I was so lost, so transfixed on her, wondering who she was and how she got there and what she did and where she was going and why, why, why, *why*....I was so focused and so gone that I forgot to hide when she turned around and looked at me.

For the longest time, we just stared at each other.

I couldn't look away, I couldn't move or speak, I couldn't do anything. Her face was long and oval shaped. Her eyes were a steely silver-blue. Her cheekbones were high and her nose long, her nostrils flared. Her dark plait lay over one shoulder. I swallowed. My throat was dry and my heart was thudding in my ears. I wondered what she saw when she looked back at me.

Neither of us spoke. Somewhere up ahead the dog was still splashing after his ball. The girl remained frozen, alarmed and yet somehow defiant, refusing to cower or hide or run. She stared me out and stared me down, her body rigid, her shoulders square. She was carrying a leather bag across her chest. I wondered what was in it.

I didn't know what to do. Was she going to speak? Was I? I opened my mouth but nothing came out. She was just watching me, in what? In fear? In anger? I couldn't tell, but I had never felt so scrutinised. My mouth snapped shut and the moment dragged on. Me and her, staring at each other. Who was she? Where did she come from? Where did she live? *How* did she live?

I resolved to speak, to ask the questions that were driving me crazy, so I moved forward, out of my hiding place and I cleared my throat and opened my mouth to address her, this strange angry looking girl.

And that was when I heard another voice. A male voice. Distant, and rising and dipping on the wind, but definitely a voice, calling and shouting. I didn't want to hang around and find out who else was on the wrong side of the fence. I lunged away from the bushes, stormed through the stream and started scrabbling madly back up the mountainside. The girl said nothing. She just stood and watched me go. I didn't stop until I was back at the top, my chest heaving, my throat raw, and then I turned and looked back. And she was still there, with the dog prancing around her ankles. She was still there, staring up at me.

I heard the other voice again, turned around and started running. No wonder I won the race at sports day, I thought, as I tore back across the land, back towards the fence, all I have done lately is run!

It was not until I was back on my side of the fence that I remembered the seed I stole and why I stole it. But it was too late now.

I couldn't go back.

15: Lies

When I got back home they were waiting for me. All three of them. And I could see right away that something was wrong. And when I looked into their faces I could tell that they were thinking the same thing about me. I fell through the door with the guilt and the questions all hanging from me, making it hard to put one foot in front of the other. I didn't know where the other Lissie had gone. Lissie Turner the fastest girl in school. That's right. That's her. This Lissie was different; lost and confused and angry and scared. She wasn't me. Or was she? How was I to know? I looked at my family and could not decide what to prepare for them; questions or lies.

Grandma Elizabeth was awake and chattering in the bedroom. She sounded like a bird, caught and squawking.

'Lissie, we need to speak to you,' my mother said, pushing the bedroom door shut and nodding towards a chair. I slunk towards it, tired and bowed, searching through my mind for words and finding none.

'Nothing they can do about it!' Grandma Elizabeth's voice shrieked through the door, and we all winced at the madness in it. 'Ha! That'll show 'em! Nature will win! Nature always wins!'

I sunk into the chair, dropped my bag at my feet and braved a look at my father. He folded his arms over his chest and bit at his lower lip as a frown creased his forehead.

'What's wrong with Gran?' I asked.

Mum and Dad swapped looks, before Mum sighed and stepped

closer to me. 'Well she won't stop yabbering on,' she said. 'She's been at it for ages. Talking about you and some tree!'

'Tree?'

'You mustn't lie to us, Lissie,' said my father, and his voice sounded choked, his throat swollen. 'I don't want to hear any lies.'

'What am I supposed to be lying about?' I asked, feigning utter confusion.

'Where you have been going after school,' Mum told me, and I swear my heart stopped. I tried to swallow and speak but I couldn't. I just stared at her and thought oh no, she knows, they all know! 'Lissie?'

'Why? What has Gran been saying?'

'She keeps talking to you,' Mum went on. 'About you going behind the fence? Leaving the Province and finding some tree?'

'I found a hole,' I said miserably, knowing there was no way back from this now. 'In the fence. A few weeks back.'

My dad dropped his face into his hands and made a strange noise behind them. 'Oh, Lissie...'

'Well, what's so bad?' I questioned him, sitting up straight. 'We're not prisoners, are we? If there's a hole in the fence why can't I go through? What am I doing wrong?'

'Nature is winning!' Gran cried out from the other room, making us all jump. 'All this time! Ha!'

It was my mother who crouched down before me and took my hand into both of hers. I stared into her face and saw nothing of Grandma Elizabeth. It was like there was no connection between them at all and never had been. She looked dark and anxious and pained.

'You should have told us,' she said to me softly. 'That is the worst thing about it. You lying to us. You should have come and told us right away.'

'And what would you have done?'

'Told the guards to fix it,' she replied instantly. 'But that's not the point.'

'Your lies and your secrets are the point,' my dad chipped in, looking right at me. The look on his face was even worse. Pure disappointment. 'Why didn't you tell us, Lissie? Even if curiosity got the better of you and you went exploring, why didn't you tell us about it? Why?'

I shook my head. 'Gran...' I started to say. My mother's hands tightened on mine.

'She fills your head with nonsense!' she snapped. 'Always has done!'

'You told her about going out of the Province?' asked Dad. 'You told her, but not us. Why Lissie? I can't understand it. I can't understand the deceit. Don't you trust your own parents? I feel like I don't know you at all!'

I shrugged my shoulders and felt a tear bulging at the corner of my eye.

'I thought I'd get in trouble. I felt guilty. I knew it was wrong...I knew...but what I don't understand is why?'

'Well there are many reasons why!' my mother said harshly,

now dropping my hand and straightening back up. 'It is forbidden, Lissie, for your own safety. For everyone's, and why would you want to go out there? When you have everything you need right here?'

'How do I know what I need?' I whispered, staring down at my feet.

'You're talking in riddles,' said Mum, jerking her head towards the bedroom. 'Just like her. Honestly Lissie, I thought better of you. Can't you tell she is losing her mind? She is dying. *Dying*. And I know how much that hurts and scares you, but you must remember her mind has gone. She does not know what she is talking about! You can't let her get inside your head.'

'Or we'll have to make other arrangements,' my father said then with a weary sigh. 'Have her admitted to hospital where she will be more comfortable and less of an influence on your young mind.'

I didn't say anything, because there was nothing to say. I kept my mouth shut and my head down and waited for them to finish.

'What did you do over there?' my mother wanted to know. 'What did you see?'

'Nothing,' I lied to her, not looking up. 'Just walked a bit. Sat down. Came back.'

'That's it?'

'Yes. Honestly. There's nothing there. Just grass. I just walked and sat.'

'But why?' Dad again. 'Why did you feel the need? Don't you know the dangers? Don't you understand what our ancestors fought so hard to build here?'

'I didn't know it was dangerous...'

'Well of course it is!' Mum shouted at me, making me jump again. 'You could get lost, or hurt and no one would know where you were! There might still be diseases out there! Wild animals! Who knows!'

'Have we got to stay here forever then?' I asked, risking a look into their eyes. 'Is that what the ancestors wanted?'

My parents did not answer me. They looked down at the floor, out of the window, and then briefly at each other. My mother spun away, clicking her tongue and stamping her foot. She went to the stove to put on the coffee.

'For goodness sake child...I've never heard anything so ungrateful.'

'We've got everything we need here,' my father said slowly and patiently. 'That is what they worked so hard to achieve. A society that works. People who are happy, safe and fed. Jobs. Good health. How do we know any of that exists out there?'

'The scavengers,' I started, quietly and unsurely, barely daring to look at them. 'They go out there all the time...'

'Yes and some of the time they don't make it back!' my father snapped at me, his face leering closer to mine. 'They explore unknown territory, girl. Places even the guards don't go. Trying to find things to help us. Scavenging is a highly dangerous job!'

'It seems safe there...' I tried to tell them. The tears were falling freely now, but their faces did not change. Hers, tight and angry, and his, creased and hurt. 'It's okay out there really. Just grass and sky, nothing wrong. We could explore, couldn't we? Now things are settled in the Province? It's better than it's ever been Mum, you're always saying that! Why can't we explore outside the fence? Just for fun? Just to learn things?'

My father was shaking his head at me.

'Lissie, you are talking nonsense! Yes, things are better, and yes it is better than it's ever been, but that does not mean it's safe out there yet! No one needs to go outside the fence Lissie, my girl, *that* is the point. Everything you need is here.'

'But the guards and the scavengers!' I tried again, getting angry now, though the tears continued to fall. 'They go out! People who go to Province 1 to see the central government! They do! So, it must be safe, it *must* be! We could at least go where they go!'

'They risk their lives to do this for us,' he said this to me now through tightly gritted teeth. He took another step towards me, and he was angrier than I had ever seen him before. I heard a wail from Grandma Elizabeth and I longed to go and comfort her. 'Just like they did back then. The first people Lissie, our ancestors, who survived war after war after war, who saw death and destruction and horror for decades and decades, who saw the evil that humans were capable of...they made it here, they fenced it off and they started again. From scratch! Bit by bit rebuilding homes, and buildings and lives and hope! Starting a society again. Just like the other groups who did the same, up and down the country. Salvaging what they could. Putting the past behind them. No more wars, Lissie!' And he raised his fist and actually shook it at me. 'No more guns or bombs! No more killing! No more needless dying! Food for everyone! Jobs for everyone! And they risked everything, just like the first scouts did, risking disease and

119

starvation every time they left this place to search for food, materials, more survivors....'

'Harlan...' my mother was back at his side, placing her hand on his shoulder. 'That's enough. We'll send her to bed without supper and talk again in the morning. Tomorrow is an important day.'

'Why?' I asked, getting to my feet and grabbing my bag, and only then remembering the lies inside of it; the secret diary and the stolen seed. 'What's happening tomorrow?'

'There is to be a meeting in the square,' my mother told me, her hand still steadying my father, as he trembled beside her, his fists remaining clenched at his sides. 'The Governor has announced it. Everyone is excited, Lissie. They are expecting good news.'

I wanted to say so many things. I wanted to tell them that their explanations were not enough for me anymore. That none of this was enough. School and duties and tokens, and the Governor and the domes, and the square and the meetings. None of it was ever going to be enough for me now. I had been out of the Province. I had seen a dog. I had met a strange girl. I knew things. I felt it shivering inside of me; defiance and some sort of strength I didn't know I had. I wanted to tell them that they had not explained anything, and that they had not won. Instead I asked them a question.

'What would happen to me?'

'I beg your pardon?' my mother tilted her head at me.

'If they knew. The guards and Governor Lancaster. What would they do?'

'Breaking the rules is against the treaty.' She said it simply and coldly. 'You would go to trial, Lissie. Once you are fourteen, that is. Once you become an adult. Crimes against the treaty go to trial.'

'But that is not going to happen to any child of mine!' My father warned me darkly. 'We are going to forget what you did, and put it behind us, do you understand? No one else knows and that is how it will stay.'

I wanted to tell him that this made him a criminal too, but I didn't. I just nodded bleakly and went into my room. I felt cold and empty. Like I wanted to cry but also scream. The room, in fact the entire hut seemed impossibly tiny and suffocating. I closed the door behind me and threw my bag onto the bed. I could hear Gran snoring loudly. Her arms were dangling from the bed, her fingers scraping the floor. I went to her and eased her gently back up and into her covers.

'Thanks a lot,' I told her in a whisper as she snored on. 'You've turned me into a rebel and then dropped me right in it. Weren't we supposed to keep quiet about the tree?'

I sighed and turned away. I had a strong urge to read the diary before that was found out too. So, I climbed into my bed, pulled my covers over me and dragged out the book. I lay down and opened the book and had the heaviest feeling of not being able to trust anyone. In my head, I saw the girl and my stomach flipped over. If my parents knew about her...

Desperate now for answers, I read on. Grandma Elizabeth was now fifteen years old and things were changing around her faster than she could keep up with;

'*My dad was saying for years that the news you want is never online. The internet is free, and everyone is addicted to it, logged on*

121

and tuned in, but they are not being told the truth. I grew up listening to him say this, and now it is starting to make sense. If you looked for news online, you would believe two things. One, that everyone was happy and content and grateful for free usage when energy prices are sky high. And Two, that the increasing number of rebel groups were to blame for any bad news and violence that you did hear about. Without the Internet my dad and his groups are forced back to ground roots level. Him and his group, and all the other groups. They have different names, but they are all fighting the same thing.

I understand it more now and I try to tell my friends at school, and I try to tell my teachers, but either people do not care, because they are too busy living their lives, or they look scared and tell me to be careful. It started with the seeds, he says. It started with that and has led on to so much more. They are taking our rights and our freedoms all of the time and no one notices, he says. Laws are slipped in and passed and the news is not reported, the truth is not told. No one knows. All they know is that their food is getting more expensive, and it is getting impossible to buy new seeds.

The first domes were built just after I was born. They were hailed as a great innovation. The saviour of mankind. Food grown vastly and safely, without disease, without risk of attack. They wanted control of the seeds, my dad say, even back then. If they control the seeds, if they own the seeds, if they have designed and patented and altered the seeds, and if they have made the seeds theirs, then they have won, and they have everything. They have control of it all. And still he says in his deepest darkest moments...people still do not care. People are glued to their screens, ignoring the truth, ignoring the dangers. We are the only ones that care and we have been labelled mad, dangerous, unstable, crazy.

I am scared. I do not want him to get arrested again. I do not want to lose him. I ask my father, what can I do to help? What should I do? And he says two things. I can do these two things now and I can do these two things forever and I should only stop when I am dead. I can plant things. And I can tell the truth.'

There was a noise outside, a commotion at the door, so I pushed the book down the side of my bed. As usual the diary had my head in a whirl. I longed to wake Gran and asked her to explain her words. What did it mean to me? Why was it important to me now? But I couldn't ask her because something was happening. My father had opened the door. My mother screamed.

I ran to my door and she was there, pushing me back in, holding up her hands. 'No Lissie! Get back in!'

'What? What is it? What's wrong?'

My father had gone outside into the night, shouting, yelling, swinging something. I tried to get past my mother but she held me tight and battled me back, and I thought what can it be? What on earth was happening? What was it they have seen out there?

And then I heard him bark.

Charlie.

He had come to find me.

16: Truth

My father shut the door on us. I pushed past my mother and reached out to open it, but she grabbed me and spun me around.

'What on earth is wrong with you?' she was yelling and shaking me. I just thought, well it's all gone wrong now. It might as well all come out.

'It's the dog! I know it! But it's fine, it won't hurt you!'

My mother tightened her grip on my arms, refusing to let me go. 'What are you talking about, Lissie?'

'It's just a dog,' I tried to tell her, turning my face to the door. 'Dad! Listen to me!'

Mum shook her head, gritted her teeth and moved me firmly to one side.

'My girl,' she was saying, as she opened the door just enough to poke her head out. 'This is something else you have been hiding from us! Harlan!'

'It won't hurt anyone,' I said from behind, hopping about urgently. 'It's nothing to be scared of Mum, you have to tell Dad!'

'Be quiet,' she hissed back at me. 'Stop shouting and get back into your room right now!'

'Just don't let him hurt it...' I begged, the tears starting again, much to my disgust. 'Just tell him, *please* tell him not to hurt it!'

'He will do what he has to do Lissie! He will do his job!'

'But what does that mean? What is he going to do? Mum, *please*!'

My mother shoved me hard towards the bedroom. I'd never seen her like that before. Her eyes were wild, her face flushed, and her hands were shaking. She looked like she wanted to kill me. She lifted one hand and pointed rigidly to my room.

'Get. In. There. *Now*.'

I had no choice. I was in enough trouble. More trouble than I had even known was possible. I slipped back into the bedroom and closed the door behind me. Sobbing quietly in useless shame, I went to the window and leaned over Grandma Elizabeth. She murmured and stirred in her sleep, but for a moment I ignored her. Instead my eyes strained into the darkness and I was sure I could just make out my father up ahead, walking briskly. Dragging something behind him.

Oh, my heart just dropped to the floor. Just fell right out of me. All I felt was hopelessness and despair, and horrible gut wrenching guilt. This was all my fault. That was all I could think as I stared into the blackness. My mind was racing ahead, trying to work things out, trying to find an answer. My gut told me to get out, to run after him and beg him to see reason. To pull Charlie free if I had to. But my head was telling me to stay put and wait. My head forbade me from moving, from doing anything. My head bound me in paralysing fear. Part of my fear concerned what was going to happen to the dog. The rest of my fear concerned what was going to happen to me.

'Lawrence?' Grandma Elizabeth croaked suddenly beside me. I jerked back from the window and stared down into her pinched little face. She looked tinier than ever, like a fragile hunched little bird. I grasped her hands with mine. Somehow right then, she felt like my last

125

hope.

'Gran, it's me,' I whispered, bringing my face down and resting my cheek against hers. 'Gran, can you hear me? It's Lissie. Please help me.'

Slowly, her hand rose falteringly and fluttered lightly down onto my head. I closed my eyes and sighed deeply, and her fingers rustled gently through my hair. I could feel her mouth smiling against my cheek.

'I hear you, child,' she moaned softly. 'I know...'

'Dad has the dog... Dad has him.'

'Not his fault...' she rasped breathlessly. 'He has to do what he is told...'

'Dad? What do you mean? What will he do?'

'Dogs are not allowed...like the seeds, they are not allowed...'

'Oh Gran,' I gasped, now burying my face in her neck. 'I'm so scared! I don't know what to do Gran...I don't want to hurt them but...'

'You can't help it either,' she said to me, stroking back my hair. 'Not your fault what is inside of you.'

'What does that mean, Gran?'

'Fire...But you didn't know that until now.'

I wanted to tell her that her words were as mystic as ever, and not much help to me at all right then. But I didn't. I had the strongest feeling that our time together was running out, slowing down, fading. I felt the urge to tighten my grip on her in case she should slip between my fingers, before my very eyes. I just held her, my face against hers, her hand in my hair. My heart beat against her heart and I could feel her ragged breath in my ear.

'There is going to come a time when they will make you choose...' she said to me, and I waited, listening for more. 'You will have to choose...go or stay...be like them, or fight back.'

'I don't even know what you mean,' I was sobbing at her. 'I don't even know what to fight back? Who to fight? Why?'

'You know how they do it...' she went on, ignoring my pleas. 'They steal power by giving people what they want...they did it back then, and they are still doing it now.'

'I don't understand, Gran...'

'No, but you will. You will my child. You'll understand everything. You have to finish the book before they find it...'

I wondered if she was right about this. I sat back, finding the stool with my backside, and wiping both hands down my face, collecting the tears on my palms. Gran's eyes were closed, and her breathing was laboured.

'You know you have to behave,' I whispered to her then, my eyes flicking to the door and back. 'They want to put you in the hospital after today. Then I won't even be able to see you.'

'They can't shut me up that easily,' she replied with a toothless grin. 'In the book Lissie. Read the book.'

I didn't get much more out of her after that. She drifted into sleep and dreams. I went back to my bed in misery to drag out the cursed diary. I felt like a slave to it. Not wanting to read it, not wanting to know any more, but feeling like I was forced to. As I climbed into bed and ran my fingers over the aged pages of her words, I knew one thing was true. What they'd told us was a lie. What they had fed to us at school and at home, was a lie. Whether this was by accident, because they just didn't know what actually happened when my great-grandmother was a girl, I just couldn't say. Not yet.

I jumped forward a few pages, telling myself that I probably didn't have much time. Dad would be back at some point. I would have to face my parents and they would have to face me. What if they decided to search my room and found the diary? Would they haul it off and hand it in like the dog? Somehow I just couldn't imagine them sitting down with me to read it. They already thought she was mad. Words from the past were not going to change a thing.

I turned a few pages, scanning the lines for something juicy;

'*It's funny how people make do and help each other out. Mum says there is always something to be proud of in the human race, despite all the horror. While the great war rages overseas, the gas is running out for ordinary people who can't afford it any more. The governments say they are fighting for us, fighting for the oil. My dad says, we don't want your oil! We just want our seeds so we can look after ourselves! Where we live, the lights are slowly going out. People are returning to the forests to scavenge wood and start fires to keep warm. There is a strangely defiant community spirit. Dad and his pals collect wood now they are all out of work and can't get online. They make these bonfires outside and cook food. They say they will prevail.*

More and more cars are abandoned every day. No use for them now. Only the very rich can fill them up and make them move. I walk home from school and they are all lined up along the roads, dumped and going nowhere. Horses are the new big thing around here. Carts too. And if people need to get into town, and don't have the money, then they might offer something else, like wood, or food, or home brew! My dad says we are not beaten yet. They have not won yet. He says the day they come and take his seeds away is the day he will fight to the death. I laugh when he talks like this but mum says, don't encourage him, he is not joking!

I don't really understand all the law stuff. But I do know that dad says they are making little amendments here and there, hoping people will not notice. They tell you it is for your own good, he says. That patenting the seeds protects them. It means scientists can play with them and engineer them to grow into bigger and better plants, so that food is cheaper for everyone. They say that when the oil is completely gone, the food prices will be even higher and people will starve. They are trying not to let this happen, they say. Trust us, they say. All the effort must go into the domes. More and more of them springing up all over the country to feed us. People are so relieved. There's one near us, they say, there's going to be one I can walk to! We'll be okay! My dad says they are wrong about this on many levels, but at the very least there should be choice. If you want to eat that food then fine, but if you want to grow your own and replant the seeds or swap the seeds with your friends, then that should be okay too. So at the moment he says it is not illegal for him to have a garden that produces food. But it is illegal for him to sell or give his seeds away to other people. Figure that out!

There is another protest next week. This time it is a local one so Mum and Dad say I can go too. Lots of people from the village are going. All the people who do not trust what they are told and want to stick with nature. A massive march will begin here and go through town and then onto the next town, and then onto the next. We will ride horses and bicycles and go on foot. We don't care about their oil or their wars. We just want to grow our own food.'

I decided to leave it there and rest my eyes for a bit. It was too dark to read, and I didn't want to disturb Grandma Elizabeth by lighting a candle. She had the curtains open, as always, but there was no moon out there tonight, just a bleak endless sky. I hid the diary down the side of the bed and stared at the ceiling.

I thought about Ned and wanted to cry. I thought about the dog, Charlie, and my guts heaved and wrung themselves out. And I thought about her. The girl in the stream. Was she out there looking for the dog? Her dog? What if she found her way here too? Would my father drag her off in the middle of the night as well?

I must eventually have fallen asleep, my eyes too heavy to keep staring at nothing. I jerked back awake violently when the front door was closed with a bang. I lay still, frightened, confused, wishing Gran was awake, and on my side. My father wasted no time. He came straight into the room, and walked stiffly over to my bed.

'Are you awake?'

'Yes Dad. What did you do-'

'Hush. You have no questions to ask me, Lissie. I want you to keep quiet and just listen to me for once. Do you understand? This is very, very serious.'

'Yes Dad.'

I looked up at him but the room was so dark I could barely make out his face. Just the silhouette of his head and his tufts of beard.

130

I sensed my mother lingering anxiously behind him but she did not say a word. He cleared his throat.

'Lissie, you have broken the rules. Our rules as your parents, and the rules of our home, Province 5. You have lied and lied and you have hidden things from us. You did not tell us about that beast out there, and now the entire community is at risk. Those things were thought dead and extinct decades ago. They brought nothing but disease and destruction. They mixed and bred with other wild things and became so dangerous we had no choice but to hunt them down, one by one. I had to take it to the guards, who will alert the Governor in the morning.'

I desperately wanted to speak. I wanted to answer him and question him and make him understand. But I couldn't. I bit down on my lip until I could taste the tang of blood. He cleared his throat again and shifted slightly, sliding away from the bed and towards the door.

'We'll talk again in the morning, young lady. But I wanted you to know what will happen. After the town meeting we will go to Governor Lancaster and explain everything. We will tell the truth Lissie, because we have nothing else to hide. The creature will be taken care of. There will be some sort of punishment for you, but I cannot say what. You have brought this on yourself. If there is anything else you need to tell us, if there is anything else you have been hiding from us then you must tell us before we see the Governor. I will give you the rest of the night to think about this.'

I said nothing. There was silence and hostility between us. I felt this awful thing inside of me. This tightening, this hardening, this pushing away. Part of me tried to scramble back to them, part of me clawed at the distance that was gaping between us, desperate to put

131

things back to the way they were. But too much had happened, and I could feel it inside of me, curling up and solidifying. Too much had changed. They knew it and I knew it.

When they'd gone, I was relieved and resigned to seeing the Governor again. I was glad. I had lots of questions for him myself.

17: The Meeting

The next morning, I was ordered to get dressed and eat breakfast. My mother had been crying. My father maintained a wooden expression. I felt that hardening again and I struggled to understand it. I wondered why I no longer felt the urge to cry or crawl onto their laps. I kept telling myself that I was almost fourteen. Almost an adult. Maybe we were just simply preparing to let each other go. Before I was marched out of the door, I grabbed the chance to read one more extract from the diary.

Grandma Elizabeth's father was arrested at the protest. Hundreds were. She and her mother escaped back home to lay low. The village rallied around them, providing food and wood, and their friend Elias stationed his eldest son Lawrence at the gate, convinced that danger was close. A few days later she wrote again, her words smudged by tears. Her father was sentenced to ten years in prison for conspiring to riot, among other things. She was devastated. Somehow, all those years and decades later, I could still feel her pain and her grief. The groups and the protesters were labelled 'rebels' and 'terrorists'. They were accused of trying to wreck the Government's plans to safeguard the country's food supplies. They were accused of attacking the domes. I took the stolen seed from my bag and pressed it into my palm.

I hid the diary under the rug this time, and hoped that its secrets would still be there for me to find when I returned. *If* I returned. I waited outside the hut while my parents bustled about inside. I stared down at the hard flat earth beneath my feet and I remembered the seed in my hand. I did it without thinking; scuffed up the dirt with my foot,

The Tree of Rebels

dropped the seed, and pushed the dirt back over it again.

Just then my father stepped out and slipped an arm around my shoulder and for a brief moment I felt the tears threatening. He pulled me close for a hip bump, before letting me go again. I heard his juddering sigh and I wondered what this was like for him. Turning his daughter in. On my other side my mother stared straight ahead, wearing her best dress, with the soft leather shoes she saved for special occasions and her hair in a neat bun.

We walked on in silence, until we spotted Ned and his parents up ahead. My father's arm dropped away from my shoulder and when I looked up at him he gave a quick nod of his head, letting me go. Ned and I fell behind, side by side, while our parents linked arms and walked on chattering nervously.

'What's it all about? Any idea?' Ned was asking me. I shook my head.

'I don't know. But afterwards I'm seeing the Governor.'

He stared at me quizzically. 'My mum said you were in trouble. Is it...?'

'Not the diary. Say *nothing* about the diary.'

He nodded, looking at me and then at them. We all marched on towards the square. I glared at their backs, thinking that I did not recognise them anymore. We trudged on in silence. I wanted to speak to Ned but I didn't want to draw attention to him either.

'The dog...' he whispered and I shook my head at him quickly, my lips clamped shut. I can't do this anymore, I thought then, I can't take the not knowing anything! He gave up, stepping morosely along

134

beside me with his head hanging and his hands balled inside his pockets.

When we reached the square, it was full of people. The entire Province had turned up. A wooden podium was set up on the forecourt just outside the Governor's office and I could see him there already, surrounded by his guards and cohorts. I thought about the jail cells under his offices and wondered if Charlie was there. We trailed in behind the other families, my parents holding hands now, casting anxious glances my way.

Governor Lancaster stepped up onto the podium and instant quiet fell over the square. I gazed around at all the faces staring back at him in thankful awe. Mothers were smiling gushingly, while fathers stood with their backs straight and their shoulders square, grasping the hands of their children. My stomach felt sick and heavy. I could barely lift my own head, but I forced myself to. I followed suit and looked up at Governor Lancaster. You won't want me in your garden anymore, I was thinking, you won't want me there when they tell you what I've done.

He cleared his throat and smiled at us reassuringly. He was so good at that; putting everybody at ease. He must have got that from his ancestors, I thought as I watched him, that ability to spread calm. My father's hands came down onto my shoulders and stayed there. I blew my breath out and waited for it.

'Province Number 5!' he called out to us, his voice clear and strong as it echoed around the square. 'Good morning to you all, and what a beautiful morning it is too!'

Murmurs of agreement rose from the crowd. Smiles grew wider. Shoulders relaxed.

The Tree of Rebels

'Thank you all for being here. I know you are all busy, industrious people, so I will not take up your time for long. I have two announcements to make. The first regards this year's annual Day of Thanks, taking place as ever on the first of June, the day the Peace treaty was signed. We have sign-up sheets inside the lobby of my building. You can sign up for making food or drink, or providing entertainment. I am sure the children of the school will have something magical up their sleeves as usual! There will be the annual parade, followed by speeches, song and food! I know you are all looking forward to it as much as I am.' He beamed out at us and the crowd murmured again, shifting feet, grinning and nodding in his direction.

'The second announcement is something rather different,' he said now, and his voice changed, dropped down a tone or two, and I sensed the crowd react accordingly. This was serious. My father's hands tightened on my shoulders, and my mother slipped her arm through mine, holding her breath.

'I have good news for you all this morning,' Governor Lancaster called out. 'I have heard from Province 1, and I have been asked to pass on the following statement. I shall read it to you now.' He coughed, then raised a piece of yellow paper up in front of his face. 'The central Government of Province 1, hereby announces the end of the one child per family law. From this day onwards, the people of every Province are permitted to have *two* children per family.'

There were breaths drawn all around me, as mouths dropped open and eyes widened. 'We can confirm that produce from all the domes has exceeded expectations. We are training more and more doctors and nurses. We are relearning the simple skills of the past. Becoming more efficient at producing clothes, furniture, paper, beeswax candles, tools, medicines and so much more. The people of
136

this New World are industrious, honest, hard-working and I know that the future is indeed bright for all. Congratulations people, you have earned this!'

The Governor lowered the paper and faced the crowd and before he could even utter a word, they erupted.

Cheering, hooting, cuddling and crying. All around Ned and I. Our parents too. Pulling us in for hugs, kissing our heads. My mother had tears streaming down her face and she was saying over and over; 'I told you, Harlan! I told you it was coming!'

'Amazing, how amazing!' Hilda Fleck was chanting, wringing her hands before clapping them and flinging herself at her husband. In all of this, Ned and I stood and stared at each other.

'Looks like we're about to be replaced,' he said wryly, raising one auburn eyebrow into his hairline. I smiled back because I was pleased for them really. I knew how much it meant to my mother especially. But then I looked back at the podium, because he was still stood there. Still there, and staring silently back at me.

It took a long time for the crowd to disperse. Although everyone had jobs to get to, they were not in a hurry, instead lingering as long as possible to soak up the atmosphere. There was a party vibe in the air. People were group hugging and slapping hands. Eventually though, the square started to empty out, and that was when my father took my hand in his and nodded towards the Governor's office. My mother had gone off a little way with the Flecks and when Ned attempted to come towards me, his mother reached out and grabbed his arm. He stopped and watched me, blinking in the sun.

'Come on, let's get this over with,' my father said, as we walked towards the building. 'You must tell the truth Lissie,' he warned me. 'About everything. I am sure they will see you are just a young silly girl who got bored one day.'

'Okay, Dad,' I followed him through the front doors. 'I'm sorry, Dad.'

He looked back at me and sighed. 'It will all be okay,' he said, but he looked less than certain about this. He approached the desk where Miss Harper was laughing with Governor Lancaster. To one side, stood Saul and two of the guards I recognised from around town. Saul was stood loosely yawning, but he straightened up when he saw us coming, and his eyes narrowed in on me, his forehead crinkling in wonder. My father cleared his throat and smiled sheepishly at them all.

'Sir, excuse me sir?'

Governor Lancaster held up his hands when he saw us. 'Oh Mr Turner! How lovely to see you. Do we have an appointment?'

'Well no sir, but I thought, I mean, I wondered if we could speak with you. After...yesterday? Last night? We were wondering...'

'Of course, of course,' the Governor shook his head and put down his drink. 'How silly of me. I didn't mention it in the speech as we don't want to alarm anyone, do we? But let's go and discuss it.' he smiled at us and beckoned towards the door that led upstairs. 'Come on Mr Turner. Lissie. Come on upstairs. Miss Harper? Some refreshments perhaps?'

She bobbed her head and disappeared to find something, while my father and I followed the Governor solemnly up the stairs. I remembered the last time we were both there, when my father was thanked for his services to the town. I found myself wondering if the
138

guards thanked him last night when he turned up with Charlie.

We walked down a white tiled hallway and were ushered into the room with the balcony. Governor Lancaster closed the door behind us and strode towards the open doors that overlooked the square. The breeze from outside immediately played with his tall, white hair. My father bowed his head, his hands fumbling at the front, his knees sagging. I felt a sudden surge of rage and frustration. Why did he look like that? He hadn't done anything wrong! Why did everyone feel the need to bow down to this man? I looked at him now and remembered that his father was Governor before him, and that more than likely Saul would take his place one day. My stomach lurched with an urge to vomit. My feet were twitching, my toes curling and uncurling, my knees dipping and rising, willing me to move. The strongest urge. The strongest urge I had ever felt just to turn around and run.

Where would I go? It was easy. The hole in the fence. The other side. Find her.

'Mr Lancaster, Governor,' my father spoke up then, seemingly unable to put things off any longer. 'We've come to explain about the dog, that is, Lissie has.'

Oh, the betrayal. I mean, that's what it was, right? He didn't have to do this, did he? It didn't have to be like this. I gritted my teeth and stood my ground, even though my feet wanted to fly me out of there. The Governor turned around and those steely eyes were on mine. I remembered sports day. Beating Saul. Winning. Flying.

'I want to ask something first,' I said, and my father gasped beside me. But Soren Lancaster did not gasp. He tipped his head ever so slightly to one side and a smile formed on his lips. It was strange, that smile. Like he was inviting me into a secret place, a place that was

139

only to be shared between me and him. His eyes twinkled, daring me.

'Go on Miss Turner. You may have your say.'

So I did. While I still had the chance. 'What's happened to that dog? Where is he?'

'I'm afraid it was destroyed last night, Lissie.'

No. I didn't say the word because my mouth had clamped shut on me. I tried to open it but my lips refused. It was almost like they knew how much trouble I could get myself into if they opened even a tiny amount. My father said nothing. The Governor looked regretful.

'I'm sorry, Lissie,' he said to me. 'Let me take a moment to explain.' With that, he went to his desk and pulled out the chair. I watched how he moved. So light on his feet, like his shoes were oiled and his limbs were fluid. He slipped into the chair and smiled softly, while his eyes remained on me. 'Not many dogs survived the wars, Lissie. Obviously. When times became chaotic, what was once man's best friend became just another creature fleeing for its life. But yes, some did survive. Those that did became feral, wild. Of course, they also bred with other creatures, and became even more dangerous. They would kill you as soon as look at you. My father killed many back then. They would send out hunting parties to bring down packs of them so that the people in the settlement would sleep safely at night. Basically, the beginning of the job your father now does so well.'

'He wasn't wild or vicious,' I spoke up, my words like grit. 'Did anyone give him a chance? I did! He wouldn't hurt anyone. He was fine.'

'Well maybe he was,' the Governor went on, his voice a soothing, hypnotic purr. 'But that is not the only issue, Lissie. They

140

also carry disease. They did back then, and so we cannot take any chances now. Our ancestors saw many deaths even after Peace had been declared. Can you imagine how awful that must have been? To have survived the near destruction of mankind only to be killed off by a dog carrying a disease?'

I said nothing. What was the point? I just held his gaze and waited.

'How long had you been playing with the dog?' he asked me now. 'Assuming that's what you did with it?'

'I didn't play with it. I saw it and it followed me. That's all.'

'Where did you first see it?'

So here was the moment. The moment when I had to decide whether to lie or tell the truth. I swallowed. Opened my mouth and then closed it again.

Suddenly, my father interrupted. 'She saw it a few days ago when she was walking home.'

He stepped forward and slipped an arm around my shoulders. 'I guess she was scared, but maybe more curious, sir. She has an amazing imagination, just like her Great-Grandmother. I think she wanted to play make-believe a little longer, you see, sir. Keep it to herself. And then last night it turned up at the hut sniffing her out.'

'You didn't have to kill it,' I said, and my father's arm dropped from me in shock. I suppose now it was his turn to feel betrayed. 'I mean, you could have locked it up. Kept an eye on it. I've been around it. Are you going to lock me up, in case I have a disease?'

The Governor was silent for a few moments. He placed his

elbows on the desk and raised his hands towards his face. I could see that his fingers were long and slender. They cupped his chin and hid his smile.

'Well, Miss Turner,' he said eventually. 'What to do with you, is I suppose what we are here to decide.'

I shut up and waited. He knew what I thought, and so did my parents. I decided that I did not want to get locked up. Not yet. Not over this. This was not enough. There were so many more things that they did not know, and so many more things for me to find out.

'I'm so sorry, sir,' my father was saying now, shaking his head. 'I don't know what's got into her lately. Maybe it's the fourteenth birthday on the horizon. Sometimes it affects them a bit, doesn't it? I've heard people say it. They get a bit scared. A bit anxious. About all the changes?'

'Yes, that is common,' Soren Lancaster agreed smoothly, now raising from his desk and walking slowly towards the balcony with his hands inside his pockets. 'There is a lot for them to get used to at this age. There is a lot that we ask of them. For the good of everyone, of course.'

'Of course, of course, and Lissie knows that, she really does. She's always been such a good girl. Very conscientious really. Such a help, especially with her Grandmother.'

'I can imagine,' the Governor replied, and then he turned around and his shoulders slumped very slightly. 'Okay, this is what we will do,' he said. 'Lissie Turner, I cannot lock you up. You are thirteen years old and not yet an adult. You have made a grave mistake, not telling anyone about the dog the first time you saw it. But like your father says, this is a time of transition for you, and so perhaps this once, we can allow you this indiscretion. This moment of madness, shall we say?'

'Well, thank you sir, thank you so much-' my father started gushing but the Governor stopped him with a hand held up briefly.

'*But* there must be consequences, otherwise how will she learn?' he asked, and I saw my father nodding at him, head bobbing helplessly on his shoulders. 'Lissie must be under house arrest for the next two weeks. She must not leave your hut. At all. Are we clear?' he asked, hands now on his narrow hips.

'Of course sir, yes,' my father replied. 'That's understood.'

'And as for the breaking of rules. The *lying*.' Governor Lancaster looked me right in the eye now and I did not look away. 'For this Lissie, you will no longer be required to come here for your duties. I need to know I can trust the people who work for me. And you've proved that is not the case. Your father will have to seek out some alternative duties for you. Helping him in his Animal Control work would be my strong suggestion.'

My father nodded and so did I. I wanted to get out of there and fast. House arrest. My head was spinning. I couldn't. I just couldn't. I needed to get back there...I made moves towards the door, nodding and bowing and scraping just like they all do, looking as sorry as I could just to please them.

'What do you say, Lissie?' Dad grabbed my arm.

'I'm very sorry, sir,' I said the words they both wanted to hear, and I stared at the floor in shame.

'Off you go,' the Governor dismissed us. 'What a shame this wonderful day had to be slightly tarnished for you, Harlan.'

'I know, but thank you, thank you sir, it is an amazing day, amazing! We are so thankful!'

We were leaving, we were going, making our escape, getting away from him, when he called out one final command;

'And Harlan? I seriously recommend you place that dear old woman in the hospital where she can be more comfortable and where vulnerable young minds cannot be confused. Does that make sense, Harlan?'

My blood froze. Dad gripped my hand and pulled me on.

'Yes sir,' he called back over his shoulder. 'Perfect sense.'

18: A Girl

I had one chance and one chance only. It came that very night, and so I took it, because my punishment started immediately. That night, there was to be a dance in town. It was announced in the square, while father and I were talking to the Governor. All the men and women of child bearing age were invited to intend. There was to be music and dance and food and drink. My mother spent the rest of the day in a state of dreamy excitement. Every time she looked at my father she seemed to melt. Her face was soft, her eyes dewy. Just before I had my bath, I caught her in her bedroom, holding a tiny pair of white knitted boots. Mine once, I presumed. I wondered how soon they would start trying for a second child.

We'd had the talk just last year in school. We'd all sat there, blushing and cringing, as Miss Branksome explained to us how babies were made and not made. At the time, I had not really noticed how much of an emphasis she had placed on the measures that were used to *not* make a child. I had just gone along with it, like everything else, because it was a rule, and rules were rules, just like all the others. It was there to protect you.

'A whole new generation,' my mother said dreamily over dinner. 'Just think.'

They made sure I was tucked into bed and left a candle in the window for me, before they left, arm in arm. They didn't think to tell me to stay put. They seemed so happy, so caught up in each other, I guess they didn't pay me and my mistakes a second thought. I suppose they had no idea how deceitful their first-born child could be.

I watched them from the window for a while, leaning over

Grandma Elizabeth, listening to her shallow breath. 'They want to send you to the hospital,' I said softly, not sure if she could hear me or not. 'Governor Lancaster suggested it, Gran. What do you think about that?' I glanced down at her but she slept on, her mouth hanging open, her pale old gums on show. Her hands rested like feathers on her tiny chest. I wondered for the millionth time how many breaths were left inside there.

There was no time to waste, so I wasted none. I pulled a warm coat on over my night clothes, shoved my feet into boots and stole silently from the hut. Outside, the night air was cool and sweet. A bird called somewhere closeby. I left the door on the latch, and hurried out into the darkness.

As I ran towards the hole in the fence I pictured them all in the square. My parents, and Ned's and all the others desperate for another child. I imagined them dancing and swaying to the music, soft in each other's arms. I wondered if the Governor was watching them from his balcony. He was a single man since his wife died in childbirth. I wondered if he had ever wanted another child?

No time to think, just time to run.

Run, and run and run.

I reached the fence, gasping for breath, filled with fear, heavy with guilt. I wished Ned was with me, but I couldn't risk him getting into trouble too. He turned fourteen two weeks before I did. I found the hole, almost surprised to see it still there, but of course, only my parents knew about that. They didn't betray me totally, I reasoned, as I squeezed myself through. But they would probably come to regret that pretty soon.

I was on the other side and running again. What if she was not there? What if I never saw her again? She would never find out what happened to her poor Charlie... I gulped down my guilt and dismay and kept running, as that seemed the best thing to do. Just keep moving, and drinking in the air and the freedom. I felt like I was escaping, running away from all of them...

I reached the mountainside and began my careful descent down. I moved slowly, trying to get my breath back, trying to get a hold of myself. I didn't know why I felt so desperate, so giddy and agitated. I took deep breaths, calming myself, telling myself she might not be there. But she was. I heard her right away. Splashing through the stream, just like before.

'Charleeeeee....'

Oh no. Poor Charlie. Suddenly I felt horribly sick. But I kept coming down, letting the loose stones and dirt scrabble down with me. She heard me, so she stopped calling and she stopped walking. She stood in the river, staring right at me. I bit my trembling lip, and keeping my head down, I kept coming, kept moving towards her. I didn't think I had ever been so frightened before in my life.

She stood and watched me come. She had some kind of belt across her chest, and around her back. I could see a water bottle hanging from it. She folded her arms across her chest, and the moonlight danced in her silver-blue eyes. Her face was calm, almost expressionless as I reached the stream, and started to approach. I had so many questions that it was suddenly impossible to speak. I could not even open my mouth. I feared a tirade of nonsense might tumble out of it. I didn't have any faith in my ability to form words and speak them correctly.

But she had no such qualms.

'You again,' she stated, looking me slowly up and down. I watched her face, trying to decide if she was friendly, or hostile. 'What's your name?' she asked. I nodded at her. It was a good place to start.

'Lissie Turner.'

'Lissie? What kind of name is that?'

Her question confused me. Her tone was curious, and yet slightly insulting. 'It's from my mother,' I tried to tell her. 'And my Grandmother. Beth. Elizabeth. We pass names down...' I trailed off and stopped speaking. She was sort of frowning at me. There was a slight smile upon her face. I looked at her and thought she was quite beautiful. With high cheekbones and that long elegant nose. She appeared to be waiting for me to say something, so I tried following her lead. 'Who are you?'

'Aisha,' she said instantly. 'It means One Who Lives.'

'Oh. So where do you live?'

'Here. There. Everywhere.'

'But where?'

'It's not *where* you live that matters little girl, it's *how* you live.' Her mouth turned up at one corner, mocking me. I swallowed and glanced away from her. The stream was trickling past, weaving through our legs, its gentle waves shining in the moonlight. There was so much to ask this girl, so much to tell her that my words kept getting strangled in my throat. She stared at me with her brow creased, her head tilted and her arms crossed, and then I remembered the reason I came. And as tragic as it was, it was a starting place.

'I came to tell you something,' I say.

'Tell me what?' she asked, her chin lifting up slightly. I swallowed. My throat was dry. I didn't know how to do this.

'The dog,' I muttered, looking down at my boots, soaking up the stream. 'Charlie?'

'I can't find him,' she replied sharply, leaning forward. 'He never wanders off for long.'

'Something bad happened...I'm so sorry...but they don't understand, they didn't know he was friendly...and he followed me, he turned up at my home and...' I braved a look at her face. Aisha. Her expression remained confused but slightly softened.

'We need to sit down,' she said, and so we did. I followed her over to the apple tree where the land was dry and we sat down beside each other with our knees bent, and our arms hugging our legs. She stared at the stream, her eyes glistening. 'Is he dead?' she asked then. 'Did your people kill him? Is that what you're saying?'

I nodded helplessly and sorrowfully. 'They told me. He followed me you see. Turned up in the night and my dad panicked and dragged him off to see the guards.'

'Guards?'

'Guards...they work for Governor Lancaster. They keep the peace, that sort of thing. You go to them if there's something wrong, if someone is breaking the rules.'

'Like the police?' Aisha murmured beside me. 'That's what they used to call them in the Old World.'

'I know. My Gran tells me about the Old World. She likes talking about it.'

'She must be pretty old if she can remember back that far.'

'She is. She's my great-grandmother actually. Anyway, I'm so sorry, really I am. I came here to tell you, because I figured he was yours...'

She sat there for a while in silence, just hugging her knees and staring at the stream. I felt dreadful, I really did. Her eyes were fixed on the water, her shoulders hunched and her top teeth biting at her lower lip. Eventually she sighed and dropped her gaze.

'Yeah he wasn't really mine, we were just friends. He followed me about. I've been trying to train him up, but to be honest, I don't think he really had it in him.'

'Train him up for what?'

'For hunting of course,' she said, as if it should be obvious. She turned her head to look at me and a knowing passed over her face. 'Oh, of course. You have domes? They grow all your food in there, right?' I nodded in reply. 'Right, well. It's different out here. We're different.'

'I didn't even know...' I said, shaking my head. 'I came over here by mistake...I'm in so much trouble because my parents found out, and then the dog...I'm just so sorry. I tried to stop him, you know. I did try.'

Aisha blew her breath out slowly. 'Don't worry,' she said to me. 'It's not your fault about Charlie. Poor Charlie. I'm gonna' miss that stupid dog.'

'I'm so confused,' I blurted out then, suddenly terrified that she would get up and walk away from me, and leave me there with all this turmoil in my head, terrified of what was on this side of the fence, and terrified of what was on mine. I dropped my head into my hands and my fingers clawed at my hair. I squeezed my eyes tightly shut. 'I don't know what to do...I didn't even know, I didn't even know any of this was here!'

'Excuse me,' she said a little bluntly. 'How can you not know? What did you think was on the other side of your fence? And why do you even have a fence?'

'I don't know,' I shrugged at her. 'To keep us safe?'

She pulled her head back. 'Safe from what?'

I shrugged again. 'From disease. Starvation. Wild things...like...'

'Dogs?'

I nodded at her miserably. It all sounded so stupid when you tried to explain it. Suddenly I was overcome with the desire to know about her world, and her life, out there. 'There are more of you? Out here somewhere?'

'Yes,' Aisha smiled. 'More than you can imagine. They don't tell you this? They think we are all dead? Or they tell you we are?'

'They don't tell us anything!' I exclaimed, throwing my hands up in despair. It was frustration I felt most though. Building and surging inside of me, rising up from my guts and threatening to blow my head off. I could almost picture it happening, my mind exploding with all this new information, with the endless, endless questions. 'I didn't know there was...anyone else. They tell us about Peace,' I took a deep breath and started to tell her. She looked at me with wide eyes, her lips clamped shut. 'Peace...after the last war, when there were just handfuls of people left around the country...When they fenced themselves in close to a dome, and made themselves safe, and started to grow...'

'Grow?'

'The society,' I told her. 'The town, and the people, and school and work and...' I stopped, breathless, my heart thudding so hard it hurt to breathe.

'But you didn't know about us.' Aisha stated this calmly. 'They never told you about us.'

'Maybe they don't know about you?' I asked, shaking my head at her. She bit her lip and looked at me in pity.

'Wow,' she said. 'You really don't know much, and you say you go to school?'

'Yes. But not for much longer. When you are fourteen you leave and get a job. Soon after that you leave home too.'

'Where do you go?'

'You get a hut built for you, your parents help, neighbours help. That kind of thing. It's meant to be this huge exciting day. Setting up home.'

Aisha licked her lips very slowly. 'Yeah, and then what?'

'What do you mean, then what?'

'What happens next? To you?'

I opened my mouth to answer her, and then promptly closed it again. What did happen then? I swallowed, trying to swallow it all down, the frustration and the fear and the shaky gut wrenching explosion building inside of me. It was almost impossible. 'You just go to work,' I mumbled. 'Go to your job and earn your tokens.'

'Tokens?'

'To buy stuff with?'

'Oh you mean, like they used to have money? Coins and notes?'

I shook my head. 'I don't know about that. We have tokens. Slips of paper really. You swap them at the stores for things you want, or need. Like a new dress or new shoes if you have enough tokens. Everything else is basically taken care of. They deliver our water, you see. They give you the right amount of firewood. Food. Everything.'

'Wow,' she said, whilst looking anything but impressed. 'Really sounds like a lot of fun. Hang on. What do you actually do for fun?'

I shrugged. Another good question. 'Life is busy,' I told her. 'They have dances. I mean, sometimes they do. They're having one tonight, that's why I snuck out! They're having a dance for all the parents to celebrate the fact they can have another child now!'

Aisha frowned deeply. 'What? Wait. Your Governor or whoever he is, tells you how many kids you can have?'

'Only because there wasn't much to go around,' I found myself explaining to her desperately, because I didn't like the look upon her face, like she pitied and looked down on me, like we were all stupid or something, like we were all wrong. 'They had to ration everything. But things are getting better. There is way more food. They're getting better at everything, you see.'

'But you can't grow your own food,' Aisha said with a small

laugh, her tone suggesting this was simply the most ludicrous thing she had ever heard. 'I mean, that's what I heard. Is it true?'

I nodded. 'We don't need to...' I started to explain but I stopped when I saw the look on her face. I knew I didn't have long. I didn't want to get caught. I wriggled on my bottom, my whole body squirming with the desire to run back home, and with the whirlwind of information and confusion I was having to swallow. 'I have to go back,' I told her. 'I'm under house arrest for breaking the rules. I don't want to get caught. And this is breaking the rules. But you've got to tell me more, before I go. Who are you people? Why don't we know about you?'

Aisha got slowly and gracefully to her feet. She swiped at her backside with one lazy slender hand and looked down at me with a sigh. 'We might not be here for long,' she said. I got up, practically leaping to my feet in front of her. 'We pass through. We wander on. If you want to know more, you'll have to come back another day.'

'But I don't know if I can...I don't know when!'

'I'll come to your fence then,' she shrugged. 'Is there a place I can talk to you through the fence without anyone seeing?'

I thought hard. The part where the hole was would be too risky. I tried to think about the rest of the Province. Which part was the most deserted?

'I know,' I said suddenly. 'There are old ruins. On our side. Not much left now, just bits of walls and bricks. We play on them sometimes. There are swings. It's down a slight hill. Out of sight, if no one else is there. But you can see the ruins from the fence...'

Aisha nodded at me briskly and turned to go. 'I'll see you there tomorrow night.' She gave me a brief wink, and then she was gone. She slipped away and into the night, leaving me all alone. I was filled with hunger and panic and fear, and all three seized me at once, wringing me dry. I turned and ran.

I made it back to the hole and squeezed through, looking this way and that, utterly convinced that mum and dad would see me, or would have set the guards on me. But there was no one about. The sky was black, dotted with stars. From the square, I could hear faint strains of music and I imagined them all there, singing, dancing, laughing and loving. I wondered how many babies of the next generation would be created tonight, and a soft smile moved my lips. But not for long. I started running and did not stop until I was home and inside the hut.

They were not home yet. I ran to the window and gazed out. No one was out there. All the kids tucked up in bed, and all the adults down in the square, partying, celebrating the rule change.

My shoulders dropped with fatigue and I slouched off into the bedroom. Grandma Elizabeth was awake. She was sat up, gazing out of the window. The night air tousled her hair, lifting and dropping it gently from her scalp. I slunk in and went to her sheepishly.

'Saw you coming,' she said, not looking at me. 'What were you running from, child?'

'I don't know Grandma,' I said, releasing a mammoth sigh and throwing myself over her lap. 'That's the problem.'

'Sneaking out?' she questioned with a rumble of laughter in her bony chest. 'Breaking more rules? Lissie Turner, the rebel. Who would have thought?'

'I've met someone,' I said, my face buried in her blankets. 'The someone you told me not to be scared of. There are people out there Grandma. People living on the other side of the fence.'

Another weary chuckle escaped her. 'Scary people?' she wondered. 'People who mean you harm?'

'No Gran, I don't think so. Just a girl like me. Aisha.'

Gran murmured and her hand slipped into my hair. 'Lovely name.'

'She said there are more of them. She said so many things Grandma. But I can't tell Mum or Dad, can I?'

'No, no, no,' she said instantly. 'Think of what happened to the dog...'

I shuddered. And then once I started, I could not stop shivering. She wrapped her tiny arms around me. Her head bumped down upon mine, and she was shaking too.

'You have to be secretive my girl,' she whispered above me. 'Read the book and keep your secrets close. Be on the outside what they want you to be. That's all the advice I can give you right now.'

I wanted to ask her more. Of course I did. But I was so tired. So physically and mentally worn out. I closed my eyes and before I knew it I was sleeping deeply. I only awoke slightly in the night when my father's arms closed around me before carrying me to my own bed.

19: Rebels

'September 2078

Don't have much time to write. So much to do. My arms ache, my back is killing me, got blisters all over my feet from the walking. Had to sell the horse. No food to feed it. Elias and Sophie sold theirs too. Lawrence sometimes gives me a piggy back. Spent all weekend helping him dig the hideout and the tunnel. Crazy stuff all the time. Write to dad to tell him but have to use codes. Mum not sure they even give him the letters. People in town like zombies. You know the ones. You've seen them too. Unless you are one of them? If you are one of them then I guess you think you are fine. You can't see yourself, that much is for sure. So we are living a lonely life, a desperate life, us and the others. We're not what we were. We are what dad warned we would become, everything he warned has come true and Lawrence says worse is to come.

So overseas all across the middle east the war is raging still. They are looking for men all the time to send over there to die for oil. It's ok the zombies say. The zombies tell you it will all be ok because we will win the war and win the oil and then the food prices will come back down and everything will go back the way it was. Lawrence and I laugh at them. Or run from them. Their faces haunt my dreams. Dad was right. Their souls got swallowed up online. They still get their time, you see. Long as they are good and still. They get their time on line to play their games and talk to their friends and rub their eyes asleep and pretend that NONE OF THIS IS HAPPENING. Ok then. Go back to sleep zombies. We will die in your shadows. You cannot see or hear us anymore.

They call us rebels now. Traitors. Sceptics. Outsiders.

The Tree of Rebels

Troublemakers. People to be wary of, people to shut up. Shut down, shut away. Like dad, and the others. Gone. Poor mum. She goes on. Like a ghost, like a machine. Barely eating or sleeping. The house so cold. The vegetable patch her only source of comfort or joy. But they will come for it Elias warns. In time.

Then we will starve. We cannot buy food. We have no money, no jobs, no means. The zombies still have theirs, but they cling to it desperately, feverishly. It will all be all right, they chime and repeat and drone and repeat. It will all be all right because bad things do not happen to people like us.

Lawrence says the storm is coming. He says the days are near. The storm will chase us all to the gutters he says, and who will be left? He says this to me before he kisses me quiet. That same mouth that speaks of the end days and destruction it seals my lips shut. I love him.'

I was crying silent tears when there was a knock at the door. I shoved the diary down the side of the bed, sniffed and wiped my eyes with the back of my hand. I went to answer the door, but not before I pressed my lips against Grandma Elizabeth's soft sagging cheek.

It was Ned. I let him in and closed the door behind him. He looked hot and dusty. I guessed he had just finished his duties.

'You okay?' he asked me, as we traipsed into my room and perched on the edge of my bed. I sniffed again.

'Not really, Ned. Bored. Scared. Fed up.'

'Sad?' he asked, leaning forward and peering into my face. 'You've been crying.'

I didn't try to deny it. 'Just been reading,' I shrugged. 'Not much else to do while I'm locked in here. I know who Lawrence was now

158

anyway.'

'Who?'

'Her boyfriend,' I sighed. 'She loved him.'

'So where are you up to? What's going on?'

'Massive war over seas,' I said, dropping my hands between my knees and leaving them there. 'Getting worse all the time. More and more countries getting dragged into it.'

'What's it all about?' Ned asked softly.

'They're being told it's about oil,' I replied. 'But the weird thing is, while the Government are sending people to fight this war and win this oil and everything, they are also building the domes. These massive glass domes. All over the country.'

Ned was silent for a moment. I could almost hear his brain ticking over. Eventually he blew out his breath and touched my arm. 'You mean like our domes?'

'Yes. Like all the domes. They started building them then. While the war went on. They told the people it was so they could grow more of their own food and not rely on exports from overseas.'

'But what? Your Gran didn't believe that?'

I shrugged my shoulders and glanced over at her bed. She was lying there like she always did. Like a ghost, barely there, barely anything. She rarely spoke, and I was not sure if this was just her trying to appease my parents, or whether it was because she had nothing left to say. I'd whispered into her ear for hours now, told her all about Aisha wanting to see me again tonight, asked her questions about Lawrence and the rebels and I'd had nothing back. Not a word.

The only good thing I could say about her silent wasting away was that my parents had stopped talking about moving her to the hospital. 'Her last days are upon her...' my mother murmured when she tucked in her blankets.

'She doesn't talk anymore,' I told Ned. 'Not a word. Just time now, they say.'

Ned's gaze moved across the room to Grandma Elizabeth's bed. A slow sigh eased from his lips. 'The trouble is,' he said softly. 'No one talks Lissie. Not really. I've been trying to listen lately. To what people say. But they don't really say anything.'

I looked at him. 'What do you mean?'

'They don't talk about anything. Nothing more than work and school and duties and family. That kind of thing. I tried asking my dad what his grandfather might have remembered from the Old World. He looked at me like I was mad Lissie. Why are you going on about that, he said. I said, because I want to know more about it. What it was like back then, what happened to the world. But he said all I need to worry about is right now. I tried to tell him I was interested in the things from the museum, you know, the technology things, and he got so mad he sent me to my room! They're dangerous, he said.'

'My parents are the same,' I nodded. 'If you go off course they get all twitchy. All my mum cares about is another baby, while my dad, well...if you'd seen him that day in the Governor's office Ned. He was worse than that dog, you know. Might as well have been licking the man's shoes. Saying sorry over nothing.'

'I've been trying at school too,' Ned went on. He talked slowly and softly, his eyes still on my Grandma Elizabeth. 'Asking questions.

Putting my hand up. Everyone knows about the dog now, you know. They know why you're being kept in.'

I snorted and clasped my hands together between my knees. 'I bet Saul Lancaster has something to say about that.'

'Hmm, not much. He's not been at school. Turned fourteen last week.'

'Us next...' I murmured, looking down. 'Bet our parents can't wait to get us out and make room for the new babies when they start coming.'

'Hmm,' he said again, lightly drumming his feet against the floor. 'I'm kind of looking forward to it. Me and dad picked a spot out for me today. It's near those old ruins you know, where we used to play? No other huts nearby. Could do with some privacy.' He looked at me and raised one eyebrow. 'How about you?'

'Haven't even thought about it. I don't want to have to leave Gran...' Then I looked at Ned sharply. 'Did you say your hut is going to be near the ruins?'

'Yes. Started work on it.'

I bit my lip. 'Ned, I'm meeting Aisha there again tonight.'

Ned's eyes grew wider. 'Aisha? That's her name? The girl we saw?'

'Yes. I found her again last night. I had to tell her about Charlie...'

Ned's eyes blazed into mine. 'Full of disease they're all saying. Lucky it was only one. My dad reckons guards have gone out on patrol, in case there are more.'

'There are more,' I told him. 'More of Charlie, more of Aisha. Living on the other side of the fence Ned. She's got so much more to tell us. I have to sneak out again somehow.' I looked at him pleadingly, thinking about his hut. He narrowed his eyes.

'You need a plan.'

'Ned, I'm scared for you though. I don't know what will happen if anyone finds out about this. About her. I *have* to see her again. She said they don't hang around for long.'

'Your parents and mine are having dinner tonight,' he said wonderingly.

'Are they?'

My heart was racing now. I sat forward, my hands clasping together against my chest. Ned licked his lips and glanced at the shape in the bed.

'I'll knock for you,' he said softly. 'Twice at the window once they're all eating. I was going there anyway. Wheeling some wood over.'

'Okay Ned, let's do it. We'll be rebels one more time!'

'It probably will be the last time,' he sighed. 'We'll be in work before we know it, Lissie. No time for all this. No time asking questions...or anything.'

We'll see about that, I wanted to tell him but I didn't. I just smiled and patted his arm, while inside I was swelling up once again, everything galloping and thundering around inside of me. I felt two things very strongly. The end of all of this was upon us. And one way or another, things were going to change forever.

For the rest of the day it was just me, the diary and Grandma Elizabeth. Mum had left strict instructions regarding her care. Every hour I was to dip a cloth into sugared water and wring the droplets into her open mouth. Then I had to lay the cloth over her forehead. Every two hours I would move her position on the bed. This was not difficult as she now weighed far less than me. I kept the window open just the way she liked it and I read to her from the diary the rest of the time.

'With every bomb that falls the Government make more rules and are able to justify them. The law was finally passed last Monday night. What dad and the others have been fighting against for so long was passed in seconds, unknown and uncared about by everyone but us. The troublemakers. The outsiders. The blamed. It is now illegal to own seeds. Any seeds. To plant them or swap them or sell them or give them. When we head the news we all stood out in the garden, staring at the crops. Mum was crying. Elias was fuming. Lawrence and I held hands.

The food in the shops will soon be cheap again, we are promised. Now we have control. The domes are protected and our people will not be affected by this war any longer. But all over the world people like us are saying no. No. You cannot have our seeds. You cannot take this away from us. And they are grouping and marching and fighting back. We will do whatever it takes, Elias says.

Everywhere you go, you see the fear in people's faces, yet they do not join us, they do not say no. They take it, and why? For their freedom, for their easy lives, for turning a blind eye and assuring themselves that it does not matter. It's okay they say. They know what they are doing. Let them get on with it. They will grow the food and it will be safe and protected. All will be fine'

The Tree of Rebels

I stopped reading when I caught sight of a passing shadow. Light falling and moving just outside the window. The soft tread of movement on dead grass. I leaned over Grandma Elizabeth and I saw nothing. No one. I gritted my teeth and looked down at the book in my hands.

'Read it, Lissie...' her voice bubbled up from below. I peered down at her, and her eyes remained closed, her mouth hanging wide open. I patted her hand and read on.

'*Now we have to move on. There is simply no choice. They came in the night and destroyed the garden. Elias was arrested in the confusion and the violence. Mother and me hid, and then ran in the night, with Lawrence by our sides. We are scared they will arrest us too. There is no choice but to find others and run. Every day the war is escalating. London is being shelled. Chemical weapons have been unleashed on Manchester and Liverpool. Are the Government protecting us? There is chaos in the streets. I write this in an underground cellar of a pub somewhere near Ringwood. We have no transport. We don't know where to go. We have what food we could grab. Lawrence is determined. We won't be beaten. We won't give in. He takes me by the hand and we go into the forest and he shows me all the things we can take and eat. It is marvellous, mum says when he shows her. He shows her not to give up hope, not yet, not ever. Keep fighting, he says, with his pockets full of seeds. And everywhere we go we will spread the seeds, we will keep them going, we will fight back...*'

When my parents returned home from work, I hid the book, kissed Gran on the head and went out to see them. My mother prepared me a meal of soup and bread and left it on the table for me. She nodded at me to sit down, and still I felt the ice coming from her all the time, the silent fury, the unspoken accusations. How dare I ruin things? How dare I risk what she has waited so long for... She stroked her belly when she thought I was not looking. I did not speak. I ate my food and watched them get ready to leave.

'Ned's hut is on the go,' my dad told me, and I nodded in reply. 'I've been thinking. Maybe we should build yours adjacent to his. Perhaps he can keep you out of trouble, my girl.'

I nodded again and smiled at him thankfully. 'Yes, dad.'

'Right well,' he lingered at the door, rubbing at his stubble. 'I hope you've been thinking about everything, Lissie. We'll need to have another talk at some point.'

'It's all right, Dad,' I told him, with a barely audible sigh. 'You don't have to worry. I've learnt my lesson. I won't let you down again.'

Those were the words he wanted to hear and you could see the relief all over his face, as his shoulders dropped and his head rolled loosely on his neck. 'That's a good girl, good girl Lissie,' he said, and I waved him goodbye, and her. 'We won't be long,' he added, as they left. 'Just got so much to celebrate right now, Hilda wanted to put on a spread.'

'Have a great night,' I said, and they were gone.

I waited.

I went to Grandma Elizabeth's side and watched over her, while the cool night air stole in through the open window, bathing our faces. I stroked her powder puff hair away from her face. I thought about her and Lawrence, on the run, all those years and decades ago. Before all of this. When their world had been turned upside down, taken over and set on fire. I thought about how terrified they must have been, running.

The Tree of Rebels

I stroked her hair and thought about her words in the diary, about Lawrence cooking them meals on the fire, of things called dandelions and daisies and nettles and plantain. I didn't know what these things were, or why we didn't eat them now. Lawrence knew so much, and he taught them well. He kept them safe and alive and fed, and all of this was outdoors, living wild, sleeping under the sky, or in abandoned buildings, and as they fled they met others along the way, doing the same. Sharing knowledge and flouting the rules that now governed them to keep them safe, these rebels, these ragged runaways joined forces and held hands. They sought a way of life that had been stolen from them, passively at first, and then aggressively, with no remorse. Snatched and ripped away from them. For their own good.

I thought about the wars raging on after that. One after the other. Countries invading other counties. Fighting for oil, fighting for land, fighting for food and water. It went on and on. No one knew how to stop it all. I didn't know how they survived, but they did. Thanks to Lawrence.

'I want to know what happened to him,' I whispered into her ear. 'Your saviour. Your Lawrence. He saved you all but he didn't save himself.'

Just then she opened her eyes.

Her mouth stretched open, revealing no sound, only air. I saw the sadness in her eyes and it broke me up inside. I wanted to wrap my arms around her and scoop her up and hold her tight and safe forever.

Her eyes were wet and filmy, she blinked and blinked, trying to clear them, trying to see me again. I stroked her hair and held her hand and finally she gasped out a sound.

'Sacrificed himself...to save us...to lead us here...It was his plan all along.'

'I don't understand, Grandma.'

'We were dying...no food left to scavenge...they had burned it all...nothing left...just dust.... except in the domes...we needed to...we needed to access the domes...'

'That meant coming here?' I asked, and although she was incapable of nodding, I knew what her reply meant. 'He led you here to save you? This place was already working?'

'After the last war, the last bomb, the last explosion, there were still people...survivors...It took years and years for them to group together....'

'But they did,' I answered for her. 'Like dad says, human nature, survival instinct. They moved near to the domes and started again. Lawrence knew joining was your only chance to live?'

Grandma choked and closed her eyes, moaning softly, as tears leaked from her, sliding down into the crevices of her sagging neck. I shushed her and rubbed her hand and tucked her blankets up under her chin.

'You don't need to talk anymore,' I whispered. 'I know all I need to know. I am going out soon Grandma. To speak to Aisha again. I won't be long though. You just sleep, and I will be right back.'

I heard a noise outside the window and looked up sharply. Nothing there but a noise, a knock, twice against the wall. I grabbed my coat and boots and got ready, not taking my eyes off Grandma as she lay there silently. Before I left, I leant over and kissed her cheek and she opened her mouth and said one more thing to me;

167

The Tree of Rebels

'You are one of us Lissie. One of us.'

20: Betrayal

Ned and I met in the darkness and moved quickly. There was no time to lose. I was not scared of being caught, or getting into trouble. I only knew that I needed to know more. I needed answers. I walked on, head down, moving fast, silent. I had the strongest sense of things shifting under my feet. Even as I moved and breathed and thought, things were changing, things that could never be changed back again.

Ned led me through the centre of town, keeping to the shadows, keeping to the dark. Light on our feet, we felt like traitors and criminals. We did not speak, not once. He led me out of the other side, beyond the square, past lines and groups of huts, where yellow light glowed from candles in the windows. We passed through them all silently, darkly, unseen. If they knew what we were thinking...if they knew anything...

The huts grew scarcer, and we pushed on, over land that was dead and dusty, where nothing had grown, where nothing was permitted to grow. Above us the sky was black tinged with blue, just nothingness and silence, watching us as we crept on.

We found the ruins. Brick walls blown apart, parts of buildings scattered. Strange metal objects tied in concrete to the ground. Whenever I was there I imagined the people that died. The people that lived here before us, in homes, in buildings, in a past we knew barely anything about. People like Grandma Elizabeth and her parents, and her friends. Going to school. Driving cars. Going to work. It filled me with so much sadness I didn't think I could stand it. They were all here once, I thought, looking around at the dark shapes. They were all here like us, living their lives. And then...nothing. Over. Gone. Not even anything to remember them by.

No wonder people made up their own version of history, I thought. You could understand it. There was nothing left but a handful of survivors and a world of devastation. They must have felt so shell-shocked. Humiliated, even. They did this to their world. Destroyed it, and for what? Why? We still didn't know *why*.

I bit my lip and looked for Ned. He had wandered away into the darkness.

'Lissie, here,' he called to me softly. I found him surrounded by wood and rubble. In the dark it was hard to see how any of it was useful, but then when I stared, I could see the circular trench had already been dug out. They had started the process. Building him a home, setting him up, letting him go. I bet they can't wait, I thought sadly and my shoulders hung.

'This will be all mine,' he said then, hands on hips, voice fragile and yet defiant. 'I wanted to be over here, you know. Far from them. They didn't argue.'

'They've got their minds on other things,' I reminded him.

He sighed. 'Oh well. This is how it goes. This is how it is meant to go. Two more weeks and I start work with my father. That's it then.'

I didn't know what to say to him, so I kept quiet. Inside my head though, I was arguing back, telling him; no, shut up, don't say that. It doesn't have to be. Nothing *has* to be. Things can happen. Things can change.

170

Like a rustle in the darkness. Like an owl call that is not really an owl. Like fingers laced through a chain link fence. Like eyes shining in the darkness, seeking us out. Me and Ned.

I put my finger to my lips to shush him, and I took his hand and led him away from the rubble of his future home. We went deeper into the darkness until we found the fence. How did they build the fence, I wondered. How long did it take them? Was it the very first thing they did? The very first urge they had? Keep us in, keep them out.

Ned's hand was cold inside mine. I held on tighter and took him to the fence. The owl who was not an owl called us again, and we moved towards it. We moved towards Aisha and her eyes. I felt strange as I got closer. I felt lighter. Like weight and sadness were dropping from me as I walked. Like my chest was able to move upwards again, taking in air, allowing me to breathe. My nostrils flared, inhaling the unknown world beyond the fence, her world. And she was there. Like before. Her eyes, shining through the fence and watching us come.

We reached Aisha side by side, holding hands. 'This is Ned,' I said, tightening my grip on him.

Aisha nodded, and ran her eyes up and down him briefly before shrugging. 'Hi Ned.'

'Hi,' he said, and his voice was small with wonder. He peered behind her. 'Are you alone?'

'Actually, no,' she conceded, before releasing a shrill whistle that made us both jump. We heard rustling behind her as she looked back at us with a smile. 'You brought a friend, so did I. Funny, hey?'

We watched as another human form emerged from the

171

darkness behind. He was taller than Aisha, towering over Ned and I. As he reached the fence and grinned down at us, I could see a blond stubbly beard, a big toothed smile, and crinkled up eyes. His hair was down to his shoulders. He was wearing a long dark coat and I could see a makeshift belt around his middle, holding what looked like a massive knife.

'Connor,' Aisha bumped him with her shoulder. 'Meet Lissie and Ned.'

Connor shook his head, rolled his eyes and leaned into the fence. 'Bloody mad,' he breathed at us. 'Can't believe this...There you are! Bloody mad!'

'Same,' Ned stuttered beside me, his eyes like saucers.

'Thanks for coming,' I said to Aisha, wanting to bring things back on track before any time was wasted. 'Nice to meet you, Connor.'

'Had to come,' he said, with another shake of his head and roll of his eyes. 'Dangerous, yeah. But had to come. Had to see you folks with my own eyes. Been a long, long time since I've seen anyone new!'

'What do you mean, dangerous?' asked Ned, his hand slipping from mine. Connor and Aisha swapped a look.

'There's a lot you don't know,' she said finally. 'Maybe we should all sit down? How long have you got?'

'Not long,' I said quickly. 'Not if I don't want to get caught. My parents are having dinner with his. So...'

'We won't mess about then. You know you can't leave, right?'

Ned and I sunk slowly down to the ground. This. This was

worse than I thought. The heavy feeling was back. I settled my backside into the ground and stared at them, as they sat themselves down on the other side of the fence.

'Some people leave,' Ned argued. 'Well, not leave. But the guards and the dome workers, they leave and come back every day. And the scavengers…but there aren't too many of them these days…My dad says it was getting too dangerous. But the rest of us, I mean, no one ever wants to, do they Lissie? Why would they want to leave?'

To this, Connor scratched his neck and laughed. 'Yeah, mad, you got everything you want, yeah?'

'Basically,' I told him, pulling my knees up to my chin and hugging them. 'It's all taken care of. It works. People go to work. They all have jobs. They all get food and everyone has a hut. Ned's getting his own hut too soon...over there.' I pointed to the land behind us, but they seemed oddly uninterested.

'Hmm,' said Aisha, licking her lips. 'Well, no one wants to leave, or that's what they tell you, right? Well that's a lie, and everything else is pretty much lies too.'

I couldn't look at Ned and he couldn't look at me either. I had the strongest desire to get up and just walk away. The thing was, the thing I wanted them to know, the thing was...it *hurt* to hear this. It hurt badly. It was like poison seeping slowly through me, infecting my insides, tainting them black, curling them up as they died. It was horrible.

Ned and I sat, not breathing, not speaking. His leg fell against mine and stayed there. We waited for them to speak and we did not want them to speak. We did not *want* to hear it. We did not want to be poisoned. We did not want to die.

But it was like a slow death hearing it, and it happened.

'It's the same all over,' started Aisha. 'All the Provinces are fenced off or walled off. Only the officials move between them. Some of them even started that way, you know? They were built like that, before the wars ruined everything else.'

'Course some got blown to smithereens and they had to build them again, put up new fences and so on,' said Connor. 'But some survived intact. They were built that way to start with, you understand? Just like the domes.'

'Not all of them survived the wars either,' Aisha went on. 'But the intention was they would. All the Provinces have domes just outside, right? Crops in some? Livestock in others? Convenient. Or planned?'

We said nothing, Ned and I. We sat and waited and we soaked it all up inside of us, all the horrible, seeping, messy betrayal of it.

'Pretty much the same wherever you go,' Connor told us. 'Same system. Domes. Food provided. Like you just said! A good life. But you can't leave. No one wants to leave, right? In all these years, no one has ever got bored and wanted to leave? No one has ever wondered what else there is to see out there?'

'Disease,' Ned murmured. 'Wild animals...'

Connor laughed brashly and shook his head. 'Do we look like we are diseased? Or ravaged by wild animals?'

'How do you know we can't leave?' I spoke up. I felt dark

inside. Dark and twisted and in so much pain...

'We know because some have escaped,' said Aisha. I looked into her face and I wanted to sob. She was making it sound like we were in a prison! 'They've told us what we know. We've seen and heard things. We don't stay still out here, like I told you. But we're not locked up. Not like you.'

'This can't be true,' Ned looked at me. 'Can it? Do our parents know? Are they all in on it? What happens if we just try to walk out?'

'You'll be apprehended and taken into custody,' shrugged Connor, apologetically. 'That's what we've been told anyway. I don't know man. Try it!'

'Don't be stupid, Ned,' I said, touching his arm. 'Calm down. We need to think about all this. Let it sink in.'

'True,' nodded Aisha. 'Wise words, Lissie Turner. Don't go crazy. And whatever you do, do *not* tell anyone about us.'

'Whoa no,' agreed Connor, looking concerned. 'Don't do that. They don't like us. Not one bit.'

I wanted to ask how he knew that, but I didn't, because I thought I could probably figure it out for myself. I looked down at my hands, linked over my knees. My throat felt stuffed tight and full. I opened my mouth to speak, but nothing came out. I felt Ned beside me, as stiff as a board, all the strings in his body pulled tight.

'Tell us everything,' he said.

Aisha sighed and looked sorry. 'Brace yourselves,' she warned. 'You're only young. What, twelve? Thirteen?'

'Nearly fourteen,' said Ned. 'Nearly adults.'

'They call you adult at fourteen?' Connor sounded enthralled. 'Really? What's that all about then? That's mad!'

'It's so they can get you out into society, right?' Aisha spoke, her eyes on mine. 'Get you working? Keeping the wheels oiled? Keeping the system going?'

'*System?*' I croaked.

'It's a system,' she shrugged. 'Most societies are, or were. Back in the Old World they had a dominant system called capitalism? Do you know anything about that?'

'There's not much information,' Ned told her, his voice low and throaty. 'A couple of photos and things in the museum. Some of those laptop things, and phones. They keep them in glass cases. No one ever wants that way of life back again.'

'But I've got something else,' I remembered then. 'My great-grandmother kept a diary from back then. A journal.'

Connor made an 'o 'shape with his lips and looked at Aisha. She was still staring into my eyes, her expression barely changing.

'Impressive,' she nodded. 'I guess that's what got you going? Coming over the fence?'

'I found a hole one day,' I started to explain. 'When I followed Charlie. I'd never thought about the fence until that day. I'd never really noticed it.'

'They keep you busy, hey?' wondered Connor.

'It's not so much that,' replied Ned, before I could answer.

'They keep you happy. That's what it is. Or at least, you *think* you are happy. That's right, isn't it Lissie? Like our parents tonight? Since the meeting?'

I nodded slowly. 'Happy and grateful. My dad says we are living in the best times ever. Everlasting Peace. No more war since the treaty. The human race finally got it right.'

'Well,' Aisha said, raising her eyebrows at us and reminding me of one of the teachers at school. 'Never mind all that. That is a discussion for another day. You're entitled to your opinions, but we just wondered if you wanted to know some truth. They obviously don't educate you much in there.' She pushed her hair behind her ears and when we did not speak, she went on. 'Your officials don't like us,' she said grimly. 'They never have. Your people may talk about Peace, but there is a still a fight and it has been going on for over one hundred and fifty years. Your Grandmother might remember it if she is as old as you say. I suppose it depends whose side she was on.'

I thought about sides, and I thought about seeds, and Grandma's diary, and I opened my mouth to tell Aisha all this, but she suddenly looked nervous. Her eyes shot from one side to the other. All around us the skies had grown darker. She frowned.

'We can't be much longer,' she whispered and nudged Connor with one elbow. He got up on his knees, peered into the darkness behind him, one hand going to his belt. Aisha looked back at me.

'I'm getting a bad feeling,' she explained. 'You know, in my gut? Always trust that, my father says. Like the animals do. Anyway, listen. You *have* to understand something, okay? You might think your Governor and all the other ones care for you and want to protect you, but the sooner you forget that stupid idea, the better.' She looked at us

177

each in turn, defiant. 'They don't care about you and they never have. They care about the system, about their own survival and about control. You're all cogs in the machine and don't think for a minute they wouldn't eliminate you if they had to. They wouldn't hesitate. And it's always been that way. Okay?'

Okay? How did she expect us to think that was *okay?* Ned's lips were quivering as he stared down at the ground.

'Everyone says what a nice man the Governor is,' he said in a low, careful voice. 'They all love him so much.'

'Well, that's how they want it to look, obviously. And another thing. They know about us. Your Governor, and his guards, they all know. They don't tell you of course, but they've always known. They don't trust us and they don't understand us. They fear us, and if they could destroy us they would in a heartbeat. You need to understand that, guys. They will tell you it is to protect you and your little society here. They will tell themselves this too, and they will believe it even. But the truth is guys, they have been fighting us for generations.'

'*Why?*' I heard myself asking her.

She got up then, silently and smoothly. Connor had already drifted back into the darkness. Aisha smiled at me and winked.

'They call us rebels,' she went on. 'Outsiders. They will tell you we are dangerous. But there is really only one reason why they fear us and want to destroy us.'

'What?' Ned rasped beside me. We clung to each other, hauling each other back to our feet and Connor had disappeared and Aisha looked at us for a moment as if she simply pitied us. And then she stiffened and straightened and her chin jutted out and her eyes were
178

fierce and I thought my goodness, Grandma Elizabeth, how much you look like her!

'We said no,' she told us. 'We said no back then and we are still saying no now.'

We moved forward instantly, our mouths falling open, our hearts in our throats, desperate for more, desperate to reach through to her, to touch her, but she was gone. Just like that.

Ned fell back, breathing heavily, his eyes staring, his mouth hanging as if he could not muster enough breath.

'Unbelievable,' he whispered and I agreed. 'Will we ever see them again? Lissie?'

But I was gone too. I ran. Running faster than Ned could ever keep up with. Running back through the black, past his rubble, and towards home. Running faster than anyone else in town, because I was Lissie Turner and I was the fastest...and I ran and ran, and I could hear him calling me from behind, as he raced after me. But I kept going and I did not stop and I did not look back because I had to get home, because my heart felt clutched and squeezed and because there was fear alive and crawling inside my throat, strangling the breath from me, because I had the worst feeling in the world, the worst fear....

I thundered through the night and Ned let me go.

I raced towards home.

I *had* to get home.

I rolled through the door, I fell over my feet and I landed with a thud in a panicked heap. I laughed out loud at myself and dropped my head into my hands for a moment. Calm down, I told myself, calm

179

down, don't be so stupid, what is wrong with you? Nothing, nothing, calm down, calm down. Stupid girl. Nothing is wrong. Nothing has happened.

So, I went into my room to see her, and the cold hit me first, the window open as usual, the air colder than I left it, the curtain fluttering around her. One hand lying outside the covers, dangling down to the floor. Fingers. Cold.

I went to her and I saw her covers tucked up to her chin, but the curtains were fluttering in the way and I shoved them back and closed the window, and I saw her, but her hand was hanging down, out of the bed. And it was so cold in there.

I went to her and I saw her face and her mouth was stretched wide open, and her eyes were open too, wide open but she was not seeing me. Grandma Elizabeth was staring at nothing. Oh, no, oh no, oh no, no, no, oh no, please no, please *please* no....

But she was staring and she was cold and when I touched her she did not move, and her face felt stiff and her eyes were like glass and her skin was like cold rubber and her hand was hanging down to the floor. I would sob over her, I would gather her up, I would cradle her in my arms as she used to cradle me, I would kiss her mouth and her cheeks and my tears would fill her open staring eyes but I didn't, because I saw something on the floor, and I sank down to it, I sank so slowly down to the floor.

My knees first. Smack. And then my backside on top, and then the rest of whoever I was, falling and sagging and sinking down low, and my hand reaching out for it, and I should have kissed her, held her, letting my tears soften her body, but I was down there, down on the floor and reaching for it, reaching.

180

I picked it up and held it. I held it in front of my eyes and the tears blinded me and it was a stark

pink blur and it was soft and delicate in my hold and I wiped my tears away. I sat and held it, the dusky

pink petal, the soft petal from the dusky pink flower

21: Endings

I was still sat there when they came home. It might have been minutes later or it might have been hours. I was huddled next to her hand as it stretched towards the floor, and I was still holding the flower petal. It was hot and pressed into the palm of my hand.

They came through the front door. They came in laughing and jolly, and then whispering and hushing, and then they stopped. They must have heard my hopeless sobs. My father peeked his head around the door and frowned. My mother, right behind him.

'Lissie? Lissie...what?'

'Grandma,' I moaned, and that was all I could say. 'Grandma, Grandma.'

They came in, side by side, my mother reaching for her, my father reaching for me. He pulled me to my feet by my arms and he forced me into his chest. His hand cupping my skull. His other hand rubbing my back.

'Oh no,' he said to my mother. 'Oh no...'

I glanced through my hair and my mother was stroking her face, and feeling for her pulse. But she knew, like I knew, that time for her had ended. She released a sob and covered her face.

'Oh no,' my father said, still rubbing my back. 'Oh Beth...Lissie...I am so, so sorry.'

There was nothing left to do.

She was gone, and it was over.

There was nothing left to do, so we covered her up and I got into bed with them.

I should have told them about the petal in my hand but I didn't.

The next morning my father got up early. I watched him from the doorstep. I sat there with a cup of warm milk clasped between my knees. I stared at the hard, dry dirt under which I had buried a stolen seed. There was no school, no work. When someone died, everything stopped. They put up the flag. The black flag went up the pole, and soon everyone would know, and people would start to come. First the Flecks, and then the next neighbours, and then the next. They'd come to see us, and they'd bring food and drink and kind words. They'd come and see her to whisper their goodbyes.

My father made two fires. One indoors and one outside. He put a pot on to boil so that there was a large supply of coffee for the visitors. Doctor Tanner had been and gone. Soon would come the Flecks. It would go on like this all day, until it was done. And then the men from the cemetery would come to claim her.

I sat on the step and watched my father. He smoked his pipe and wiped his brow. He gave me looks and sighs and ruffled my hair. I said nothing. Mum was inside the house. Blowing her nose. Touching her belly.

I listened to them all morning. When the people came, I heard the same things said over and over again.

'She had a good innings...a long, long life.'

'Oh my, what a good age, what a grand age to reach.'

'She saw so many changes.'

'Such a long, long life.'

'We must be so thankful for how long she had.'

'It was her time. Her time to go.'

'We are so sorry for your loss.'

'But what a long life...what a blessing.'

'She saw so much.'

I thought about the diary. Yes, she did. She saw so much, so much more than these people knew.

So, I sat on the step and I watched them come and I watched them go. When the Flecks arrived, there were murmurings and kisses dropped onto my head and when I glanced over my shoulder, I saw Hilda and my mother, heads together, hands on bellies.

Ned dropped down beside me. His face was white and his eyes circled with black. He sighed so heavily it was like he was sinking into the ground beside me.

'I'm sorry, Lissie,' he said to me eventually, as the people came and went. 'You knew. Didn't you?'

'I had this feeling...' I shrugged. It was the first time I had spoken all morning. My throat ached from the crying.

'What a night,' he muttered beside me. 'I feel like I am going crazy. I mean, seriously Lissie. What are we supposed to do with all of that? What are we going to do?'

I wanted to tell him this was not the time or the place, but then

184

I thought twice. Because maybe it was.

'I think I know what to do,' I said to him, 'but I might be crazy. You tell me.'

'What do you mean?'

'I need to talk to the Governor.'

Ned froze beside me. He stared at me, shaking his head. 'What are you, crazy? No Lissie! What about everything they said?'

'It might not be true,' I fired back. 'And if it is, how do we know? How do we find out? What do *you* want to do Ned?'

It was a good and fair question. Why was everything always down to me? Why did Grandma Elizabeth have to lay all of this onto me? Why did she ever have to give me that diary?

'I don't know,' he said angrily. 'I haven't slept all night thinking about it. I want to ask my parents, but you know what they're like. I want to ask *someone*.'

'But she's dead,' I said softly, gritting my teeth. 'The only person we could have asked is dead.'

'What about the diary? Have you got to the end yet?'

'Nearly. It ties in with what they said last night though. It's like they were telling the same story. We've been lied to Ned. That much is true.'

'Well, then we should leave.' He kicked his heels into the dirt. 'We should say no thanks to their little huts and their duties and jobs, and we should say we are going out there.'

'I wonder what would happen...'

'So do I. I can't believe no one has ever tried it before. Just walked out. Upped and left to go and live somewhere else.'

'Fear,' I shrugged. 'They don't know what's out there. They know they're safe here. Provided for. They know things are getting better all the time. More food. More opportunities. More babies. If they left, wouldn't they have to start all over again with nothing?'

'I don't know,' he grumbled, looking away and kicking at the ground again. 'I don't know anything, Lissie. *They* live out there, don't they? *They* survive. I wonder if that's all true, what they said about it being dangerous. I mean, you think about Soren Lancaster and you can't imagine him being dangerous, can you? To them? I mean, Aisha and Connor are not hurting anyone by being out there?' Ned just shook his head and lifted his hand to rub vigorously at his eyes. 'I don't know,' he groaned. 'I just don't know. I don't know anything anymore.'

'I'm going to ask the Governor,' I nodded firmly.

'Yeah, and how are you going to do that? What are you going to say?'

I was shaking with the effort it took not to scream. My fist was closed so tightly my fingernails were digging into my skin. I felt the shudder in my palm, which worked its way up my wrist and all the way to my shoulder. I had to use my other hand to help me; peeling back my fingers one by one to reveal it to him.

He gasped when he saw it. The pink petal in my palm.

Ned gasped when he saw it because he had never seen anything so vivid before.

186

My hand was shaking and I clasped my wrist still with my other hand and I pushed the words out through my teeth so that no one else would hear.

'I found this on the floor. Next to her bed.'

I looked up then, as the last words left my lips. There was no time to explain anything to Ned, there was no time to let him touch the petal or to ask what it was, what it meant, how it got there. There was no time because here came the Governor, Soren Lancaster. Today he wore a black suit and a black wide brimmed hat, and his meat faced son trailed behind him looking bored. As he walked his big clumsy feet kicked up clouds of brown dust.

I closed my fist and dropped my hands between my legs. Ned stopped gaping, closing his mouth up fast and leaning back in the doorway. I stared at Soren Lancaster and he stared right back at me. Just like on sports day. Just like when I was the fastest girl in town.

He was met by my parents. They rushed past us to meet him. They were so thankful, so grateful to see him. He spoke to them softly, and then they all trailed past us on the step. He said nothing to me. His head was low. His shoulders meek. They went inside to see Grandma Elizabeth.

I tightened my fist around the petal.

At the end of the day, the light in the sky started to die. The men from the cemetery arrived and everyone moved to one side to make space for them. They went inside the hut and were in there for some time while my father offered everyone coffee, and my mother brought out a big pot of soup to share. Friends and neighbours hovered in the dusk, murmuring and hugging. The atmosphere was heavy with anticipated sadness.

When they brought her out, my mum and dad found me and pulled me to them. Everyone hushed, and there was total silence as she was carried out inside a simple wooden box. I felt an urge to run to her then. I wanted to see her one last time. I wanted to hold her hand and kiss her cheek and brush her mad white hair from her face. But I couldn't. They were holding onto me, and I held onto the petal still, and all we could do was stand back and watch.

It was sombre and still. No one moved or spoke.

She was carried out and carried away, and then slowly, one by one, we started to follow. Mum and Dad in front, me just behind, and then everyone else. As was tradition, we walked slowly behind the men carrying the box, holding hands. I tried to look for the Governor but I couldn't see him anywhere.

We walked on silently, heads bowed. We walked through the square to the cemetery. It was the place where they started burying the dead, all those years ago. They told us all about it in school. They had to put the bodies somewhere, so a group of survivors nominated themselves for the duty. It was surrounded by crumbling white bricks. There was a sort of gravel path leading through the opening and we all traipsed through behind the men and Grandma Elizabeth. My father slipped his arm around my shoulders, and my mother started quietly sobbing into a tissue. I couldn't help but wonder if she would start to feel a little bit free now that Grandma was gone, now that she was unburdened. But I didn't say this, because nobody spoke.

I stood there under my father's arm, as they lowered the box into the ready-made hole and then started to place the dry twigs on top

188

of it. Some people went up and helped, and some people stood back and watched. Maybe they were all thinking about their own lives, and their own deaths one day. How this ending would come for all of us. It was all silent, but their words were still in my head from before. A great life, they said. A long life. It was her time to go. It was her ending.

But what if it wasn't? What if she wasn't meant to go yet?

I stood there watching them light the twigs and set her on fire. I remembered what they said in school; how it took too long, and was too exhausting to bury all the bodies, so they started burning them instead. A tradition that stayed with us. I stood there with my fist closed around the bright pink flower petal which should not have been anywhere near my grandmother.

There are always those who say no; she told me this once, there are always those who rebel.

You've got fire in your veins, she told me this too. You are one of us.

I stood there and watched them set her on fire and I was thinking no, no! Don't do it! Something is wrong! She wasn't supposed to go yet! Something happened to her! I wanted to scream, but she was already burning, it was already too late.

And the pink petal was burning a hole in my hand.

22: Goodbyes

'You're shaking,' my father said to me on the way back home. The death was over as was the burning. All that was left was the service tomorrow. The dead were always honoured in a service the day after their burning. Everyone would return to the cemetery and make a circle, and people were invited to go into the middle of the circle and make speeches about the departed. But for now, we all went home. We all trudged sadly back to our huts.

I felt vile as I was led away. Dad kept his arm around me. Mum walked just in front, as if she was eager to get back. I thought briefly about how she had been acting since the announcement in the square that day. Nervous, distracted, always biting her lip or sucking her hair or trailing away mid-sentence. Now I watched her scurrying home. I wondered who would speak tomorrow for Grandma Elizabeth. Mum or Dad. Or me.

'I'm all right,' I told Dad when he hugged me closer. 'Just cold.'

'We'll soon have you home,' he responded, rubbing my shoulder. 'Back in the warm. Do you want to come in with us again? You can if you like. Just like when you were little.'

'I remember that,' I said with a slight smile.

'Yes, every night. You would wake up saying you had a bad dream, or you were too hot, or too cold, and could you please sleep with us? Of course, we didn't mind. Scooped you up and all snuggled up together, didn't we?'

I nodded wearily. I didn't have the heart to tell him the truth. That I would go to Grandma Elizabeth first. That I would try to wake
190

her, try to climb in with her, but she wouldn't wake up to let me. So, I would give up and go to them instead.

'Do you think you and Mum will have another baby soon?' I asked him then. He took a deep breath before answering.

'We don't know yet, Lissie,' he said carefully. 'But we hope so. Oh, we do hope so. Your mother especially. She believes strongly you know, women were born to bear children. To be mothers. She's felt so restless all this time, and I think that is why.'

I nodded and we walked on, following her as she hurried home. The silence stretched out for a while and we both just allowed it to. There were noises all around us, people crunching their way home, trudging and sighing. A sad day for all. I heard an owl call far away in the distance and I shivered again, more violently this time, from head to toe. My dad felt it and rubbed my shoulder again.

'Oh you're shaking Lissie. Poor girl. It might be the shock too. I am so sorry darling. So sorry that we were not there...'

'I'm sort of glad I was there.' But of course I wasn't there, was I? I was at the fence with Ned, and Aisha and Connor.

'She meant a lot to you, Lissie. I know that. We both know that. You can talk about her any time you want. I know you two had a special bond.'

We met inside our heads, I thought.

'Do you agree with Mum?' I sighed. 'Are women born to bear children?'

It seemed a good idea to change the direction of the conversation. Dad tilted his head like he always did when he was thinking about something.

'Hmm, well.'

'Is that what Ned's mum thinks too?' I went on. 'Would they both have liked lots and lots of children, if they'd been allowed?'

'Hmm, well. They understood, like we all did, that was not possible before.'

'And is it too late now? I mean, can they only have one more baby?'

'Well yes, just one more at the moment. I mean, one more for every couple that want one anyway. In every Province, of course. So, the more people we produce, the more people there will be to work and grow food and harvest food and bring it here and so on. It should all work out fine.'

I didn't agree with him anymore. That was the thing. I didn't agree with any of them. The more and more I thought about it, the less sense any of it made. I wanted to ask him now, why we couldn't grow our own food. Why we couldn't have a garden, like Grandma Elizabeth's father used to grow. Why we couldn't grow what we liked in it, and cook and eat it ourselves, and then have as many children as we wanted to have. I didn't ask him though, because I did not dare. In my head, I saw that day in the square, when he turned me towards the Governor's offices and off we went. When he delivered me. When he slobbered and slathered at the feet of that man. *That man.*

I was shaking from head to toe. With the petal in my hand, and the knowing gnawing away at my guts, and the anger, the thrumming, building, gut wrenching anger clawing its way up through my chest and into my throat. I looked around at them all; at all the good,

192

hardworking people, trudging home after watching Grandma Elizabeth burn. All the people, doing what they were told. Living their good lives.

I thought of that man and I burned from the insides.

You have fire in your veins, she said to me and she was right.

'So everyone is happy,' I said as we got closer to home. My father held me near and I looked up into his face and saw his broad whiskered smile.

'Grateful,' he agreed. 'Although today is such a very sad day. But sometimes days like this remind us how far we have come. How tightly woven together we all are. Look how everyone stops what they are doing and comes to pay their respects. Look how they came to our home all day, bringing food and gifts and kind words. And tomorrow...It will be a sad day Lissie, but we will all do her proud I promise.'

'I'm not under house arrest anymore,' I reminded him, and I felt him flinch.

'No, that's right. That's all over with Lissie. All done and dusted. Don't you worry.'

'Few more weeks and Ned gets his hut. And then me. No more school.'

'That's right my girl,' he said, and his voice was a little bit tighter and his arm around my shoulders a little bit stiffer and I wondered why. Was it my tone? 'Big changes ahead for some of you kids. Saul too, I hear. All change. Lots to be thankful for. You'll all be out there, standing on your own two feet as you are supposed to.

Stretching those wings!'

'Taking our places,' I added.

'Yes, I suppose so, yes. Replacing us when the time comes eh?'
He gave a little chuckle and went back to rubbing my shoulder. 'Day
of Thanks coming up too. And after your birthday, you can go to the
Coupling Dances...That's something to look forward to isn't it now?'

'Of course. And the baby...'

My father looked down at me and smiled before ruffling up my
hair. 'You'll be an amazing older sister, Lissie,' he grinned. 'You'll be
able to teach him or her so much!'

He said this rather blindly I felt. I was thinking about holes
under fences and running after dogs and hiding diaries, and stealing
seeds...

The conversation ended. We were home. We went inside. My
mother had already put the pot on to boil.

'Warm soup before bed, I think,' she was sighing as she scuttled
around the stove, tying on her apron. Her cheeks were flushed from
her hurry home. My father slipped into his chair and tugged me onto
his knee. I didn't resist; for a moment, I felt young again. Small, and
loved. He felt big and warm and rough and whiskery and my heart
ached for it, because it felt like somehow I was going to have to leave
it all behind. Out of choice, and out of necessity? I mean, they made
you anyway, didn't they? They made you leave.

So, I pulled away. 'No thank you,' I said to Mum, shaking my
head at the idea of the soup. 'I think I'll just go to bed actually.'

'Oh all right love,' she said, coming towards me. Her anxious face softened slightly as she cupped my chin and then kissed my cheek.

'I am sorry, Lissie. I am so sorry my love. It's been a very hard day for you and you've dealt with it so bravely.'

I'm going to miss her, I wanted to tell them. I was going to miss her so, so much.

I swallowed my tears and I slipped away. I thought, that is what I will become good at doing, slipping away from them. Soon, I will be gone. I will be out there on my own, just like Ned and Saul and whoever else turns fourteen. They would have their new babies. Their new starts. And we would have ours.

In my room, I stood for a moment, and the room without her seemed huge. Empty. The window open as usual. Her bed stripped. I opened my mouth to take a breath and a half sob emerged, so I slapped my hand over my lips and stopped them. I wouldn't cry for her. Oh no. I glared at the bed and gritted my teeth and still I was holding the petal in my hand. I won't cry for you Grandma. But I will do something for you...

I went to where I last hid the diary. It was time for my final reading session. I was nearly there now. I was so close. And even though she was gone, tonight for one last time I could curl up under my covers and read the words she wrote when she was young. I could read about running, and about wars, and I could read about Lawrence and her love for him, and all the things he taught her...

But when I slipped my hand down under the mattress there was nothing there.

Nothing.

It had gone.

I stood back, blinking, seething, shocked and hating. The diary was gone and I knew who had it.

23: Questions

I didn't wake up the next morning, because I had not slept. At least, not properly. I spent half the night in my bed, lying there rigidly, too torn up inside to relax, and I spent the other half of the night in her bed with the window wide open. I couldn't sleep there either. Her bed should have smelled of her, but it didn't. Why did they have to strip it? Why couldn't they have left it how it was? I would have been able to climb in and smell her one last time.

They took that from me too, I seethed.

Today was the big day. There were lots of big days coming up now and I would have to choose my timing carefully. I could not rush in with my anger and my churned up guts. No. I could not say or do what I really wanted to. I had to keep it all in. Truthfully, I was not too sure what I would do, or say, I just knew that I would, that I had to. That it would happen anyway. Everything I knew was a ticking time bomb inside of me.

That morning, I got up and went to the wash room to get cleaned and dressed. I was not hungry but I sat down and ate the porridge my mother prepared. She pasted her hand across my forehead and frowned.

'You don't look very good Lissie. Didn't you get much sleep? Do you feel unwell?'

I shook my head at both questions. She had that soft look on her face again. She went back to the stove and took the kettle off to make the coffee. Dad was outside chopping firewood. There was a strange mood in the air between them. Sadness, tinged with relief.

Impatience. They were ready for her to go, I concluded, eating my breakfast. They were ready for the next chapter of their lives. That's what it was.

'You're very quiet lately,' my mother said with her back to me. 'Since the whole dog thing, I mean. Not just since yesterday...' Her words softened and faded towards the end of her sentence. I felt this sharp jab to my heart. It was getting harder and harder to swallow my food. I didn't know what to say to her. What did she expect me to say? What did she want from me?

'Just thinking a lot,' I decided to tell her.

'What about?'

'About everything. Just...everything. Didn't you at my age? Didn't you wonder about it all?'

She kept her back to me and sighed. Here I go again, I thought miserably, watching her. Disappointing them. Just like Ned. So, wouldn't it be better for all of them if we just left? Went beyond the fence and tried a different life? Of course, the thought made me tremble and filled me with fear. Or was it fear? I didn't even know anymore. I couldn't say I felt brave enough to just leave, just go and never come back, but I also couldn't bear the thought of never seeing Aisha and Connor again, never finding out more.

'When I was your age Lissie,' she said to me, stirring the coffee in the pot. 'Life was harder than it is now. Food was rationed. They were still learning, you see. Still learning what to grow and how to grow. People were starving all over. Everything was scarce. Food, water, medicine, knowledge. This is what you forget. This is what you don't understand.'

198

'Didn't you want to go outside the Province, Mum?' I shouldn't have said it, but I couldn't help it, I just couldn't. Her back was stiff now, her shoulders rigid. 'Didn't you want to go and help in the domes? Or go to the other Provinces and learn about them? Or be a guard or a scavenger?'

'Of course not Lissie! Why would I want to risk my life? It wasn't safe! People learnt that the hard way!'

'What do you mean?'

'Sometimes I wonder if you've ever paid any attention my girl!' She finally turned to face me, shaking her head from side to side. 'Did you listen at school? Did they teach you anything?'

'It wasn't safe,' I said. 'Because of disease and wild animals. Everyone was safer here. Being looked after.'

Mum pulled her head back and frowned at me heavily. 'Why do you say it like that?'

'Like what?'

'Being *looked after*,' she sneered. 'Like that. Like it's a bad thing. I don't understand you!'

'Sometimes Mum, I just want to learn about the rest of the world. I just want to go out there. I just want to find it for myself. I just want to-'

I stopped. My father appeared in the doorway, sweating from his brow and rubbing at his chin. He stared at me for a moment and then he looked down and grunted.

'It's just today,' he said to her, waving a hand at me. 'It's going to be a hard day for her. Let's not talk about this anymore.'

'But I want to,' I told them. 'I don't see why we can't talk about it. It's not against the law. I just want to talk to you!'

'Maybe after,' he muttered, striding past me to the stove and picking up the pot of coffee. 'But for now, Lissie, this conversation is over.'

The service took place at mid-day. People from all over the Province wandered back to the cemetery to pay their final respects. There was always the sense that it really was final. That grieving and crying ended here, today. Once it was done, it was done. Acceptance of death was vital. So, we all went back, and when we got there the ground where she was burned was still smoking.

My last sob was a shuddering which started in my shoulders. I wanted to let it take me over. I wanted to lose control. I wanted to sink to my knees in the dusty, smoking ground and I wanted to plunge my hands into the ash and scoop her up one last time. I wanted to throw my head back to the sky and scream out. It wasn't her time! Someone was there! This is all wrong! All of you are wrong! I wanted to make a scene and drag it out and carry the pain and the grief around with me forever more, on my face and in my shoulders. Like Hilda Fleck had done for Woody. I saw her stood on the other side of the circle beside her husband and her son. She was not paying attention to the service. She was biting her lip and then smiling and then biting her lip to stop herself. You can't wait, I thought, staring at her, you can't wait to see if the next one is better than Ned! And there was the Governor, stood beside Deputy Bradley, both with their heads bowed in respect. I didn't think I could bear it.

I lowered my eyes and stared at the ground. My father went forward to speak. I could barely hear him. I was not listening. I was not there. I did not want to do this. I was too full up, you see. It was like I could not think or breathe. I was too full up of everything; of Charlie and Aisha and Connor, of rebels and wars, and seeds and domes, and I just wanted her back, so, so badly, I just wanted my Gran back, so that we could meet in our heads again, so that she could whisper in my ear. I wanted her back. And I wanted her diary back.

In the end, I couldn't do it. I couldn't stay there watching them blink tears away while they read out their thoughts. I didn't want to hear what they had to say about her, because I knew they didn't want to hear what I had to say about her. So, I left. I turned slowly when no one was looking and I slunk away between the people, out of the crowd. And for a moment I was free. I was alone. Just me, heading away, getting away.

I could breathe again.

I kept walking and breathing. I had to do something. I had to.

Before I knew it, I was back in the square and no one was in sight. I stood for a minute and took it all in. It was eerie, to say the least. I thought about the first settlers, those ragged and bloodied survivors of the last war on earth. It was mind blowing when you thought about it. How they survived out of all those billions and billions of people. I stood for a minute and tried to picture them, limping here, seeing the domes and heading for food. And my Grandma Elizabeth was one of them. But I would never find out what happened when they got there. I would never find out what happened to her Lawrence. She said he was sacrificed, but what did that mean?

And suddenly I knew what I had to do.

I marched on, with purpose now, right up to the Governor's offices. I went to the door and pushed against it but it did not yield. I knocked instead, loud and clear. I pressed my face to the glass and spotted movement behind. Here she came, Miss Harper, scurrying out from behind her desk, pencil behind one ear, forehead creased in confusion.

When she saw it was me she looked at first pleased, and then concerned. I suppose I had not turned out to be the star pupil she had hoped for. I smiled at her reassuringly and she unlocked the door.

'Hi Miss Harper. Thanks.'

'Lissie Turner, what on earth can I do for you? It's your grandmother's service, why aren't you there?'

'I couldn't stay,' I told her breathlessly. 'It was too hard. I need to see the Governor.'

'But he's at the service!'

'I know. I was hoping he'd come back here after?'

'Yes I believe he intends to, but-'

'Can I come in and wait for him?'

She opened her mouth in surprise and then closed it again. 'Um, well...'

'Please,' I said, my body already half way through the door. 'It's important Miss Harper. I can't tell you how important. I wouldn't be here if it wasn't. Please.'

'Well, all right, all right,' she waved a hand and let me in rather begrudgingly. 'But you will have to wait right here with me young

202

lady. I can't just let you wander around, and I don't know exactly when he'll be back!'

'Thank you, thank you!' I headed to the wooden chair near the window. 'I'll just sit right here and behave myself I promise. I won't say a word. You won't even know I'm here.'

'Hmm,' she said, before locking the door and going back to her desk.

I sat there and tried to keep quiet. I was so many things. Thrilled and excited. Glad to be breaking the rules again, glad to have fire in my veins. Scared. Terrified, in fact. Confused. All these words and conversations in my head. All the things my parents believed in. All those people out there, kind and good. All the things they believed in. I sat there and squirmed.

I sat there and kept quiet like I said I would, but Miss Harper seemed to find this harder to do than me. She shuffled a few papers, took a sip of her hot drink and then tilted her head at me.

'You know it's a shame really,' she announced, so I sat up straight.

'What is Miss Harper?'

'That you couldn't come back for more duties. I liked having you around.'

I offered her a smile. 'I'm sorry about that. I broke the rules.'

'Hmm,' she said, giving me a sort of stern look. 'Well, you were a little misguided, shall we say? What was it like though? That dog thing?'

I shuffled forward on the chair. 'It was lovely Miss Harper. He was lovely. He didn't do anything wrong. He didn't hurt me.'

'No, well that was lucky, wasn't it? But disease. It might have been diseased. You really should have told your father right away.'

'Well, I was curious. Is it wrong to be curious?'

She sipped from her drink carefully. Perhaps when she lowered it, there was the smallest of smiles upon her lips.

'I don't really know,' she said. 'I suppose it depends on the situation and on the damage that can be done. But thankfully for you, your father was on hand, and everything is all right.'

'Unless there are any others,' I shrugged at her. 'You know, out there.'

She looked shocked and uncomfortable, one hand fluttering to her chest. 'Oh Lissie Turner do not say that! What a horrible thought!'

'Well, I can't help being curious. Sorry.'

'Well, the Governor was sending out patrols, last thing I heard. I'm sure they will do everything in their power to check there are not any more of them out there! Lay traps or something, I expect.'

At this, my body grew cold. It grew even colder when just two minutes later the door opened and in walked Soren Lancaster.

He stopped when he saw me. A flicker of concern seemed to pass over his smooth face. And then he smiled and he was the same as he always was. Calm and contained. At peace with his world. He removed his hat and held it in one hand, as he closed and locked the door behind him. All the time he kept his eyes on me.

'To what do I owe this pleasure?' he wondered.

'Lissie needs to talk to you urgently,' Miss Harper reported from behind her desk. 'I only let her in because she seemed so very desperate.'

'Well, of course, of course,' he nodded, pleasantly. 'What is it, Lissie? What can I do for you?'

'I need to speak to you,' I told him. My voice did not come out the way I wanted it to. It was cracked and unsure. His smile reached his eyes and he nodded his head towards the door that led upstairs.

'In private I assume?' he asked and I nodded. 'Well come on then, child. Lead the way. You have my full attention.'

I got to my feet. Ugh, my legs had turned to jelly. My feet filled with lead. I could barely walk, but I had to. I went ahead of him as he suggested. My throat was dry. My knees wanted to drop me down to the floor. But then I thought about Grandma and her diary, and the bright pink petal.

Somehow I made it to the top of the stairs, and then he sidled lightly past me to push open the door to his personal office. We went in and he closed the door behind me. He seemed remarkably unruffled. He placed his hat on his desk and went to the window to open the shutters.

'Look,' he said from there, so I walked towards the other window and looked out. 'All those people...'

The square was full again. They were mostly heading back to work, or back home, but they were slow, talking and hugging, stopping to chat, catching the elbows of passers-by.

The Tree of Rebels

'All those people turned out for that remarkable old lady,' he said and when I turned to look at him he was stood beside me with his hands linked behind his back. 'An amazing day,' he said. 'An amazing turn-out. And your mother and father said some beautiful things...But of course, you missed that. How strange.'

'I needed to talk to you more than I needed to listen to them say goodbye,' I heard the words leave my lips and I could barely believe I had spoken them. I looked back out of the window.

'This must be important,' he said. 'For you to miss your own great-grandmother's service. Missed your own chance to speak about her too. And she was the last one, you realise? The last survivor from the Old World. Yes. Quite a day really. Quite a day.'

'Well, it's her I need to talk to you about.'

'Oh?'

'You were there, weren't you?'

There, I said it. And now he knew what I knew.

There was silence from him. He remained at the window, hands behind his back, and then he swallowed a smile as he turned to look at me. I folded my arms over my chest and glared back at him. In that moment, I was not afraid. I felt many things, but for some reason, fear was not one of them.

'You were there,' I said it again. 'I found a petal from a flower next to her bed. One of your flowers, Governor.'

His smile was soft and gentle. His eyes were amused. I wondered what he thought when he saw me there like that. Challenging him. I bet no one had ever done that before. But yet, still
206

no fear. I just wanted answers. For her.

'Let me get this straight Lissie,' he said. 'Are you accusing me of something?'

'I'm saying I know you were there. In my hut. The night she died.'

'But child, you were there yourself, isn't that right? You were still under house arrest. You were there in the hut when she died. Your parents told me this. *You* were there Lissie.'

'No, I wasn't there,' I told him, and I stepped forward, and my fury was doing it, my utter fury was pushing me towards him. 'I wasn't there, and you know that, and I know that. Just like we *both* know you were there!'

He laughed. He closed his eyes briefly and laughed at me. Then he turned towards me and tipped his head and his expression was full of pity.

'Oh you poor child,' he purred. 'What a muddle you have got yourself into. You know, you really do intrigue me. I have never known one quite like you before. Then again, you are her great-granddaughter, so I suppose it is to be expected.'

'Are you denying it?'

'Denying what?'

'Being there! Being in my hut when she died! *Killing* her!'

He took a step towards me and held a finger up to his lips. 'Lissie Turner. I suggest you control yourself. You are to be an adult very, *very* soon. With a job and responsibilities. Now I can accept that

207

this sad day has got to you. You are not yourself.'

'Yes I am, I am myself. And I want you to answer me, Governor Lancaster. *Were* you in my hut that night?'

'You want to know where I was the night she died?'

'Yes.'

'Hmm,' he said, stroking his chin in mock thought. 'Well then. Let us bargain. Let us trade secrets. If you tell me where you were, I will tell you where I was. Does that sound fair?'

I forced my teeth down over my tongue. I couldn't tell him where I was. I couldn't tell him about Aisha and Connor.

'I was out walking,' I lied instead, hoping this would fool him. 'I needed a break from the hut. I went out and walked for a bit. Then I came back and she was dead, and the petal from your flower was on the floor!'

'If there *was* a flower, what makes you think it belonged to me?'

'You're the only one who has them!'

'You say you were out walking?' he questioned, moving to his desk now and picking up his hat. I nodded at him. 'Alone?'

'Yes alone.'

'But you can't prove that. You can't prove anything young lady, which is where this matter sadly must come to an end.'

'But-'

'No buts, Lissie!' He stepped towards me quickly, his voice

louder and harder, his eyes bright with life. I stepped back and I felt in that moment that I had lost. I had lost momentum, and I had lost courage. He held his hat and regarded me cooly. 'No buts. This matter of yours comes to an end right here and now and neither of us shall ever mention it again. You do not want your parents to know you left the hut that night. You do not want your parents to know you lied to them. You do not want them to know you left her alone and went out searching for more rules to break. Also Lissie, you do not want *me* to find out where you really were.'

I was ruined and this was over. But I had not finished with him. 'Are we free?' I asked him. He blinked at me.

'I beg your pardon?'

'Are we free? Can we leave? Can we get out of here?'

'Out of the Province?'

'Yes. Because that is what I wish to do. I can't stay here anymore knowing what I know about you.'

'I think this is a discussion for another day, child,' he said, trying to dismiss me now, trying to let me know he had won and this was over.

'No. I need to know now. Or maybe I might start talking. I might show my parents the flower petal. I might show Ned. I might-'

'You might land yourself in a lot of trouble Lissie,' he held a hand up to me. 'Let's be honest about this. You are already on thin ice. You have been breaking rules all over the place. If you want to stand here and suggest you know things about me, how would you like me to suggest what I have been learning about you? You need to be very careful, that is the thing. Once you are fourteen, there will be no more protecting you. It will be out of my hands,'

'Protecting me?'

'Treason is a very serious offence.'

'Treason?'

He smiled very gently. 'I have a dossier of complaints against you, Lissie. I have been watching you a long time. Before you came onto my radar I was watching her. Until she got old, of course. But it seems she was still able to spread her poison even from her death bed.'

I shook my head at him. I was appalled. So angry I was out of breath. 'Don't you, don't you...'

'I've been watching your family for years, Lissie Turner. And you have the gall to stand here and make accusations? Your parents are good people. This much is true. *You* on the other hand seem to take after the old woman. You cannot be satisfied, is that right? You cannot be grateful.'

I couldn't answer him. I couldn't speak. I was so angry. So enraged. My fists were balled up at my sides. He pointed outside.

'Look out there. Go on look. Look with your eyes. See for yourself. A peaceful, calm society. Where everyone has a job, Lissie. Where everyone has a home. Where everyone has enough food and water and heat. Where everyone is appreciated. Where everyone is kind and warm. Do I lie? Is this not the truth?'

I tore my eyes away from him and gazed out at the square. 'It might look that way to you...'

210

'How do you see it then?' he asked in amusement. 'What am I missing?

'At the moment,' I said through gritted teeth. 'Right now, I see a prison.'

'A prison?' he sounded amused. 'Really? How interesting. Well Lissie, I might suggest to you that you have no idea what a prison truly is. And neither do you want to.'

I was bored of this. Going around in circles, getting nowhere. He was talking in riddles the whole time, trying to throw me off course. I stood my ground, put my hands on my hips and stuck my chin out at him.

'You took her diary. I want it back.'

24: Answers

Governor Lancaster stared at me and smiled. His eyes narrowed slightly, as the smile pulled his lips up towards his ear lobes. He looked like he wanted to laugh at me but was attempting to control himself. I remained still, standing my ground, like my ancestors tried to do back then. See, I know all about it, I wanted to tell him! I know all about what my great-great-grandfather tried to do!

'Diary?' he said very smoothly. 'What diary?'

'She had a diary. It was in our room. Now it's gone.'

He laughed. He threw back his head and chuckled. 'Oh my, my my. What a vivid imagination you have, Lissie! So, let's get this straight. First, I was in your hut the night she died, and left a flower petal there for some strange reason? And secondly I found an old woman's diary and stole it? Why would I do that?'

'You just said yourself,' I replied, evenly. 'You've been watching our family for years. You were watching her, like your father before you. She said not to trust any of you! She was right! Everything she said was right! And when I think about it, why did you invite me to do duties in your garden, anyway?' I stepped forward, thinking back, trying to make sense of it all. 'Was that part of watching us? Did you want to keep an eye on me? See how I'd react?'

Governor Lancaster put his hands back behind him and began to walk. He walked very slowly and cooly around his desk, past me, and then around again. There was something more menacing about him now, there was no denying it. He did not take his eyes off me, and he looked hungry.

'Why don't we deal with one question at a time, Lissie? So, what was in this precious diary that makes you so worried about it?'

'I just told you. Everything she said. The truth. And she said not to let anyone find it. And now I know why. Now I'm learning more and more.'

'Well, you could put it like that, or you could suggest that you are getting more and more confused. Have you ever considered the fact that maybe the diary was a story? A work of fiction?'

'No,' I shook my head at him vehemently. 'It was her diary. From when she was a kid. It's the best history book I have ever read!'

'And if this is all true, what makes you think I would want it, Lissie?' He was walking past me again, now slightly stooped forward as he frowned down at me. 'What would I do with it? Why would I care about it?'

'You tell me!'

'Oh no. No, no, no, Lissie.' He stopped just behind me and spoke directly into my ear. '*You* tell *me*.' I jumped and moved away from him.

'Because it's got the truth in it,' I said to him, backing myself up towards the window. 'Because she was the last survivor, because she knew what *really* happened to the Old World, who really destroyed it and why! Because you don't want people to know all this. We're not taught it at school. We're not taught the truth!'

'The truth is always open to interpretation, Lissie,' he said, with a sad little shake of his head. 'That is something you learn as you get older. Nothing is black and white. Truth for one person, is not the same truth for another. It gets bent out of shape over time. It depends on your perspective and what you are protecting.'

'You're trying to confuse me. You can't even answer my simple questions!'

'You don't have simple questions, Lissie Turner, and there are no simple answers. I'm going to do something for you now. I am going to end this silly pointless charade.' He sighed softly as he moved towards me, and I wanted to move back, but I couldn't, because I was at the window, my back pressed against it. His face was so strange. Like he was full of regrets and torment. Was he faking it?

'I just want the truth from you,' I tried to tell him. 'I just want you to tell me the truth and then I will go. I'll leave and you'll never see me again. I won't hurt anyone. I won't tell anyone.'

'That's a lie, only you don't know it, Lissie.'

'What?'

'You will tell people and you will hurt them.'

'I won't if I say I won't!'

Again, that sad smile, that long sigh. He was as close to me as he could get without treading on my feet. Our faces only inches apart now. To my horror, he reached out and cupped my chin in his hand. He lifted my face up to meet his, and there was no escape.

'I'm not accusing you of lying,' he said, and his tone was so friendly now, so calm and reassuring. His eyes seemed to narrow and yet deepen at the same time. They moved quickly, taking me in, running all over my face. 'It's just you are so young, and so confused, and you have no idea what you will really do with your information. I

214

can't blame you for any of this, Lissie. Truth be told, I am actually very fond of you. You're one of a kind just like she was. I can't deny there is something about you...' He bit his lip, and his eyes were pentrating now, as if he were trying to see deep inside my soul. Then suddenly he dropped my face and clapped his hands, making me jump again. '*But* I have my orders you see.'

'What orders?'

'Never mind that for now,' he said. 'Let's just end this. You will feel so much better if you just let it end. So,' Soren Lancaster placed one hand on the glass directly behind my head. 'I am going to give you something, Lissie, so be quiet and listen hard. I am going to give you one opportunity only. Just one. It starts right now. You are being given one opportunity to put all of this behind you. To forget about the petal you found. To forget about this diary. To forget about what you *think* really happened in the Old World, and to forget everything you *think* is so wrong about this one. Do you understand what I am saying?'

I opened my mouth, willing words, ferocious words, but none arrived. I just opened and closed my mouth like a fish looking for air. He smiled patiently.

'You can leave here now, Lissie. You can go back outside, join your family and cry one last time for your great-grandmother. You can go back to your hut and your life. In due course you can have your own hut and your own job and your own family. And we will never bring this up again. I will not ask anything of you and you will not ask anything of me, do you understand? In short, Lissie, we will have a deal. A mutual understanding that will benefit us both, and more importantly than that, everyone else out there. All those good and innocent people. Now what do you say?'

I cleared my throat and moved slowly away from the window and away from him. I understood what he was saying, of course I did. He had made himself perfectly clear in every way. He would let me get away with what I had done, if I let him do the same. It was an admission of his own guilt and I hated him for it.

'What if I say no?'

'I can't exactly tell you,' he turned to me and sighed again. 'I guess it's up to you to find out. Now what about we both sleep on it? Think about everything and meet again tomorrow? I am happy with that if you are?'

'I don't want to be anywhere near you,' I hissed and headed quickly for the door.

'Understandable,' he called after me. 'But think it through anyway. No decision that affects so many should be taken lightly. One way or another, the course of your life could be about to change very dramatically, Lissie Turner. If you do have any further questions you know where to find me and I will certainly make time for you.'

'Yeah, I bet you will...' I muttered before yanking open the door and getting the hell out of there. Outside his room I stopped for a second, closed my eyes and breathed. And that was when the fear finally hit me. It was like it had just been hiding there the whole time, just ducked down below the surface waiting to rear up and whack me right over the head. It sent me reeling from that place, flying down the stairs, out of the door and back out into the square.

Once I started running I couldn't stop.

The fear, the horrible bone shaking fear took control of me. It threw me on, and my legs were a blur, and my throat was raw and I

216

kept running and running. Lissie Turner, I was Lissie Turner, I was Lissie Turner and I was the fastest girl in town.

I didn't stop running until I reached the fence. By now I could barely breathe. I threw myself at the fence, gripped on and let my legs give way. And then I used the fence to haul my trembling body along. I was looking for the hole. Where was the bloody hole? I couldn't breathe, I couldn't breathe, the stink of him, the smell of him in my nostrils, in my throat, my lungs, all heaving, choking and my stomach twisting and lurching. I felt so alone. I never knew it was possible to feel so alone. Where had the bloody hole gone?

It had gone. What did I expect? I could climb over! I stood back and looked up. The fence was fifteen feet high and my body was wrecked. I needed to find another hole. I needed to dig another hole, I needed to get out! Why couldn't I get out? I just wanted to get out!

'Calm down,' I told myself, whimpering slightly. 'Just calm down, calm down. Think. *Think*!'

I didn't know what to do, so I just kept walking. With one hand on the fence, and my head hanging low, I just kept walking. They said it took an entire day to walk around the perimeter of the Province. Almost twelve hours exactly. I didn't know if this was true because I had never tried to do it. Maybe now was the time to try. Maybe now was the time to just walk.

So, that's what I ended up doing. Walking. On and on and on. Keeping right next to the fence. Trailing my listless hand along it. Every now and then I tripped, stumbled and fell. My legs were that weak, my steps were that uncertain. Every now and then I burst into pointless tears. I cried them out, because no one was there, no one could see. And I kept walking. I walked through lunch time, and I walked through dinner time, and I walked until my knees throbbed and my feet screamed in protest and my head hung heavy on my neck. I walked and cried, and walked and seethed and fumed and feared. I thought about my Grandma Elizabeth, now just ashes in the air, and I looked all around me, thinking of her, wishing she could see me or speak to me, wishing she was still there to guide me.

The fence was really the dullest thing in the world. It went on and on, curving around our tiny little world of busying people, and it revealed nothing, nothing great or grand or sad or terrible. Just one long, high, dull forever fence. Was it here when the first survivors arrived, or did they put it up? How did they put it up? Where did they find the wire and the poles? Or, like the domes, was this already put in place as the Endless War gobbled up its last victims?

As the night drew in I was calmer. I could breathe again. Think again. I placed the facts apart from the fears inside my head. I collected my thoughts and pushed away my fury. I thought about what I knew, and about what I didn't. I never got to finish the story, I thought. I didn't know what happened next. I wanted that diary back. I *needed* that diary back. I needed a plan, I needed to think, to calm down and think logically. What did she tell me? What would she want me to do? Who could I trust?

Instantly and sadly I ruled out my parents. I ruled out every grown up I knew. I thought of Ned and Aisha and Connor. That was it. But Aisha and Connor were gone. I considered this for a while as I plodded slowly and painfully on. The more I thought about them, the more I pondered what was going on. What were they doing so close to the Province anyway? If what they said about our people fighting them was true, then surely they would keep as far away as possible? What was Aisha doing there that day, down by the tree with Charlie? What

218

were they still doing there now? Did our people know? What about Deputy Bradshaw and the guards? Or was this part of my betrayal still a secret? How much danger were Connor and Aisha in right now? Unless they had already gone? Maybe they had. Maybe I would never ever set eyes on them again, or anyone like them. Maybe this had all been a fluke and an accident, something that was not supposed to happen, something that would never occur again. I should just let it go. Just carry on. Like I was supposed to. Grateful for the peace, and the food, and the work and the home. And be happy. Like they all were.

This, I realised, was what the Governor had just offered me. Leave it all alone. Let it be. Let go.

And if I never saw Aisha or Connor again, then that was what would happen, right? I mean, what could happen if it was just me? Just me against all of this, against everything? Just me wanting the truth? Just me believing that Governor Lancaster murdered my grandma and stole her diary? Just me.

The loneliness hurt so I sunk to the ground. I was nearly home. My knees hurt so much they felt swollen. I wondered if I had ever walked so much in my whole life. I walked alongside the fence where I first saw Charlie. That day felt like a lifetime ago, like I was a different person then, and this was a different world.

I walked on, and soon enough I saw my hut. It was this little round mound of home, shining in the distance. Candles glowing in the window. Their stooped figures silhouetted inside. I stopped and sat down on the ground. My legs stuck out in front of me, my hands sat limply in my lap. I was thirsty, hungry and exhausted. They would have missed me. Maybe searched for me. I didn't care anymore. This much was true. So much had changed. I wished I could tell them that.

And that I still loved them.

I sat there for a long, long time just watching my hut. I sat there and watched the sun going down behind it, this perfectly round ball of marvel and colours, spreading and deepening across the horizon. The hut sat gloriously in the middle of it all. It looked like it was on fire. I watched them moving about inside of it, and I got this dull ache in my gut. I remembered falling down the step when I was a little kid and my mother sitting me on the table inside to see where I was hurt. I remembered all the nights we sat outside under the stars, while my father stoked the fire and we drank soup and ate biscuits. I remembered the stories he used to make up to amuse us. I remembered falling asleep in his lap and him carrying me back to my bed. I remembered the day I started school, and how they walked me there, holding my hands on either side of me and we met Ned and his parents along the way. Haven't they grown, they all said and smiled, where did that time go?

I sat and watched them moving about the hut while more tears fell slowly from my eyes. I let them fall, not blinking them away or rubbing at them. Just letting them come. Just letting it go. I needed a plan, I needed to think, I needed to decide.

What should I do?

What did I want to do?

The thing was; did I want to stay or go? I wasn't even sure I could go. I wasn't even sure I would be allowed. Arrested and taken into custody, they said. I can't even tell you what will happen, the Governor said. But if I could, if they let me, or if I got out, if I could leave the Province, would I? Would I do it? Did I want to? What did I actually want?

More than anything, more than the diary, more than the night Grandma died, the petal, the Governor and everything else, more than all the mysteries and lies, I needed to know this, I needed to work out exactly what I wanted. I needed this answer before I needed any of the others. Otherwise it was all pointless.

I sat there and sniffed as my tears dried on my face, and I watched the hut, my heart beating hard for those people inside, who had loved me and nurtured me. I watched them moving about in the candlelight and I wondered what they were doing and saying and thinking, and then I knew what to do. I knew the answer. I would go to them. Show myself to them. Offer all of this, all of what I was, of what I had become, to them. My parents. And then, only then would I know the answer.

I took the biggest, deepest breath of my life and I got up from the ground and walked towards home.

25: Time

I went to them with the intention of confessing. But their reaction when I reached them surprised me. First my mother rushed to me, grabbing me and slamming me into her collar bone. My father put down his mug of coffee and hurried up behind her. My breath was pressed from my body as she crushed me into her own. I could feel her heart beating against mine. Whatever words I planned to share with them dried up on my tongue.

'Oh Lissie, Lissie, we've been so worried about you! Oh, my girl, oh my child, my girl...'

'It's all right,' my father told me from above her head. I was so confused and he must have seen this. He gave me a cautious frowning smile. 'It's okay. The Governor said you would need time, so we tried not to panic, but oh Lissie, we are glad you are home!'

I managed to nod against her bosom, and she squeezed me once more, harder than ever, before gently easing me back as if to inspect my existence.

'Oh you worried us, we were so worried!'

'I was walking,' I started to tell them. Dad patted my shoulder rather clumsily and ushered me to the chair he had vacated.

'It's all right, we know, we know. The Governor told us. He said you would be all right, and he was right! Thank Goodness.'

I was eased into the chair by my mother's shaking hands, and then she knelt in front of me, tears in her eyes, creases all over her face as she tried to keep the crying in. She grabbed one of my hands and

222

held it between hers.

'Oh my girl, my girl,' she said. 'I was so worried. It's been killing me just waiting!'

'The Governor said,' Dad repeated from behind her. 'He did say Beth. He did say she would be back. Give her time, he said.'

'Well, time feels like forever when you are waiting for your only child to come home!' she snapped back at him. I sat limply in the chair, my heart going mad, my legs aching even more now they had been rested. 'But you're okay, you're okay,' she said to me. 'Oh thank goodness. You've been gone so long.'

'I went for a walk...'

'Yes we know, we know,' said Dad, nodding and looking eager and serious at the same time. He looked like he was bursting with things and holding them down, holding them back. 'Governor Lancaster said you were walking. He said to leave you be. Said it would do you good. And has it, Lissie? Has it?'

'Wait,' I said, my head lolling back into the chair. 'When did you see him? What's he been saying about me?'

'We couldn't find you after the service,' said my mother, still clasping my hand in hers, still battling with those tears. 'We looked all over and no one had seen you, and then the Governor found us in the square and said he had just been talking with you.'

I stared back at them in wonder. It seemed like years ago that I stood there by the window and tried to trade secrets with him. Dad blew out his breath dramatically and shook his head at me.

'He said he'd found you very upset and took you up to his

office for a chat.'

'That's right,' I nodded vaguely, and I tried to remember now what my intention was. What I had wanted to tell them. But they kept talking and soothing me.

'He said not to worry,' Dad said. 'He said you were very upset at losing Grandma Elizabeth and he had suggested a long walk to calm you down.'

'Is that where you've been, Lissie?' Mum asked, and I looked down into her face, nodding.

'I walked around the entire Province.'

Her eyes widened. 'The whole way? Lissie...'

'Quite an achievement!' grinned Dad. 'You must be exhausted!'

'And hungry!' Mum let me go and pushed herself up to her feet. 'I saved you some food. Just you hang on a minute my girl.'

'I just kept walking and walking,' I said to them. And as I said it, I started to feel it. All the ground I had covered, all the air I had breathed, all the thoughts I'd had, and I felt my body weakening, my mind drifting off, my eyes shutting down.

'You're exhausted,' Dad stated as a fact. 'You need sleep. It's been a quite a day. How nice of the Governor to look after you like that!'

'He's a good man,' Mum agreed from the stove. 'A good and kind man. We're lucky to have him. What on earth made you walk all day, Lissie Turner? My goodness you are a funny girl with your head in the clouds.'

'Just like Grandma, hey Lissie?' Dad was smiling down at me. 'Two peas in a pod we always said, didn't we Beth?'

'I miss her too, Lissie,' Mum said. 'We will all feel the loss for some time to come, but she had a long, long life. An amazing life. The things she saw. And she died exactly as she wanted to, right here in her home, in her own bed.'

This jarred inside of me and I opened my mouth to protest, but she was already in front of me, pushing soup and warm bread onto my lap.

'Get that down you and then off to bed! You'll sleep for days!'

Dad reached out to ruffle my hair. 'Fancy walking all that way. I don't think I've ever done that! Nope. Too busy. Oh well. It did you good, I can see that Lissie. You seem calmer now.'

I dipped the bread into the soup and ate it slowly. I was too tired to talk. Too tired to think. Too tired to do what I'd planned to do. I just sat there and ate and tried not to spill the soup on myself because I was so tired... I just ate it slowly, chewing carefully, trying to look at them, and into them. Trying to see them. They look so good, I thought. Good enough to eat. Watching me, wringing their hands, touching me, loving me. How could I do it to them?

I was going to tell them about the diary. I was going to tell them about the seeds and the wars and the rebels. I was going to tell them about Lawrence and Elizabeth. Aisha and Connor. Me and Ned. I was going to tell them about the petal on the floor beside Gran's hand and I was going to tell them what happened when I went to see Soren Lancaster. He told me to think about it. He gave me time. But I couldn't open my mouth, I couldn't speak, or think.

The Tree of Rebels

I let them take care of me. I was nearly an adult, but that night they did not treat me like one. She wiped the soup from my chin. He took the bowl when it nearly slipped from my lap. She brushed the crumbs from my clothes. He lifted me up in his big strong arms, and she opened the door to the bedroom and fussed around the bed before he dropped me into it. She wiped my hair from my face and kissed my brow, and he leaned in from behind her, one arm around her waist as he tipped me a wink and instructed me to have sweet dreams, and then they tucked me in like a small child and left me to sleep.

I couldn't say anything. I couldn't speak.

I lay there and thought about them. I loved them. They loved me. But something had changed. Then I realised that I'd expected them to be angry with me, disappointed yet again. And in my defence I was going to tell them everything to give them a chance to do the right thing. I had not been prepared for this onslaught of parental devotion. I was floored by it. Thwarted. And then I remembered him.

The Governor.

Talking to them. Telling them not to worry and to give me time. And I saw him how he really was. He is the puppet master, I thought, leaning arrogantly over his tight little world. Pulling the strings and making all the puppets dance to his tune...

I didn't think much longer. I fell into the deepest sleep of my life.

When I woke up the next morning I made a decision. I wouldn't tell them everything. Not yet. I would play it his way, but with my eyes wide open. I would take the opportunity he offered me in his office and I would play it out. I would let them continue with their little game, their little dance.

I stayed in my bed and watched my toes wriggling at the end of my legs. I couldn't even bring myself to look over at her bed. Just thinking about her made my heart lurch in pain. But I tried something. I swallowed it down. I took a deep, new breath. I thought about playing it his way, and the best thing was, he would not know. He'd think he had won, for now. I'd let him think this. I'd be cowed and afraid. Beaten. I'd give up and give in.

Because I needed time.

He was right about that, you see. I did need time. I was wrong to think I could burst in here last night and hit them with everything like that. They would not have coped. They would have over-reacted. They would have been terrified. Only now could I see how controlled they were. It was like my eyes were wide open. Like Grandma said. They were all performing monkeys.

So, I'd take his time. Thank you very much, Soren. Thank you for this opportunity to calm down and think things through. I'd take it with both hands and use it wisely. I'd take his time and I would bide my time. But I would never, ever forget about that petal on the floor next to her cold stiff hand....

26: Ned's Last Day

The Day of Thanks was nearly upon us. So were our last days at school. It felt like everything was happening at once. We were in the middle of a whirlwind. As it came upon us, Ned was always frowning, scuttling and nibbling his nails. I was a hard, small, unknown thing they did not see coming.

'Are you all right?' he asked me whenever we were alone. 'What's going on? What are we gonna' do? What about the rebels?'

I just shook my head at him. I shushed him. 'Forget about it.'

'Forget about it?'

'Yes. For now.'

He blew out his breath and kept quiet.

School was a hive of activity. Everyone buzzing around, brimming with excitement, talking about the first of June. Everyone loved this day so much. The first of June, the day the Peace treaty was signed. People gave presents and everything. They were planning the biggest party yet, right in the middle of the Province. The same thing would happen in the other Provinces, and across the world, we were told. But how did we know? I found myself wondering this as the big day loomed up. How did we know those other places even existed? How did we know we were not the last people left on earth? But then I remembered Aisha and Connor.

On Ned's last day of school, we walked slowly in together. His head was hanging and he dragged his feet. We started off in silence, neither of us knowing what to say, and then he began murmuring the

Song Of Thanks beneath his breath.

'For no more war, and no more fear, we thank you all, we thank you all.'

It sounded eerie and cold coming from his clamped lips on a dull morning. The sky was silent in response. It felt like nothing was moving or living except for us. I had got a constant lump in my throat that I couldn't swallow. It was called Province Number 5.

'For food to eat and clothes to wear, we thank you all, we thank you all...'

'Stop it,' I groaned, poking him with my elbow. 'I've had enough.'

Ned sighed. 'Finished my hut last night. Me and Dad.'

'So what's it like? Do you like it?'

He scratched his ear. 'I like it, but it makes me feel sad.'

'What do you mean?'

'I like the hut. It's mine. It feels like mine. It's all set up now, and I even cooked my first meal there last night. Mum and Dad and me sat on the step to eat it.'

'Yeah, and?'

'It's just...*them*.' And he stopped walking and sucked all his breath in, pushing his shoulders up and then down again. 'They never loved me, did they?'

I didn't know what to say to him for a moment. I just examined his eyes and saw the awful sadness, and how it made his whole body sag. I sort of wanted to kick him. I wanted to scream into his ear, wake up! Maybe that was what I wanted to scream at everyone. I wanted to snap him out of it. Forget them, they don't deserve you anyway!

'I suppose they never got over your brother dying,' I said to him with a useless shrug. 'I'm sure they do love you Ned. In their own way. They've just not been very good at showing it.'

He bit his lip and kicked at the ground. 'Hmm. Well too late now hey? Big day tomorrow and everything. Off I go.'

'You'll love it,' I smiled. 'All that freedom. Can decide what to eat for dinner. When to eat dinner. I'll come over and annoy you. Oh, wait, you'll see a lot of me because Dad thinks I should have mine near yours.'

A little light returned to his eyes at this. The corner of his mouth tugged slightly. 'Yeah, my parents said that too. You don't reckon they are…?'

'What? Coupling us up?'

Ned snorted laughter and red stole across his cheeks. 'Don't be stupid...'

'Wouldn't put it past my dad,' I grinned. 'He's always going on about the Coupling Dances...and how he met Mum at one...' I made a face and Ned laughed in response. 'Anyway...' I shrugged and started walking again, and Ned trailed after me.

'I'll be okay,' he said, as if trying to convince himself.

'Course you will. Big man Ned. You can boss me about until it's my turn.'

230

'And at least, no more school!'

'No more Saul either,' I remembered, glancing sideways at Ned. He returned my gaze cautiously.

'I know. No hut being built for him though. Just his own apartment on top of his father's.'

I shook my head as we walked on towards the square. 'What do you reckon they'll have him doing?'

'All sorts, according to my parents. He's supposed to learn everything about running this place, and communicating with the other Provinces. He'll get to go to them, I suppose. Can you even imagine?'

I found myself squinting at the emergence of the sun on the other side of the Province. 'What I find hard to imagine, is people like him leaving here and doing important stuff, and people like you and me never asking if we can go too.'

'Yeah, that's been playing on my mind.'

'No one wants to,' I said. 'No one even asks. I mean, even being a scavenger Ned, it's seen as the job that no one wants, isn't it? It might have privileges, but no one wants to be one when they grow up, do they? What does that mean Ned? I mean, what does that actually mean?'

He looked at me quizzically. 'What?'

'Well, does it mean they are scared to for some reason? Scared to wonder? Scared to ask? Or scared to go out there? Or does it mean they just don't think of it, they just don't imagine it, or wonder about it? Does it mean me and you are different?' I couldn't resist holding his hand as we walked. I was talking faster and faster, and I felt the urge to grip onto him, to hold onto him while everything else I knew and trusted seemed to fade away. 'Is there something wrong with us, Ned? Me and you? If we're the only ones asking questions? If we're the only ones who feel trapped?'

'I don't know,' he admitted. His hand was cold and small inside of mine. 'But Lissie, I've always felt different. Haven't you? I mean, no one at school ever gave me the time of day except you.'

'Was Grandma the only other one?' I asked him. 'The only one who questioned things? Governor Lancaster thinks she poisoned my mind, you know.'

'Are you going to tell me what went on between you two?'

'Not much,' I replied. My head feels so full of it all, I thought. There was this constant roaring between my ears. 'He denied being in my hut. He denied knowing anything about the flower petal. But where else would it have come from, Ned? Where?'

'I still can't believe you went to him. You're mad, Lissie Turner.'

'Maybe I am. I wanted answers. I wanted something. All he gave me was time.'

'Time?'

'He made me an offer. I would forget about his secrets if he forgot about mine.'

'Well that's as good as him admitting something!'

'No, not really. He's got one over on me Ned. It means I can't tell my parents or make a fuss about the diary or the petal, or they'll all find out I wasn't there that night.'

Ned looked confused for a moment, but then he nodded his head quickly, understanding. 'You think we'll ever see them again?' he asked, lowering his voice as we got closer to the square.

'I don't know, but they definitely didn't seem keen on anyone else finding out about them, did they?'

'Makes me think about the poor dog...'

'I know, and with the diary gone we have no chance of finding out what happened once Grandma Elizabeth and Lawrence arrived here.' I shrugged my shoulders and lifted my eyes, taking in the Governor's offices as they loomed up before us. 'Maybe I'll have to ask him again.'

'No,' Ned, clutched my arm. 'You can't, Lissie. Who knows what he is capable of? What if Aisha and Connor were right about people being arrested?'

We stopped walking. We stood in the middle of the square, half way between the Governor's office and school. People moved about slowly, yawning their greeting to the start of their working day. Kids like us, dragging their bags behind them in small groups, murmuring as they scratched at their hair. I couldn't help get the feeling that something had changed. It was almost like people were trying not to look at me.

Like...there! Maggie Henshaw who worked with my mother at the hospital, looking at me and then looking away when I caught her. I turned in a slow circle, taking them all in. One by one I saw heads turn, eyes averting to the ground, or to the sky or to each other. Near the school gates two mothers staring launched into an animated

233

conversation with each other as soon as I looked their way.

'People know something,' I whispered to Ned. He linked his arm through mine. 'They're all staring at me and trying not to stare. Can you feel it?'

'Yeah. I think so. Although Saul isn't trying not to stare at you. Look.' He jerked his head towards the Governor's building where Saul Lancaster suddenly appeared. He came towards us, hands in pockets, elbows poking out to either side. His hair was slicked back, revealing his large shiny forehead, pocked with blemishes. His eyes sneered, but his lips twitched in a smile.

Ned and I did not move, and we thought he was going to walk around us, or past us, but he didn't. He walked into us, nearly knocking both of us flying. With our arms still linked we held our ground and he leaned over us, his eyes coming to life, his smile lifting to reveal his teeth.

'What's your problem Saul?' Ned asked him. He had no time for Ned. It was me he had his sights on.

'Lissie Turner,' he hissed into my face. 'Lissie Turner the traitor. Get out of my way.'

'How is she a traitor?' asked Ned in disgust. 'What are you on about?'

'Shut up Fleck, you maggot,' growled Saul, his eyes still on me. 'I'm talking to the traitor, not you. My last day at school today, *traitor*. I'm an adult tomorrow, do you know what that means?'

'I'll let you tell me,' I told him evenly, refusing to flinch. 'Seeing as it means so much to you.'

234

'I'll be my father's second in command,' he said, his eyebrows. 'And you know what that means?'

'Course I do Saul, you'll take his place one day. Everyone knows that. That's what always happens.'

He looked satisfied for a moment, drawing back and smiling a grimace. 'And what else happens on that day is the new governor calls a meeting and gets to draw up a new rule sheet. Did you know *that*, traitor?'

'No one ever changes the rules,' said Ned, glaring at him. 'They've always stayed the same!'

'Well that doesn't mean no one ever can,' Saul replied fiendishly. 'And the first thing I'm gonna' do is crack down on ungrateful traitors like you, Turner.'

'How do you know anything about me, Saul?' I decided to ask him, my voice growing louder now as the stares began to return. 'Your father and I had a private conversation, so if you know anything about me Saul Lancaster, it means your father has gone back on his word!'

He closed his mouth and stared at me in amazement and confusion. I had no idea where those words came from, or why I said it. But I could feel him watching me, and my skin was crawling from it. He was up there, behind his windows, watching all of this. He should have told his idiot son to keep his mouth shut, I thought viciously. He shouldn't have told his dumb brat anything!

Ned nudged me back to reality and there they all were. The people of the square staring at me. I felt a rush then, inside of me, this black surge of rage and disappointment and frustration, frothing forth all at once, taking me down.

'You can't just come at me and call me a traitor,' I growled at Saul, shoving him in the chest. If they want a spectacle, I thought, I will give them one! If they want to stare, I will give them something to stare at! Something to talk about for once! Ned grabbed my arm and started yanking me away, and towards the school. 'Do you even know what that word means?' I asked Saul. 'Who have I betrayed? How have I betrayed anyone, Saul?'

'Shut up,' Ned spat through his teeth as he tried to haul me away.

'You know what it means, Turner,' said Saul, fat cheeked and smug and licking his lips at me. 'You know what I'm talking about.'

'Well let's talk about it then!' I yelled back at him. 'Let's all talk about it! Let's all talk about stuff no one ever talks about! Like why we can't go over the fence! And who caused all the wars before the peace, and why people like you just get to be in charge and none of us get a say!'

'Oh my goodness, Lissie, shut up, just shut up!' Ned, dragging me on. Me, digging my heels into the dust, laughing and smiling at the people all around. At their saucer eyes and gaping mouths.

'Shut her up, Fleck,' Saul stayed where he was and yelled after us. 'Shut her up before it's too late!'

Ned manhandled me through the gates and into the building. His face was bright red from the effort and I was still shouting. I'd lost control. I'd lost something.

'I want to talk to someone!' I shouted, and my voice echoed back at me in the lobby. 'I want someone to talk to me! Talk about this! Right now!'

236

'Lissie, I don't want to slap you, but in a minute...'

'All out there staring! Staring at me! Traitor, am I? Traitor because I want to know more! I want to know everything! Why is that so wrong? I just want to ask questions!'

Ned tried to shut me up, but it was too late. The damage had been done, and I wondered later, if

that had been Saul's intention all along. The head-teacher Mrs. Batton strode towards us with a face like

thunder. I thought she was going to shout, or yell, or demand to know what the hell we were up to, but

she didn't. She simply seized me by the top of my arm and dragged me away from Ned, out of the

lobby and into her office.

27: Isolation

'Lissie Turner, I've heard all about you.'

I sat in the chair opposite, with the desk between us. She rested her elbows on the desk and clasped her pudgy hands under her chin. Her thick black eyebrows were frowning down over her eyes. I heard the children coming into the lobby, heading to their classrooms. Their shoes smacking against the hard earth, their voices shushed and awed. And me at the centre of it all. Me, shouting at Saul in the square. Losing it.

I decided to tackle her head on. It was too late to play the game. She was a human after all. She was a child once. A girl, like me. I leant forward and grasped the desk.

'Mrs. Batton I am sorry. I'm sorry for shouting. But I *have* to ask you something! Can I ask you something?'

'Lissie, calm down. *Slow* down.' She shook her head at me slowly, soothingly. Her brow creased in concern. 'Take a deep breath. Just sit a while and breathe.'

'But all that, out there! I need to say it! I need to talk to someone!'

Mrs. Batton squirmed slightly in her chair before fixing me with a patient smile. 'All right Lissie, if you're that desperate then go ahead. What can I do for you?'

There was so much to say, so much to ask that I didn't know where to start. 'What have you heard about me?' I remembered her words, and Saul's. 'What are people saying? Saul called me a traitor!'

'Did he now? Is that what that was all about?'

'No, more than that. Much more than that. But why am I a traitor, Mrs. Batton? Who has said that about me?'

'Well there are concerns and rumours, I won't lie to you Lissie, but it was your very own parents who came to speak with me. They've been concerned about you for a while now. And I can see why.'

I sat back and stared at the floor. I felt dazed and swamped. All the words and questions fading away, dissipating inside of me. 'I've let them down...' I murmured.

'You've had a hard time,' Mrs. Batton declared. 'This can be a difficult time in any child's life, but you've also had the loss of your Grandma to deal with. They say you were extremely close to her.'

'I was. But they think she poisoned my mind,' I sighed. 'The Governor thinks so too. But all I want Mrs. Batton, all I *really* want is some answers. I can't help it, you see. All these questions in my head, and I don't know who put them there, and I don't know why no one else seems to ask them, but that's all I want, that's what I need. I need to ask them.'

Mrs. Batton relaxed in her chair. She looked pleased with me. As if I had finally given her something she could work with.

'Well, that's what I am here for, sweetheart. Ask away. What is it you want to know?'

I looked back at her, and my cheeks were getting hot. In fact, all of me was. There was too much of it, you see, too many questions and too many fears and too much anger rumbling inside of me. I was burning up from the inside. I was scared to open my mouth in case I

239

exploded.

'Take your time,' she told me firmly.

'They never taught us in school,' I said, looking right at her. 'Who started the wars in the Old World. What they were about. Doesn't anyone know?'

She shifted slightly on her chair, cleared her throat and forced a smile.

'Well, Lissie there are a few reasons for that my dear. Perhaps the most important one being, why does anyone need to know? The past is the past and it is better left that way. The lessons were learnt. We are no longer at war. We no longer suffer; we no longer kill. We are at peace and everyone is provided for. The lessons have been learnt and the evil has never been repeated, so what good would it do bringing it up?'

'Talking about it wouldn't mean it would happen again,' I pointed out. 'It's just it would be interesting to know. I mean, why? Who was fighting who? What for?'

'It doesn't do anyone any good to worry or wonder about *that*,' she replied. 'All those people are long dead. What matters is the survivors decided *no more*. No more war. They started again, with the best of intentions, and that is our legacy. That is what we are all carrying on.' She brushed back her hair, her expression satisfied. I could see that this was enough for her. She believed this and she loved this.

'So you don't know?'

'I beg your pardon?'

'You're the head of the school and you don't know what the wars were about? No one ever told you? You don't know what happened back then?'

'Lissie, I know what happened! There were wars...the human race almost wiped itself out...'

'But why, *why*? You don't know why? Because I do! My Grandma told me Mrs. Batton. She told me everything she could remember from when she was a girl. Why was she the only one who did that? Why does no one else know the truth?'

I could see what I'd done to her now. Her pleasant face was a ruin. She was shifty and restless, her chair suddenly uncomfortable, her eyes unable to meet mine. Her cheeks were growing red. She pouted at me and then sucked in her lips.

'I don't appreciate your tone, young lady. I invited you in here to calm you down and help you. There is no need to speak to me like I am a fool.'

'But you don't know,' I just chattered on at her. 'I know, and you don't. Do you see how crazy this is? Mrs. Batton, I even know why my Grandma was the only one who wanted the truth to be passed on. I know why she told me who started the wars and what they were about, and who was killed and why...I know!'

'Don't raise your voice at me, Lissie Turner! I will not sit here and be shouted at by a thirteen-year-old girl.'

I bit my lip and nodded at her. I could feel myself losing it again and I forced myself to take slow, deep breaths. Somehow, I had to get through to her. I had to get through to someone! I was beginning to feel like the crazy one.

'Okay, I'm sorry, Mrs. Batton,' I tried to tell her, but in my heart, I could feel it was too late, it was useless. Her guard was up now and she was back to doing what she did best. The bossy head mistress keeping us all in line. 'I just had questions and I wanted to ask them. I'm sorry.'

'You should be sorry, really,' she snapped. 'I am trying to help you. Just like your parents and the Governor have been trying to help you. Now Lissie, what you need to come to terms with is that your Grandmother was extremely old, and very fragile in her later days. You simply cannot take everything she told you to heart.'

'She told me not to tell anyone else.'

'Did she now? Lissie-'

'She told me you are all performing monkeys.'

'Lissie Turner!'

'She told me she only came here because she had to, because they were dying and they saw the domes, but this wasn't for them, this place was a prison once they got in!'

Now she stood up and her hands hit the table, palms down, fingers splayed.

'Lissie Turner, I am warning you!'

'She told me a different story, Mrs. Batton, a different story to the one we've all been fed, but none of you want to hear it! None of you want to know anything!'

'You need to stop this right now, young lady.'

Her eyes blazing. Her jaw jutting out at me. Her chin frozen.

Her breath hitched in her chest.

'Why though?' I begged her. 'Why can't I say it? Why can't we go over the fence?'

'If you want to go over the fence, then go over the fence, Lissie Turner! You might find yourself over there quicker than you think if you carry on like this! Now, up you get!'

I stood up slowly. 'Didn't you ever want to go out there Mrs. Batton? When you were a kid? Didn't anyone else ever wonder what is out there, other than the scavengers?'

'There is your answer child. The scavengers reported back to us, as they still do now. There is nothing out there worth seeing. Nothing but a massive wasteland of bones and dust. Until you reach the next Province, where my lady, you will find everything is exactly as it is here. We are provided for. We are safe. Why is that not enough for you?'

I shrugged limply. I felt weak and tired. My time here was over. I had failed. I made my way around her desk towards the door.

'I wish I knew,' I said to her. 'But it's not.'

'Ungrateful,' she shook her head at me sadly. 'And deluded. I am sorry the old woman did this to you, Lissie. But you need help.'

'I need answers. No one can give me any answers.'

'Answers to lies, Lissie. Lies. Her words over ours, I guess. I can't help you with that. But I don't think you better come back here again, do you?'

I opened the door and looked back at her. I tried to work out how she felt about this, but it was hard to tell. Her cheeks were still rosy with anger. Her eyes searched me and I could see how much I confused her. So maybe it *was* me. Maybe she was right.

'You're expelling me?' I asked, just to make sure I'd understood her correctly. She nodded grimly and looked away.

'I can't have you upsetting the other students. I don't know how to deal with a child like you, Lissie. I am sorry.'

I gave her a weary smile before I went. 'Don't worry Mrs. Batton. You're not the only one.'

I went out of the door and walked, slumped and alone, out of the school.

Without even thinking, I went to the cemetery. My only wish right then was to be close to Grandma Elizabeth. This world, full of time and order and duties, was dragging me further and further away from her. I sat in the dust and I tried not to think about what had just happened. My head was a thumping hell of pain and frustration. I felt like I was truly going mad.

Behind me, their lives went on regardless. School, and work and duties. They would all take their lunch break at the same time, the entire Province breathing a satisfied sigh of relief as they undid their lunch boxes one by one. After eating, they would all return to work. Were they performing monkeys, or just people grateful to be alive? To be eating food? Going to school? Waking up each day? I had no idea. Not anymore.

Expelled from school. My parents, my poor parents, was all I could think. What on earth would they make of this? Of me? I put my hands into the dust and swallowed tears. No point crying, I told

244

myself, what's done is done. I sat and curled my fingers into the earth, digging with my nails, scratching at the land. I thought of her and my sobs wanted to tear loose. They wanted to climb up from my guts and claw their way into my raw, dry throat. They wanted to stretch open my mouth and roar out, but I couldn't let them. I clamped my lips shut. I ground my top teeth down upon my bottom. I sat there and I was lost. No words, no thoughts, nothing. All I could do was keep my eyes shut and scratch at the ground.

I took deep breaths. One at a time. In and out again. Minutes passed, and slowly but surely my mind started to clear. I could open my eyes and let my teeth unclench. Mrs. Batton was still in my head, but I was letting her go, fading her out. I don't know what to do with a child like you...

Ned's last day, I remembered. Ha, he'd be tickled to think it was mine too...I smiled bitterly, released a sigh and started to move. I needed to get up. Find my way back home somehow. Wait for my parents to hear the news and come running to find me. I could just imagine their distress. I had the strongest feeling that this was the end.

I pulled my knees up and put one hand behind me to push myself up. It was then that I realised I was not alone. Someone was standing right behind me. Someone had stolen up behind me so silently I had not noticed. Or was I too caught up in the turmoil inside my own head? With my eyes closed and my body trembling?

I turned my head and looked up into his face.

Had he been there the whole time?

Maybe he had been there in school, listening while I ranted and raved. Maybe he was there in her office, standing like a ghost behind me. Then he followed me here and watched me tearing at the dust. Stood over me and sniffed my despair.

'What do you want Governor Lancaster?' I asked him, while a cold chill crawled out slowly across my body.

His hands were in his pockets. His head was tilted. His expression was dreamy. He smiled his secret smile.

'Why don't you and I go for a walk, Lissie?' he asked me pleasantly. 'It's such a beautiful day.' And he held his hand out to me. 'Come on, little one. What do you say?'

28: Walking

I didn't suppose I had much choice, and anyway, I wanted to talk to him, didn't I? I wanted to be heard. I didn't take his hand, as I got up slowly, wiping the dust from my palms down my legs. I looked one more time at the place where she was burned, and then I followed Governor Lancaster out of the cemetery.

We went out the back way. Not back out into the square, but through some trees and down a path that led away from the centre of everything. He walked beside me at my pace, with his hands behind his back. The day was getting hotter. I felt sweat breaking out across my forehead and my shoulder blades. We walked past a cluster of huts and a woman looked up at us from her doorway, where she was sweeping the step with a baby strapped to her front. Her eyes lit up when she saw the Governor and he responded with a tip of his hat and a friendly nod.

'Morning, Freda,' he called out to her as her face broke into a grin. 'How is the little one?'

'Keeps me up at night!' she called back, propping the broom to one side as she stared down into the baby's sleeping face. 'But she's worth it!'

'Keep up the great work,' he said, and we walked on.

I looked up at him and he was still smiling that placid smile. I had never seen him angry, I realised, not even that day in his office. I had never seen him break. Whereas, look at me. Look at what I had become.

'So did Mrs. Batton call you?' I asked him. There seemed little point in hanging around, dragging this out. Governor Lancaster bit his lip slightly.

'Ooh yes, well, I was in the area. Saul left home in a hurry this morning and I had to catch up with him.'

'He was after me that's why.'

'Oh?'

'Called me a traitor. Right in front of everyone in the square,' I said, looking up at him, looking him right in the eye. 'That was what started all that. *Him.*'

The Governor bit his lip again before smiling. 'Oh dear. I must apologise to you then, Lissie. I wondered what he was up to when he dashed off so quickly. My son can be a bit of a hot head at times. I am hoping he matures and learns to cool down.'

'And what if he doesn't?' I asked. 'What if he stays like that and he's running this place one day? Because that's how it works isn't it?'

'Well no, not really, Lissie. It's not quite that simple. Yes, it is my job to help shape and mould Saul into a decent governor, but at the same time, if he does not meet the requirements when the time comes then he will not be the governor. Simple as that.'

I frowned at him, disbelieving. 'I didn't know that.'

'Well, there is much you don't know, Lissie, which is why I decided it was time we talked again. Talked and walked, what do you say?' He reached out and patted my shoulder. I didn't flinch, but I looked at my shoulder as if it had been tainted.

Another cluster of huts was coming up. This time I saw a small boy playing in the dust. He wore the simple hand-made clothes we all bought from the dressmakers with our tokens, and his feet were bare. He was using a piece of wood to dig through the dust. He had a little tin bucket next to him, and as we looked on, he snatched up something from the ground and hurled it into the bucket. I remembered doing that when I was little. Digging for treasure. Anything, but especially coins from the Old World. We used to collect them and swap them with kids at school. The coins all had dates engraved on them, and the older they were, the more power you had when bartering. From another door-way a weary mother looked on, sipping from her coffee.

'Morning Tilda!' the Governor called out, tipping his hat again and waving. 'He looks busy!'

'Morning Governor!' she yelled back cheerfully. 'He was ill yesterday! High temperature and in bed all day. Fine now though!'

'Glad he is on the mend!' he replied. 'Have a good day!'

We walked on. I felt him looking at me and my face warmed under his gaze.

Eventually he said; 'what are you thinking, Lissie?'

'I am thinking lots of things,' I replied coolly. 'Why do you ask?'

He laughed softly. 'You intrigue me...'

Wow, I thought, I was not expecting that. I pushed my hair back from my face, stuffed my hands into my pockets and walked quickly. I thought about that day I walked around the entire Province, and then returned home with the intention of coming clean.

The Tree of Rebels

'So, you were saying Saul might not take your place...'

He grinned. 'I am hoping he will, of course. He has a lot to learn though. Patience, among other things.'

'If you want to know my opinion, I don't think he will ever be ready. I think he would make a really bad governor.'

To this, he laughed out loud, his head going back, his hand banging at his chest. I want to make you angry, I thought as I stared at his gaping mouth, I want to make you break.

'He's a bully,' I said, getting braver. 'And he is not very bright.'

His head snapped back down and his eyes were on me, luminous and daring. 'All right,' he said, his lips moving upwards again. 'That's probably enough. I will take your comments on board. You needn't worry about Saul. I have my eye on him too.'

'So who gets to take your place if he doesn't make it? How does it work?' I shrugged and kicked a stone across the dust. 'I mean, I have no idea how it all works. They don't teach us stuff like that in school. I've actually just realised that they don't really teach us anything.'

'Oh really? Is that so?'

'Basically. It's because *they* don't know anything.'

The Governor's mouth dropped open in surprise. 'Is that what you think? Is that what you said to Mrs. Batton?'

I shook my head. 'Not really, but it is true. They don't teach us stuff because they can't. They don't know it, do they?'

'They teach you plenty, Lissie. Otherwise this place would fall apart.'

250

'Oh yes they teach us how to live here,' I nodded, my eyes narrowed. 'Then you have duties for your position and then you leave school and you are ready. They teach you what you need to know, yes.'

'And that is why it works here, Lissie...' he said this calmly and patiently, his hands back behind him. He glided alongside me, his head slightly lowered to take me in. I stared ahead. We were passing through another cluster of huts.

'You only tell people what you think they need to know,' I said, and he sighed in response.

'You say it like it is a deliberate thing, a planned thing. But it's not, Lissie. It's just the way we have survived up until now, and who knows how things might change and evolve as time goes on?'

'So in that case, I should have been able to share her diary...' I looked back at him, and this seemed to catch him off guard, as for a moment a strange, quick look passed over his face, touching his eyes slightly before vanishing again. 'I know you took it,' I added quietly, firmly. 'I know you were there. No one can hear us out here. You might as well admit it.'

I could see him thinking this over. He blew his breath out noisily and a great frown creased his smooth forehead.

'Ooh,' he said. I felt the anger frothing up from my guts again. He was there, I knew he was. He was there, and he took her diary.

'No one can hear us,' I reminded him in a whisper, and to this he looked around us, at the miles and miles of dusty land that stretched out since we had left the last group of huts. He sort of shrugged, and then maybe my whispering brought him towards me, into my confidence, maybe it was what he had desired all along. Because he wrapped one arm around my shoulder to hold me close to his side, and that way we were joined, we were one, four legs marching at the same pace, kicking up the dust under the great unknown sky.

'That diary was a crime,' he said. I tightened under his arm. Every muscle stiffening, tensing, longing to shake him off. I forced my teeth together and waited for him to go on. He sighed dramatically and waved his free hand at the air. 'This is how you have to look at it, Lissie; the old woman should never have kept it. She should never have shown it to a young, impressionable girl. I had to take it, I am afraid. I had no choice. And your parents would understand this, I can assure you.'

'How did you even know about it?'

'Oh I knew, I knew. Many signs, over the years. Many murmurings from her old lips in my direction. And then Saul was walking past your hut that day and heard you reading from it.'

My mouth dropped open in protest. That rotten sneak! 'I knew it!' I spat, ducking away before he could stop me, freeing myself from his arm. 'And then you came back didn't you! You came back and stole it and you killed her!'

'I still don't understand what makes you think I killed her...' he said this with a soft laugh. 'She was dying anyway, Lissie. She was on her deathbed. Yes, I stayed and talked to her. I held her hand and brushed her hair from her face and she spoke to me too, you know. But she was dying quite nicely all by herself. Why do you think I did something to her?'

'You shouldn't have been anywhere near her!' I roared at him,

252

and I stopped walking, stopped playing along. I stood firm and stood my ground, hands on my hips. 'She wasn't doing you any harm! I knew that flower petal was yours! You're the only one allowed to grow anything around here!'

Governor Lancaster looked at me calmly. He reminded me of my father, gazing down at me in weary patience. 'Yes well, it must have fallen from my lapel.'

'I want her diary back! I was reading it!'

'Yes I know, Lissie, and that is why I had to take it, because like I said before, that diary was a crime. A criminal offence. An act of treason, full of lies.'

'Lies?'

'Yes lies. Or at least one person's interpretation of the truth...'

'Well tell me yours then. What's different about yours?'

He looked at me shrewdly, those eyes narrowing in on me. 'How much did you read?'

'Nearly all of it,' I said in triumph. 'And there is nothing you can do about that! You can't take away what I know! You can't wipe my mind!'

'Well that brings us back to the question of what we should do with you, Lissie Turner,' and he was smiling at me once again, the calmest, coolest man in the world. It's not fair, and it's not right, I thought, and I want to do something about it.

'I'm expelled from school,' I said. 'That means I only qualify for the lowest duties.'

'Well you can't say I didn't try to warn you...'

'Your son wound me up! Called me a traitor!'

'He gets hot under the collar,' he shrugged. 'He is very passionate about this place, as am I. He feels like I feel. That the people of this place deserve to live in peace.'

'In ignorance you mean. Even the teachers have no clue, do they? What really happened back then? What really destroyed the Old World? Why do you keep it from them Governor? It's in the past and people have learnt their lessons. We say it all the time! So why can't they know how it all happened? Why can't they know what's in the diary? About them banning the seeds?'

The Governor looked a little bored now. He blew his breath out again, licked his lips and decided to walk on. 'Come on,' he said. 'Walk with me.'

'You haven't answered the question,' I said, hurrying after him. 'Why are you allowed to know, but no one else is? What are you so afraid of? Are you afraid people might want to plant their own seeds?'

'It's not about fear, Lissie,' he yawned. 'And it's certainly not about seeds. It's about protection. We've got a chance here can't you see? Three generations now born into a peaceful world. It's still a tough world. We still have so much rebuilding to do, and while we're doing that, we're still all trying to figure out how not to make the same mistakes again. You talk about myself and Saul, and my father. You think it's unfair that Saul will take over from me? We only leave it that way while it works, Lissie. We only muddle on, as best we can, overseeing, looking back, making decisions and adjustments, trying to figure out how to do this. How do you imagine those last survivors

254

started again? They had to group together for one thing. Find each other, as well as food and shelter. And then they had to elect a leader, and make decisions. Life and death decisions. It is no different now. We have moved on, we have learnt so much from our forefathers and mothers, but it's still such early days, child. Central government would like to start a voting system, where candidates for Governor are put forward and people get to choose who they want. Would that please you, Lissie?'

'You're fobbing me off,' I said, and I stopped walking again and glared up into his face. I saw it again then. That quick panicked look passing over his neatly controlled features. A chink in his smooth armour. A crack in his shiny facade. I'd worked him out and he didn't expect that. A small smile pulled at my lips. 'You're buttering me up. You're sweet talking me.'

'My goodness child,' he said, looking dismayed. 'I truly did not realise how bad things had become with you. How much she has infected you. How cynical you have become.'

'I've got my eyes wide open. I'm questioning everything, Governor. Not like the rest of them. And I know what you are doing right now. Trying to talk me round. Make me see sense. Just like the Day of Thanks and all that.'

'The Day of Thanks is very important, Lissie.'

'Yes I know it is. I know *why*.'

'I am still trying to help you, Lissie. I am trying to stop you from making any more mistakes. Can you imagine your poor parents when they hear the news about school?'

'Tell me about the rebels.'

255

His mouth.

It gave him away. It dropped open. And then he tried to save it, he tried to gulp air, bringing it in, but it was too late and he snapped his mouth shut instead. I knew and he knew.

He took a few moments to gather himself together. There was a hard look in his eyes. His mouth smiled, but it was thin and cold. It reminded me of that day in his office when he leaned over me next to the window.

'I am running out of options with you, Lissie Turner,' he said. 'I am trying to warn you once again. I am trying to get through to you. I am trying to calm you down.'

'I am not a traitor for wanting to know the truth. I am not a criminal for wanting that diary back.'

'Yes you are. You are. Saul was correct about that. You are trying to rush things. You are taking the twisted words of a messed up old mind and you are trying to force them upon all these good people. You have no idea of the damage you would do.'

'I just want people to wake up...'

'So what are you saying to me? I detect a threat in your tone.'

I wondered if I had him. If I really had a hold over him. Power.

'I want the diary back or I will start talking. I don't care what people say or think about me. I will start talking. You don't want them to know what I know.'

'Rebel, eh?' he said, with a slight sigh. 'Just like she was...'

'They didn't want to even come here. They wanted to live life their way. But that was all destroyed, wasn't it?'

He sniffed, as if it offended him. 'Are you attempting to make me a deal, Miss Turner?'

'Give me the diary or I talk.'

'And what if I give you the diary, and you *still* talk?'

I shrugged. 'That will be your move Governor.'

'I would arrest you and put you on trial.'

'You can't do that until I am fourteen.'

He leaned in then, quick and hard like that day in the office. His hands looped back behind him, his eyes burning into mine. 'I won't give it back to you, until after you are fourteen.'

It was the last thing he said to me.

He turned on his heel and walked back the way he came, and I was left out there in the dust, watching him go. Was it right that I felt victorious? Was it safe that I felt I had won?

One more week and I was getting the diary back.

29: Day Of Thanks

On the morning of the Day Of Thanks, my mother prepared the breakfast table with a pinched look upon her face. She was in a strange mood which I found hard to fathom. Of course, after my expulsion from school, they were barely talking to me. But beneath the rigid anger that clouded her eyes, something else was quivering. Her lips bunched up and then smoothed out. She took deep breaths when she thought I was not watching.

I, on the other hand, remained resigned and silent. For the moment, there was just waiting. First I would endure the Day Of Thanks. And then I had wait until my birthday. Wait until I was cast out into the hut they'd been building me close to Ned's. Wait for the Governor.

'Utter disgrace,' they called me last week. I sat at the kitchen table and took it all without flinching. 'Cannot believe you would do this to us. What is wrong with you? You are so ungrateful. Your ancestors would turn in their graves. Shamed the family. Everyone talking about us. Can't look anyone in the eye. Why, Lissie? *Why*?'

I only had one answer for them and it was a simple one.

'Grandma's diary told me a story and for now I am choosing to believe it, as no one else here can give me any answers.'

To this, my father had exploded.

'Answers? What answers? The answers are staring you in the face my girl! The answers are all around you! In jobs and houses and education and health and peace Lissie, *peace*!' This was always the word that he clung to when all else failed. This was the word he

258

dragged up and threw out at me, again and again and again. Peace. Everlasting Peace. The Declaration of Peace. The Day of Thanks. Peace, peace, peace. It meant so much to him; it was the beat in his brain, the pulse in his veins. I couldn't blame him. It was what they had drummed into him since he was born. The terrors of the past replaced by a new, clean humanity. No more wars. No more guns. No more bombs. The past was dangerous; the future was bright.

For now, we existed in a tight silence. They washed and dressed and ate in silence. They murmured between them, and cast the odd anxious look my way. They talked about my hut but did not include me in its plans. They talked about Ned and his new life and how well he was doing, but they did not look at me with the same hope. They talked about today, the Day of Thanks and they smiled in relief that it was finally here.

After breakfast, we left the hut together. Barely a family any more, but a trio of ghosts, walking stiffly towards the square. Along the way we met the Flecks, and pleasantries were exchanged. Nothing was said to me, but eyebrows were raised and heads were tilted in sympathy for my parents. No one had been expelled from the school before now. No one knew what to do with me. No one could understand where it had all gone so wrong... All they could do was blame the dead old woman.

My mother and Hilda Fleck linked arms and wandered ahead of the men, leaning into each other, giggling and whispering behind their hands. The two men walked behind them with their hands in their pockets and their heads low. I was last. Trailing behind, feet dragging, heart heavy. She was in my mind even more than usual. She would not depart easily. Grandma Elizabeth. If the Governor had his way no one would ever know the truth. But did they really need to know? Would it make a difference if they did? I asked myself these impossible questions as I walked behind the adults. I looked at the dust where nothing was allowed to grow, and I looked at the huts which we made ourselves. I walked past each one and the simple, honest life that was lived out behind every door, and the square and the buildings that survived the wars, and the buildings made from scratch, and the museum where all the things from the Old World were locked up. Did they need to know? Would it change anything if they did?

This whole world was weighing on my shoulders as we walked. And in the square the excitement was building. The crowds were gathering tightly. Picnic benches dragged out and dotted around. A stage set up. Banners and streamers and paper chains made by the children in school. Little ones dashing about squealing, squeezing through their parents' legs.

Ned found me and took me to one side, though his parent's eyes were immediately upon us.

'Naughtiest girl in the Province,' he said with a grin and a sparkle in his eye. 'Whatever will they do with you?'

I crossed my arms and watched my mother and father placating the Flecks. 'They don't know what to do with me,' I said. 'Because this has never happened before.'

'I guess it had to happen sooner or later,' he shrugged easily. 'No one could be perfect forever, could they? Someone was bound to throw a spanner in the works. Personally, I blame your Grandma. I think she was feeding ideas into your head while you dreamed.'

I reached out and punched him lightly on the arm. 'Ha ha. Very funny.'

260

'Well, that's what I've been telling my parents, anyway. Only way they will let me anywhere near you. Your parents, on the other hand now think that *I* will be a good influence on *you.*'

'Let me tell you the latest,' I said, and suddenly I had his complete attention. My eyes drifted towards the stage where I could see the Governor talking and laughing with his guards. 'He and I had another little chat.'

'Oh yeah?'

'Yeah. After I was chucked out of school he found me. We had a long walk around the Province together. Sort of came to a deal.'

'You're joking me? What kind of deal?'

'I will keep my mouth shut about what was in the diary, *if* he gives it back to me.'

Ned shook his head. 'I don't get it...'

'I get the diary back so I can finish reading it. As long as I am quiet and good until then.'

'Until when? When is he giving it back? And so, you were right about him being in your hut when she died?' His eyes were growing wider by the second. I gave him a polite nudge with my elbow.

'Don't make a scene. They're always watching me. I'll get the diary back as long as I shut up and stop making trouble...'

'Okay....and then what?'

'Well, I don't know. He won't give it back until after I am fourteen.'

Ned's eyes widened even more. His mouth fell open and then snapped shut again. 'Oh Lissie. You'll be an adult. He can treat you as an adult.'

I shrugged. 'Basically what he said. I won't know what that means. I won't know until then.'

'And neither will anyone else,' he said in wonder. 'Because this has never happened before...because no one has ever broken the rules like this before...'

'No one has ever been a traitor before,' I said grimly. 'Which is what he says I am. The book itself is a crime he says.'

'Why though? What will it do? What will happen if people read it? I don't understand, Lissie. I don't think I have ever understood.'

I licked my lips and gazed around us. Our parents were watching nervously. Their eyes flicked from us to the stage, and back again. On the stage the Governor prepared to talk to the crowd, and sensing this, the people began to knit tighter together, their conversations hushing up.

'They'll know that the people that destroyed the Old World are the same ones in charge of us now.' I hissed these words into his ear, into his skull, into his brain, and then I moved away, I moved backwards and away from him and the poison I had infiltrated him with. I could not stand to watch the terrible truth dawn in his eyes. I could not stand to see the devastation and the fear.

I slipped away, I slipped backwards, easing my way carefully past the elbows and the shoulders, backwards, backwards, away from them all. And he took centre stage, where he belonged, and they all began to clap their hands and stare at him adoringly.

262

'Good morning!' he bawled out at them, his face one big beaming smile. 'Good morning and what a beautiful morning it is! Happy Day of Thanks, Province 5!' To this the crowd erupted into explosive applause. There were hoots and cheers and whistles. No one noticed me as I kept moving backwards through them, and away from him.

'To get us started!' he called out over the cheers. 'Please welcome the children of Year One!'

There were enormous cheers and clapping as he moved away from the stage and a gaggle of small children were herded energetically on by their teacher Miss Evans. I remembered her in Year One. Doe eyed and sweet hearted. Tight blonde curls and freckles across her nose. She had barely changed at all since then, but I wondered if she would ever recognise me.

The children were four and five years old, chubby cheeked and full of proud smiles and waves for their parents. They all clutched little Province 5 flags in their hands and waved them about madly. I remembered doing that too. I remembered desperately scanning the crowd for my parents, and taking what felt like forever to spot them. They had been to the side, arms linked and eyes bursting with pride.

With Miss Evans standing just to the side, the children awaited her cue, and then burst happily into song. The crowd were quiet and still as every parent's eyes simultaneously filled with tears.

'For no more war, and no more fear, we thank you all,

We thank you all!

For food to eat and clothes to wear, we thank you all,

We thank you all!

For Everlasting Peace and Joy, we thank you all,

We thank you all!'

I was now almost at the back of the crowd. When the children finished singing, the people clapped and cheered, and the Governor returned to the stage to introduce the next act. While all of this was going on, there were volunteers carrying trays of food and drink around the square.

'Please help yourself to a refreshing cider,' the Governor called out. 'Made with a brand new recipe I am told! All made from the beautiful apples grown in our domes!'

People took their glasses of cider and their eyes lit up all around me. Alcohol was only ever given out on special days like this. It was something they all seemed to relish and look forward to. I wondered if Ned was trying one for the first time. There was fresh orange juice for the children and plates of biscuits and cakes.

'Please now welcome to the stage the children from Year Two who have a very special performance for you this morning!' Our Governor bowed out once again, basking in their gratitude and adoration, and I thought; this is what it is all about. How thankful they all were. How grateful they were for all of this. How it was presented to you again and again from the moment you were born. Three generations now and not one single war. Not one single bullet fired from one single gun. Nothing but peace and the growing and delivering of food, and the peaceful silent building of huts and lives and children for tomorrow.

Why did it all stick in my throat, making me want to be sick?

264

Another gaggle of Province children was ushered onto stage. This time a group of six and seven-year old started acting out the signing of the Peace treaty, on this very day back in 2085. The crowd hushed again, and I kept slipping slowly, slowly back.

I recalled doing a performance like that. I played an old woman wearing a tattered shawl and using a broken stick to walk with. I was supposed to be a survivor from the last war. A survivor of all the wars that raged when my Grandma Elizabeth was young. A survivor of the famine and the diseases. A survivor who limped along with the others, picking stragglers up along the way, walking on and on through a devastated landscape, through the ruins of the world, until they found a dome that still had food growing in it...a dome that had seeds...

At the back of the crowd I felt the rubble wall behind me. All around me, adults took their glasses of cider and lifted them to their lips while their eyes shone in delight. I thought about all those hard, green apples growing in perfect unity inside their dome. Tree after tree, all grown the same, all kept in check, in neat lines, producing perfect fruit again and again and again.

And then I thought about the little rebel tree on the other side of the fence...

I thought about the scrawny, wild, little outcast and I smiled.

I could stay here, looked down on and whispered about. I could watch the rest of the performances. I could eat some cake and some biscuits. I could join my parents for the picnic, where glorious hampers of food and drink were passed out to every family. I could sit and receive my present, my gift from the Province, from the Governor. Sometimes it was more food. Sometimes it was tokens. Sometimes it was a toy, or a book.

The Tree of Rebels

I could sit here and take it all but I was not going to. There was fire in my veins and I knew this because she had told me so. There was a pulse vibrating through me, shuddering under my skin. There were silent wings upon my feet because I was the fastest girl in town. I was Lissie Turner and I would not stay here and say thank you.

I turned and ran before anyone could stop me.

Maybe they saw me go, maybe they didn't. Maybe they said; oh, there she goes again, that wild treacherous girl, running, always running. Forget about her. Let her go. She will see the error of her ways one day. Let her go. Maybe they cared, maybe they didn't. Maybe the Governor saw me go, maybe he didn't. I just hoped no one followed me.

Because I needed to go back to the tree of rebels.

30: The Rebel Tree

As I ran I heard them singing again.

Thank you all, thank you all.

I just ran. It seemed to take no time at all. Before I knew it, I was there, looking for the hole. It had been filled in, but that was it. Just dirt. That was nothing. That was nothing in the way of me and my tree. I got down on my hands and knees and remembered what Charlie did that day. Scraping at the dirt, tearing it away with my fingernails.

We thank you all, we thank you all.

Who were they thanking? What were they thanking them for?

The sun burned down on me while I dug. Sweat plastered my hair to my skull, and my clothes to my skin. My tongue stuck out the corner of my mouth while my hands clawed and pulled at the dry earth. As soon as I thought I could fit, I started shoving my body through the hole and under the fence.

What was the punishment for this? What was the crime?

No one knew. Like Ned said. No one had done this before me.

I was through and I was free, and freedom was like a hammer from the sun smashing down upon my brain and I started running. My legs were alive, never to be beaten and they threw massive strides out against the land, beating it, winning, because Lissie Turner was the fastest! My lungs took the air and my body took the fuel and my feet smashed against the dirt and the grass and I was running, running, and free, free!

The Tree of Rebels

Could they see me? Did *he* know?

I am running from you all; I am running to my tree....

Just like before, the land started to move down, sloping and guiding me gently away from the fence and the square and the rules. The air felt colder, fresher. Birds screeched across the blue skies, egging me on, screaming for me to win. I found the craggy hillside and started flying down it. I didn't think I would fall, but suddenly that was what happened. My head and shoulders overtaking my legs and feet, and the earth and stones scrabbling and skidding beneath me, and my balance was compromised, and my arms spun and I was going down, down, down.

Something hard smashed against my kneecaps. I tasted blood in my mouth as my teeth crushed my tongue. First my knees, and then my head. Dirt in my eyes. My hands grabbing and snatching, failing to find anything to hang onto. I rolled over, and then over again and again. My spine cracked against rock. My body tumbled like a bowling ball. I was amazed and saddened that I was suddenly, unexpectedly, going to die here.

But I didn't die. Not yet anyway. I landed at the bottom in the cold, clear water and I was on my knees with my head hanging low, and I saw my own face gazing back at me. My shoulders heaving, my breath coming out ragged and shallow, close to sobs. My eyes stared back from under the water. Bright blood shone in my hair and around my mouth. I blinked at myself. I sat and caught my breath and waited for the pain to start.

The fear arrived first. There was no time for it during the fall. But now it came and shook my body from head to toe, wringing shivers from my bones and sweat from my pores. I'd landed, but only now was I terrified of falling. And then came the pain. Slowly at first. A stinging around my nose and mouth, an aching at the back of my head. I sat back on my feet and looked up at the sky. Something wet fell from my face and landed in the water creating ruby red circles that grew bigger and bigger.

My elbows hurt. My knees were in agony. My spine felt raw. My ribs groaned when I tried to move. I opened my mouth and coughed up a pitiful sob. You stupid girl, I heard them all telling me inside my head, stupid girl with your head in the clouds! Now look what you have done! I stared around me in dumb shock and thought, I could have died, I could have died...

I leant forward slowly, wincing and gasping in pain. I slid my hands into the water and splashed it up onto my face. My skin screamed in protest and bright blood flowed onto my reflection. I wanted to cry but I refused. I bit down on my tears and rubbed them out of my eyes. It was okay. I was okay. I would try to move in a moment. I would get up and remember why I came. Remember what I ran from.

I used my scraped hands to push the rest of me up. My back hurt the most. My back and my head. I rubbed at it slowly, taking deep breaths as the pain ebbed and flowed. I attempted walking. My steps were hesitant and weak. Every step was a nightmare. I brushed dirt and stones from my hair and when I looked at my hand there was blood on the finger tips. Oh, I will be okay, I told myself, I will be fine. I would go back in a minute and face the music yet again, and my mother would be finished with me, but surely she would patch me up first?

I paddled through the stream and looked back over my shoulder at the way it twisted tightly around the bottom of the hillside.

269

I thought what fun it would have been to play here when we were little kids. Mum could have brought us here if she had known about it. We could have kicked our shoes off and waded in. We could have raced from one side to the other. We could have built bridges out of sticks. We could have made boats and floated them. We could have had a picnic under the tree and watched the water shining as it tumbled by.

Ouching and oohing, I stumbled awkwardly over to the apple tree. There were still a few apples left so I picked one and held it in one hand, savouring the weight of it, and the texture of its bumps and scars against my stripped skin.

'You're still here then?' I asked the tree.

The tree stood silently and proudly, its spindly arms reaching out to each side. It made me wonder about everything that had been stolen from us. I stared around me, taking in the lush greenery and the smell that filled my nostrils. It was like existing in another world entirely. How did the seeds know not to grow on the other side? Or did they just not let them? The government sent their patrols out daily to murder them, that was the truth. The seeds were locked up just like us, I realised. Inside the domes. Watered and fed. Heated and tended. Cared for until they grew, until they did what they were supposed to.

There was a noise in the water behind me and I whirled, my breath catching, and fresh pain flaring to life in my head.

'Whoa!' she said, holding up her hands, her feline eyes widening at the sight of me. 'What the hell happened to you?'

Aisha. Alone. Bare footed and with a bow and arrow slung over one shoulder and two dead furry things draped over the other. I blinked at her until my knees went weak, and then I sank down to the soggy green ground under the apple tree. I dropped my head into my hands and closed my eyes. Everything hurt. How was it possible to feel this much pain? It felt like it would overwhelm me now.

She arrived beside me, calm and sure. She rested her dead things and her weapon on the ground and slipped a cool arm around my shoulders.

'You're okay,' she told me with certainty. 'You can come with me, Lissie. Have you run away? We will hide you. You can be one of us.'

She said this in a warm soothing voice, and I thought; she is trying to make me feel better, she is trying to help me. I looked up at her, my face breaking with the tears.

'I just fell,' I managed to mumble at her. 'I fell about half-way down.'

'Oh,' she winced, withdrawing her arm. 'For a moment I thought they did this to you. That you escaped.'

'They wouldn't hurt me,' I assured her, but I could see the blank look in her eyes. The not believing. The constant questioning. I looked down at my legs, where blood had caked around the knees and the skin was swollen and tight underneath. 'I didn't escape anyone. I just couldn't stay and join in their Day of Thanks.'

'Day of what?'

'It's this special day. Same day every year. The day they signed the Peace Treaty? We celebrate it.'

'Oh,' she looked vaguely surprised. 'Sounds great. So how have you been?'

271

'Terrible,' I moaned. 'Horrible. Everything has gone wrong, everything is ruined. I don't belong there anymore Aisha. I don't belong anywhere!'

'That's not true,' she said with certainty. 'So what's happened since we last saw you? I've been back a few times you know. Here. And to the fence near Ned's hut. He sees us sometimes; does he tell you?'

I shook my head. 'I am barely allowed to speak to him. They all hate me. Call me a traitor. I've been expelled from school. No one has ever been expelled from school! They don't know what to do with me...'

Aisha exhaled her breath with a whistle. 'You better start at the beginning.'

'When I last saw you,' I said with a massive sigh. 'I had this terrible feeling suddenly. So, I ran home to her, my Grandma Elizabeth. And when I got back home that night she was dead.'

'Oh no!'

I nodded grimly, folding my sore, stiff arms on top of my knees, and then placing my chin down on my arms. 'She was dead. I mean, they all said it would happen. She was the oldest person left...'

'She knew the truth about everything...' Aisha breathed out beside me.

'Yes. I know. And she was trying to tell me everything, and it was all in her diary. I hadn't finished it yet, but when I looked for it, it was gone. He took it.'

'Wait a minute. He? He who?'

'Soren Lancaster. The Governor.'

'Oh I've heard about him,' she said gravely. 'I've heard about all of them. They're all the same you know.'

'I don't know. All I know is he was there in my hut when she died. He took the diary, and he will give it back to me when I turn fourteen as long as I keep my mouth shut and behave myself until then.'

I turned my head to look at Aisha. She was frowning quizzically back at me. She looked alarmed and intrigued, but not scared. Not like me.

'He said that to you?'

I nodded miserably. 'We've had some chats, you see. He knows I know everything I'm not supposed to, and he wants me to keep it quiet. He has no idea that Ned knows too.'

'And what do you think will happen when you turn fourteen?'

'He'll give it back to me. Or so he says. So, I can finish it and find out what happened. But then, I don't know. He wouldn't say. I'll be an adult, so...'

'He could arrest you,' she said with finality. 'That's probably what he will do. Charge you with treason or something like that. Do you know what the punishment for that is these days?'

'It's never happened before,' I shook my head.

'It's happened plenty!' Aisha retorted, her eyes flashing. 'Especially with the first-generation survivors, when some people didn't like who they were being bossed around by! Nothing had really changed they said.'

'So what happened? What did they do to traitors?'

'Well, officially they were banished...' she said this with wide eyes and a secret smile. A finger rose to her lips as I stared at her in horror.

'But?'

'They were hung.'

'Hung?'

'Yes. By the neck. Until dead. Best way to deal with them, they thought. They weeded out the troublemakers and disposed of them. I guess your Grandma Elizabeth must have heard wind and kept her thoughts to herself, eh?'

I couldn't speak because I felt sick. It was suddenly all rushing up from my guts. Putrid and hot and gagging me, filling my mouth, coming out of nowhere... I sat forward and vomited a violent stream of porridge lumps. Aisha squirmed away to one side and whistled at me.

'Probably the bang to your head.'

I couldn't speak. Couldn't think. Couldn't move. I just sat there and retched and gagged and heaved. I cried while I was doing it. Like a little baby child. Like a little lost child without its mother. I moaned and sobbed and vomited. Just when I thought there was nothing left, it rushed up again, and my guts twisted and tightened, forcing it up, forcing it out. A hot lumpy rush into the water. I rubbed the heel of one hand into my eye where I could feel the skin swelling and growing. My throat was raw and dry and aching.

I wanted to go to sleep. I wanted to curl up right there and close my eyes and suck my thumb and know nothing. Hear nothing and see nothing and say nothing. I didn't want to know. I didn't want to know any of this...

31: News

I'd started to think I was a big, tough girl. I liked to make out I didn't give a damn and nothing scared me. But none of it was true. I was turning fourteen in three days, but that meant nothing to me right then. Instead I felt about four years old. Thwarted and weak and so confused. At some point Aisha slipped her arm back around me, and some time after that I gave in and rested my head upon her shoulder. I must have fallen asleep like that after a while, because when I jerked awake again, the light had changed and the day was older.

She was still beside me though. With her legs crossed and her bow and arrow across her lap. She was sharpening one of the arrows with a thick handled knife. The dead creatures from her shoulder were lying on the grass behind her, and as she worked, she frowned and her forehead gleamed with sweat.

'What are you doing?' I asked her, rubbing at my eyes.

'Making this one sharper,' she replied, holding it up for me to see. It was very impressive, I had to admit.

'You make these yourself?'

'Yep. Everyone does.'

'What for?'

'What do you mean, what for? For hunting, of course.' She grinned lazily and nodded at the furry bundle behind her. 'To catch those fellas. My mother makes the best rabbit stew ever.'

'Rabbit?'

'Yeah rabbit. Like those.' She stared at me while a thought dawned on her. 'Oh right. You don't have rabbits? You've never seen these wild?'

I shook my head slowly. 'Animal patrol shoot anything they see. To protect us from disease.'

'Well, well,' she said with a sigh. 'Luckily for us these things are running wild out here. Everywhere you go. Plenty of the little buggers. All they eat is grass and there is plenty of that the further away from here you get...'

'I can imagine my Grandma doing that,' I said, raking my hands slowly back through the mess of my hair. It was thick with knots and dirt and dried blood. 'When I get her book back I will find out what else happened.'

'Yeah. And then what? That's the thing. You've got a lot of thinking to do kiddo.'

'You said about your mum?'

'Yeah?'

'Who else is there? Where are you all?'

Aisha put her newly sharpened arrow carefully down onto the grass and then lay her bow next to it. Her hair was loose and she shook it back over one shoulder before turning to look at me. 'There's my mum, and her brother, my Uncle Thomas. There's my older sister Violet and her two kids. There's Connor and his parents, and his younger brothers. There are others. Sometimes we wander alone, sometimes we join up. Sometimes we stay still for a long time. Sometimes we keep moving and moving. Depends what happens.

Depends on a lot of things.'

I tried to swallow the lump in my throat. 'Is it dangerous out there?'

'In some ways,' she shrugged. 'Yes, it is. My dad didn't make it.'

I stared at her, unblinking. 'What happened to him?'

Aisha scratched at the back of her head, her eyes on the stream. 'He fell ill,' she said distractedly. 'I don't really remember it, because I was little. He got a fever. Had an infection. They tried everything...'

'I'm so sorry.'

'Hey, it's okay,' she shrugged lightly. 'It's the way it is. I guess you have medical supplies and schools and stuff?'

'My mum works in the hospital. They do pretty well most of the time.'

'Well, anyway...That's us. Out here. Doing our thing.'

'Do you always get this close to a Province?'

'No, we try to keep as far away as possible actually. But we hadn't been down this far South before. Fancied being near the sea, you know? Took a risk. Moving on again soon. Put some distance between this place and us...'

'The sea? Where is the sea?'

She blinked at me before shaking her head slowly. 'Wow, you really do live in a bubble, kid. It's about ten miles that way.' She pointed behind her. 'That's where we're camping. Down on the beach.

It's gorgeous, Lissie. You should see it.'

'Seen it in books...'

'You need to see it for real. You need to *smell* it. Breathe it in. Run down the sand and into the waves!'

'Maybe one day...'

But who was I kidding? This place was not ready for change like that. Not yet. These people were not even ready for an old woman's diary. They weren't even ready for the truth of the past. And who was I anyway? What business was it of mine what they were ready for? Battered and bruised I got slowly to my feet. I had to go. Aisha jumped to her feet beside me.

'You sure you're ok? I can take you to the beach, if you like? If you can walk that far? My mum will know how to help you.'

I shook my head. I felt numb. 'I have to go home, Aisha.'

'And what about him? Your governor? What are you going to do?'

I started to walk painfully slowly through the water. 'I don't know. I'll have to wait and see. I'll have to see what happens.'

'Even after everything I've told you? Lissie, you don't know what he is capable of. These people are ruthless! Always have been!'

I stumbled, wincing, wondering how the pain could possibly be getting worse. 'He's always been really good to us...' I murmured.

'We're moving on in a few days,' she blurted out, grabbing my shoulder. I nearly cried out with the pain. Sitting down too long had made my spine stiffen up. My whole body felt locked into place. 'You won't be able to find us again, Lissie. So, if you decide to leave, you need to decide quickly. Or we'll be gone.'

'I don't think I can just leave them,' I shrugged regretfully, when the idea had been in my head all along. 'I'll come back on my birthday,' I told her then. 'Three more days. Then I'll know more.'

She nodded and bit her lip and moved slowly back, until she was standing under the apple tree again. I looked at her and the tree one last time before I began my climb. I thought how strong they both looked. How much they looked like they belonged there. The breeze was in her hair, lifting it free from her shoulders and sending strands across her nose and into her eyes. She shook her head and lifted one hand to push it back behind her ears. I thought about our lives as opposite things. I'd been planted and encouraged to grow the right way. I'd been watered and fed and nurtured. I'd had a glass dome over my head the entire time, only I thought it was the sky. Whereas she was a seed that the wind had set free. She had blown on the wind to wherever it took her. She had made her own roots and had grown taller and stronger because of it. Aisha, and the tree. On the other side of the fence. Breaking the rules.

Walking back to the fence became the longest walk of my life. Tears fell from my eyes and were dried by the sun onto my cheeks. Every inch of me ached and groaned from my magnificent fall. I knew I would have to tell my parents the truth. From the start to the finish. How on earth could I not? They deserved to know the truth. They'd cared for me and done their best for me. They deserved the truth and the chance to make up their own minds. A tiny glimmer of hope clutched my heart; maybe they would want to leave too? Maybe we would pack up and leave here together.

Back at the fence, I lowered myself to the ground, crying out in pain and frustration. I almost expected the Governor's deputy and guards to arrive suddenly, their gloved hands reaching for me. But somehow I knew it was not going to work like that. So far he had been true to his word and I got the feeling this was important to him. I knew he would bring me the diary on my fourteenth birthday, and I knew he would allow me to read it. What happened after that was enough to make my skin grow cold.

I squeezed myself slowly through the hole, and then kicked the dirt back into place before stamping it down. With that done, I turned around and began the weary trudge home. I wondered if they were there, waiting for me. If they'd realised I'd disappeared and came looking for me. Or if they were still in the square, saying thank you.

For the longest time, I was just a broken body walking. I wandered on with my head hanging and my eyes on the ground, and my mind was so full of her. Of Aisha. I didn't want her to be gone. I wanted to see her again, and again after that. I wanted to meet her family and her friends. I wanted her to teach me how to shoot rabbits with the bow and arrow. I wanted to *see* rabbits. I wanted to see the beach.

I walked home, knowing that I lived in a cage.

When I got there, the door flung open and they came at me. At first it was with anger and resentment. Their lips pinched up, their eyes dark with fury, their hands clutching, wanting to tear at their own scalps. And then they saw the sight of me and their faces fell into despair. I stumbled on wordlessly and they received me in a panic, dragging me indoors and slamming the door shut on the world.

'Oh Lissie, Lissie! What have you done? What happened to you? You stupid girl!' My mother eased me into the chair and she was switching fast between rage and fear. She wanted to hug me and strike me. She felt love and hate simultaneously, I could tell. She could barely touch me, although she knew she had to.

'What now? What *now*?' My father moaned and shook his head and there were tears glistening in his eyes. I wondered how much more of me he could take.

'I'm okay,' I tried to tell them with a massive sigh, followed by a sharp intake of breath as my mother laid her hands on my head. 'I fell down. I was running too fast. I tripped. I'm okay.'

'What have you been doing?' he demanded, banging one fist into the palm of his other hand before pulling urgently at his lower lip with his thumb and forefinger. 'Where have you been, Lissie? You are beyond a joke! What the hell is wrong with you? One minute you were there, the next you are gone! Drawing attention to yourself yet again!'

My mother came at me with a wet cloth. 'Do you know what they are calling you? Do you? Mad! And traitor! You are one or the other! They have all decided!'

'Utter disgrace,' he said, hands over his eyes. 'I can hardly bear to look at you or even call you my daughter anymore, Lissie...'

'Well, that's fine,' I replied tensely, taking the cloth from my mum's hand. 'I can do that myself.'

'You won't even let us help you? Where did you go? Where did you fall to end up like this?'

'I'll tell you everything,' I offered. 'But you won't like it. And all I can tell you is I am sorry. I never wanted to hurt either of you.'

My father looked at my mother and shook his head, because he didn't want to hear it. She covered her mouth with one hand. He placed his hands on his hips and glared at the floor.

'No,' he told her.

'What?'

'No, we don't need to know. We don't want to hear it, Lissie.'

'But you have to! You must know the truth Mum, Dad! The truth about everything! The truth about this place! I have to tell you about the diary Gran gave me! That's what changed everything, you see! You need to read it. Then you can make your own minds up!'

'Just go to your room,' my mother muttered, turning away. 'We will deal with you tomorrow. Just *go* and stop disgracing yourself.'

'You heard her,' he said.

'You don't want to hear it?' I asked, incredulous. 'You don't want to know the truth? About why I am mad, or a traitor? I am neither, and you need to hear it!'

'You'll implicate us,' he said, shaking his head and walking in circles. 'So no, we don't need to hear it. If you find yourself arrested, you have no one to blame but yourself!'

'I'll show you the diary then,' I said, finally heaving myself up from the chair. 'When the Governor gives it back to me on my birthday. You can see for yourself what Gran tried to warn us all about. She never wanted to come here you know, her or her husband. They were forced. And then her husband Lawrence was killed by the people here. People like *you*! People who just follow orders because they can't think for themselves!'

It was a cruel thing to say, but it was also the truth. They didn't want to hear it though. I limped away from them, smashed and aggrieved, hating them all.

'Suit yourselves,' I muttered in disgust. 'I hope I am arrested. I don't care what they do to me. They can kill me if they like! Call me a rebel and a traitor and kill me with you all watching! But at least I will die knowing the truth!'

I didn't care anymore. Forget it! Forget them! They wouldn't listen, and they would never understand. I was too different. I was like Grandma Elizabeth. With fire in my veins. I was a rebel. They would never understand this, so what was the point?

I headed to my room, stamping my feet. The pain all gone now that I was filled with hot dark anger. Come and get me now Soren! Drag me away screaming! I'll make sure I cry out as much of the truth as I can while I go! I'll tell anyone I see, anyone who will listen! You are all liars here! All complicit with the bending of truth. All deniers! Performing monkeys dancing in the fog.

It came out of nowhere. Her soft frightened voice.

'There is something you should know.'

I looked over my shoulder. Hating them both. Him, with his head down and his eyes glaring, and her with her drawn face and her hands across her abdomen.

'We have to play it safe, Lissie. For the sake of the baby...'

Chantelle Atkins

32: Fourteen

For the next few days, we shuffled around our lives, barely speaking to each other. Each of us trapped in our own shock and confusion. We were like fish; opening our mouths and gaping, our lips yawning to put words to our hurt and fear, but failing every time. My mother took the time off work, stating that she was unwell. In truth, she took the time to tend to my battered body. On inspection, it seemed I'd been lucky not to break anything. She said my spine was bruised like my ribs. The gash on my head needed three stitches which she put in herself under candlelight. The rest of me she washed and bandaged up. I would survive. I was less sure about our family.

During this time, I longed to speak to her in my father's absence. I kept thinking about what she said, and what she meant. *We have to play it safe.* Strange words for a woman excited about a new baby. The sort of words I never expected to hear from her lips. But every time I opened my mouth to ask her, I couldn't bring myself to start it all again. I was just so tired and for the time being and it was so nice to not be fighting with her.

My father went to work every day, his head low, his jaw tight. They were both torn in half. So many unsaid things lay between us that I wondered if we would ever be able to heal the rift that had grown. As for me, I stayed in my bed as instructed. I stared at the ceiling and watched the shadows on the wall. I did as I was told, and just waited.

I waited for my birthday, and I waited for him to come for me. In the background, my father murmured about my hut being ready, but I didn't know when I would get to live in it. I watched the walls and waited, and the passing of time had never seemed so painful. I lay

285

there and thought about Soren Lancaster, and the secrets we held. I wondered what time he would come, and if it would be him with the diary or a messenger. I wondered how much time I would be given. I wondered how fast my battered body could run.

When finally, the day arrived, I woke up to a grey morning. I saw from my bed that the sky outside was ominous, promising rain. I shivered under my covers. Even the sun has vanished on me, I thought, rolling over and pulling my blanket with me. I strained my ears to the sounds beyond my room. I heard them up and moving about. The stove was being lit. The door opened and slammed. Footsteps crunched beyond my window. My father swung the axe into the wood. My mother made puking noises.

I decided to move. I could not bear them coming to me with that terrible pity and yearning in their eyes. It made me want to scream when they looked at me. It was like they could hardly bear to see me. They were tortured by my existence. And still they avoided the truth. I got up slowly, wincing with the pain. Then I opened my door and shuffled slowly out to meet them. He was still outside, swinging the axe. She was sat at the table with her head in her hands.

'Mum?'

She looked up at me and smiled grimly. It was a sick smile, and there were dark circles below her eyes. 'It's okay,' she groaned. 'It's just morning sickness. I was the same with you.'

'Oh. Okay.' I came up to the table and eased myself down onto the other bench.

'Still sore?' she asked me, her head returning to her hands.

'Not too bad.'

'Happy birthday, Lissie.'

'Oh. Yeah. Thanks.' For a moment, I had forgotten.

'So, all grown up...' she said unsurely, with a hiccup. 'I never thought the time would go so fast.'

'When is the new baby going to come?'

'After the winter. In the new year. Same as Hilda's.'

'What, Ned's mum is pregnant too?' This was news to me. My mother smiled weakly, and shifted to look at the kettle now whistling on the stove.

'Lissie, do you think you could get that for me? I don't think I can move without puking at the moment.'

I got up and limped over to the stove, picked up the kettle and brought it back to the table. 'I didn't know that,' I said. 'About Mrs. Fleck. Does Ned?'

'Yes, he knows. We decided to tell you both the same day. The day you...Well, the Day of Thanks. We were so excited to tell you both, you know. So much to be thankful for.'

I slid back onto the bench and gazed at her cautiously. I could still hear my father smashing the axe into wood outside. 'Mum,' I whispered. 'Do you truly believe that?'

She looked first alarmed, and then resigned. 'Oh Lissie...'

'I know, I know, we're not supposed to talk about it. We're all supposed to love this place and want to stay here forever. But I just want to ask you one question, Mum. On my birthday. On the day I become an adult. Just *one* question. Please.'

287

She did not speak. But she nodded her head. I picked up the kettle and poured the water into our waiting cups.

'Was it just me Grandma Elizabeth tried to get through to? Or did she tell you stuff too?'

'You mean about her diary and everything in it?'

They were words I was not prepared for. I was not ready for the look on her face either. For the first time, I looked at her, I looked into her eyes and saw Grandma Elizabeth there. It was like she was there, alive, and shining right back at me. Did you miss me, Lissie?

'I always knew about the diary, and what it said,' she whispered.

'You knew about it? But she said you didn't! She said not to tell you!'

'Well, she got forgetful. Confused. Yes, Lissie, is the answer. Yes, I knew about it, and yes she tried to get through to me. And my mother.'

I was so shocked I could barely breathe. 'But?'

'But what? What can you do? What is the answer? What is the alternative? That is what you must ask yourself, my girl. That is what you need to decide.'

'But he has it now Mum, the Governor has it...'

She held a finger to her mouth, shushed me and glanced at the door. 'No more.'

'But Mum!'

'Not now. No more. Just think about what I said. What is the alternative, Lissie?'

The door opened and my father strode in. At once, the atmosphere darkened. He could not meet my eyes. I felt it then, more than ever. He saw me as a traitor. And I was forever tainted. But my mother had given me something. Something I never expected in a million years.

'Tea is ready,' she said to him. 'What do you want for breakfast? I don't think I can manage anything myself.'

'Bread is fine.'

'I'll do it,' I offered, thinking about Mum's sickness. But he waved me away, shaking his head.

'No, I will. Thank you, Lissie.' He wiped his hands down the legs of his trousers and turned towards the stove. 'Happy birthday,' he added, with his back turned.

'Thanks. When can we go to my hut?'

'Whenever you're ready,' he replied softly. 'I've got the day off, so...'

'I would say sooner rather than later,' Mum interjected. 'Just that it looks like rain, and I know I won't have much energy later.'

I nodded at her thankfully. She must have known how much I wanted this day over with. Moving on. Moving out. It was supposed to be something to celebrate. But it didn't feel that way today.

'Congratulations, by the way.' I said this to them, and he turned slowly to face me. 'I'm sorry,' I added, looking into his eyes. 'I really am. About everything. But I mean it. Congratulations about the baby. I'm really happy for you both.' They said nothing, so I got up from the bench while they swapped looks with each other. 'I'll get washed and dressed, then we can get going. Might as well move me in today.'

I limped off to the washroom and only silence followed me. Truth be told, I wanted them to say no. I wanted one of them to call after me, to say don't be silly, Lissie! There is no rush! There is no rule about when you must move into your hut for good! For most people, it was a gradual transition. But not for me. The sooner I got out of there the better, and we all knew it. Too much had happened. Too much had gone wrong. But as I washed and dressed, for the last time under my childhood roof, I couldn't get her words out of my head. What is the answer? What is the alternative? What did she mean? But she knew. That was the most shocking thing. I kept shaking my head, trying to take it in. She knew the whole time. She knew Grandma had a diary full of truths about the Old World and this one, and she knew Grandma was trying to tell me things. Had she wanted me to hear them too?

What was the answer?

When we were all ready, we left the hut. I couldn't help looking over my shoulder as we went. I'd packed up all my things, just a bag full, but it felt like everything I really wanted to take was back there in that hut. My home and my family. I could have wept. Maybe it was the pain that still plagued my every step and breath. Maybe it was my mother, holding her belly protectively, yet unable to look back at me. Or maybe it was my father. This tall proud man, who was no longer either. Leading the way, a few steps beyond my mother. Leading me away. Giving me to the Province.

Should we tell him? About the diary? About the Governor

290

coming for me? About Aisha in the wild with her family? About our ancestors coming here in peace and hope only to find that it came at a cost? That something basic and natural had to be first cast aside. That they had to go to sleep and close their eyes, and only open them to look at good things. Safe things.

I couldn't think. I couldn't breathe!

And yet we went on. We walked on and on, through the Province, keeping to the edges with our heads hanging low. Every now and then we could not avoid walking through a cluster of huts. Where there were people, hanging out washing, or pushing warm bread into children's hands, there were also dark eyes. Accusing eyes. Resentful eyes following our progress. We didn't look at them. We didn't respond to whispers. We just kept going.

I felt like I was being cast out. Banished. Maybe that was what the Governor had in store for me once I had read the book and learnt the whole truth. Banishment. Would I welcome it, or fear it? I thought about Aisha, and finding her again, one last time. She wanted me to go with her, I remembered. She wanted me to see the beach...

When finally, we reached my hut, my father swallowed and turned to me on approach. 'Here we are,' he said, and his words were almost a gasp. As if everything was killing him. I looked at him in pity, and longed to fling myself one last time at his legs. Sorry Daddy, I am so, so sorry!

'It's lovely,' I said bravely instead, and walked on ahead of them. My hut had been built not far from Ned's. We would be able to call to each other from our doorsteps. And there he was. Waving slowly and unsurely from his doorway coffee mug in hand, work clothes on. A man now. I waved back and kept walking.

My father had done a good job. I ducked inside and stopped in the main room. It looked clean and fresh and smelled of damp mud and dry straw. Beautiful. Somehow it made my heart ache. I could be happy here. He had made me a long, narrow table, with a bench on either side. The stove was next to the window, which he knew I would like. He had fashioned two wooden stools and placed them on the rug. Besides them, a rocking chair with a fat blue cushion on it. All the windows were decorated with blue curtains. I imagined my mother sat up night after night, sewing them for me, and I wanted to cry again.

'Look at your room,' she croaked from behind, and so I did. Pushing open the door which creaked back at me. Immediately I saw the bed. Right under the window, just like Grandma's. A wooden framed bed, complete with hand-made patchwork quilt and two pillows. Just gorgeous. Against the wall sat a little desk and stool. There was another rug on the floor. I just shook my head and tried not to cry.

'I love it,' I told them, and I did, I really did. I hadn't expected to feel like this. I hadn't ever thought or imagined the work they would put into it. I was not being cast out. I was being set up. Made ready. Prepared. I suddenly felt immensely grown up. I giggled and wiped a tear from my eye. 'It's really lovely! I really love it!'

I turned around and found them with my arms. I could tell this surprised them both. At first they tensed, and then they let go and we blended into each other. We held on. We were arms and bodies entangled and breathing, eyes closed and squeezing out tears. My mother's cheek pressed against mine, and I could hear and feel her heart thudding. My father stroked my hair from above.

'Oh my girl,' he was saying, his voice muffled. 'Oh my girl, Lissie...I don't want to let you go.'

'I'm going to be fine,' I replied, hugging him back. 'I promise. Just fine. Me and Ned. We're going to be good.' I didn't know if I should promise him this, but in that moment, I did mean it.

'Coffee!' my mother exclaimed suddenly, breaking free and wiping her eyes. We all laughed nervously. 'Or tea?' she asked. 'Lissie, I filled your cupboards, and your water and wood were delivered yesterday.'

And then she was all efficiency. All my mother; dragging me around by the hand, making sure I knew where things were, reminding me what days of the month things were dropped off. The whole time I was listening to her and nodding, as my father grinned in the background, but I was thinking about the words in the diary. Of vegetable gardens and banned seeds. I was thinking about the stolen seed I pushed into the dirt and how nothing happened, because I did not know how to make it happen. And about how nice it would be to plant a seed here and watch it grow. To see it from my window. This life that I had nurtured. But I could not say it. I could do them no more harm. I would not spoil this precious time for them. I would be what I now was. An adult. One of them.

And so, we played our roles out.

I made the hot sweet tea, and we sat on the doorstep together, all three of us. And then my father chopped me some wood and made me a fire to boil the pot over, and my mother kept her arm around me, and wiped tears from her eyes.

'Mothers never want to let their babies go,' she nodded her head at me. 'But we have to.'

'I'm not gone,' I told her. 'I'm not far. You can come any time you want. I'll make us all dinner, how about that?'

She bumped me with her shoulder, and I thought how odd it was that I felt closer to her then than I had ever done before. It's what she said, I thought. What she said about the diary. What was the answer though? What was the alternative to all of this?

I had the rest of the day to ponder this question. Their parting gift to me was enough tokens to

feed me for a month. They kissed my cheeks and ruffled my hair and then they left me there by the fire,

as the afternoon slid on towards evening. I sat and waited. I sat by my fire and drank cups of sweet tea,

and waited for the Governor.

33: A Visitor

I am fourteen years old. I am an adult and this is my home. I am Lissie Turner and I am going to find the truth.

I kept thinking these things while I sat outside my hut beside the fire, watching the light slowly die. I was lying on the ground, with a pillow under my head, watching the sky. It was so massive, so huge, so endless and unknown. It stretched its mottled blue and blacks from one side of our world to the other. The clouds were moving fast. Heading home. Tucking up. The moon was out and shining brightly and I thought about all the ages it had seen. From the beginning of time and people, to now. To what we had become. I thought about all these things while I waited.

The people of the Province were good people. This, I knew. I thought about the reasons why and how I knew this. There was no violence. The people were kind. They looked out for you. If you fell over, there were always hands to lift you back up. It was safe. Children could run from one end of the Province to the other if they wished. They could run and climb and play and scramble before returning to the warmth of their hut, where the fires never stopped burning.

They were good people. The parents were good. The teachers were good. The guards were good, watching over us all, keeping the wheels turning. And the people of the domes were good. Weren't they? They planted and watered and grew the seeds. They brought us the food. They brought us the water from the reservoir. They delivered us the wood so that we did not cut down the wrong trees. They did these things for us, to keep us happy.

And what did the people in the Provinces do in return? They raised their children to believe in Peace. They raised their children to believe in Now. They sent them to school where the teachers carried on this praise of the present. They believed in good fortune and lessons learnt. Salvation. Progress. They went to work. All of them. One by one, as soon as the children were old enough to go to school. They went to work in the store, in the office, in the hospital, on patrols, in school, doing so many things, so many duties that all kept the wheels turning.

It was a deal, you see?

They kept us happy, and we kept them in power. I nodded and smiled when I'd worked this out. I was going to tell him this when he finally came. It was strange how I was feeling much stronger than before. Maybe it was being here. Becoming an adult. Being forced to believe I was one.

I was lying there staring at the darkening sky when I heard a noise and sat up, wondering if it was him. But it was just Ned, stealing softly across the dry earth towards me. He carried an old cracked plate with some bread and cheese on it.

'Well, look at us,' he sighed, dropping down beside me and placing the plate down. 'All grown up and living on our own. How's it been?'

I propped myself up on one elbow and took a piece of bread. 'It's been okay actually. Better than I thought. I sort of like it here. I felt terrible when I woke up, but not now. What about you?'

He smiled gently. 'I'm getting used to it. So, you know all about the babies then?'

296

'Yeah. They told me. Are you happy for them?'

'Can't not be,' he shrugged. 'They're happy. They're different already.' He shook his head and waved a hand. 'Whatever. I'm out of there.'

'A new beginning for everyone eh?'

'I suppose so. So, you've made things up with them? Shut up about the diary like they wanted?'

I smiled at him wickedly. 'Well, no not exactly.'

'Lissie?' Ned rolled his eyes and then dropped his head into his hands. 'Oh what now? What have you done?'

'I haven't done anything Ned! Just listen.' I sat up straight and shuffled closer to him. The sky was darkening rapidly and the shadows in the distance could be anything. Anyone. 'He hasn't been yet, you know, so just, keep quiet. Keep your voice down.'

Ned's eyes widened as he gazed around us fearfully. 'You think he'll come here? Now?'

'That was our agreement, remember? He'll give me the book back today, on my birthday. Then once I've read it, I find out what it has cost me.' I glanced over my shoulder, before moving even closer to Ned, so that our legs were touching. 'So shh,' I warned him. 'We don't know who is listening.' Ned sucked his lower lip in and clamped it down with his teeth. 'My mum let something slip this morning,' I whispered into his ear. I put my hand up to my mouth, shielding us, directing my words straight into his head. 'She said she knew about the diary all along. Probably read it too. Gran tried to get through to her and her mother. Not just me.'

Ned pulled back slightly and stared into my face. 'Eh? I don't get it. Why would she get so angry with you then? If she knew all along?'

'I don't know. We didn't get a chance to talk because my dad came back in. He obviously knows nothing. But she does. I think she's scared, Ned. I think she doesn't want to talk about it. She hasn't chosen rebellion, that's for sure.'

'And you have?' His voice was a croak in the darkness, his eyes gleaming back at me. I didn't know the answer to this.

'I don't know yet,' I shrugged. 'Depends what happens next I suppose. My mother said I had to think about something. What is the alternative? That's what she said. What do you think she means, Ned?'

Ned pulled his legs up to his chin and wrapped his arms around them. The fire crackled and spat, throwing shadows on our faces. 'I guess she means the alternative to *this*. To living here in Everlasting Peace.'

I pulled a piece of bread apart with my fingers. 'Well, Aisha was telling me all about that on the Day of Thanks.'

'So that's where you went? How did you get hurt?'

'Fell down the hill,' I told him with a sheepish grin. 'For a moment I thought I was going to die Ned! It was like I was flying for a bit. I just kept going!'

Ned whistled through his teeth. 'You're an idiot, Lissie Turner. I'm telling you.'

'I know, I know. But I had to get out. I couldn't stand it that day. All that gratitude. Made me want to puke.'

298

'Well you just drew attention to yourself yet again. Everyone thinks you're mad. Or bad. Either way, what will you do for duties?'

'Dad wants me to help him, of course. Hunting down innocent animals no less. I mean, we can't have anything here that doesn't belong, can we?'

Ned visibly winced at the bitterness in my voice. 'Shh,' he warned. 'He could be close.'

'Scared?' I teased. He rolled his eyes again.

'Of course I am. I'm not going anywhere though.'

'Don't be stupid. No one knows you know anything. We better keep it that way.'

'So what else did Aisha say?' he asked, ignoring my statement. 'Can't believe they're still out there...'

We did the exact same thing at the exact same time. We looked over our shoulders and stared into the darkness beyond our huts. Back there, past the ruins, at the fence. An owl was calling. Ned shivered. I looked back at him and took a deep breath.

'She told me how they live. Who she lives with. Where they go. She told me about a beach, Ned! There's a beach, not even that far from here.'

Ned looked wistful for a moment. 'Wow. I've seen pictures but...'

'Sometimes I get mad Ned, when I think about everything they have kept from us. Dogs, and trees, and seeds, and beaches! And why? What for? Aisha is safe out there! Why can't we be? Why do we even need a fence anymore? Back then, yes, I get it. But not now! They go on and on about Everlasting Peace and yet here we are living in a prison! Fenced in! When we have no enemies!'

'Well that's a matter of opinion,' a voice came suddenly out of the darkness. We froze. Ned and I. Our muscles locking, our heads pressed together, our eyes wide and guilty. 'Please,' the voice went on, smooth and low, purring towards us. 'Don't mind me. Your conversation sounds very intriguing!'

With slow jerky movements, I raised and turned my head. And there he was. The Governor of Province 5. He emerged like a shadow, sliding out from the darkness, barely making a sound. Cat like, he strolled loosely towards us, before waving a hand at the ground where we sat.

'May I?'

I nodded dumbly, before nudging Ned away from me. We looked like two naughty kids caught doing something we were not allowed to do. I cleared my throat, smoothed down my hair and shoved some bread into my mouth. I could feel my cheeks blazing, and sweat had crept out across my skin. I was not sure if Ned was even breathing.

'You shouldn't creep up on people,' I mumbled through my mouthful. To this the Governor threw back his head and laughed. He wiped his eyes and then sat down beside me, with his shoulders still shaking.

'Oh Lissie Turner, if you aren't the funniest girl I have ever come across...'

Ned and I looked down into his lap, where he held a cloth satchel, presumably with Grandma Elizabeth's diary inside it. Ned sniffed, pushed his shoulders back and lifted his head.

'You've bought the book back,' he said, dumping himself in it even more. I rolled my eyes at him but it was too late. I could see on his face that he didn't care.

The Governor regarded him curiously. 'Yes, young man. I had a feeling you were somewhat involved in all this. Of course, I was dearly hoping to be wrong. Been led astray have you, Ned?' He smiled softly at him. 'What a shame for you. You should have picked your friends better.'

'He doesn't know anything,' I butted in, before Ned could open his mouth. 'Leave him out of it. Go on, Ned. Go on home.'

'I'm not going anywhere,' Ned replied through gritted teeth, while his green eyes glared out at the Governor. 'I've been in on it all from the start, sir. You might as well know. And I stand by Lissie and her Grandma. I believe them.'

Governor Lancaster clicked his tongue and sighed.

'Oh dear me. That is a shame. Well, if that is the case, Ned Fleck, you had better stay put and listen on. This involves you too.' He then turned his attention back to me, and his expression changed suddenly. Gone was the smooth smile, the gentle teasing eyes. Instead, his muscles hardened and his eyes cooled. He sat like us, with his legs up and one arm wrapped around them. With his free hand, he patted the satchel he was still holding onto. 'Kept to my word Miss Turner, and you kept to yours. Well,' he flicked a look at Ned. 'In a manner. But nevertheless, here we are. Where none of us wanted to be. Happy birthday by the way.'

I dropped my legs and crossed my arms over my chest. 'Thank

301

you.'

'Alas, not *quite* the day of celebration your parents would have liked, I imagine,' he went on regretfully, his eyes burning into mine. 'A sad day in fact. Welcoming you to adulthood and letting you go with such regret and disappointment.'

I wanted to argue with him. I longed to tell him that my father was only disappointed because he did not know any better, because he really did think I had gone mad, because he did not have the fire in his veins. I wanted to tell him what my mother said. What she knew. But I couldn't. I held my tongue prisoner behind my clenched teeth and forced myself to think about the tiny life stirring inside her belly.

'You still want this?' he asked me, nodding at the bag.

'Of course I do.'

'All right then.' He slid his hand inside the bag, tugged out the book and passed it to me. I felt something tremor through me as I took hold of it again. Her words and her thoughts back where they belonged, in my hands. I pressed it to my chest and wrapped my arms tightly across it.

'Thank you.'

'What happens now?' Ned was quick to ask him. Governor Lancaster was already getting to his feet. We watched him stand up and brush the dust and the grass from the seat of his trousers.

'I'll give you overnight to read it, Lissie,' he said briskly, not looking at me as he straightened out his clothes. 'I trust that will be sufficient time?'

'Yes,' I nodded in reply. 'I was nearly finished before you took it.'

His eyes met mine, and we crashed there together, and it was like a bang in my chest, in my heart. The truth staring me in the face. We were enemies. Something was festering between us. Something that was quickly turning rotten and black. Something we could not take back. I shivered, but I refused to look away.

'I will return with my guards in the morning, Miss Turner,' he said to me, standing straight and tall, his chin tilted upwards so that his eyes appeared like slits. 'I will ask you one question there and then. You will have one final chance to end this madness and return to your normal life. I will give you the choice Lissie, and mark my words, it is *you* who will be making the choice, not I. What I do after that will be dictated to me by the laws of not only Province 5 but by the laws of New England.'

'What question?' I stared right back into his face. The shadows from the fire danced across his features. First one eye gleamed, and then the other. And then it was his teeth that shone as his lips parted.

'Based on what you read tonight, you will come to a decision, Lissie. And that is what I will ask you. Rebel or conform. I bid you goodnight.' And that was all he had to say. He tipped his hat, turned on his heel and began to walk away.

'What happens then?' Ned called after him, but we both knew it was pointless. He had said what he came to say. He quickly disappeared into the black and all that marked his exit was the screech of an owl, making us both jump violently. Ned reached out, clutching at my hand. 'He'll arrest you!' he said fearfully. 'He said he'd come with his guards! We should go...we should get out!'

'Let me read it first,' I told him as calmly as I could. 'Nothing is definite until I have finished the book, Ned. You want to keep me company?'

He nodded fiercely in the light of the fire. 'You bet I do.'

34: The Diary

Inside my hut, we closed the door, drew the curtains and lit the candles. We did not speak. It was as if she was there with us, so we did not need to talk. She was going to do the talking for us. We went into the bedroom and I sat on the floor with the book on my lap and Ned climbed onto the bed and laid down with his hands laced across his stomach. I lifted the book to my face, opened it up and inhaled. I could smell her again. I closed my eyes and smiled in relief. From the bed, Ned sniffed and I wondered if he was crying.

'Are you sure about this Ned?' I decided to ask him one more time. 'You don't have to do this you know. You can go now and not be involved. He said as much.'

'Don't insult me, Lissie,' he croaked in reply, sounding angry. 'If you really think I would do that to you, then you don't know me at all.'

'Sorry Ned. I'm just saying...I feel bad that's all. I don't want you to get into any trouble because of me.' I shrugged, not knowing what else to say. 'You've got to think about it, that's all I'm saying. You might be about to wreck your own life.'

He let out a growl then, surprising me. 'Damn it, Lissie. Don't argue with me. Don't you understand, I need to do this too?' I nodded, waiting. He ran his fingers back through his thick, red hair, blowing out his breath in frustration. 'I need to do something,' he went on. 'Who am I, otherwise? Who am I, Lissie? I'm no one. I need to be...someone they remember.'

He stared up at the ceiling, his cheeks twitching. I turned back to the diary. 'All right, Ned. I'm sorry.'

'Just read it, Lissie. Let's get this over.'

'Okay. Sorry.' I cleared my throat, opened to where I had last read, and started reading out loud;

'We finally arrived last night. Lost three on the way. Another two probably won't make it. We are all sick and need clean water badly. We waited at the gates to be let inside, and oh what a relief, seeing human faces, being ushered inside and offered food, water and medicine. We are sleeping in a makeshift barn. The roof is half missing. The people here are busy making new homes with whatever they can salvage. They send volunteers out daily to bring materials back. Last night Lawrence was whispering in my ear; we will rest and feed and then we will make a plan. We will overthrow them, he said, and set the people free. I didn't know what he was talking about. There is barely anyone left, doesn't he realise? The whole world was on fire, and when the fire stopped burning there was nothing left but ashes. But he says it was no accident that the domes survived. No accident that they have put fences up already. I cannot bear to think about it. We will do what he says. Eat and rest and then leave.'

I stopped for a moment to turn the page and glanced back at Ned. He was lying with his arms behind his head now. 'Few weeks later,' I told him.

'They have taken good care of us. It is surprising what supplies they have here and what skills. Nurses and doctors. People in charge. I am relieved to be safe and alive, relieved to be still, not walking any more, but I look at Lawrence and I see fear in his eyes all the time. Something is not right, he tells me. I try to soothe him. We have been given our own shelter now. Very basic, but the people here go out in

306

small groups to bring back supplies. Sometimes they are gone for days, or weeks. Sometimes they don't come back at all. Sometimes they bring other survivors back with them. There is still food growing in the domes nearby and people go out and bring it back. They have a few horses they are building up. They have a bit of everything really. But Lawrence does not trust the one who seems to be taking charge. He argues with him a lot. Challenging him. We don't need people in charge, he tries to say. I agree with him, but I warn him to be careful. We have a lot to lose.'

Ned sat up on the bed then and swung his feet down to the floor. 'Sounds like the Governor's ancestors were taking charge from the start,' he mused. 'I guess that makes sense. Someone would have had to.'

I shrugged and look back at the book. *'In some ways things are good here. It has been a few months now and the people keep talking about peace. Peace forever, they say. The guy they have crudely elected to be mayor or whatever it is, he holds these meetings in the square. People listen to him because he has a way with words. A charisma. Just like Lawrence. Only Lawrence is viewed with suspicion, like an outsider. People say he is trying to stir up trouble. This other guy harps on about how lucky we are. How we must never allow that stuff to happen again. War is over forever he says. No more guns and no more bombs ever again. Let's work together, he says. Let's build this place up and start again. People are enthralled with this promise. They are so grateful to be alive, to be part of this; building a brand new world where people have finally learnt that war is not the answer.*

'Lawrence does not buy it and neither do I. We will leave soon and find our people. These are not our people. These are sheep.

307

Scared sheep, desperate to be told what to do and how to do it. They will do whatever they are told because they want to live. They have lived through horror. They are shell shocked and traumatised. They would believe anything right now. They just want to be told everything will be all right. No more fear, they say. No more war.'

'Bet my ancestors were just like that,' Ned muttered from behind me. 'Doing whatever they were told.'

'You can understand it,' I looked up. 'They'd been scared for such a long time. Fed lies about who was causing the wars too. These people still thought the government were trying to protect them by building the domes, not take their rights away.'

'Go on,' he said, nodding at the book. 'What happened next?'

'Okay. *We are leaving as soon as we can. We just need to save enough rations and make plans to head in the right direction. Lawrence has been talking to others who are not happy here, not so convinced. They want to find their loved ones. They want to try other places. They say they used to grow their own food once...before it was stopped. They talk wistfully and in whispers. They say, wouldn't that be nice again? To plant a garden and watch it grow? Lawrence has asked. Can't we have some seeds? Can't we start a garden? Like in the old days? The people in charge said no. That was when we knew. The one running this place are the same as before. Lawrence is convinced something is going on. He has so many theories, each one more crazy than the last, but each scarily believable. They razored the world to the ground on purpose, he says, obliterated us to win their war. To win ultimate control. Who is in charge, he asks me and the others. Who is leading us here? Telling us what we can and can't do? Just look! They wanted slaves and sheep and that is exactly what we are giving them!*

He tells us we either leave or overthrow. But there is a spanner in the works. I am pregnant.'

With weary tears in my eyes, I looked up at Ned's pale drawn face. 'My Grandmother,' I told him. 'Mum's mother, Bessie.'

'Go on then,' he urged. 'It's nearly at the end, isn't it?'

I nodded glumly. 'I feel sick Ned. I really think I might throw up.'

'They were right, weren't they? Aisha and Connor?'

'Looks like it.'

'Keep reading Lissie. Please.'

'Okay. You asked for it...This is a few months on again… *So, it has happened. What we feared. We should have left when we could. But Lawrence became obsessed with rebellion once again. What would be the point in leaving and dying somewhere else, he said? These people need taking down now! These sheep need waking up. We can free them. We can free nature. Take off the chains once and for all. And they were all for it...except for the one who was spying all along.*

So, they came for him this morning. My Lawrence. My love. Just as they came for my father all those years ago. They say Lawrence is a traitor, and a criminal. They held a meeting in the square and I tried to stand up, I tried to say NO! But I was taken aside and advised. They know about the baby. Stay safe, this man said to me. Live here and stay safe. You will be safe. I saw the faces of the people all around and they were so frightened. The leader stood up there and told them lies which they gobbled up hungrily. This man was not just a traitor but an enemy in our midst, he said. This man was plotting against us, plotting to kill us, plotting to start it all again, the violence and the hatred. He knew what to say to wind them up. I couldn't bear it. They were shouting for justice. Set an example, they were screaming!'

I stopped reading and bowed my head into the pages. 'There's only a few sentences left, Ned. This is the saddest thing ever...'

He sat there, clenching his fists in his lap and staring at nothing. His eyes looked odd. Glassy and cold.

'Planned it from the start,' he murmured. 'Wars to end rebellion. Blame the rebels, blame the people they want rid of. Get control. Total control. Start over. Plant us.'

It made sense, but all the same, he was scaring the hell out of me. I looked back at the last words my Great-Grandmother ever wrote in her girlhood diary. It seemed amazing to me now that she carried it about with her for all those years. That she saw her world set on fire. That everything changed in her lifetime alone. Old World to New World. I took a deep breath and finished it.

'I can write no more. I have no words. The baby was born last night. Bessie. I will tell her the truth when I find the courage. For now, I have only anger and pain. My Lawrence. My love. I miss you so much. You led us here to save us and sacrificed yourself to these people. And to see them now you would never know. You would never believe they could have done it. Building homes, rebuilding ruins into buildings, educating the young children, aiding the sick and the elderly, and everyone is so grateful, Lawrence. So, thankful for no more war. They are all so happy now. I hate them for it. And yet after everything I have seen, I cannot blame them for it. Goodnight Lawrence. Thank you for everything you taught me out there. Thank
310

you for the fire in Bessie's veins. I will tell her about it. I will tell her what it is for.'

I blew out my breath, closed the book and placed it carefully onto my lap. Outside the open window an owl hooted urgently. I thought vaguely of Aisha, and then shook the thoughts away and looked at Ned. He was pale and small and shaking with something.

'So that was it,' I said to him. 'They killed the last rebel who wanted his freedom. Kept everything as they wanted it all along.'

'Sickening,' he said tightly. 'And those people out there, my parents, all of them. They're all sick too!'

'But they don't know,' I reminded him gently, heaving myself up onto the bed beside him. 'They were born here, just like their parents before them. It's all been wiped out. I don't know why they allowed Grandma Elizabeth to live really. Knowing what she knew.'

'They knew she had to protect her child,' he whispered back. 'She had no choice, Lissie. All she could do was tell them. Bessie, and then your mother. And you.' He looked at me now, his expression dark, his lips trembling. 'She risked everything by keeping this. She could have been found out at any time.'

'I wonder what she hoped would happen...'

'I don't know. I guess she wanted the truth to come out...but she must have known the danger that would put you in.'

'Hmm,' I said, getting up again. 'Maybe not.'

'What do you mean?'

'Well, Soren Lancaster is not the same man who ordered

311

Lawrence be killed. He is a descendent of that man, but times have changed. He said so himself.'

I left the bedroom and wandered into the main room to find something to eat. I heard Ned's feet hit the floor behind me as he followed.

'You're not making any sense, Lissie.'

'Maybe I'm just trying to convince myself everything will be okay,' I replied, hunting through the food my mother had left for us on the table. I found two tomatoes, some cheese and some sliced ham and started to make us a late-night snack.

'You think you can reason with him?' Ned frowned.

'Maybe. Who knows? We're not our ancestors, Ned. We're different people. I can try talking to him. Make a plan with him.'

'Bargain with him?' Ned shook his head in disbelief. 'He won't want to know, Lissie. Not now you know all this! And me! Why would we stay quiet about all this?'

'No one would believe us anyway, if we just went out there shouting about it,' I pointed out, passing him a plate of food. 'Besides, what else is he going to do? Kill us? I think our parents would have something to say about that!'

'No one did back then,' he pointed out, staring at me in wonder. 'It'll be the same thing happening all over again Lissie! You can't trust him.'

I sat on the bench and nibbled at the food. 'I don't trust him. I just think things are different now. There is room to talk, that's all I'm saying. What other option is there?'

312

'We can leave!' he cried at me, throwing up his arms. 'Now! Just get out of this place and find the others!'

'I've thought about that,' I said, nodding gravely. 'But I don't want to cause problems for them. I don't want them hunted down or anything. The Governor might not know anything about them. We have to try and keep it that way Ned.'

'Protect them and sacrifice yourself? Just like back then, Lissie. You're insane if you think it will be any different.'

'I just want to give him a chance,' I tried to explain, as he stood there glowering, refusing to sit down or eat. 'I just want to give these people a chance. I mean, maybe there is an opportunity here to change things! He said as much to me the day I got kicked out of school. He said it just takes time to implement changes. He said that they want to change the way it works. That we will be able to vote in our leaders, that sort of thing!'

Finally, Ned sat down. He rested his head in one hand and listlessly picked up a slice of cheese. He looked exhausted, with dark circles beneath his eyes.

'He was trying to get around you then,' he reminded me wearily. 'He was trying to get you on side. It's different now. Couldn't you feel that when he was here earlier? I've never seen him like that before, Lissie. It was like he wanted to eat us alive or something. I swear it. I couldn't look at him.'

'We'll talk to him,' I looked him right in the eye and nodded at him as confidently as I could. 'We've got lots to talk about. He can't deny that. We'll make a bargain. Ask to leave if it comes to it. But I think we should act as grown up as possible, don't you?'

'I have no idea,' Ned sighed miserably. 'I really don't. But I'll trust you Lissie, if you really know what you are doing.'

'I'm not sure that I do. Not one bit. I just know that I need to confront him. I have to hear it all and know the truth, one way or another.' We ate in silence, and fell asleep right there with our heads upon the table.

35: A Choice

Things happened fast in the morning.

We were not given any time to wake up, to talk or to think. There was no time for breakfast or for the brewing of coffee. There was no time to rub the sleep from our eyes. We were awakened suddenly and torn violently from our dreams by the banging on the door. Our bones creaked in protest as we moved our limbs from their strange places. Our necks, cracking and cricking into place.

Ned looked at me and I looked at him, and we knew that it was now.

'Come in,' I said, before the door got knocked down. Ned turned slowly, wincing in pain. I cracked my knuckles on the table top and got quickly to my feet.

The door opened, and Soren Lancaster walked in with Deputy Bradshaw and two other guards right behind him. One of them was his son. Grinning spitefully across his pimply face, Saul carried a large wooden baton under one arm. I felt instantly sick and all the moisture evaporated from my mouth and throat.

The Governor was cool, brisk and to the point. Outside, the sun was a golden ball placed on the horizon, rising slowly to awaken the people. He stood there with his hands behind his back and his expression calm yet firm.

'Lissie Turner,' he addressed me. 'Did you finish the book?'

I nodded firmly, my chin jutting out, my hands going to my hips. 'Yes I did, Governor. I read every last word.'

The Tree of Rebels

'Well, Miss Turner, before I ask you the question I need to know the answer to, I think I better update you on last night's events.'

This was not what I expected to come out of his mouth. I glanced at Ned and he frowned back at me.

'What events?' I asked nervously. Governor Lancaster raised his eyebrows, first one, and then the other.

'Last night our people were intercepted on their way back from the domes with this morning's delivery. A fight occurred.'

I was lost. 'What?'

'It's all right. No need to panic. We fought them off and captured one. We have him in the jail right now.' A thin smile tugged at his lips, but he fought it back and contained it. His face remained cooly smug. 'One of those rebels you were asking me about, perhaps?'

'I don't understand...'

'Well all that is by the by, Miss Turner. I need to ask you a question, don't I?'

I looked to Ned, who stared back at me, his lip quivering, his eyes questioning. I thought about Aisha and Connor and owls hooting urgently in the dark. And so, the Governor asked me, because he wanted to know what I would do next.

'So what do you have to say to me this morning, Miss Turner?'

I glanced once more at Ned, as he turned to me with a slight smile upon his lips. He looked how I felt; wrecked and afraid and defiant all at once. I remembered about the tree and I licked my lips and looked squarely back at the Governor.

316

'I don't choose to conform to lies, Governor,' I told him clearly. 'I choose to stand up for the truth.'

He did not hang around.

He motioned to his men, and all three of them came for us. Saul and Bradshaw on Ned. The other one on me. Their grasping hands seizing our limbs, twisting our bodies, pulling our wrists behind our backs where they were promptly handcuffed. Click. Snap. Lock.

'Lissie Turner and Ned Fleck I am arresting you by the powers vested in me by the state of New England and charging you with the crime of treason and intent to overthrow the immediate government of Province 5.'

These were the things he said as they bundled us towards the door. I wanted to laugh into his face. It was both funny and terrifying. It happened so fast that we could not breathe. We barely cried out. We were theirs.

He didn't say anything else. He didn't need to. He had us. There would be a time for talking later. We were moved, propelled violently and urgently forward. I looked over my shoulder and saw the Governor closing the door to my hut behind him with Grandma Elizabeth's diary in his hand and then, whistling softly under his breath, he caught us up. He gave me one sympathetic look before dancing out in front, leading the party back to his castle.

I watched his back and there was an initial rush of energy and adrenalin as our limbs were manhandled and our bodies hurried on, but now there was something else and I had block it out; I had push it away. Now there was this small mewling girl, this child, eyes streaming, crawling up from the pit of my belly crying out in terror,

The Tree of Rebels

Mum! Dad! Mummy! Daddy! I tried to bite her down, swallow her, keep her at bay. But there were tears in my eyes anyway, especially when I glanced back at Ned, with one guard and the terrible Saul hauling him along. I felt guilt hammering me down. Oh, Ned. Poor Ned.

We were bundled towards the square. Some of the huts were stirring, with smoke billowing from the chimneys, and candles being lit on the inside behind curtains. But there was not much else. As far as we knew, no one saw our disgraced journey through the Province and into the square. I thought about the person in the jail cell and I was not sure if this was a good thing or a bad thing. What if we all just vanished? Oh, it made my guts hurt when I thought it...What if what Aisha said was true? Hangings? Oh no... He wouldn't. Not to us. We're just children, I wanted to cry out at his harsh turned back. Yesterday I was a child.

As we were marched across the deserted square I wondered if we ought to cry out in protest. Try to wake them all up. Would they let it happen anyway? Would they stand back and watch just as they did all those years ago when Lawrence was arrested? Would they just stand by, shaking their heads in pity and disappointment? What about my parents? I was so scared, but somehow I knew I must not show it. I must not let him see. I must not break. And neither must Ned.

I looked back at him to check as we were dragged around to the back of the Governor's office. Oh, not the front door for us. Not now. No Miss Harper or trays of refreshments, nothing like that for us now. The Governor unlocked a door at the back adjacent to the stables. I remembered the day Saul had me mucking them out and it felt like another lifetime ago. Had he known back then? What he was being groomed for? Had he known about my family and the rebellions and

318

the sacrifice? It would explain a lot, I thought, looking at him now, as he sneered down into Ned's reddening face and then kneed him in the back to move him forward.

Oh, how I wanted to lunge at him, to fly at his slab of a face and dig my nails into his flesh. But I was spun around and pushed on. The door was opened and we went through and then immediately down. It was dark. The only light came from the beginnings of the day outside. There were narrow steps and I sensed cobwebs brushing against us. The light dwindled the further down we went.

Down we went. There was a strange damp smell. Earthy. Stagnant water. Dust. I blinked rapidly, fearfully, trying to make sense of the space around me. We were all pushed up together in a small space at the end of the steps. I heard keys. Metal. Our scared, laboured breathing. Something shuffling, feet dragging. A whimper.

Then suddenly a ball of light. The Governor lit a candle and our faces were illuminated. Mine and Ned's, staring and pale, our eyes huge. The guards, strangely resolute, hardened, accepting. And Soren Lancaster's. Proud. Triumphant. Knowing. He opened a metal door and we were pushed through.

Beneath our feet the floor was wet and cold. I could feel the damp musty air clinging to my shins and my wrists and my neck, and I had an urge to shake it away, to shake myself out. To be free of it. The metal door closed behind us by Saul. No one spoke.

We were in another small space. I could feel cold brick walls on either side, my elbows spiking them as we were pushed along, following the ball of light carried by the Governor. The ceiling was low and his head was bent on his shoulders. Silence now apart from the ragged terror that drew through our nostrils. Ned and I. Pushed along, for what felt like forever. A right turn and another narrow corridor. Wet walls. A rotten smell. Another hopeless whimper. Every hair on my body standing on end. I wanted to open my mouth and say something to them. I wanted to say stop, please stop, what are you doing to us? This has gone far enough. This must be a joke. But I was afraid to even open my mouth, afraid of what might come rushing up from my guts, threatening to consume me. So, I bit my lips and sucked air through my nostrils and on we went with no one speaking.

We turned another corner and finally stopped. My feet were freezing. There was no natural light. I heard keys jangling and I peered around the Governor to see another metal door. A jail cell. Not just one, but three. Lined up in a row. Each perfectly square. Each with no window, no light, no air. Each with nothing inside it except a bucket. My mouth hung open now, desperate for air. It inhaled for me, bringing up my ribs rapidly before releasing them again in a frenzied panic. But each breath was not enough. Each breath only served to frighten the next one.

The Governor unlocked one cell, and then another. We were forced towards them, Ned and I, and it was only then, in the ball of light created by one stubby candle that I saw that I was wrong. The cells contained more than just a bucket. One contained Connor. And another contained Charlie.

36: Prisoners

Three cells. Connor sat in one with his back to the far wall. His hands dangled limply between his knees. His face looked white and his eyes seemed huge gazing blankly back at us. I could not tear my eyes away from the bright red gash across his forehead. Ned was un-cuffed and shoved into the cell beside his. The Governor slammed the door and locked it with a long silver key. Charlie looked pathetic. Skinnier than ever and weak and wobbly as he got up from the floor and staggered up to the cell door. Finally, I found my voice.

'Charlie! What have you done to him? I thought he was dead!'

'Hmm,' the Governor said, his tone curious. 'Couldn't make my mind up about it. Been putting it off. Wondering how I can make use of the thing. Anyway, in you go. Say hello to your old friend.'

Deputy Bradshaw un-cuffed me, and pushed me forward into the cell. I slipped down to my knees and plunged my hands into Charlie's greasy, matted fur. He remembered me. He stuck his nose into my ear and splashed his tongue across my lips. I felt the tears filling my eyes and tumbling down my cheeks. The cell door slammed and locked, and there we all were. Connor, Ned, Charlie and me. And on the other side the Governor, his face dead, no expression there at all.

'Leave us for now,' he said over his shoulder, and off they shuffled, his men and his terrible son. My shoulders dropped. My backside hit the floor and Charlie sagged against me, his sides heaving, his ribs digging into my leg. I pulled him onto my lap, resting my face on his head, trying to offer him comfort. In the cell beside me

Ned remained at the door.

'Will you tell our parents?' he asked in a dull voice which echoed eerily around the dark, dank space we'd been hoarded into. The Governor flicked his hand at his suit, as if the very air offended him. His expression still blank, he did not look at Ned as he replied;

'My next stop. I will tell them in person of course.' He placed his hands behind his back. 'No doubt they will be destroyed.'

'This has never happened before,' said Ned. 'They won't stand for it.'

'They'll have to,' Soren Lancaster replied with a yawn. 'It's not me, Ned. It's the law. You are adults now and you have broken the law.'

'How?'

'Do you really need me to explain it to you?'

'Yes! We read a book! We found the truth!' Ned was angrier than I had ever seen him. His hands now curled around the bars of the cell. His face pressed against it, his breath coming hard and fierce.

'You've been talking to people on the outside,' replied the Governor, placidly. 'And that's just one of your crimes. Plotting to overthrow the government of Province 5 is the biggest crime you can be tried for. And you're right, no one has ever broken the rules like this. This has never happened before.'

'We didn't know there were people out there,' Ned went on. 'No one ever told us! We've broken rules we didn't know existed!'

The Governor merely raised his eyebrows.

'What happens to us?' I asked, staring up at him from the floor. I could already feel the damp clinging to my clothes. My skin started to shiver. I glanced across at Ned and Connor, and the lack of blankets, and felt guilty that at least I would have Charlie to cuddle up with. The Governor looked rather bored, examining his nails and removing dirt from them.

'Tomorrow evening I will allow you and Ned to see your parents, one at a time, up in my office. You will have just a few minutes to say goodbye to them.'

'What about Connor?' asked Ned, still clinging to the bars of his door, his eyes burning into our jailor. 'You can't just keep him here for no reason!'

'There is a reason,' the Governor replied calmly. 'He and his party attacked our delivery convoy last night with bows and arrows. And if I were you Ned, I would be careful about what you say. Every word you utter furthers the case against you. You knew of the rebels and yet you did nothing to warn us? You let your own people be attacked.' He shook his head in mock sorrow.

Connor sniffed from his cell. 'No one attacked you, you liar,' he sneered, barely lifting his head. 'I was all alone. Minding my own business. You just needed another reason to boost your propaganda.'

The Governor cleared his throat and waved a hand dismissively. 'You'll all have your chance to be heard. You will all be given a fair trial. That is how things work. Of course, I can't promise your defence team will be up to much. No one has had any practice of this you see! Well, certainly not from this Province anyway. There are always little skirmishes in the larger Provinces.'

'People who want to leave, you mean,' snarled Connor. 'We've got a few who made it. They didn't like the way things were going. They wanted to be free.'

Governor Lancaster narrowed his eyes at Connor. 'Hmm, if you're talking about certain scavengers, then I can assure you, action has been taken. We will not be made fools of. I have not announced it to the people yet, but the scavenger position is no longer needed. The job is obsolete.'

'What are you *talking* about?' Ned shook his head violently. The Governor rolled his eyes.

'No time to discuss it all now, young man. I've got places to be, people to see.'

'We'll tell our parents everything,' declared Ned, his chin up, his eyes blazing. 'They'll tell the whole place. You'll have an uprising on your hands!'

'Oh dear,' Soren chuckled in response. 'You really have been spending too much time with the Turners! Uprising, you say? What do these people have to rise up against Ned? Jobs? Food? Water? Homes? Oh no! How terribly they are treated! I ought to be scared!'

'You're a liar and a bully,' Ned growled back at him. 'And the truth will come out, we'll make sure of it!'

'Well, we'll see about that.' The Governor lowered the candle down to the floor and then stood straight, with one hand rummaging around in his back pocket. We watched him silently, wonderingly. Charlie whined and buried his nose in my arms. 'Ah, what have we here?' He had something in his hand. It looked like a flower, and something else, a biscuit? I looked at Ned and his shadowy face
324

looked back at me, not understanding. 'Oh come here boy,' the Governor said cooingly, crouching down in front of my cell. He slapped his thigh and held out the biscuit and the flower.

'What are you doing?' Ned asked. Connor sat up, watching intently.

'Oh come here boy, you must be hungry!'

Charlie caught a whiff of the biscuit, and in a shot, he tore himself from my lap and threw himself at the bars. His ragged tail beat back and forth, and thick drool ran from his lips. He was starving and desperate. The Governor held back the biscuit and showed him the flower. The dog snatched it and swallowed it whole. He then backed up a bit, confused and unsatisfied. Smiling widely, Soren threw him the biscuit and he caught it and gobbled it in one.

'There's a boy!' he said, before dusting off his hands and standing back up. He left the candle on the floor and I wondered if it would be our only light.

'What was that?' Ned demanded. 'What have you done?'

But Soren Lancaster did not answer him. Instead, he laced his hands behind his back and grinned at the dog. I looked at Charlie and saw right away that something was wrong. The drool ran from his mouth so fast that he looked like he was leaking. It frothed around his jaws, and the more he licked it the more it foamed. He vomited. Once. Twice. A third and then a fourth time while we all looked on in horror. And then he collapsed.

I moved to him, grabbing him and yanking him back onto my lap. His eyes rolled up into his head. His tongue was twisting. His sides heaved violently. I looked up.

'What have you done?' I screamed. 'What have you done to him?'

Connor was on his feet now and at the bars to his cell, just like Ned.

'Poison!' he cried out. 'He poisoned him!'

'No!' I was screaming now, crying, hugging him to me, but I could already feel that it was too late. His eyes never rolled back down again. His sides stopped heaving and his heart stopped beating. It was that fast.

'You're evil!' Ned shout. 'Evil!'

There was nothing I could do. I held him to me and shook him and pleaded with him not to die, but it was too late, he had gone, that quick. That fast. Seconds! I buried my face in his greasy fur and wailed.

'No! Why did you do that to him? Why did you do that?'

'Call it a demonstration,' the Governor answered, tilting his head to one side. 'Also, an interesting experiment. I've been feeding him various flowers for weeks now. Looks like I finally hit the jackpot.'

'Murder!' Connor yelled.

'Murderer!' Ned joined in. 'You didn't have to do that!'

I held Charlie, begging him to fight back, begging it not to be real. But he had gone. He was soft and floppy. I looked up at the Governor with tears streaming from my eyes.

'Why? Why?'

He rolled his eyes as if we were boring him. 'A demonstration Lissie. Of how easily I can rid myself of problems.' He raised one eyebrow at me and then winked. And then I knew. It hit me so hard I could not breathe. I opened my mouth but the words wouldn't come out, because they were too big, too monstrous, and they were stuck in my chest and in my throat.

Grandma Elizabeth.

'No...' said Ned, and I looked at him and he saw it in my eyes and he remembered what I said. The petal on the floor. The flower petal.

The shock was too much. I wanted to lie down. I wanted to curl up. I couldn't do it. I couldn't fight this man! I couldn't even look at him! I didn't even want to believe in him!

Knowing I was wrecked, the Governor turned his attention to Ned. 'When it comes to your parents, you have a decision to make. Your mothers are both carrying children. I would think very carefully if I were you, about what you tell them. Perhaps just tell them you are sorry?'

'You *killed* her...' Ned was saying it for me, but even his voice was gasping and strangled. 'Lissie's great-grandmother. You did it.'

'She was a problem I should have sorted out long ago. But for a long time, she was silent and good. I think in the end old age destroyed her mind. She got tangled up in the past. Not her fault. I bear no grudge. Now, her interfering daughter Bessie was another matter altogether!'

Bessie?

The Tree of Rebels

My grandmother.

The breath was knocked from me again. My stomach cramped and I had to lean away from Charlie's body to be sick.

'You killed her too?' Ned talking for me.

The Governor exhaled noisily in amusement. 'Well, no, not me personally. I was just a child, of course. About the same age Saul is now. I watched though. Imagine that!' He gave a sick little giggle while we watched on in utter horror. 'I mean, I'm not sure you could even say my father *killed* her. She was in the hospital anyway, you see. She was very ill. And she *had* been warned. She was very meddlesome. Probably not her fault either really. Her mother would have been poisoning her mind from birth just like she poisoned Lissie's. She was a feisty one though, Lissie. You remind me of her!'

I wiped my mouth and stared at the ground. I couldn't look at him. I couldn't...

'Murderer,' whispered Ned. 'And none of them know....'

'No, none of them.' He sounded smug, I thought. Self-satisfied and proud of his work. 'I keep a tight ship. Things are known on a need to know basis. Like my guards, you see. They know that there are dangerous armed rebels out there and that there always have been.' He shot a cold-eyed look at Connor. 'The guards watch out for them. Hunt them down if they can. In order to protect the good people, we serve and watch over. And they know that every now and again descendants of these rebels get silly ideas in their heads and need to be watched too. Most of the time these things fizzle out. Sometimes we have to get heavy handed.' He shrugged. 'Part of the job I am afraid. My father and grandfather, and his father before him all helped prepare me of course.'

'It's all lies...' murmured Ned. 'Everything. Everything they do and say and think. It's all lies. It was your people that started the wars in the first place. You destroyed most of the world in order to win. In order to keep control. Isn't that right?'

'You've got it Ned,' Connor said from behind him. 'That's exactly what happened.'

'Well, anyway,' the Governor was backing off now, his hands behind his back, his smile intact. 'I think we'll leave it there for now. I haven't got time for a history lesson. You've got a big day in front of you. Best get some rest. And remember, both of you,' he stopped and looked back at Ned and I. 'When you say goodbye to your parents, remember what happened to the dog? Yes?'

We didn't answer him. We looked on in shock and hate and fear. He smiled and then he was gone, leaking back into the shadows, shuffling down the corridor away from us.

We were left there in the dark.

Connor turned slowly and walked back to the wall, where he slumped down and took up his previous position.

'Monster,' he muttered, before falling silent. I looked once at Ned, but it was too much to bear. I buried my face in Charlie's fur and started to cry.

37: Waiting

For the longest time, none of us spoke. Connor sat against the wall, his head hanging, his arms folded on top of his knees. Ned remained standing at the bars to his cell. It was as if he could not bear to turn around and look at it, as if once he did that, it would all become real. His fingers were curled around the bars. His eyes flitted from me to Connor, never settling.

It all ran through my head, so fast and hard that I could not bear it. Poor Charlie, locked up there in the dark, so scared and alone, so hungry that he ate poison! And Grandma Elizabeth's last moments...with him, *him*! Leaning over her bed, pressing the petal to her lips. I could not bear it. How was I to bear it?

And Bessie...my mother's mother. They'd always said Bessie died of a chest infection when she was twenty-six years old. She suffered badly from asthma and could not fight back. My mother was a two-year-old child. She never knew her own mother. Maybe she'd had her own suspicions? And what about Grandma Elizabeth? Did she know the truth about Bessie's death? Did she keep quiet to keep my mother safe? My mind was racing and spinning; I thought of the flowers, I thought of my duties for the Governor. Did the deadly flower grow there? Right under my nose? Perhaps all along he'd been plotting to kill me too…

The candle was going out.

Oh no. *No*!

It flickered. Some unseen draught playing with our only source of light. I watched it with eyes wide and fearful. Charlie's body hardening on my lap. The flame danced and then it went out. Blackness swamped us instantly. I took a deep breath and began to cry again.

'Don't cry Lissie...' Ned said in the darkness. His voice shook. I could not see him anymore. My eyes were wide open and staring but I could not see a single thing.

'Your eyes will adjust in a minute,' Connor called out from his corner. 'Just hang on. Don't panic.'

'She's probably in shock!' Ned cried out uselessly. 'What that man just did!'

'They're all like it,' said Connor darkly. 'They train them to be. We try to avoid them like the plague. Ha, *us* attacking *them*? No way. That's mad! We stay away!'

'What will happen?' Ned asked him, his voice trembling. 'What happens at these trials?'

'Not much from what I hear. It all happens in Province 1. That's where they'll take us as soon as they can.'

'Will they lock us up there? Kill us? What?'

Ned was veering close to panic. He was still at the gate, hanging on. I stayed sat on the cold wet ground, holding Charlie for warmth. But there would not be warmth for much longer. He would grow stiff and cold.

'I don't know for sure,' said Connor. 'Just try not to panic.'

'We might be killed, but don't panic?'

'Panicking won't help, is all I'm saying. Sit yourself down and take some deep breaths. This is all designed to mess with your mind, you know. The cells, the dark and the cold. No blankets. No food.'

'They can't treat people like this,' Ned mused. I could hear him moving now, heeding Connor's advice and sliding slowly down the bars so that he was also sat on the ground. 'It's freezing in here,' he said, teeth chattering. 'I might just have to keep talking to stop myself panicking. I hope you guys don't mind.'

'Good idea,' Connor told him. 'You carry on. I'll do the same. Lissie? How you doing over there? You're not alone okay? We're right here. Right here.'

'Shuffle over to the bars,' said Ned. 'Come and lean against me. We can keep each other warm. Lissie?'

I wasn't sure I could answer. My throat hurt so much. I pressed my face one last time against Charlie's fur, before pushing him slowly from my lap. I was still sobbing quietly. My chest hitching and my stomach lurching every time. I crawled away from Charlie, away from his cloying vomit and I reached out for Ned, clawing at the bars.

'Shh,' he said softly, finding me, wrapping his hands around my wrists and pulling me closer. We pushed our arms through the bars and clung to each other. 'Sorry Connor,' he said with a little chuckle. 'We've got a hug thing going on here. If you get too cold just shout, and I'll come over your side and give you a turn!'

Connor laughed in reply. 'I'll survive. Got warmer threads than you guys. You hold on. Hold onto each other. That's the other thing they want, you know. If they can turn you against each other, get one of you to crack, then they've won.'

'We know,' Ned sighed sadly, his cold cheek protruding

through the gap in the bars and pressing against mine. 'We read the rest of the diary last night. This guy Lawrence? He was set up by some people. They turned him in and got him killed. Maybe the same thing happened to Bessie? What happened to your mother's father, Lissie? Who was he? Do you know?'

I sniffed. 'He was called George. They said he was so distraught about her death that he killed himself. That's why Grandma Elizabeth brought my mother up as her own. She had no one else.'

'Hmm,' Ned growled, tightening his grip on me. 'How do we know any of that is true? The Governor probably did something to him too!'

'All I know is these people are crazy,' Connor spoke up. 'Crazy for power. They got it and they don't want to ever let it go.'

'And it's really the same people? I mean, the people who started the wars back then?'

'Oh yeah. Yeah, yeah. The people in charge, whoever they were, probably spread right around the world, eh? They knew where to hide when it all kicked off. Near the domes for one thing. Major cities for another. That's why all the Provinces are where they are. No accident. They were built up on the remains of the biggest cities. The bastards survived, mostly. Passed the power onto their offspring. No elections, see? What they wanted all along I guess.'

'And they make out we are so lucky...' Ned said softly. 'They go on and on about it from the moment you are born. *So* lucky. Born into Peace. No more war. Not ever again.'

'They got no one to fight!' Connor laughed. 'They're in charge. Got the reins on you guys. Happy days!'

'He said there were sometimes problems in the bigger Provinces...'

'Guess there's bound to be. Bigger populations. More room for disquiet, I suppose. More chance of rumours spreading before they get shut down. More chance of people wondering how else things can work, maybe?'

'More people like Grandma Elizabeth,' I muttered into Ned's cheek. He shuddered against me.

'What are we going to do, Connor?' he called back over his shoulder. 'When we're taken up to see our parents?'

Connor exhaled sadly in the darkness behind us. 'It's up to you, kids. I don't know. He could be bluffing about hurting them, I suppose. How would he explain your disappearances and their deaths? But would that stop him? You know him better than me.'

'We don't know him at all,' Ned growled. 'I used to think he was...He was...He's like a god or something, Connor! They worship him!'

'I used to think he was nice,' I said, pulling my face away as the cold bars numbed my skin. 'Nicer than his rancid son anyway.'

'Ugh, did you see his face Lissie? He was loving it. So, he's known all along. His whole life he's known the score. Unbelievable.'

'And the flower garden,' I reminded him. 'Why did the Governor let me see it? All the time I couldn't work it out...couldn't understand why he would pick *me*...'

'Hold on, what flower garden?' Connor asked.

'He has this secret, private garden,' I replied, my teeth chattering as I spoke. 'Up there somewhere. We never knew. No one is allowed to grow anything you see. No one ever has. You've seen it. Just dust. But we have these duties you see...'

'Duties?'

'Jobs,' I tried to explain, realising that Ned was right to keep us all talking. It was taking my mind away from poor Charlie behind me. 'When you turn fourteen you leave school and home and get a job. Usually the same or similar job to your parents, but before that, before you're fourteen, you do these duties for people. Like job experience I suppose. To see what you're good at and earn yourself some tokens.'

'Tokens? Like money?'

'Yes, you can save them up and exchange them for things. Anyway, I was given duties at the Governor's office, up there. It was a bit of a surprise, but now I get it all right. He was keeping tabs on me and my family, wasn't he? Seeing if I was anything like Bessie?'

I could feel Ned nodding against me. 'It's like he was testing you. Showing you the flower garden to see how you would react. Keep quiet or demand to know more.'

'What about these flowers then?' Connor prompted us. 'They're the same ones he just finished Charlie off with?'

My heart lurched at the mention of him. I closed my eyes tightly, squeezing out the last of my tears. 'Poisonous,' I hissed. 'Maybe all of them. Maybe that's the whole purpose of them!'

'Poor Charlie,' said Ned, wistfully. His hands were right around me, laced together at the small of my back. I had my arms around his shoulders. I was not sure who was shaking the most. 'All that time we thought he was dead. We thought they'd killed him.'

'Aisha really loved that mutt,' said Connor. 'Not that he was good for much. Not the brightest one we've had.'

'He must have been so scared and alone and cold down here...' I glanced back, just once. I could just make out his still, shaggy form.

'Connor, tell us about out there,' Ned announced suddenly, lifting his head. 'Tell us what it's like. Where do you live? How do you live?'

Connor shuffled in the blackness, changing his position. 'We live off the land,' he told us softly, and I pictured his eyes glazing over as he imagined where he came from. 'We're born under the stars. We shelter in tents, wagons, dens, whatever is needed, whatever comes to hand. Over the years my family and Aisha's have set up camps in various places. You know, places we can head back to. Places where we know what grows. But in between we wander.'

'You don't want to stay still?' I wondered. 'Build houses and make homes?'

'No,' he said with a sad shudder. 'Not really. The people before us, they never thought that was safe. Once they knew about the Provinces and the domes and the power in place, they decided to stay clear, stay away. It's been drummed into us for years. They are the enemy.'

'So what were you doing so close to here?' asked Ned. 'Why was Charlie there that day? And Aisha?'

'We've had people go missing before,' Connor explained

gently. 'People not turn up where we expect them to. People who go off hunting and never come back.'

'Like you, now?' I asked.

'Yeah. Like me now. There's been disquiet about that, you know. Unrest. What do we do? Allow our loved ones to be picked off one by one? Or try to find out what is happening to them?'

'You were sent here, like scouts?' I sat taller now, my coldness and fear almost forgotten.

'Yeah. Kind of. Me and Aisha sometimes. Sometimes others. Just looking, you know. Hunting and gathering, and nosying I suppose. My brother Tate went missing from near here about a year ago. So...you know. I might get to see him now, eh?'

'Oh my god,' said Ned. 'It just gets worse.'

'They want to gather you up, one by one,' I said then, a cold chill crawling down my spine. 'Get rid of the enemy once and for all. Then the rumours will stop inside the Provinces. People won't want to get out if there is no one there to get to.'

It all made a horrible and ghastly sense, and we fell quiet. I wondered if my parents had been told yet. I wondered how hard it would be for my mother to keep the fire out of her eyes when he told her what had happened to me. I wondered what my father would choose to believe. Down here, it seemed impossible that life carried on up there without us. It was like we had already been banished. Buried alive. Wiped out. I started thinking about all the other people who may have shared these cells before us. The lies just went on and on.

And we sat like that not knowing what time had passed. With

337

no light and no sound, we had no way of telling what time of day it was. I wondered if this place was designed to make people disappear and the fear took hold of me all over again. What if they didn't come back? What if they didn't tell our parents they took us? What if no one knew and no one came? We would sit here like this forever, dying and then rotting. No one would know. I had to bite my lip to stop myself from screaming.

At some point Ned fell into a fitful sleep against the bars. And then some other nameless time after that, I did the same. I only knew this because it was the light and the noise that woke me up. The door at the end of the corridor was pushed open and as we all stood on our wobbly legs, rubbing our eyes, we saw a circle of light coming our way.

Ned slid his hand towards mine and I took it thankfully. As the light got closer, Connor got to his feet and came to the front of his cell, wrapping each hand around the bars and watching curiously as our worshipped leader reappeared. Governor Lancaster was alone.

'Just you, Miss Turner,' he announced primly. 'Aren't you the lucky one? Ned's parents couldn't bear it, you know. His mother took a funny turn.'

Ned leapt at the bars instantly, pressing his face through them. 'What did you do to her? What did you do!'

'She fainted Ned,' Soren replied cooly, barely giving him a glance. 'The shock and the shame no doubt. You only have yourself to blame. We had her admitted to the hospital where she is being looked after. Your father is with her. We said he could still see you but he declined.'

Ned drew back, his arms falling to his sides, his head slowly dropping.

'Probably lies, Ned,' I told him quickly. 'You know we can't believe a word this man says.'

'Oh Miss Turner, shush now. We don't have much time. Come along.' He was at the door and unlocking the cell. I didn't know what to do suddenly. I had a moment of freedom, a chance? To do what? Run at him? Try to overpower him? I looked him up and down, considering it. He seemed to sense this and laughed softly.

'I'd think about poor Mrs. Fleck if I were you, Lissie,' he advised, before crooking a finger and beckoning me out. 'You'll come quietly or she'll be delivered a very special bouquet of flowers before the night is done.'

'You leave her alone!' Ned yelled then, back at the bars suddenly, his teeth gleaming in the candlelight. 'You better not touch her!'

But it was no use, because the Governor only had eyes for me. He took my elbow and led me out of the cell and down the corridor towards the door at the end.

'You'll see your mother,' he said to me then. 'And I hope you make the right decision here Lissie. I really do. So many lives may depend on it...'

I looked up at him and his face was yellowed by the light, and he was smiling.

38: A Mother's Tears

He was still smiling when we reached the end of the corridor. Instead of turning right, which was the way we came in this morning, we turned left. There was another door, which he unlocked with another key. There was a brief, breathless moment when he let go of my elbow to turn the key, but I did not move. I could not move. My limbs had turned to jelly. My body so full of fear and anger crashing about inside of me, that I couldn't seem to function. It all felt so unreal. I really, truly started to wonder if I was dreaming. If maybe all of it was just a dream?

With the door unlocked, he took my arm again, and pushed me slightly ahead of him. We started to go up a very steep and narrow staircase. It dawned on me that we were now above ground level again, and climbing higher. I wanted to say something to him, but my throat wouldn't work properly. I tried coughing and clearing my throat, but it did nothing. I just couldn't find the words to say. It was madness. All of it was madness, and surely not real?

Governor Lancaster and I walked up the stairs, turned left, and walked up more stairs. As we got higher, natural light returned and he blew out the candle. I tried to imagine how he might be feeling. Was he scared of what I might say, or do? Or had he got it all worked out? Because nothing ever seemed to ruffle him, did it? Nothing ever seemed to get under his skin. He wore that same cool, knowing expression on his face all the time. And then my throat forced something out at him.

'You're a monster. And none of them know it.'

He glanced down at me with a calm smile tugging at his lips. 'You see things in black and white Lissie, when really things are rather more grey.'

'What is that supposed to mean?'

We went through another door and came out somewhere I recognised. The hallway right outside the door to his office. He pushed it open and guided me inside. I held my breath, expecting to see them there, but it was empty. He shut the door, keeping a firm hold of my arm.

'Miss Harper will bring your mother up.'

'Why just her? And what do you mean, things are grey?'

He moved his tongue around the inside of his mouth as if searching for some piece of food he had lost. Then he tilted his head towards me, drawing me into his secrets.

'There are governors like me in charge all over the place,' he explained. 'And we follow orders. It's as simple as that. It's the way things work. I tried to explain that to you once, but you didn't want to listen. I tried to tell you that things can and *will* change, in time. But you chose not to believe me.'

I could hardly believe what I was hearing. I pulled my arm free of his and stepped away from him. I didn't want to be any nearer to him than I had to be.

'You're trying to make excuses for yourself! You can't try and convince me now Governor! It's too late!'

'Too late to listen to reason, Lissie? Yes, you are probably right.'

'You didn't have to do that to Charlie!' I spat at him hatefully. 'You didn't have to keep him down there like that!'

'Oh so we're back to the animal, are we?' He stroked his chin in amusement. 'It's very strange to me how attached you are to it.'

'You're not just following orders,' I told him in disgust. 'And if it were just that it would be bad enough. But you're enjoying this. I can tell.'

'Hmm.' He walked past me with his hand linked behind his back. 'There may be some truth in that. I must say; I have been watching you for a long time to see if I had anything to be concerned about. Your mother gave us no joy, for example. She's no Bessie, is she? A bit of a disappointment to the old woman I should have thought.'

'Been looking forward to the chance of a bit of action?' I snarled, backing away further. 'Looking forward to locking people up? Sacrificing them like your ancestors did to Lawrence?'

'Yes, maybe you have a point, Lissie. Who can blame me? Life is so ordinary here, don't you find? The same routine day in day out. Who can blame a man for feeling excited when things are shaken up a bit?'

'You make no sense. Things are shaken up all right, but now you're going to stamp us out. No one will know and it will all go back to normal. That will be a disappointment for you, won't it?'

The Governor lifted his hands and dropped them in amused exasperation. 'At the end of the day Lissie, I have my position to consider. Obviously, I enjoy my standing and I intend my son to enjoy it too. I must follow orders. There are bigger people than me at play,
342

you know.'

'You don't scare me,' I informed him, and in that moment, it was true. He did not scare me when I saw him like this. He was too much like his son. Power hungry and yet somehow weakened by it.

'I may not,' he agreed with a wink, as we heard urgent footsteps coming along the hallway towards the door. 'In fact perhaps once you arrive at Province 1 you will look back on me fondly and wish you had taken all the chances I offered you.'

I glared at him, outraged. There was a timid knock at the door. 'Governor? Sir? Mrs. Turner is here.'

'Let her in.'

At once the door opened, and in she ran. I had expected fear, reluctance, caution, but there was none of this. Just my mother, Bessie's child, running at me. Her arms wrenching me forward into her body. Her chin on my head, her heart against mine. And he walked to the door and looked back at us.

'You have ten minutes. I will be right outside the door.'

When the door closed, my mother pulled back, took my chin with her thumb and forefinger and tipped my face up to hers.

'Oh Lissie...' It was all she could say before the desperate tears consumed her. I sensed that I must take control.

'We don't have long,' I said, staring into her eyes. 'Remember all of the things your mother and her mother told you. And so will I. There have *always* been people who say no. There have always been those that rebel. There *always* will be.'

She shook her head while her eyes leaked and her hands clawed at my shoulders.

'No, this can't be happening. He can't take you! Your father is in bits... The whole Province is in shock... He called a meeting earlier today in the square. It was compulsory to attend!'

'What did he say?'

'That rebels had attacked the delivery convoy and tried to steal food and kill. One was caught and is under guard here until he is taken to central Government tonight. He said you and Ned were helping them, aiding them! On their side! Trying to overthrow him! Everyone is in such a panic, Lissie!'

'It was a boy called Connor,' I told her. 'He was picked up by them, Mum. Attacked and brought here. He did nothing wrong. They took his brother a year ago. The rebels Gran told us about, Mum, they are still out there. They mean no harm! They don't want to overthrow anyone. They just want to be left alone.'

She found my hands and took them into hers. 'Hilda is in the hospital...'

'I know. He told me. He will kill her, Mum, he will kill you too, so you have to pretend and keep it up, okay?'

'I can't let them take you...'

'You have to. Listen to me. You have to walk out of here sobbing and apologising to him. Apologise for me and ask to be kept updated about my trial.'

'Lissie...'

'No. Listen, Mum.' I gripped her hands back, my face against hers now, my urgent words whispered into her waiting ear. 'You walk out of here like you believe him. Like I am guilty and you are sorry. Hang your head in shame wherever you go. Don't let anyone see the fire in your eyes. Promise me!'

'But why? What can you do? What should we do?'

'I don't know yet...But I have faith in Grandma Elizabeth and somehow whenever I don't know what to do, she always seems to be there in my head.'

My mother sighed a smile against my cheek, her tears running down our faces. 'I always said you two had a special connection.'

'It must be true. That's how it feels anyway. I want to go with them, Mum. Ned and Connor and me. We'll go peacefully. I'll finally get to leave this place like I wanted!'

'But not like this Lissie, not like this. You don't know what they are capable of! No one does!'

'I want to see the world out there. Even if it is just once. For the last time.'

'Don't say that!'

'Just have faith,' I told her, pulling my hand free and wiping away her tears. 'Okay? We'll be all right. I promise you that. You can believe that.'

'I feel like I've let you down, Lissie...' Her eyes fell away from mine.

'No, you haven't. You did what you had to do to keep us all

345

safe. Just like Grandma Elizabeth did back then when they took her Lawrence. She had Bessie to think of so she kept quiet and kept safe. You know all this, don't you?'

She nodded slowly. 'Whispered to me by my mother. And then my grandmother. Harlan knows some of it Lissie but he chooses not to believe. He believes in this place. In Everlasting Peace. His parents taught him to...he can't help it.'

'I know he can't, Mum. It's all right. Not his fault. Just go along with it for now.'

'I don't know if I can...I might never see you again!' She started to cry fresh tears all over again. I pull her face onto my chest and hold her tight.

'Just sit tight,' I tell her. 'Just stay calm. Think of the baby.'

A fresh burst of sobs erupted from her. 'But you're my baby...you're my baby, Lissie!'

It was no good after that. I couldn't say any more to her, or her to me. We just held each other tight and she sobbed against me. For some reason, I remained dry eyed. Perhaps it was because as she sobbed I was mostly thinking about him, on the other side of the door. I was thinking about his cool eyes and his thin smile and his hands linked casually behind his back. And I was thinking about Charlie, cold and scared and hungry in the dark. Charlie, writhing and dying in pain.

I held my mother and stroked her hair back and thought about all of this. I didn't understand where my courage came from, but I knew I was right about Grandma Elizabeth. She'd always been there for me. That would not end with her death. With her murder.

346

The door reopened before either of us were ready. My mother pulled back slowly, her eyes begging me, but I shook my head at her and she nodded back at me.

'I'm sorry to interrupt,' the Governor said from the doorway. 'But I am afraid we have a schedule to keep, Mrs. Turner.'

She drew back, remembering what I said, patting my arm one last time before turning from me, with her head dropping low.

'It's all right sir,' she mumbled. 'I'll be on my way.'

'Of course,' he said smoothly, respectfully. 'Are you going to the hospital to visit Mrs. Fleck?'

'Yes,' she replied before him, her eyes to the floor. 'I am heading there now.'

'Please pass on my regards and let her know I will be in to visit her myself later.'

'I will. And I'm...' she trailed off, shuffling humbly past him and into the hallway. She looked back at me one last time and her breath hitched in her throat. And then she did exactly what she promised to do. She looked up at him and said; 'I am *so* sorry, Governor. So sorry for all of this...'

'You must not blame yourself, Beth,' he replied gently, brushing her shoulder with one limp hand. 'This is not down to you or Harlan. We all know that.'

'You'll make sure she is taken care of? Given a fair trial?'

'Of course. I will keep you updated about everything. I'm so sorry it must come to this. But you see how my hands are tied...'

347

She did not answer him. She merely sniffed her last tears, turned slowly and shuffled away. When she had gone, he strode quickly over to me, smiling a fresh, sweet smile.

'I hope you did the right thing, Miss Turner,' he said, snatching up my arm again. 'For all their sakes.'

'I expect you were listening, Governor. Did I do the right thing?'

'I heard nothing,' he said, frowning into my eyes. 'But I will soon know. I will be watching your parents very closely, Lissie. Now, let's go.'

And with that, he pulled me from the room.

39: Moving On

Seeing my mother did something to me. There was something alive and beating in my chest, fighting to get out. I could feel my heart going bang, bang, bang. With every thud, it seemed to be getting louder and fiercer. No fear any more. No fear. Holding my arm tightly, the Governor led the way back down the corridor. My top lip curled when I looked up at him.

'Back to my cell, is it?' I asked, my voice loud and booming down the hallway. A muscle in his cheek twitched and he hurried me on. 'Back down into the pitch black? Is it like that on purpose? Is it supposed to break us? Make us more afraid?'

He did not answer me, just gave a little roll of his shoulders and marched us on. His fingers, tight against my skin, were thrumming with electricity. I could feel it coming from him, whatever it was, nameless, intent. And he could feel it coming from me. Fire in my veins.

We arrived at the other stairs, the ones I never knew existed, and he started dragging me down them, his feet flying faster than mine. The anger was in us both. Equal. Trembling. At war. I tried to yank my arm back, away from him, but he held on tighter.

'Why the dark and cold?' I demanded, as our feet clattered down, away from the light. 'What's that about? Do they make you do that? Is that in the rule book? Keep prisoners in the dark and cold? Is that what they tell you to do? Aren't we innocent until proven guilty by the trial? You can't treat innocent people like that!'

'I'm doing everything by the book, Miss Turner...' His voice was crushed by his teeth.

'Oh! Oh, I see, yes! Your rulebook! I never realised you were such a puppet, Governor!'

To this he yanked me back, pulling my arm up above my shoulder. 'You keep quiet girl! You keep your insults to yourself!'

I stared into his eyes and saw what I had done. I was not exactly sure how, or why. He was ruffled. His top lip quivered.

'Touched a nerve,' I told him softly. 'Always thought you were such a leader, a man of the people, lording it over everyone. Everyone's best friend. But you're not anything like that. A puppet for your masters! Dancing to their tune!'

His face loomed close to mine, his eyes bulging. 'You keep quiet. You don't push your luck, girl. Your little rebellion here is almost over. Not that it ever got started. Come on.' He walked on, hurrying down the stairs, hauling me with him. I laughed at him and kept laughing. I felt like I had found a thread and wanted to keep pulling at it. He had a wound, and I wanted to get a stick and poke it into his flesh.

'All your ancestors too,' I laughed, as we went down into the darkness. 'And next your son! Do you have to call them sir and madam? Do you have to bow to them? What happens if *you* break the rules, Governor? What happens then?'

'Unlike you and your kind I have no need to break the rules,' he grunted at me, fumbling in his back pocket for his candle and matches.

'My kind?'

'Troublemakers. Mean spirited meddlers. Never satisfied.

Never happy! Always want everything your own way, even when things are working just fine the way they are.' He dropped my arm to light the candle, but again I did not run. What I told my mother was true. I did want to get out of the Province and see the world beyond it. With the candle lit, he grabbed my arm and off we went again. 'You can't deny it works this way, Lissie,' he said into the darkness, and I detected the smile in his voice, the cool returning to his veins. They were words well known and well-rehearsed. They formed the lullaby that had sung us all to sleep for so long.

'Works for who?' I asked.

'Works for everyone! Tell me, who is badly treated? Who is unhappy? Everyone is provided for!'

I snorted in disgust. 'Everyone is asleep. At least you think they are. You *hope* they are.'

'What does that mean?'

'It means, how do you know Governor? How do you know who else feels like I do? How do you know who whispers in the night? How do you know there aren't more diaries written by the old and hidden by the young? How do you know this will be over?'

I'd got him now. I'd really got him. If I was lucky and clever and brave, maybe I would get all of them. Maybe, just maybe....

He chose that moment to fight me back, and if he couldn't fight my spirit than I guess he had to fight my body. His hand left my arm and seized my neck. The candle bobbed in and out of sight as I wrestled and struggled and punched back at the hand and the arm that held me. He held on tighter, squeezing my neck, crushing my throat, forcing my scream of protest back down into my guts. We went on like

351

that. Him and me. Dancing our violent dance through the dark and back towards the unknown cells. The cold was back there waiting for me. Clinging wetly to my legs. Settling on my hair.

'Oi, hands off her!' Connor started yelling from back there.

'Get your hands off her!' Ned too. 'I'll kill you!'

Under the hand, past my crushed throat, I laughed. I laughed at him and his lack of control. I laughed at him and the seeds of doubt I had settled into his mind. I laughed at all of them and everything they stood for.

Unceremoniously I was slung into my cell. My knees hit the cold wet floor, and finally my laughter was released. He slammed the door on me, and pointed a finger.

'You'll be made to regret everything, Lissie Turner!' he hissed through the bars. 'Soon enough! You will regret everything!'

He turned and left, taking the light with him.

I crawled to the bars to find Ned, coughing and sucking up air, and reaching out blindly for him. He found my hands and pulled me towards him.

'You okay? Lissie!'

'What happened up there?' Connor demanded from behind. 'What set him off like that? He's a bloody madman!'

'Got under his skin, I guess,' I replied, rubbing at my neck with one hand, whilst holding onto Ned with the other. 'Wondered if I could make him tick...really wasn't hard...he didn't like what I was saying!'

'Why, what did you say?' asked Connor.

'Just that he's a puppet for the people in charge. Follows their rules and orders. He didn't like that one bit!'

'Well it's true!' exclaimed Ned. 'That's exactly what he is!'

'And I warned him that it might not be as easy as he thinks to snuff out rebellion.'

Ned gasped. 'What?'

'Just planted the idea in his head. It's something he needs to think about! Just because he shuts us up doesn't mean it's over!'

'Way to go, Lissie!' laughed Connor, clapping his hands. I grinned in the darkness. My neck hurt and my heart ached for my parents, but then I thought about the Governor losing control, and pushed that all away.

'How was your mum?' Ned asked me softly. I thought for a moment about his own mum in the hospital and his father refusing to come. I rubbed his hand with my thumb.

'She was okay. Upset, but she listened to me. He left us alone for a few minutes.'

'What did she say? What's going on out there?'

'He called a meeting this morning in the square. Told them rebels had attacked the food convoy, and one was caught. And that you and me had been helping them. Making contact and feeding them information because we were trying to overthrow the Governor.'

Ned blew his breath out slowly. 'Wow. So, now they all know there are others out there? Beyond the fence?'

'Yeah. They're all in a panic, Mum says. He filled them all with fear. Of course, they all believe everything he says. He gets to ship us out of here and it's all over. All swept aside. Job done.'

'But what about your mother?' Connor asked.

'I told her to play along. No choice.'

'So when will they move us?' wondered Ned. 'How long are we stuck down here for now?'

'Nightfall,' Connor said instantly. 'Bet you anything you like. They'll move us when it's dark.'

'You'd think he'd want to parade us,' sniffed Ned bitterly. 'Show them what happens to people who break the rules!'

'Too risky,' I said. 'Some of the people might get twitchy. We were only kids just days ago and this wouldn't have been allowed. Better to do it unseen. Keep it all secretive. That's how they've got away with so much for so long...'

None of us spoke for a moment. My anger was still there, pulsing under my skin, but it had died back a bit, calmed down. The cold darkness wrapped itself around us and I could not help but think about poor Charlie lying in the shadows behind me. I swallowed and took deep breaths, and tried to stir the feeling up again, the feeling of the fire running through my veins. Inside my head I took up a silent chant for Grandma Elizabeth; no, no, no, no, NO.

I clung to Ned and he clung to me, and Connor breathed noisily behind us. My gut thrummed with fear and yet I was alive with excitement. How could that be? I closed my eyes and thought about Soren Lancaster's face. His muscles twitching. His shoulders rolling. What was he doing right now? What was he thinking? Did he know what would happen to us out there?

This thought brought me back to our predicament and our fate. A cold tremor clung to my spine. A terror clawed at me from the inside, reminding me of sacrifices and hangings. But I had to squash this down. I had to bat this away. I was finally going to leave the Province. I would get to see the outside world. Even if it was just a glimpse. Even if it was not for very long. Even if we were transferred somewhere worse than here, and tossed back down into darkness. I'd have it with me in my head.

I thought about Aisha and her beach, and I leaned against Ned and dozed...

I don't know how long any of us slept, but somehow we all did. We were woken up by the hairs that stood on end upon our necks and across our arms and down our legs. It was like being pricked by a pin all over. We shuddered from our dreams and faced the blackness once again.

'Someone is coming...' Connor whispered from his cell. And he was right. We strained our ears and sure enough there was the sound of footsteps coming down those stairs again. Next came the metallic clang and scrape of keys being turned and doors being opened. A short while later the candlelight bobbed along the narrow corridor towards us. Slowly, we eased ourselves up and onto our feet, Ned and I still with our hands linked.

The Governor came first. Behind him Saul, and three guards, all with their helmets on. All dressed in black and padded out and uniformed and somehow inhuman, terrifying. I looked into the Governor's face and saw that he was unsmiling. He looked all business.

'Time to go,' he told us calmly, and unlocked my door.

I pulled away from Ned and stumbled curiously towards the night. I wanted to say something to the him, but I didn't know what. What good would it do now? So, I just stared at him, and I guess something in my eyes must have said it all, for he looked down, and looked away.

'Put out your hands,' snapped Saul, stepping forward now. I immediately sensed his hunger. He buzzed with it. He could not wait to get started. To practice his skills. To hone his craft. I held out my hands and he snapped a pair of metal handcuffs onto my wrists. There was a long chain running through them, and he held the weight of this in his hands, before pushing me towards the other three guards.

The Governor was silent as he unlocked Ned's cell, and the same scene was repeated. Ned stepped out, offered his wrists, and was cuffed like me. The chain ran between us, and the final stretch of it was saved for Connor. He came sullenly from his cell and before the cuffs were placed on him he spat viciously into the Governor's face.

Immediately he was knocked down by Saul, battered at by the handcuffs and the chain, and then a shiny wooden baton that came down upon his shoulders and his back. He did not cry out, but curled up, covering his head. I gasped and looked at the Governor, who was slowly wiping the spit from his cheek.

'That's enough Saul,' he said to his son, and the beast was reined in for now, shut down. He straightened up and looked at his father.

Everyone seemed to be holding their breath. Wondering what he would do. He stepped forward, leaned down and stroked Connor's damp hair back from his head. The light from the candle illuminated the blood seeping from his hairline. For a bizarre moment, Soren Lancaster looked gentle and sorrowful, as he gazed into the young man's face. Connor stared back up at him, panting heavily.

'You can't help it,' he purred, looking sorry. 'It's how you were raised, poor thing. Out in the wild...without rules or order...poor, poor boy.'

And then the Governor's face changed. He displayed a face I had never seen before, and I thought I had seen many. This face was the face of an animal. His lips parted and the top lip curled into a snarl, and the saliva strung out between his teeth as if his rage was too much and he was choking and drowning on it. His hand stopped stroking Connor's hair, and instead gripped it, yanking him up to his feet by it, as he pushed his red raging face into his.

'Dirty, filthy, savage little animal, you will pay for that!' They were words hissed out through his clenched teeth, words barely audible, words throaty and guttural, conveying his hatred. 'I will wipe out every last one of you!'

Saul stepped forward and cuffed Connor's wrists together. He then swung his baton into his gut and down he went again.

'Stop it, you're killing him!' I cried out. 'You monsters!'

To this, Governor Lancaster threw back his head and laughed. He lifted one foot and placed it upon Connor's back. 'Well, isn't this a turning point for us all then? Hey? What do you think? Our masks have all slipped and here in the dark we are revealed.'

'Just leave him alone...' I muttered, my eyes on Connor, as he groaned and coughed and tried to get back on his feet. 'You've got

357

what you wanted. You've won. We're out of here.'

'Revealed to be evil,' Ned said behind me, his face gaunt and pale in the shadowy light thrown by the candle. 'And no one knows...they all think things are so good here...'

'Things are good if you leave them alone!' the Governor barked back at us. 'Things are good if you know your place! Things are good for those that are thankful! For those who are not...' he lifted a finger and dragged it across his own throat, before laughing at us again. 'Let's get you on your way gang! You've got a long journey ahead of you!'

And with that, we were hauled on and pushed forward. The chain linked us together. The Governor and his son chuckled and murmured. The light got brighter as we climbed those stairs again. On the other side of the door we expected to see the night, but we only got a glimpse of it before we were bundled into the back of a wagon.

We were on our knees. Connor bleeding and groaning. Ned trembling next to me. I looked around. I could smell the horses. Hear them stamping their feet and snorting their breath. Two of the guards climbed into the back of the wagon with us, and the chain was attached to a metal hook in the floor of the wagon. We were not going anywhere. We were a circle.

The Governor remained outside, his hands linked behind his back. His face was smooth and trouble free and smiling once again.

'Have a good trip!' he called to us, as the horses were lashed at. 'Don't do anything I wouldn't do!'

Oh, how I wanted to cry something back out at him. Something to wipe that smile from his face, something that would freeze his blood. But I had nothing.

40: Beyond The Domes

Slowly, the wagon pulled away. The Governor was left standing there in the darkness, watching us go. He smiled and raised a hand in a slow wave. That was the last thing we saw, before one of the guards pulled shut the cloth entry. Governor Lancaster waving us off.

So, we did not get to see the Province as we left it. We did not get to see the great iron gates opening to spill us out. We did not get to see the dark land ahead of us as the horses dragged us away from our homes and our lives and rumbled us on and into the unknown. We did not get to say goodbye.

Inside the wagon it was dark and hot. Our stomachs rumbled and our mouths were dry. We were all sat with our legs crossed. I looked at the guard nearest to us. I remembered him from school last year. He was only a year older. His name was Harold Evans.

'We haven't had any food or water, Harold.' I informed him hopefully. He kept his helmet on. They all did. His dark eyes looked angry when he turned them upon me.

'Shut it,' he said. Just like that. I licked my lips. Now that I'd remembered how long ago we ate and drank, the urge to do both seemed incredible and overpowering.

'You can't not feed us,' I tried to tell him. But I was not sure if this was true. How would I know what they could and could not do?

'He said shut it,' the other guard snapped. He was older than Saul and Harold, perhaps in his late teens. I thought his name was Griff, or something like that. I just stared back at his impassive face and thought about how his father would have been a guard before him, and his grandfather before that. They were both seated at the door, wooden batons in hand.

I decided to try one more time. 'We just need a little food and water,' I said with a helpless shrug. 'You must have some on board.'

'You'll get fed and watered when we get there, now shut it,' was the answer he gave. He lifted the baton up just in case I wondered what would happen if I did not shut it.

'We can't ask any questions?' I looked at Ned, surprised he had spoken. The guards glowered, warning him. 'Okay forget about food and water,' he said to them pleasantly. 'But you can't blame us for being curious. Come on. We've just got to sit here in silence?'

The younger guard looked at the older one, and sniffed. 'What sort of questions?'

Ned glanced at me, his eyebrows lifting in surprise. 'So, like where do you train?'

The younger one, Harold, frowned. 'Where do we train?'

'Yes! I'm curious. I've always wanted to know. Where do you train? How do you even get picked to be a guard?'

'Same as you get picked for any other job,' he replied, as if this should be obvious. 'Your father does it. You get duties and see if it fits you too.'

'Did you *want* to do it?' was Ned's next question and again I looked at him in alarm. What was he playing at?

The guards looked uneasy. The older one grunted and waved a

hand, as Harold looked back at Ned. 'Course I did! What kind of stupid question is that?'

'Sorry, just...just a thought. You like it then? How do they train you for it? Did your dad teach you?'

Harold glared beneath the visor of his helmet. 'We train out at one of the domes actually. It's a strenuous process.'

The older guard, Griff, looked confused and uneasy. He peered at Ned carefully, and then at me, before turning his attention back to Harold.

'No need for chatter,' he said, brusquely.

'I'm sorry,' Ned said, and his voice came out so sorrowful, so childlike, that it almost brought a tear to my eye. There was a lump in my throat. And then I looked at him and I could tell that he was putting it on. 'It's just I wanted to talk to pass the time...being so scared and everything...' He sniffed and lifted his manacled hands to wipe at his nose. Beside him, Connor said nothing. He just sat slumped in the darkness, his head low and his jaw tight. I wondered what on earth must be going through his mind. Somehow by examining his face for just a moment I could tell that it was his brother.

There was no reply from either guard so Ned spoke again. 'Really scared,' he mumbled with another sniff. 'Don't know what's gonna' happen to us...No one will tell us...we don't even know what we did wrong.'

Again, his pitiful voice was met with silence from the guards. I just sat and waited, wondering if he knew what he was doing. His lower lip trembled and tears started to fill his eyes.

361

'Did they even tell you what we did?' he asked, mournfully. 'We've been down in the cells and we don't know, they didn't even tell us...what we did wrong...why they arrested us, did they Lissie?'

He stared at me expectantly. I coughed and looked away. 'No. Nothing.'

'Well you know what you did wrong!' Harold cried at us, incredulous. 'Everyone knows now! The Governor told us this morning. You helped this fella here, you helped him try to overthrow us!'

'Not true,' said Connor, and it was the first time he had spoken. We all looked at him in wonder, and he was still staring at nothing. 'I was just hunting. Just looking for food. We don't want to interfere with you people. That's all lies.'

'Shut it, I said!' yelled Griff. Harold looked confused.

'Yeah,' he agreed. 'Shut it. You're not supposed to be talking.'

But Ned was not ready to give up yet, and now I understood what he was doing. He was trying to get through to them. He must have had more faith in them than I did. With his lip still quivering, and his eyes shining back at them from the shadows, he whimpered;

'But we didn't do that! We didn't do anything! We just talked to him through the fence! We didn't know we couldn't do that...honest sir, honest, we didn't know that...We were just trying to be friends!'

'Well,' Harold said unsurely. 'That's what a trial is for, isn't it? So you can put your case across. If you didn't do anything wrong, then you don't have to worry.'

'They'll let us go?' Ned asked him desperately. 'They'll let us come back here?'

'Yeah, of course.' But Harold sounded even less sure about this.

'What happens at a trial? How does it work?'

Harold fidgeted and looked to the older man. 'I don't know,' he shrugged. 'Griff? What happens?'

'I don't know, do I?' the older man snapped back at him. 'I've never been to one! They don't let people in, do they? Now shut up, all of you! You're driving me mad!'

'That's your answer,' Harold nodded at Ned, his fierceness restored. 'Shut it!'

'They giving you trouble back there?' called a voice from the front of the wagon. Saul. For some reason, a shudder wrung through me. I looked at Ned pleadingly and he nodded in reply and finally shut up.

'No,' Griff yelled back. 'All under control, sir.'

Sir? Since when did Saul become sir? And to an older, more experienced guard? A knot tightened in my stomach. There was something wrong about all of this. I felt strange, like nothing was real, least of all us, sat in the back of a wagon going who knew where. Why had the Governor abandoned our fate to a bunch of kids? I looked at Connor and found no reassurance there. He looked like a dead man walking. Like he knew exactly what was going on. Ned chewed at his lip, looking like he wanted to say more, but every time he looked at me or opened his mouth I shook my head at him. No.

Silence fell, and the wagon rumbled on. Taking us.

Up front, Saul and the fourth guard drove the horses on, and I listened to them talking and laughing. No help there. No pity. What if we were not going anywhere? What if there was no trial? What if we'd just been left for Saul to deal with?

I forced myself to think back to school, and the years I'd known him. I tried to remember something nice about him. I tried to recall him doing something sweet, something kind. Helping someone. Caring about someone, or something. I was desperate to find it. I was desperate for it to be there, but it wasn't.

When I thought about Saul Lancaster all I could think about was his leering slab of a face and how much we had always hated each other. That was the only way I could see him, that was the only truth there was. Hate. But why? How far back did it go? When did it all start? When had his father starting training him for this?

In silence, we rumbled on. The ride got bumpier. The new day was dawning beyond the wagon. We heard birds screeching, crying, singing. I longed to see what was outside.

'Have we passed the domes yet?' I asked at one point, but I was glared at in response, no answer given. I would have liked to have seen the domes up close, and the people in them.

Our stomachs grumbled and growled but no food or water was offered. At one point Connor seemed to nod off, with his head upon his knees. Ned complained that he felt sick and needed the toilet, but the guards refused to answer him. I wondered if he would start crying again, start trying to arouse their pity. But he didn't. He leaned against me and shivered.

Finally, just at the point where my stomach was cramping in

pain, and my mouth and throat were so dry, so desperate for water that my lips hung apart, craving moisture, the wagon stopped. We sat up, looking at each other, wide eyed. This was good. Or was it?

'Are we getting fed now?' Ned begged them. 'I'm gonna' pass out soon...'

The cloth opening was flung back, and there stood Saul, excited and gloating. The other guard was tall, thin and pale faced. He looked to be around sixteen years old and again, I remembered him from school. His name was Mason. He looked tired and bored. No pity there either. Harold hopped out the back of the wagon, and Griff unhooked our chain from the ring on the floor.

'Up you get,' he said gruffly, and we obeyed.

I didn't know how long we'd been travelling. Only that my backside had gone to sleep, and my legs were weak. I felt weak all over in fact. Desperate now for water. Getting water had suddenly become the most imperative thing. One by one, Connor, Ned and I stumbled blindly from the wagon. Our feet landed on damp grass. It tickled my nostrils. I blinked and looked around, shaking my head lethargically. The landscape was so strange; it was hard to take it all in. On the one hand, it was green. I mean, greener than the Province. Green and bright and fresh like the land I discovered beyond the fence. There were trees in the distance. Tons of them. All different heights and colours. I could hear birds. Birds in the sky and birds in the trees. But something was not right. The picture was all wrong. It was like someone had drawn something beautiful on top of something ugly and jagged. I could see strange things jutting out at strange angles from the horizon and among the trees. It looked like metal. Edges of broken buildings. Stuff that roared up from the grass, breaking free like teeth trying to devour the beauty. I couldn't tell what had been there first.

'We need water,' I could hear Ned pleading with them. 'It's been so long now...you can't do this to us...we're innocent.'

Griff walked around to the front of the wagon and climbed aboard. What was going on? He threw down three packs, and Saul, Harold and the other guard picked them up.

'Where's he going?' asked Ned, his mouth gaping.

'He's going back home,' Saul replied with a wide, happy grin. 'What's it to you?'

The three of us looked around. We had no idea where we were or how far from home. The landscape was strange and troubling.

'Where are we?' I asked.

'Halfway between 5 and 1,' Saul told me brightly.

Griff smacked the reins and the horses started moving again. We stood and watched in wonder and awe, as the two horses pulled the wagon around in a circle, before heading back the way we came. Back to Province 5.

'We don't get a lift the whole way,' sighed Connor, as if he cared little.

Ned stepped towards Saul, straining as far as he could on the chain that linked us. 'Saul, please, we can't go on without water. You have to give us water!'

'Keep your knickers on Fleck,' laughed Saul. 'We've got a drink for you right here.' He grinned at us as he pulled one water bottle out from the inner pocket of his black body jacket. 'Here you go,' he said

366

and threw it at Ned.

Ned caught it, fumbled and dropped it while Saul and the other two guards looked on, laughing. Finally, he had it, opened it and drank three mouthfuls before passing it to me. I took it quickly, my thirst overtaking everything else now. It was not much water between the three of us, and the four quick mouthfuls I took seemed to do little to slake my thirst. I passed it to Connor, and the three of us huddled closer together, passing it back and forth until it was gone.

The guards stood to one side, positions lazy and relaxed as they watched us. 'What's going on?' I asked Connor. 'Why are we here?'

He shook his head. 'I don't know. I recognise it though. Passed through a few times. We usually stick to the coasts, though.'

'Are we really halfway to Province 1?'

'I don't know. It would make sense.'

'Right, that's enough!' Saul barked suddenly, lunging at us and snatching the water bottle from my hands. 'You've got five minutes to do your business, then we're off.'

'Where do we do it?' Ned asked, mystified.

'Here!' Saul laughed at him. 'Don't worry, we'll turn our backs. But hurry up! No messing about. We've got to get a move on.'

I stared at him wonderingly. 'Why? What's going on? Why did he take the wagon?'

Saul's smile stretched from ear to ear, and his piggy eyes shrunk to slits in-between. He stepped towards me, and I could smell his warm breath, sweet and cloying.

'We're walking,' he said reasonably, as if walking while chained together was the most pleasant thing in the world to do.

'Walking?' gasped Ned. 'Why are we walking there?'

'Don't ask questions,' Saul snapped at him, pointing to the ground. 'Just get on with it and then we're off.'

'You can't make us walk...' Ned muttered, turning slowly to face me, whilst trying with his cuffed hands to undo his trousers. 'Why are you treating us like this?'

The attack came out of nowhere. Saul was still smiling, and his body was still loose and relaxed, friendly almost. But he swished the wooden baton through the air and it collided with the side of Ned, and Ned was flung away by the force, stopped short by the chain, and then crumpled by the blow. He lay there, wordless, gasping, coughing over pain.

'What the hell?' yelled Connor. I got down on my knees, trying to reach him and while he coughed and spluttered and his eyes bulged with the agony, I looked back up at Saul.

'Why?' I asked his laughing face. 'Why are you doing this?'

'Because I can,' he answered me quickly and simply. 'Because I can!'

41: Ruins

After that we did what we were told, and we did it quickly. Connor and I helped Ned get back onto his feet. The boys relieved themselves, but for me this was far trickier. In the end, the boys and the guards all agreed to turn around and cover their faces with their hands while I struggled. By the time I was done and my dress was smoothed down, my cheeks were burning hot with shame, and I was sure that Saul had peeked.

The guards stood for a moment, drinking their own water and sharing out a loaf of bread one of them retrieved from his pack. The smell was unbelievable. I started to drool and had to slurp the moisture back in. The water was not enough, and now they were eating right in front of us. I wanted to question them, I wanted to scream at them, but I didn't dare. I looked at the dark crusts and smear of blood on Connor's face and head, and I looked at Ned, wincing every time he moved, and I looked at the three guards. Stood there, swinging their batons. And I couldn't stop thinking, how has it come to this? How can this even be happening? I felt disorientated, despite all I had been told by Grandma, Aisha and Connor. Nothing felt real anymore. The world I knew had crumbled.

When they'd eaten the entire loaf, Saul gestured to them and to us. 'Right, let's get moving. We've got eighty miles to cover.'

'Don't see why we couldn't have the wagon the whole way,' Harold grumbled, probably without meaning to. Saul instantly glared and turned to face him. I remembered that face so well from school. The way he pushed it right into yours, challenging you, forcing you to move back. Harold did just this, as we looked on wearily. He stepped back, looking sorry.

'I'll tell you why, you idiot,' sneered Saul. 'It's so we can punish these snivelling traitors, that's why! It's so we can break them!'

No one questioned what 'break them' meant. Harold nodded his quick apology, picked up his pack and slung it onto his back. Mason, the tall thin guard did the same, and then picked up one end of the chain. He began to walk and Saul fell into place beside him. Harold dutifully picked up the other end of the chain, and we were helplessly tugged on.

'Welcome to the great wide world!' Saul called back over his shoulder with a giggle. We followed, one behind the other, the chain looping from Connor, to Ned and back to me. It was only now we were walking that I realised how heavy it was. Our hands were pulled downwards and our shoulders became rounded over. Our knees soon started to ache.

As we walked, I stared around. Behind us, nothing but dark grass. Above us, a pale blue sky. The sun was just starting to come up on the horizon. Eighty miles, Saul said. Eighty miles to walk from wherever we were, to Province 1. We kept going. One foot in front of the other. Silent except for the chinking of the links in the chain.

Ned's breathing was laboured. I listened to him wheezing from behind. I wondered if Saul had broken one of his ribs. I watched his small back and his stick like legs, and his feet shuffling through the damp grass. I longed to reach out and touch him, but I didn't dare. Not now. Maybe the best thing we could do was be silent and walk. Give them no reason to hurt us. Get to Province 1 alive and in one piece and then see what happened next.

My previous excitement and determination had faded away. In the cold light of a new day far from home, I now felt nothing but cold lonely fear. Up ahead, Connor walked better than we did. He was bigger and stronger. I watched the thick muscles in his back and shoulders moving and dipping under his clothes. He kept his head up, and seemed to be scanning the horizon intently. I wondered where his people were. Where were Aisha and all the others? Did they know he had been taken? Did they know where he was going? Was there any chance of an ambush, a rescue? I realised this was our only hope and started to do as he was. Staring all around, straining my eyes and ears for any sign of hope.

Some time later we reached a line of trees. The sun was now higher in the sky and I tried to work out how long we had been walking. My back and neck said too long. My feet were beginning to blister. When Ned turned his head to see how I was doing, I saw sweat rolling across his forehead, running down into his screwed-up eyes.

We walked through the trees, experiencing a moment or two of shade. I felt the land changing under my feet. It was getting harder. I looked down at the grass and every now and then there was a patch of it missing. I glimpsed grey. Stones. Grit. The further we walked the more this occurred, until eventually we were walking on more hard grey stuff than grass. I longed to ask about it. Was this a road from the Old World? We seemed to be following it now. Following its route, just as people would have done back then. When they drove vehicles powered by oil they dug up from the earth. I'd seen the pictures in the museum. They would put the oil in their cars and the cars would take them wherever they needed to go. The cars came in different colours and shapes and they went much faster than horses.

It was harder to walk on the rubble. The guards wore thick

boots which softened the impact for their feet. More than once I felt something sharp slicing into my shoe and opening the flesh. I kept staring around as we kept moving. It was such a strange sight to behold. Like someone had painted one picture, and then someone else had painted a different one on top. Everywhere you could see the Old World poking through. Bits of walls. Mounds of bricks. Twisted metal. Burnt out car skeletons with trees and grass growing through them. We stumbled, tripped and fell. Every time, Saul and the other guard turned and shouted at us, using the chain to yank us back to our feet.

'Bones,' Ned whispered to me once, nodding his head, and when I looked I saw that he was right. Jutting out between the grass, the bricks and the metal every now and again you saw a bone. It made my hungry stomach turn over on itself, and I had to look away. It was surreal, seeing it all finally. The world outside our home. The world that was blown away...

We kept walking, and my stomach grumbled on, guessing that we had bypassed lunchtime. I was thinking about asking for some more water, when we started to walk over a bridge. It seemed to be one of the only structures still standing, and as we went over, we had to weave in and out of hulks of burnt metal. More cars. More bones. So, they were right, I thought. They did destroy themselves. It made me feel horrendously sad. Thinking of all those people, driving in their cars one minute, blown to pieces the next. And for what? Why? By who?

I couldn't help feeling homesick for Province 5. For Mum and Dad and our hut. For the square, and the stores, and the school. For no more hunger and no more war. I had to keep taking deep, steadying breaths just to keep my feet moving. The pain was everywhere now. In my feet and my knees and my wrists where the cuffs dug into my skin,
372

and in my neck and shoulders and back, and in my head as the sun pounded down on us, and more than that, worse than all of that, in my heart. It was a desolate thing when you looked around and saw it. People blown to bits. The human race brought down to its knees. That's what we were capable of. That's what people could do.

Birds flew overhead and every now and then something scuttled away from us, leaping and scrabbling over the rubble. I got the sense of being watched as we came down the other side of the bridge and continued to follow the ruined road. I wanted to cry out. Help us! If anyone is there, please stop this...

But nothing happened and no one came.

Hours passed before they allowed us to fall. We'd travelled through the remains of a city. There was a church along the way. A cathedral, Connor told me when we finally stopped. They used to go to places like that and get down on their knees and ask the unseen entity for help and forgiveness. They taught us a bit about religion in school, and there were relics in the museum. Scraps of the book they used to hold and read. Items of clothing they used to wear. I guessed the unseen entity was not listening, or was a made-up story. Whatever it was, it didn't help them.

We sat at the side of the road, with bricks around us and the smell of dust in the air. We sat side by side, panting heavily, our heads down low, our feet hurting more now that they were still. Ahead of us sat a jagged, unwelcoming horizon. I couldn't shake the feeling that the Old World did not want us here. That none of this ruined landscape was for our eyes to see. The guards kept hold of the chain and sat down too. They passed one water bottle to us and we shared it once again. The guards ate food from their packs and gave nothing to us. It hurt watching them. It hurt my guts and my stomach and my throat, which was screaming out for food.

'How're you holding up?' Connor asked us when the guards started arguing about who had eaten more than their fair share of the bread and cheese. I raised my head and looked at him sideways. He seemed remarkably calm, I thought.

'Okay,' I told him, because I wanted this to be true. 'I'm okay.'

'Me too,' Ned piped up, nodding his head as if to convince himself. 'How much further do you think it is?'

Connor shook his head slowly, gazing around. 'I think they'll keep us moving until night falls, and then in the morning we'll go on. Be there by mid-day I think.'

'Have you ever been there?' I whispered. 'Province 1?'

He nodded cautiously. 'I've been to most of them. Unseen.'

'Will anyone help us?' I asked him. It was all I wanted to know. He smiled at me gently, while a great sorrow filled his deep brown eyes.

'I don't know, Lissie. I hope so. But I don't know.'

'Aisha,' Ned murmured between us. He didn't sound very hopeful and I couldn't blame him.

'How's your ribs?' I asked, nudging him with my elbow.

'Sore.'

'Just keep your cool,' Connor warned him softly. 'Don't give them a reason to make things worse. Okay? Just keep quiet. Keep going.'

'I'm so hungry...' Ned moaned, tears filling his eyes. I nudged him again, but he wouldn't look at me. Connor glanced up at the guards, but for the moment they were distracted. They were stood just in front of us while the chain rested on the ground. Connor reached out slowly to the grassy mound behind us. He snatched and scrabbled at the earth before bringing his hand back around and showing us. In his cupped hands were some flowers. Some bright yellow, some white with a yellow centre. He had some green leaves too. We stared, not understanding.

'You can eat them,' he whispered, tipping them into Ned's waiting hands. 'Pass them on.'

'What're you doing?' Saul barked then, staring down at us. Connor carried on. Picking with both hands and then tipping the flowers and leaves into Ned's. Ned did the same, tipping them into mine.

'Finding food,' Connor replied evenly. For some reason the three of them found this hilariously funny. They threw back their heads and then bent over clutching their stomachs, whilst roaring laughter at themselves and us. We ignored them and carried on eating.

'Are you sure?' Ned asked, chewing slowly. 'My dad kills these. He pulls these up, I recognise them.'

'Honest, they're harmless. Good for you, even. Daisies. Dandelions. Plantain. You can eat them fine. Trust me.'

I remembered Grandma Elizabeth writing about them in her diary. Lawrence found them when they were on the run, I thought, and had to stifle a laugh. I held them in front of my eyes and then sniffed

375

them. I popped them into my mouth one by one and chewed. The taste was strange; spongey and fresh. It ignited my hunger and I ate them faster. Saul, seeing this, stepped forward and slapped them from my hands, then Ned's and then Connors.

'We'll say if you can eat or not!' he yelled into Connor's face. 'And my father said not until you get there!'

'Fine,' Connor shrugged at him, meeting his gaze. 'We'll remember.'

For a long moment, they were eye to eye, just staring. Then Saul pulled back, straightened up and laughed.

'You ferals,' he said haughtily. 'You're all the same. Like animals. Is that how you survive? Eating weeds from the road side?'

'Nature has everything you need,' Connor said lightly. 'She always has done.'

'She?' hooted Saul. 'What are you talking about? You people are all crazy! None of you are right in the head! All those years in the wilderness have turned you all insane!'

'We take what we need from the earth to survive. Nothing more. We give back to the earth. Unlike your people, it is us that learned the right way to behave.'

Saul shut his mouth and his steely eyes burned into Connor's. 'Is that right? Well that's not what I hear. It was your kind of people that caused all this in the first place!'

To this Connor laughed. 'How? By planting seeds?'

Saul looked furious. His eyes were full of hate. He leaned in, grabbed Connor by the lapels of his shirt and hauled him to his feet. This action tugged Ned halfway up, followed by me.

'You're all scum,' Saul was growling. 'Wild, backwards, feral *scum*. Peasants! Good job we have so many of you rounded up now. Got you where we can control you. Your kind. Always plotting and scheming.'

Connor did not reply. He could see where this was heading and the dried blood on his face was a good reminder not to go there again. He remained calm and loose in Saul's hands, until the bully turned his eyes on Ned and I.

'And as for you two, you're even worse!' he said, spit and crumbs flying from his face to pepper ours. 'Turning your back on your family and your people! For this lot! Plotting behind our backs!'

'We didn't do anything,' I heard myself saying. 'We didn't do one single thing. We had no intention of doing one single thing. We read a book!'

'Liar!' Saul roared, letting go of Connor and turning his attention to me. 'Course you were going to do something, weren't you! Weren't you? I know you Turner! Just like your ancestors. A troublemaker. Treacherous and ungrateful.'

'Curious, maybe,' I nodded at him. 'But I would never hurt anyone. That is the difference between you and me Saul. I just wanted to know the truth. Maybe I wanted to leave peacefully and never come back, but I didn't get to make that choice, did I?'

'No, because if you break the rules you get arrested, idiot! What did you think was going to happen?'

I was closer to him now. So close I could smell the cheese on his breath. 'Where does it say you can't read a book? Where are these rules written down?'

'You should have told your parents and handed it in!'

'Why?'

'What?'

'*Why*? Simple question Saul. Why? Why hand it in? Why not read it? Because we're not supposed to know the truth?'

'It's all lies,' he sneered, his nose touching mine. 'All lies!'

'So then what did it matter if I read it? If it was all lies, if it was a made-up story then what harm could it do me reading it?'

His top lip curled and he moved away from me. 'People like you are never satisfied,' he snarled, pointing at each one of us. 'You were always looking for attention, Turner. And you Fleck, you little loser, always looking to impress your parents, eh! And these lot out here, tried to start an uprising generations ago and are still trying now!'

I saw that there was no point in arguing with him. I kept my mouth shut and waited. He was in a rage now. Spittle all over his pimpled chin, while Harold and the nameless guard looked on. Saul yanked us all, twisting the chain around his hands and waving his baton about madly.

'Get moving!' he bellowed, and there was one strike for each of us as we moved on. Back of the shoulders. The pain was blinding. 'Get moving!' he roared. 'Shut your mouths and get moving! Traitors and liars! Plotters! Filthy ferals! Stupid peasants! Get moving! I can't wait to see what they do to you!'

He was like a small child having a tantrum, I thought, and walked on. I'd kept one small flower in my mouth. I moved it around from one side to the other. Sucking it. Tasting it. Thanking mother nature, whoever she was...

42: Ghost Town

It took a long time to walk through the ruins of the city. It was both captivating and depressing. There were more signs here of the Old World. In the Province, whatever was salvaged was shut up in the museum and treated with caution. Here, everything had been left to rot. I was in constant awe as we stumbled through. Buildings, or what was left of them. Shattered homes. Glass, metal and dust. My shoes were falling apart as I walked, the soles loose and flapping underfoot. There were so many things. The twisted frame of a rusty bike. Odd shoes. Items of ragged clothing. Debris of lives lost. It was like walking through a ghost town.

'Bet you never thought you'd see all this,' Saul turned to sneer at me when he noticed me staring.

'We should *all* be allowed to see this,' I decided to tell him, but he did not want to hear. Rolling his eyes in disgust and looking away from me. 'They've no right to keep us in the Province,' I called out to him. 'We should be free to come and see this if we want to!'

'No one but you wants to leave there!' he snarled back at me. 'Everyone is happy there except for you!'

'They *think* they are happy,' I mumbled in reply, knowing it was pointless.

Slowly but surely we passed through the remnants of the city. I had no idea what it was called back then. Or if it was called anything now. We didn't see another living soul, which was spooky and sad. The land started to open up again, although mounds of bombed buildings and rubble lay in every direction. This must have been a
380

heavily populated area, I thought. Nature had reclaimed it though. Did nature win in the end? I found myself thinking about this as we were dragged on. The pain got worse with every step. Blood filling the tips of my shoes. Ned stumbled and fell more than once. To take my mind off the horror of our situation, I thought about who'd won.

As far as the eye could see, two different worlds were present. One, old and dead. Rusted, rotten and returning to dust. The other, bright, vibrant and green. Stems bursting up through concrete. Vines and trunks curling and creeping around buildings and blotting them out. Slowly, it was all turning green. Unlike back home, where everything was so dry. Here, nature was thriving. Nature was not in a box, or a dome. Cultured, cultivated and delivered. Here, nature was doing her own thing. Everywhere we passed, you could see it happening. It was stealing its world back. And yet the people who did this were still in charge...

That had to change.

This thought now dominated my mind. With every bite of pain, I allowed this thought space in my head. I allowed it to give me strength. One way or another. Something just had to change. Because look! Look at all of this! As we left the rubble of the city and the homes behind, we came out onto a landscape dotted with baby trees. There was no one living there to pull them up. The weeds and the trees and the leaves and the flowers were all coming back, all taking over, all claiming back what was theirs. I thought about the apple tree I found, and I couldn't help smiling.

That little tree. Growing on the other side of the fence. Not in the domes where they wanted it. But out in the wild where nobody knew about it. Doing what it was supposed to do. What it was planted to do. Spitting in their faces, I thought, and wanted to laugh. I wondered if all this was frustrating to them? All this green! Would they razor it flat if they could? Would they build a giant dome over all of it and keep it trapped for good? Did it drive them mad that there were not enough people left in the world to stamp nature down again? To make it theirs?

You keep doing it, I thought. You keep growing, and taking back. You keep saying no, and we'll keep marching. We'll march in there with our heads held up and one way or another, something *must* change...

These were positive thoughts and it seemed that I was not alone with them. When we finally stopped again, the light of the day was dwindling, and Connor looked at me as if he knew. Maybe it was those weeds he gave me to eat. Maybe it was the flower I'd kept chewing in my mouth when I was not supposed to. Maybe it was seeing the weeds and the trees and the bushes thrusting their way through the mess of the Old World. Saying, ok, you didn't want it, we will have it back.

Ned was the only one flagging, and I could not blame him. We were given more water to share and were instructed to take another toilet break. While we did this, our guards undid their packs and started to put up a tent. Just one, for them. We sat down, while Harold drove a wooden stake into the ground, holding one end of our chain in place. The tall thin guard wandered off to collect wood and soon they had a fire going, and the sky was black. In the distant, something howled, and all the hairs on my body stood on end.

From behind the flames of the fire, Saul Lancaster laughed at me. 'Wild things!' he said gleefully, as his teeth tore greedily into the chicken leg he held. 'Like that mangy animal you tried to hide, Turner!

Loads of them out here! Might pick you off in the middle of the night. You won't feel so high and mighty then, will you?'

I didn't answer him. Just hung my head and scratched with my cuffed hands at the earth. Like Connor showed us before, there was plenty to eat if you knew where to look. On my other side, Ned leaned weakly against him. His eyes were closed with exhaustion and his breath wheezed in and out of his nose and his pinched-up lips. I patted his knee and handed him some dusky pink flowers. He opened his eyes and frowned in confusion.

'Clover,' Connor whispered from my other side. 'Good for you.'

Ned took the small soft buds and pushed them inside his mouth. 'You okay?' I asked him. He nodded, but he winced and gasped and closed his eyes. I looked at Connor. 'I reckon his rib is broken, you know.'

Connor nodded regretfully. 'You'll be okay mate,' he told him. 'Lay yourself down and get some rest. Looks like we're settling in for the night.'

Ned ate a handful of the flowers before slipping slowly and awkwardly down onto the grass with his head on my lap. I shook my head, chewing slowly.

'I don't know how they can sit over there like that,' I murmured. 'Eating and laughing while Ned's in pain. I always disliked Saul, but I never knew he was inhuman.'

'Must run in his family,' mused Connor. 'His dad's pretty vicious when he loses his temper too.' He raised both hands to his hairline and picked off a thick piece of dried blood. 'Ouch.'

'I still can't believe what I saw,' I told him. 'All of it. I can't believe what I'm seeing Connor. All this out here. That city we passed through. It's like we were kept totally in the dark for three generations.'

'Clever how they do it,' he replied softly, pulling up more clover and popping it into his mouth. 'Make you feel you are all safe and cared for. Teach you not to question things or ask for more.'

'There's no reason, though,' I said, my voice climbing slightly higher as the anger bubbled up. 'To take all this away from people. They could leave us be...let us go where we want, do what we want, plant what we want...'

'That's not what they want though,' he reminded me. 'That's not how you keep power. You'll have to talk to my mother one day. She understands human nature better than me. Always good at explaining things.'

'Do you know where she is now?'

'Haven't seen her in a while. She went looking for Tate.'

'Do you think she found him? Do you think you will?'

'I hope so,' he sighed, looking down. 'I really hope so.'

'You guys shut up over there!' Saul screamed suddenly, hurling something at us. It landed near Connor, a greasy chicken bone. 'Shut your filthy mouths or I'll come over there and shut them for you.'

Oh, how much I wanted to answer him....

But I didn't. One look at Ned's pale, pinched face and I knew how much trouble we were in. For now, I thought, we will do as we are told. So, we made ourselves as comfortable as we could with our hands bound before us. We curled up next to each other and closed our eyes. One end of the chain was staked into the ground, while the other was chained to Saul's ankle.

'If you even sneeze in the night, I'll know about it!' he promised us before ducking into the tent.

We were left alone with the fire and the night. Ned snored gently beside me. Connor lay on his side with his hands tucked between his knees.

'It will be all right, Lissie,' he decided to tell me just as I was drifting into exhausted sleep. 'I've got a good feeling in my bones.'

'I hope you're right, Connor.'

'Always trust your gut feeling...'

It was the last thing he said before he fell asleep. I was the only one awake then. Just me and the Old World. Wrecked, ravaged and yet somehow rebellious. Unapologetic. It stared back at me, asking so what? What now? What are you going to do, Lissie Turner, with your head in the clouds? I lay on my back and stared at the stars in the sky. I felt jealous of them way up there. Untouched by human madness and the craving for power. How would I ever understand it?

In their tent, the young guards snored and rustled in their sleep. I wondered if they slept easily. If they felt guilt, or doubt. If they cared at all about what happened to us. I thought about the people back home, tucked into their beds after a hard day of work. Their firewood delivered. Their food and water on hand. Their minds clear and clean of worry or wonder. Who was luckier, me or them? And I thought about my parents and wondered if they were crying for me. Out of all of them though, it was Grandma Elizabeth I missed the most.

The Tree of Rebels

I slept until a piercing howl in the night awakened us all. I sat up, eyes wide, screams clogging my throat, and Connor was the same, shoulder to shoulder, his eyes shining in the moonlight. Howls, screams, barks. Something was there, something was coming closer.

'Dogs,' Connor whispered, his hand finding mine in the darkness. I looked down at Ned, still sleeping, curled up so small and tight. I wanted to find reassurance in Connor, but there was none to be found. He knew as well as I did that something was there, that something was close, and that something was hungry. We turned our heads, staring into the impossible darkness. There were footfalls, soft and plodding. A sound like panting, large sides heaving in and out. I moved closer to Ned, preparing to protect him.

Connor stood up slowly, so I did the same, placing my feet on either side of Ned. Connor used his hands to gather up the length of the chain. The footfalls were closer now, and it felt like we were being circled, slowly.

'Dogs!' Connor yelled suddenly, making me jump. At first I thought he was crazy, but then I understood.

There was an almighty yell from inside the tent, and a commotion followed. At least one of the wild beasts had gone inside to investigate our jailors. That did not make us safe though, and all my hairs were on end, as the shadows moved slowly around us. Every now and then I saw the glint of an eye, the shine of teeth. Low, throaty growls were building up to something.

'Get it out! Get it out!' someone screamed inside the tent. The beast itself responded with high pitched barking. And then in the middle of it all, a loud boom. A sound like I had never heard before. I hit the ground, hands over my ears, landing on Ned and curling over

386

him. There was another boom and then another, and then I heard the beasts running away, changing their minds and scrambling off into the darkness.

'Bloody ferals!' Saul was yelling, and then laughing. He came towards us then, big and grotesque in the moonlight, his shoulders shaking with laughter as he waved something heavy around in the air.

'You have guns,' Connor said simply. Saul laughed at him.

'Course we have guns!'

'No more guns,' I found myself murmuring, shaking my head from side to side. Ned had woken, rubbing his eyes in confusion. 'No more guns,' I said again, staring up at Saul. 'No one is meant to have guns!'

'Lucky for you I did,' he replied haughtily. 'Or you'd be dead meat right now.' With that, he turned around, still grinning and waving the object from side to side as he headed back to the tent. The other guards ducked in behind him and I looked at Connor, shaking my head.

'They've got guns!'

Connor shrugged. 'Looks that way.'

'So much for the Peace Treaty then!'

'I don't even know what that is,' he yawned, settling back down on the ground. 'But right now, I have to say, I'm with Saul on this. Pretty glad he had a gun.'

I should have felt the same, but I didn't. All I could think about was the lies, and the hypocrisy. Another little thing kept from us for our own good? Ned curled into me, slipping quickly back into sleep. How stupid we all were. That was all I could think. How stupid...

43: Province 1

In the morning, we were woken up by two things. The smell of bacon cooking over the fire and Saul's boot. He walked around us, aiming kicks as we jerked awake. I longed to lash out and kick him back, but I knew I couldn't. I just bit my lip and averted my eyes and tried like hell not to inhale too much bacon. It was torturous though, as was the equally divine smell of coffee.

'Up you get, wakey wakey!' Saul finished his kicking and returned to the others to enjoy his breakfast. Connor had already sought out a little pile of clover for us and we tried to eat it without them noticing. Saul however, did not take his eye off us and before we knew it, he'd jumped to his feet and stormed over. 'What're you eating?' he demanded, grabbing Connor by his hair and yanking him back so that he could see into his face. He had his wooden baton in his other hand and held it up threateningly. 'Open up! Open your mouth! What are you eating!'

Connor opened his mouth obediently and Saul peered in.

'Clover,' Connor explained before swallowing. 'It's good for you. Loads of stuff out here is.'

Saul looked utterly enraged. Like he feared losing control, which was when he was at his most dangerous. While Ned and I looked on in horror, he raised his baton and brought it down on Connor's shoulders and back. To his credit, Connor barely reacted. He curled over his legs and gasped with each blow.

We had to wait for it to be over. Harold and the nameless guard watched silently. I tried to read their faces, tried to work out how they felt about such savagery. It is not how we were raised, I wanted to scream at them! But maybe it was how they were trained...

Finally, Saul had enough of abusing Connor and returned to his breakfast at the fire, grunting and muttering under his breath.

'If I catch you eating anything else!' he yelled his warning, raising his stick again. 'I'm gonna' knock all your teeth out!'

'Do they train you to do that?'

I shouldn't have said it, but I couldn't stop myself. Saul glared murderously back at me.

'Shut your mouth, Turner.'

'I'm just curious. Is that how they train you to be guards? Do they train you to beat people who cannot defend themselves?'

'Stupid bloody question!' he roared back at me, grease smeared on his chin from the bacon. 'You're prisoners and traitors! Not *people*! How else would we know what to do out here, hey? They trust us you see. Trust us with getting you there!'

'Where you'll hand us over battered and bruised,' I pointed out. 'And that's okay, is it? You won't get into trouble? There are no laws written for our protection?'

'Your *protection*? What are you on about? You're traitors!'

'Not yet, we're not. We're going to trial. We might be found innocent.'

'I wouldn't count on it,' he laughed. 'But so what if you are?'

'I'm just asking,' I shrugged at him patiently. 'I'm just curious.

There aren't any written laws to protect us then? As your prisoners, you can do what you like to us? I just never knew that, that's all. It's just another thing they don't tell you when you're growing up. Just another secret kept from us like all the others. Like the guns! They were meant to be banned! No one back home knows they exist!'

'Shut up,' he warned, raising his baton. 'I'm warning you. Shut up or I'm coming over there and shutting you up!'

I shut up. But I did not miss the flash of anxiety in Harold's eyes. I did not miss it because it was something small and hopeful to cling to. He knew that I was right. Which meant that he knew that this was wrong...

When they'd eaten, they packed up their tent and kicked apart the fire. There was more howling now in the distance and I shivered again, wondering what else was out there.

'Stupid dogs,' Harold decided to reassure himself. Saul gloated at him.

'All sorts out there, mate. Haven't you seen them? Wolves, lions, tigers! People used to keep all these beasts locked up in the Old World. But they survived, some of them, and kept breeding. You wait. You'll see something soon enough. Right, let's get moving!'

Yanking his end of the chain, we were pulled on. Oh, how it hurt. It hurt more than I knew possible. Yesterday's blisters were opened and rubbed raw again. A few hours later I kicked off both my shoes. Ned was in the middle again, his head lower today, his eyes half closed. I was starting to get worried about him. His breathing sounded all wrong. Ahead of him, Connor marched on, and when I looked at him I always felt better. He was right last night, I thought. He had a good feeling in his bones and somehow so did I. I looked at him and thought about nature spitting in their faces, reclaiming what they tried to take. There was so much of it out here. The more we walked, the more we saw of it. Fruit trees and fruit bushes. When he could, Connor pointed things out to me that we could pick and eat if we needed to. He knew so much.

We walked through the morning, and we walked through the debris of war. Another city was approaching, as the concrete and metal began to poke through once more. But before we reached the city inside the fence, we saw something more incredible. We saw the domes. The domes of Province 1. I'd missed seeing ours when we were in the back of the wagon. From Province 5 you could catch the odd glimpse of their existence, but it was a distant, surreal sight. But now, for the first time in my life I could get close to what fed us, what kept us alive, and it was amazing and yet somehow arrogant.

I counted six, but there were probably more. I could not even fathom how large they were. Sunlight bounced from the curved glass structures. They're like eyes, I thought, as we edged closer. Eyes buried in the flesh of the earth, staring out, staring up at the sky. And inside those eyes grew everything you needed to feed a small population. Wheat, barley, oats, corn, potatoes, carrots, tomatoes, onions, cabbage, apples, plums, berries and so on and so on. Everything you could wish for. All safely contained.

I was mesmerised as we approached. It dazzled me in its size and complexity. As we got nearer we could see the activity inside of them. Tiny human ants moving about under the glass. Animals. Tall crops. Trees. The closer we got, the more we could see. You could feel the heat of it too. How it sucked in the rays of the sun and trapped them inside. It was amazing and somehow terrible. I saw them and I

392

wanted to blame them. I wanted to hold them responsible for all the damage that had been done. You're the travesty! I wanted to scream up at them.

We kept walking, shoulders hunched. My guts were doing strange things now. I could feel something getting closer. Something we could not turn back from...

I felt sick. Dry mouthed. My insides were curling up, tightening. It seemed to take forever to get past the things...and all the time my heart was going bang, bang, bang and my mouth was getting drier and drier. Ned panted and groaned in front of me and, beyond him, Connor marched on.

'Beautiful things,' Harold remarked, nodding his head at the domes. He was walking just behind me, holding the end of the chain.

'Never seen one close up before...' I said breathlessly.

'One of the great wonders of the world,' he replied confidently.

'Nature used to do it all by herself, you know,' I decided to tell him. 'She still does.'

'She? Shut up, girl.'

'I'm just saying...think about it Harold...Didn't need domes back then and we don't need them now.'

'You're instigating trouble,' he growled, looking at me darkly. 'I'll tell Saul.'

'Do you still remember the Song Of Thanks, Harold?'

'What? Of course I do!'

'No more war and no more fear…'

'I know how it goes thanks, now shut up.'

'Those words aren't true,' I looked back and told him while the blood poured from my feet, leaving ruby footprints on the ground. 'They're not being heeded, are they? Look at us.'

He stared at me, his jaw working. 'Shut up.'

'We're in fear,' I went on, glancing uneasily at the domes. 'We're in fear and we're hungry. And we're still at war…They just don't talk about it. All those words are untrue, and they drummed it into us from birth.'

'I'll get Saul,' he hissed at me then, coming up beside me. 'You don't want him back here, girl. You don't want to make him angry.'

'Think about it Harold.' I looked into his eyes, trying to find him there somewhere. 'This is not how they bring you up…We are not supposed to treat each other like this. The people back home would be heartbroken and you know it. Your own mother would, if she could see this now.'

Again, his jaw twitched. His eyebrows came down lower. He knew I was right. But he had his orders. His position. I tried again.

'No more war and no more fear… *Lies* Harold. They are lies. Bringing people up to believe in lies and not to question anything. *This* is the truth.' I held up my bloody chafed wrists and showed him. I pointed to my feet. I nodded at Ned, nearly on the point of collapse. 'We're in fear, Harold. You know this is wrong. I know you do.'

He shook his head very fast and stomped away from me. I watched him go, wondering what he would say to Saul, but he said nothing. He murmured to the nameless guard who wordlessly swapped places with him. And nothing happened. And we walked on.

It felt like hours. Torturous, agonising hours. Our feet were raw. Our bodies were broken. The chains became heavier with every step. The thirst and the hunger were all consuming and now I knew what Connor meant about this being meant to break us. Break the body, and the spirit will follow? We could barely pick our feet up. There could not be much more.

The domes grew smaller behind us, and the land became flat and hard and pock marked with rubble and debris. We followed a makeshift road of gravel and stones, and on the horizon appeared our destination. Province 1. The largest Province and the home to Central Government. Governor Lancaster's orders came from there...

What struck me first as we drew closer was the absence of a fence. Province 1 did not have a fence like Province 5. Province 1 did better than that. It had a wall. A huge, looming, grey monstrosity.

'Who built it?' I asked immediately. 'When was it built? How did it survive?'

But no one answered me and Saul swiped his baton through the air as a warning. I looked back at the wall, and the great, imposing brutality of it. There were a few dead looking trees scattered around its edges, and as we got closer a great black bird rose from one cawing so loudly I wanted to cover my ears. Was it my imagination or was there something slumped at the bottom of the tree? I squinted, trying to make it out, before checking the guards faces, wondering if they had spotted it too. Yes, there was something there. Something that resembled a pile of clothes.

The Tree of Rebels

As we drew closer, Saul ordered the guards to tighten up. I didn't know what he meant until Harold and the other guard took up the slack of the chain and moved in closer. Instead of trailing in single file, one behind the other, we now walked side by side, crushed against each other. Again, I looked at their faces, trying to work out what they thought the thing under the tree might be.

Saul grunted and then laughed. What the hell did that mean?

'What is that?' I decided to ask, nudging Connor, who refused to look back at me. He just shuddered and grimaced. 'There's something there,' I said again, louder this time. 'Something at the bottom of that tree.'

'Shut it Turner!' snapped Saul, yanking on the chain. 'I'm warning you!'

I shut up, and we all moved forward, until it became obvious what it was.

'Oh no,' I said, my voice barely above a whisper. 'Is that…?'

'That!' shouted Saul, and his voice was full of so many things right then, I could barely stand to hear it. Malice, loathing and a dripping satisfaction. He was gloating, but why? He pointed at the tree, at the small and still huddle of clothes that sat there. I could see a foot. A dirty, small bare foot, toes up. 'That is your rebels for you, Turner!'

'Don't listen to him,' Connor muttered, his eyes still averted. Ned, like me, looked on in horror. The closer we got, the more obvious it became. A small child had been tied to the bottom of the dead tree.

'They leave them here when they're sick, or unwanted!' Saul was shouting as we approached. 'This happens all over, Turner! *This* is

396

your rebels! This is your people, your cause! Look at it, Turner! Look what they are!'

'What's he talking about?' I begged Connor, unable to tear my eyes from the child. He or she seemed dead, or asleep. Lengths of rope had been tied around its waist, to the tree. Its head hung forward, a thick mass of tangled brown hair obscuring its face.

'Ferals, and how they treat their young!' Saul gloated, dropping his end of the chain now so that he could go to the tree. We all stopped walking and watched. Brandishing a knife, Saul knelt behind the tree and started to hack through the rope.

'Why would they leave their child here?' I asked.

'Because they're feral!' Saul shouted back in triumph. 'They're animals! They can't cope half the time, Turner. They dump them, leave them to die. Or tie them up where we can find them. Don't worry, though. After a bit of time and treatment, we can do something with a creature like this. We can find a place for it.' He cut through the ropes, discarded them, and started to slide his arms under the child.

Just then, the small child suddenly came to life, at first stiffening under Saul's brutish touch, and then throwing back its head and screeching like an animal. We all jumped, and he grabbed her, I think it was a her, and she bucked and writhed and gnashed her teeth like something wild and possessed.

Harold and the other guard laughed as Saul wrestled with her, finally chucking her filthy body under one arm and stomping back to us. He rolled his eyes and looked quite disgusted.

'They better pay me extra for this! Ow! Bloody feral! It bit me!'

Stifling their laughter, the other guards shook the chain to move us all, and Saul slung the girl over his shoulder. I stared on in wonder. Her tiny bare feet kicked against his chest, as her grubby little hands landed fierce blows on his back.

'Case closed!' Saul decided to tell me, his top lip rising into a satisfied sneer. 'What have I been saying all along, eh Turner? This lot out here, they're no better than animals. They're scum and they always have been! *They* were the ones who ruined the Old World, don't you know that?'

I ignored him. We had reached the wall. This was it. Province 1. The large gates were closed. I expected them to open for us, but they didn't. Instead, a small door to the left of us popped open and a bearded face peeked out.

'You took your time!' he shouted impatiently, beckoning us forward.

'It's a long way!' Saul argued back, and to this the man waved a hand dismissively.

'Come on, in you come. Quickly now.'

'And we just found this out here! One of your lot should have been checking!' Saul brought the girl down from his shoulder, holding her tightly around the waist as we were shoved towards the door. I stared at everything, trying to take it all in. The thick grey walls, what were they from? Who built them and why? When? The door was small and narrow, and we had to duck our heads to get through. The man hurried us in. He was short and squat and dressed in black, like our guards. The door closed and he scurried behind a desk to pick up some paper. We huddled together, not knowing what to expect. We were in

398

a small room with a door to the left of us and a door right in front. They looked like they were both made of heavy metal.

'Bloody newbie kid on duties, must have forgotten to check this morning.' the man told Saul as he leaned over the desk, picked up a pen and scribbled his name across three sheets of paper. 'You must be hankering for a bath and some grub,' the man chuckled and Saul nodded, wide-eyed.

'You bet we are. We've got an overnight pass and then we head back tomorrow.'

'Go on then, off you go. Go and get yourselves sorted.'

The ends of our chain were dropped to the floor. With a sly wink and a menacing grin, Saul Lancaster walked away from us, still holding onto the wild, little girl. He opened the door in front.

'Keep your eye on this lot,' he advised the bearded man, before going through the door. 'Think they're above the law. You know the type.'

The door slammed behind them, and we were left in the room with the man behind the desk. He barely acknowledged us and instead, he came around the desk, opened the other door and yelled;

'Serena! Your delivery awaits you!'

Connor and I swapped glances. Ned was barely with us. His head hung low. I caught his elbow and Connor followed my example and held his other one.

'I'm worried about this kid,' Connor addressed the man as he came back around his desk. 'He's been hurt. He needs help.'

The man ignored us. He just seemed bored. Like this sort of thing happened every day.

'Where are we?' I tried asking. 'Where are they taking that child? What will happen to her?'

'Welcome to Province 1!' a female voice boomed out at us, making us all jump. A woman walked through the door, grinning widely. I stared back at her and tried to work out if it was a friendly grin, or a hungry one. She was dressed in black, and wore a chain link belt which clinked when she moved. Handcuffs swung from one side, the inevitable wooden baton from the other, and numerous pairs of keys in-between.

She took some paperwork from the desk man. 'So, who do we have here then? Lissie Turner, that must be you,' she rose two dark eyebrows at me and I nodded in response. 'Ned Fleck?' Ned managed a nod, but he could not lift his head. 'And Connor? Just Connor?'

He nodded silently, looking her over. I did the same trying to work out how old she was. She looked about the same age as my mother, but less tired, more alert. Her thick dark hair was wound into a low bun and her cheeks were full and flushed. She signed something and slung it back at the desk man.

'There you go, honey. I'll take these lovelies down to their new home.'

'Okey dokey,' he replied, not even looking at us.

'This way,' she said, and went back through the door. We followed, slowly and cautiously, still holding onto poor Ned.

'You hang on, Ned,' I told him now. 'We're here now. You're

gonna' be okay.'

'This kid needs help,' Connor called after the woman. 'He's badly hurt. We've been beaten on the way."

'Follow me,' she called back, ignoring his plea.

Beyond the door, we found ourselves on a long narrow walkway made of metal. We looked up and saw another walkway. Down below there was darkness and the only shapes I could make out appeared to be closed doors. We shuffled along the walkway, and the metal bounced and creaked beneath our weight. I was starting to realise what this place was. We walked through the wall of Province 1 and straight into a prison. Unseen by the rest of the inhabitants. We were about to be locked up.

44: Dungeon

There was a strange smell as we moved along the walkway behind our guard. My nostrils were twitching, trying to understand it. It was wet and tangy, perhaps the smell of rusting metal and something else, something sweeter... I looked up and saw a metal ceiling bearing down upon us. It seemed to bulge in places. It looked mismatched and patched together. They must have made this place after the wars, I thought, but then, how did they build the wall? What was the significance of that? We tramped along like that, the floor springy underfoot. There was no noise except for the sound of our footfalls echoing. The light was poor.

At the end of the walkway we came to another door, which the female guard held open for us. One by one, still cuffed and chained together, the three of us limped through. There was even less light now, as we were led down a concrete staircase. The smell began to change. The wet rust being replaced with something more organic, something damp and rotten. The stairs were wet and slippery. Ned leant back on me, trying to keep his balance.

'We need a doctor to look at Ned,' I spoke out suddenly, my fear intensifying as we descended deeper into the black. 'I think Saul broke his ribs. He can't breathe. Listen to him!'

'We have to follow protocol,' the guard responded evenly. We were at the bottom of the steps and the smell was worse. It was pitch black until she lit a torch, illuminating us all. Looking around I saw that we were standing in a square space. There was muddied and rotting straw all over the floor. My eyes adjusted to the dark and I turned in a slow circle, gently easing Ned along with me. They must have kept animals down here once. The place looked like a cross between a stable and a dungeon. Again, there was that strange sense of one picture being drawn on top of another. There were three stalls, which had been adjusted into makeshift cells. No metal doors or keys down here. Just wooden beams, and a young man chained by his feet to one. He looked at us with dull eyes, barely raising his head. I winced and started to panic. He wore a piece of cloth tied around his middle and nothing else. He sat with his back against a dirty bale of straw, his legs bent and his arms around his knees. I could see his white ribs poking out. He had thick dark hair, long on his neck and almost covering his eyes.

The smell was coming from the floor. There were human faeces everywhere you looked. Vomit rushed up my throat without warning and I threw up, just avoiding Ned's feet. There was not much to bring up except water and weeds, but still my stomach heaved and clenched. No one said anything while I emptied my guts. The guard moved toward Connor and took his hands into hers. She did not speak as she picked something up from under the straw and snapped it over one of his wrists. Another handcuff. Recovering, I straightened up to watch. Working quickly, she produced a key from her belt and unlocked the other pair of cuffs. I tried to work out what he was cuffed to, but Connor did not seem to care. With the greatest of sighs, he slowly sunk down to the floor and stayed there.

Next was Ned, who was barely standing. She snapped a metal cuff around one of his ankles, uncuffed his wrists and let him fall.

'He needs help,' I said desperately. 'Please!'

She did not answer me. She merely found another cuff under the straw, snapped it over one of my wrists and unlocked the other cuffs.

'Food!' I said to her, terrified now that she would turn around and walk out of there without giving us any food or water.

'Protocol,' she replied, not meeting my eye.

I could not believe this. I didn't slip down like the others. I remained standing, staring into her face, trying to locate the human within. 'Please,' I said, my voice trembling. 'Please Serena, we need food and water and medicine for Ned...*please!*'

She met my eye and her expression was steely. 'People are coming,' she informed me, with a glint in her eye. 'I advise you to keep calm.'

I shook my head. Calm was the last thing I felt. But she was right. People were coming. There were voices and movement on the steps. I looked down at Connor and he stared right back at me, his jaw tight and his eyes dark. He shook his head just a little and I guessed he was trying to tell me something. I looked at Ned and saw that his eyes were closed. He was curled up like a small child, with his ankle chained to the floor. His face was deathly white.

'Ah, Serena,' a male voice boomed, making me jump. I turned around and there were two men in the room. The one who spoke came forward, smiling sickly. He was of thin, wiry build. He also wore black and was holding a clipboard. 'I see you have settled our new arrivals in.'

'All ready for you Sir,' she replied in a monotone voice, stepping back and clasping her hands neatly in front of her. She stood with her eyes looking ahead, and her face blank. I looked at the other man who had come in. He was older. Greying. His face wizened and

404

rough. He was the only one not wearing black.

My knees were suddenly like jelly and I wanted to sink down too, sink to the floor alongside Ned and Connor and the other young man. And someone else...I could hear them but I couldn't see them. But there was someone else there too. Sniffing and breathing in a dark unknown corner.

The man with the clipboard approached us, stepping carefully, his nose wrinkling at the smell. He examined the paper on his board and frowned.

'Lissie Turner, Ned Fleck and Connor Surname-Unknown.' It was a statement, not a question. Connor and I stared back at him, waiting. Ned snored softly on the ground. The man leant back slightly, squinting at the words before reading them out. 'You have been arrested on the charge of treason and are held under the suspicion of plotting to overthrow the acting government of Province 5. Under the law and order treaty written into the Peace Declaration of 2085, you are to be held here in Province 1 until the date of your trial. You are hereby notified that if found guilty of treason you will be sentenced to imprisonment to a term to be decided by the judge, and if you are found guilty of plotting to overthrow the government you will be sentenced to death by hanging.'

He spoke these words as if they were nothing. He just spat them out at us as if they bored him. As if he had said them a thousand times before. Perhaps he had. Like the guy upstairs at the desk, perhaps this man had seen it all before. Perhaps this sort of thing happened more than we would ever know.

He lowered the clipboard and glanced at us. 'Any questions?'

'When is the trial?' I asked without hesitation. My eyes flitted between this man and the one behind him. The older one reminded me of someone, but I was too tired and in too much pain to connect the dots in my head. I watched him, though. The way he stood back there calmly, observing proceedings with his eyes alert and hungry, while his mouth was a gently stretched smile.

'That date has not been determined yet,' clipboard man replied.

'When will we know? How long can you keep us down here?'

The man laughed a little and started to back off. He'd had enough of this place and its foul stench. 'How long is a piece of string, Miss Turner?' he said, turning to go.

'We need food and water! And medicine for Ned!' I barked these things at him as he put his foot on the bottom step.

'Serena will see to that. You will be well cared for here.'

Well cared for? I shot a look at the half starved young man with his ankles chained together and looked back at them in disbelief. The man nodded at Serena.

'Thank you, Serena. We'll leave them with you for now. Questioning starts tomorrow.'

Questioning?

'Who are you?' I yelled suddenly, before the grey-haired man could leave. He hesitated before going up the steps. His smile stretched and he lifted one hand to scratch at his head in amusement. For a moment, I thought he was going to speak to me, but then he was gone.

Serena moved quickly into action. She crossed the room and disappeared into darkness, but when she returned she was carrying a wooden crate.

'Who was that man?' I asked her, finally letting my legs sag me down to the floor.

It was foul. Wet rotten straw. I kicked at a clump of filth, kicking it away from me. She dumped the crate down and lifted out a jug. She passed it to me.

'Water. Go on. Drink.'

Cautiously I took it, lifted the spout to my mouth and drank quickly, before passing it back to Connor. I lay my hand on Ned's shoulder.

'Ned? Can you hear me? We've got food and water now.'

'He was the Governor,' Serena said then. I looked back at her.

'What?'

'The man who did not speak. He is the Governor. He always comes down to see the new prisoners.'

'He's in charge? Of Province 1?'

She nodded and lifted out a cloth package. She passed it to me and I pulled it apart hungrily. Bread, cheese, ham, apple. None of it at its best, but we didn't care. Connor and I split it into three piles and devoured it viciously. Serena took another package to the young man, and another package to the person we could not see. A tirade of unintelligible growls and grunts were thrown at her. She did not respond and came back into sight, brushing spit from her chin.

'I'll ask about a doctor,' she said, picking up the crate. And with that, she was gone. Connor and I kept eating until our share was exhausted. We wrapped Ned's up in the cloth and pushed it into his hand, but he did not wake. His breathing was hoarse and ragged.

'I'm so worried about him...' I said, tears filling my eyes. Connor patted me with his free hand before picking up the chain attached to the other one and following it back to its point in the floor. He shoved back soiled straw so that I could see. We were chained to three metal circles screwed into the floor. Connor pulled at them, twisted and kicked them. He frowned patiently while he did this. Then he pushed at the floor, searching for a weak point, before giving up with a sigh.

'I don't think we're getting out of these.'

At this point he stood up and stretched. I watched him in exhausted awe. He seemed different, I thought. Like the food and water had renewed him. He may have been chained to the floor but he was still marching on. Still believing. But how? Why?

And then he did something unexpected. He walked towards the young man who had been staring at us silently. His chain allowed him to crouch down before him and the two of them looked at each other, before breaking into soft, childish laughter. I stared in bemusement.

'Connor?'

'Lissie,' he said, looking back over his shoulder. 'Let me introduce you to Tate. My brother.'

408

45: Tate

Of course. Now I could see the resemblance. They had the same thick, dark hair which curled around their ears and along their necks. Tate was smaller, thinner, his face drawn and full of shadows, but his eyes lit up when Connor wrapped an arm around his neck, stretching as far as his chain would allow, and pulling him in for a hug. Their heads touching, they murmured to each other and I felt like I was eavesdropping. While they had their moment, I looked down at Ned and placed my hand across his forehead. He felt cold and clammy and his breath continued to wheeze in and out.

'Knew you'd come...' I heard Tate say before choking on his tears. He pressed his head down further, burying his face into his older brother's chest. Connor rubbed his hair and patted his head and soothed him. In the corner, a figure was rustling and grumbling.

I pulled Ned's head onto my lap. I was thinking about Connor and his marching on. Marching towards his brother and now they were reunited just as I'd hoped. I cleared my throat.

'How long have you been down here?' I asked him, although I almost didn't want to know.

Tate lifted his head clear of his brother's chest and looked at me. He smiled and when he did his eyes shone.

'Honestly, I don't know,' he said. 'Many months. Feels like years.'

'It's been just over a year,' Connor nodded at him, and the younger boy bit his lip and smiled through the pain, fighting back tears.

'You haven't had a trial yet? I asked him.

'Oh yeah I had one. Though I wasn't accused of treason or plotting.'

'What then?'

'Of being an enemy. A rebel.'

The two brothers finally came apart, Connor sitting back on his behind and resting against the straw bale.

'Being an outsider is against their laws,' he explained to my dumbstruck expression. Tate nodded in agreement.

'They can arrest you just for being out there, and bring you here. People always end up here in 1. They send them down from all over.'

'Are there more prisoners here?'

Tate nodded. 'Oh yeah. This place is huge.'

'So, what happened to you?' I asked, desperate to understand. 'You got arrested out there?'

'Hunting rabbits,' Tate said with a weary grin. 'Saw a wagon in the distance and started to head back the other way. Doesn't pay to get seen out there. But they'd already spotted me. There was nothing I could do but run, and they were on horseback.'

'Just as you thought,' I said to Connor and he smiled at me gently, reaching out to touch my shoulder briefly.

'We all know the dangers out there. It's the people inside the

Provinces that have no idea what's going on.'

'No idea what these people are capable of,' I added sadly, stroking back Ned's hair. 'What do they want? Do you know? What do they want in the end? When they've rounded you all up?'

'I don't know for sure,' Tate sighed. 'Maybe that's it. Round up the stragglers and be done with them, and carry on as they are. As far as it goes, people are happy behind the walls and the fences. They're provided for and they think they're safer there.'

I found myself slumping slowly down into the mucky straw, taking Ned and his chains with me. He remained asleep. Perhaps unconscious. My resolve had dwindled down to nothing. I found I was beaten down and I felt broken, like giving up was all that remained. With Ned's limp body pulled into mine, I looked at where we had ended up. A filthy stinking dungeon. Chained to the floor. No way out. Nothing could be done, surely. This was it. This was where it ended, one way or another.

'He's gonna' die...' I said, my voice trembling.

Connor placed his hand on my arm. 'No, he won't. Don't say that.'

'Why not? It's the truth, isn't it? That's what they want anyway. One less trial to deal with.'

'They might send help,' he said hopefully. 'She said she would try. You can't give up, Lissie. Not yet.'

'She's one of them,' I reminded him bitterly. 'What else can we do? This is it Connor. You found Tate, but now what? We're done for.'

'You don't know that,' he tried to argue. 'You have to keep

hoping.'

'What happens tomorrow?' I asked Tate, my eyes now so heavy I could barely look at him. 'They said we would be questioned. What does that mean?'

Tate squirmed visibly in his chains. He glanced at his brother before looking away from both of us. 'I might as well tell you so you can prepare yourselves...'

My blood ran cold. My spine tingled with new terror. 'What does *that* mean?'

'You'll go before the committee. It's basically a group of people who will interrogate you. You might be with one being questioned for a while, then you'll get switched to another.'

'What do they want to know?'

'Anything. Everything. And whatever you say, they don't believe you...'

'They think the rebels are trying to overthrow them,' Connor reminded me. 'That's the kind of information they're looking for. You know, names, locations, plans.'

'They'll keep passing you between people,' Tate carried on. 'Some will play the good guy. Offering you food or water or the chance to go home. They'll do whatever they can to get information out of you...'

'And what if you don't tell them anything?' I asked breathlessly, dreading the answer.

'Threats,' Tate said, with his head hanging. 'Bad guys. They'll try to make you break...'

'They'll hurt me?' I asked, saying the words so that he didn't have to. 'Is that it? Is that right Tate? How bad? How bad will it get?'

I could tell that he did not know what to say. He shrugged and shook his head and bit his lip, struggling with an answer.

'For me,' he said eventually. 'Somehow they found out I couldn't swim. They put me in this concrete hole, like a grave, but you could stand up in it but not get out...' He dropped his head into both of his hands and his fingers were clawing through his hair. 'So they started filling it up with water if I wouldn't answer questions...I lied in the end...told them what I thought they wanted to hear...just made stuff up to please them, but somehow they know you're lying. Thought I was dead. Then I woke up back here.'

I decided I didn't want to hear any more. 'The Governor. What about him?'

'He's a strange one,' Tate admitted. 'He never says much. It's like the other people are in control and he just watches everything. But maybe that's how he plays it. I don't know. He doesn't stop them, let's put it that way. They'll hold back food...water...whatever it takes.

'And how long does this go on?'

'Most days...until your trial. After that they kind of leave you alone. Leave you down here. Isn't that right, Jonas?'

Up until now I had completely forgotten about the person in the corner. The snuffling mumbling pile of shadows. He shook his chains in reply but did not speak.

'Who is he?' I asked Tate, and he scratched at his head again.

413

'He came from Province 5 originally. You know of him?'

I frowned, shaking my head slowly. 'There was a really old guy who had that name…but he died.'

'Hmm,' said Tate. 'Actually, according to him, he was sent out as a scavenger, right? To risk his life finding stuff to help the Province? He found some interesting things while he was out there. He found us. He found the truth, let's say. He lived for a long time with a group out there, but they got him again. He got brought back here…He can't talk to you though…'

'Why can't he?'

'He was charged with the biggest crimes,' Tate said blowing his breath out through his clenched teeth. 'Treason, rebellion, plotting to overthrow, you name it, he got it.'

'Why is he still alive then?'

'I don't know…and you can't ask him either…They cut out his tongue.'

That was enough.

That was…that was too much. Just, enough! I closed my eyes as tightly as I could and buried my face down in Ned's hair. I felt ripped apart on the inside, while Ned slumped against me, probably dying. And Tate and Connor sat in solemn silence now that the terrible words had all been spoken, and the truth was here in the room with us. A tongueless man in the corner. A dying boy. Torture waiting on the dawn of tomorrow…

Okay, I could not bear it. I could not take it. I wanted to close my eyes and just die before any of them could get their hands on me.
414

There is nothing left to do, I thought. No hope. Nothing. Nothing left to do but cry my tears into Ned's hair. No one spoke because there was no point. We had reached the end of the line and I guess we all knew it.

I had no idea what time of day it was when I woke up. My stomach twisted in hunger, my mouth was immediately dry and parched. My feet and legs were throbbing and pulsing with memories of the long walk there. I opened my eyes and peered down at Ned. What if he had gone? What if he'd died while I slept? But he was still with us, still breathing in that rasping, wheezing way. I looked around and could see Connor curled onto his side facing away from me. Tate had fallen asleep with his back against his straw bale and his mouth drooping open. I heard hacking coughs followed by rumbling snores from the man in the corner.... I shuddered.

I heard movement on the steps. Someone was coming.

I sat forward, easing Ned from my lap and peering around the bale to see who it was. I saw the torch before I saw her. The blaze filling the room with more shadows that danced and flickered on the black, moulding walls. The female guard, Serena.

My stomach flipped over. Was it now? Was it my questioning already?

'Have you come for me?' I asked her quietly as she approached, carrying a wooden tray in her arms. She propped the torch against the wall and set the tray down without answering me. 'Is it my turn first?' I asked her desperately, helpless tears filling my eyes. 'Are you taking me to them?'

'No one is going anywhere just yet,' she finally answered me, and her voice was cool and steady. No emotion. Nothing. I wondered where her humanity was. If she had ever had any.

'Did your parents raise you to do this?' I asked her bitterly, and a slight frown creased her forehead. 'To torture people?' I pressed impatiently. 'To chain them up and allow them to be tortured and then killed just because they want to live out there instead?'

'My parents raised me to heal,' she said without emotion, and from the tray she picked up some items and carried them over to Ned. 'Has he woken up?'

'No. Not once.'

She laid her cheek against his chest and frowned again. Then she lifted his shirt and ran her hands over his bruised skin. He moaned but did not open his eyes. 'I think his ribs are broken,' she said, while I looked on angrily.

'Is that why he can't breathe properly?'

She nodded, picking up a roll of bandages from the tray. 'All I can do for him right now is bandage them up. Try to keep them in place.'

'Why are you helping him?' I demanded. 'So it's more fun when you torture him?'

She refused to reply and I found my anger increasing so fast and so hard that I was shaking all over. I didn't want her to touch him. I wanted to smack her hands away from him. But I didn't. I watched her pull him gently into a sitting position.

'You need to help me,' she stated. I leaned forward, taking the weight of him against my shoulder as she began to unravel the

416

bandages. I watched in silence as she began to wrap them tightly around his ribcage. He clung to me, wincing with his eyes still tightly closed. 'I will try to get some pain relief for him,' she said, when she was done. I helped him lay back down and picked up his hand.

'But what do you care?' I spat at her furiously. 'If you're gonna' kill him anyway? Why are you helping him?'

'That should help, for now.' she said and got to her feet. She went back to the tray, picked up a cloth bag and brought it back to me. 'It's not much, but that's your rations for the day. For all of you.'

I took the bag and held it in my lap. 'Water?'

'Later,' she said, and started to go.

'How do you sleep at night?' I called after her, but she kept going, picking up her torch and moving away from me. 'How do you sleep knowing what they do?'

I got no answer. I sat back, resting my head on the bale, listening to her steady footsteps returning the way that they came. Overcome with frustration I felt like hurling the cloth bag at the wall, but I didn't. I took deep breaths and opened it up. All it contained were four apples, one brown, soggy carrot and four dry crackers.

46: Questions

They came for me in swift, brutal silence. That was how it felt. Like they were in an angry, hateful hurry. I'd dozed off and missed their entrance. I looked up in dumb shock, but I did not have a chance to see anything or anyone, before a black hood was pulled down over my head. Of course, I struggled. I struggled and called out, but it was too late, they had me, and besides, everyone else was chained down. There was nothing anyone could do to help me.

So, they took me. With my hands cuffed behind my back, they picked me up, plucked me out of the filthy, wet straw and marched off with me like I belonged to them. The terror clawed violently at my throat, and I gave up screaming. I just waited, breathing heavily into the cloth which cloaked my face. Every time I breathed in, it was sucked into my mouth and my nostrils.

No one spoke. No one said a word. They had me under the arms and by the legs. I was helpless. It seemed to take forever. I was unable to keep track of the directions, or even whether we went up or down. I could hear their heavy boots stomping along, sometimes it sounded like they were walking on more patched up, metallic floors. I started to cry a little bit. I couldn't help wondering if this was the end for me.

Finally, I was set on my feet. A door opened, and then banged shut. Still, no one spoke. I was moved forward and then pulled down into a chair. My hands remained cuffed behind my back, and I felt something strapped around my chest, holding me in place. I bit my lip as hard as I could to keep me from screaming. What was I afraid of?

How would they know? What were they going to do to me? What would they want me to say?

The hood was torn off. I blinked and looked around, but all that greeted me was the slamming of the door again. I had been strapped to a chair and left alone. I stared around at my surroundings, breathing hard and fast, almost insane with confusion. The first thing I noticed was a strange object right in front of me. It was huge, maybe thirty inches in length. It was like a massive window, its surface reflective and shiny, like glass. I peered into it and could see myself staring back. There were pieces of straw stuck in my hair and my eyes looked huge and terrified. I opened my mouth to receive more oxygen, while I stared at the strange item. It reminded me of something they had in the museum back home. They used to have these glass boxes in the Old World. They would stare into them and watch moving pictures, my Grandma Elizabeth said. She said it was part of the problem.

This thing was silent, waiting.

It was rectangular, like a flattened box. I looked around it and above it. I was in a small, dark room. That was all I could tell. There were no windows, and now that it was closed, I could not see the door.

'Hello?' I called out, testing my voice. It sounded tiny and weak, on the verge of tears again. There was no answer. Why had they put me in here with this strange, silent thing? Where had they all gone? I turned my head from one side to the next, but it was hard to see around the strange, flat box thing. I didn't speak again. I stared at the shiny glass, my head low, just breathing in and out, in and out. Waiting for it to begin.

When the thing finally did something, I cringed back into the chair, but I could not look away. It was too close, too big, too bright,

419

hurting my eyes. The blank screen had come alive. Tiny, moving black and white dots were crawling all over it. It was terrifying. I had no idea how that could be happening. There was a sudden, crunching, crackling noise, and then a voice spoke to me from behind.

'Lissie Turner, you are being offered a remarkable gift. You are about to see what the Old World once looked like.'

I opened my mouth to answer, and tried to whip my head around, but whoever it was behind me placed their hands on my cheeks and held me still. Had I missed the door opening again, or had he been there all the time?

'Look,' the voice said, and the screen had changed again. And now it was alive. It was making noise, it was emitting life, right there and then, in front of my eyes. I stared in utter amazement and horror. There was nothing I could do to escape it.

The first things I saw were too fast, too bright, too noisy to process properly. I saw snippets of life, of a world that had died. There were things I remembered from the museum. People, real people, sat in front of boxes just like this one, drinking from cups, eating from bowls, staring, just staring. And then there were people sat in front of the other boxes they used to have, the online ones, the ones that Grandma said used to link them all up, across the world so that they could speak to each other. There were people in cars. Roads choked full of them. Dirty smoke was pumping out of the back of them, and the people's faces were all tight and angry. There were buildings, houses, churches, and other things I could not put names to. So many people. That was all I could think. So many, hundreds upon hundreds of them, teeming across the land, filling up the space, shoulder to shoulder, chest to chest and none of them looked happy. While some of them were extremely fat, unable to move even, others were skeletal, wearing rags.

It was all too bright, moving too fast. Each image jumped onto the next one before I ever got a chance to register it. I wanted to shout out to make it stop. How were they doing this? How did this machine work? I couldn't understand it. These things had died with the Old World. They were relics. History. No one used them anymore. No one turned them on or made them work, because they were dangerous.

There were strange sounds coming from the machine. Getting louder and louder, so that I longed to have my hands free to cup over my ears. It sounded like a roaring, a drumming, a constant beating, angry noise. The people moved faster, like they were not even real, not even in control of themselves. There were animals too. Fast shots of dogs, and cats and other things I had only ever seen in those pasted together books in the museum back home.

The pictures kept going. There was violence. Sudden, pointless, inexplicable violence. I saw it and I couldn't understand it. I just wanted it to stop but I could not look away. I saw some young boys attack an old lady from behind, one of them throwing a foot into the back of her head to take her down. I saw the bounce of her head against the ground, and I saw the shock in her eyes, before they started to kick her in the head. I saw animals on fire, being tortured, screaming. I saw people jabbing sharp things into their arms while their eyes rolled back into their heads. I saw people living in squalor and filth, in shacks and tents, on the ground, in amongst rubbish, and I saw ragged looking people running, while other people chased them, hunted them, shot at them and killed them. I saw babies getting slapped in the head when someone thought no one was watching them. I saw girls fighting in the streets, ripping hair from each other's heads.

The Tree of Rebels

I cried and shouted out to make it stop, and then it got worse.

I saw people with guns aiming at children. I saw villages on fire. I saw emaciated humans behind fences. I saw people hanging from trees by their necks. I saw men in uniforms wielding batons at young people's faces. I saw blood and tears and death and fire. I saw planes dropping bombs. Buildings destroyed. People collapsing in the road. Children with protruding ribs and swollen bellies. Children behind fences, reaching out for food they were never going to get. I saw masses of people moving on foot with everything they owned on their backs. I saw people with signs, shouting and marching, like Grandma's father must have once done. I saw people throwing stones at them. Explosions. Whole towns and cities reduced to dust before my very eyes. I saw the death of the Old World. I saw what humans were capable of. I saw the domes being built, food being cultivated and hungry mouths being fed, and then I saw the domes being attacked, set upon by gangs and wild looking crowds with weapons and fire.

By the time I had closed my eyes, opened my mouth and screamed, it stopped. It suddenly all stopped, and then I could hear birdsong. Sweet, gentle, hesitant bird-song. I opened my eyes cautiously, worried it was a trick. The screen flickered into life again. I saw the world as it was now. I saw places that reminded me of home. People building huts, smoothing mud across the walls, chopping wood for frames. I saw children running and playing, safe behind the fence. Safe from danger. I saw people working. Walking peacefully home. Making bread. Sweeping paths. It all looked so simple. Fires burned for warmth and food and companionship, and no one hurt anyone. I cried even harder then, because I missed it. I missed it so much. I missed my mother and my father and my hut.

'No more war,' the voice behind me said, and the hands relaxed against my cheeks. He released a great, sad sigh and traced one finger from my eye down to my cheek, where it stroked the skin back and forth. 'No more fear. Food to eat. Clothes to wear.'

'Who are you?' I asked

But there was silence.

I kept my eyes closed and tears ran silently down my cheeks.

47: Darkness

I was returned to the dungeon in silence.

Connor and Tate tried to ask me what happened but I refused to answer them. I simply curled up with Ned and pretended I was asleep. I couldn't even bring myself to think about what had happened, what I'd seen. I wouldn't have known where to start. I was so confused, so frightened and worn down. It seemed better to just keep quiet and wait.

Was it day? Was it night? Down here, we had no way of knowing. Hours might have passed, or maybe days. All I knew was that my hunger could not be satisfied and that Ned showed no sign of improvement. We were all listless and silent in the shadows. In the corner, Jonas coughed, spluttered and moaned. I wondered what the point of him was. Why was he still here? How long had he been chained up? What did that do to a person? I wanted to ask, I wanted to know, but my terror held me back. I was learning that it was better not to know. Since I left my home and my parents, I was learning things I never knew possible. I tried to remember the Jonas I used to know. Old, not as old as Grandma Elizabeth, but old enough. Losing his mind, they said, towards the end. His death and his life just more lies…

I found myself thinking about it endlessly. How ironic it all was. Back home they taught us to be grateful for no more war. They taught us to believe that humans had finally learnt. The human race had nearly destroyed itself, but then rose again from the ashes, reborn. New. Innocent and pure. Doing the right thing. And for so long we all believed it. We ate the food they grew for us, we warmed ourselves with the wood they chopped for us. We went about our neat little lives,

424

scurrying from here to there, smiling and thanking.

People back home were good people, I remembered. There were no bad people there. Until us, there was no crime. The cells remained empty. The square was full of people, going to work or school, stopping to chat. Everyone knew everyone else. Everyone did the right thing. But then one day I fell into a daydream on my way home from school...

I smiled slightly now, my hunger and thirst clawing at my insides while Ned slept against my legs. Yes, that one day, when everything changed...or it seemed like it was one day. One day that I wandered home, not paying attention, lost within my own head. One day, utterly normal until out of nowhere I saw a dog. And then I followed it. Whatever came over me that day? I knew the fence was there for a reason. That for three generations we stayed on one side of it and only the fearless scavengers went to the other. That for three generations we had all been safe and provided for and thankful.

But that day I forgot all of that and followed the dog, until I found the tree. My smile stretched when I pictured that tree. Are you still there? I would love to see you again. I would love to touch you again...I would love to sit under your branches and laugh and laugh and laugh. I would do anything...

The apple tree.

The tree of rebels.

The tree that was not supposed to be there, all by itself, growing. It was audacious. It was a challenge, an insult, a rebellion. Right there, growing and living all by itself and no one knew but me. It was a seed, and then it grew. Inside the apples sat more ripe seeds, waiting for their turn, like the unborn child in my mother's womb...waiting to be planted into the earth...waiting for their turn to grow.

That day was etched onto my mind. I decided I would focus on it when they were torturing me. I would think about the rebel tree and the bounty of apples. I would imagine the stream and Charlie and Aisha and her bow and arrow. I would think about all of them, but mostly I would think about the tree when they tortured me.

It all changed on that day, or did it?

Was that the day all of this began? Or had something been rumbling underground for a long time before? I thought about Grandma Elizabeth and I was still smiling. Oh, how I loved her. The smell of her, dried out and parched, soaped and scrubbed, laughing at us all. Waving her hand at them, knowing they were lost causes, slaves to the Song Of Thanks. But not me. What was it that she said? You are one of us, Lissie. *There will always be those who rebel...*

I closed my eyes and she was there.

You are here, Grandma Elizabeth. I can see you. I can smell you. I can feel your old hands in mine. You are with me telling me something with your eyes. Me and you, against all of them, me and you, meeting in our minds just like we always did. I know you and you know me...and now I've seen it too...I've seen your world. Are you with Lawrence now? What happens when you die? Is there a part of you that can escape the flames and soar away, free? I see you Grandma Elizabeth. I see you running towards your Lawrence. I see you with your hands stretching towards his.

I smiled and dreamed, and for a small amount of time I was not chained by one wrist to a sodden, stinking, straw covered floor. Nor was I not cradling my best friends head while he dreamed and whimpered. I was not listening to the man with his tongue cut out, moaning and hacking in his dark corner. I was not cold or wet or hungry or thirsty. I was not waiting to be tortured. I was not waiting to die.

Please. Please Grandma Elizabeth. Lawrence. Mother. Father. Any of you. If you can hear me. If you can help me. Please, please, please...

I think I fell asleep. I think I dreamt about home. But when I woke up something was happening. It was very dark. Shadows were moving fast. From one side to the other. Footsteps slipping and sliding on the soiled bed of straw. Human voices whispered in hurried urgent tones. Fear gripped my heart and soul. I pressed myself back against the straw bale, as if it could shield me. As if anything could.

I cringed and whimpered. I didn't want them to take me again. I didn't want to see any more. Hands came out of nowhere in the black. They grabbed my wrist and I wanted to scream but when I opened my mouth nothing but a shaking gasp came out. I fought for it, I fought for my scream, but it was not there. Only spluttered gasps, squeaks, nothing, not enough.

I couldn't feel Ned. I couldn't hear Jonas. Where were Connor and Tate?

'It's time to go,' a voice was telling me. It was her. Serena. She had come for me in the dark, again. This was how they did it. They tore you away in the black. They tore you away terrified and confused,

427

so scared you could not even scream. And I had a feeling this time it was going to be much worse...

I tried to fight, but there were more hands on me. The chain was moving and I was moving with it. I bucked and writhed but there were hands on me, hands grabbing me, pulling me.

'Time to go,' I heard her telling me again. 'Don't fight it.'

Oh, no, but no, I didn't want to go, I wanted to stay with Ned, where was Ned? I wanted to stay with Ned, my friend, my best friend, I wanted to know where he was, and was he alive? And oh, no, no, where were they taking me now? The darkness was cloaking everything. I could not breathe. They were pulling something over my head again…

I tried to scream but I just couldn't do it. My voice box had been taken. They must have taken it from me like they took the tongue from Jonas. Ripped it out of me while I slept. I was voiceless. Helpless. They were taking me, taking me in the dark a second time, hands all over me, owning me, and I was in the dark and no, no, no,

Please....

48: Light

For a long time, there was no light and no hope, and no noise inside the hood. My hands were bound behind me. I was dragged, carried along by two, three, four people? I could not tell. I could not breathe. I thought I was afraid before, but now I knew what real fear was. Real fear was this; this tight black darkness, this dragging towards pain, towards agony, towards death. Surely before had been just a teaser, just a glimpse of what they could to do me. They'd messed with my mind and now it would be my body. I tried to drag with my feet, I fought to find something to hold onto, but there was nothing.

We didn't go up the steps. Where were the steps? Where were we? I heard muffled voices, shushing, hissing. Metal scraping. A dull thud. We stopped. A metallic bang. Echoes. And then forward again, and then down, oh no, no, no, they were pushing me down, they were putting me down somewhere...and there was nothing under my feet, and only hands pushing me down, shoving me through. Oh, no, please no...

I finally screamed out but it was not the same sound as the one I heard in my head. When I opened my mouth the rough material was shoved in and my scream became a muffled gargle. My feet hit the bottom, my knees buckled, but I was held up by arms. Shoved forward again.

I thought they were burying me...leaving me to die in a hole...but no, we were moving again, and I felt the relief shudder through me violently. I strained my ears, tried to place the noises. Feet against ground. Wet. Splash. Hurrying, all hurrying, moving quickly. I didn't know how long, and where was Ned? Oh, what were they doing to Ned?

Finally, we stopped. Footsteps halted. I held my breath inside the hood and heard them breathing rapidly. They sounded panicked. Excited. I waited. There was slow movement now. Inching forward and then another metallic scrape. A thick grating sound that ended in a high-pitched squeal. I could feel something...cold air...

I was thrust forward. Hoisted up. Someone had me under the arms. Someone else was pushing my feet. I went with it, gulping in fresh air, feeling the cold smack of outdoor air around my head. We were outside? It felt and smelled like we were. Out of the tunnel, out of the dark. I didn't know what to think. I stayed quiet, dreading, hoping.

Scuffled movements all around me. Shoes against rubble, concrete. Fresh air creeping up under the hood so that I could breathe and drink it in. I was moved again. Lifted. Feet first, and then under the arms again. I bumped down. I fell forward. Hit my head. Curled up small. No one touched me now. I heard their voices. I sensed the adrenalin. I smelled something warm, wet straw or hay. Something else. I curled up tighter, my senses strengthening. Horses hooves. A snort of warm breath. I dared not hope...

Moving. We were moving. Bumping, thumping, rolling, faster and faster and faster and finally someone leaned over me and pulled off the hood. I blinked fast, making sense. But it did not make sense. Connor and Tate looking down on me, smiling from ear to ear. Relief shining in their eyes. I struggled to sit up. Connor and Tate. Free.

'What?' I started to ask, and then I saw her, crouching behind them, her long dark hair loose around her shoulders. Her arms cradling a small body, holding his head upon her lap. Ned.

'Serena?' I asked, my voice wrecked, just a croak, just a whimper.

She looked up, meeting my eye and she nodded. Connor crouched down beside me, reached around and unlocked my cuffs with a key. I was free. Utterly confused, I blinked around at all of them. Serena, Connor, Tate and Ned, and in the far corner, hugging himself, looking as shell shocked as I felt. Jonas, the man with no tongue. I grabbed Connor by the hands.

'What's going on?'

He smiled and nodded back at Serena. 'Lissie Turner, meet Serena Smith. Our mother.'

49: Serena

I was shocked into silence. I just stared at her and shook my head, and then I stared at Connor and Tate and shook my head again.

'What?' It was all I could say. I was breathless. Shaking from head to toe as the fear slowly and reluctantly left my body. '*What?*'

'We'll explain later,' she said to me with a half-smile. 'For now we've got bigger things to worry about.'

It was then that I heard the other noises going on; horse's hooves clattering against the ground. Raised voices. Shouting, screaming and bellowing. What the hell was going on? And then I remembered Ned. I scuttled forward and the violent movement of the wagon nearly threw me from one end to the other. We all hit the floor and held on. I found Ned and touched his face.

'Is he okay? What's going on?'

'He's okay,' Serena assured me, easing his head gently from her lap. She found an old sack and folded it up to place under his head as a pillow. Then she looked me in the eye. 'We're escaping.'

'You're not really a guard? You're not one of them?' It seemed a stupid question to ask, but so much had happened in such little time that I could not quite keep up. I just stared at her dumbly, begging her to explain everything to me.

'I infiltrated them,' she explained, before changing her position so that she could see out of the back of the wagon. She reached out for a bow and arrow buried under the straw. 'We'll talk later Lissie. We're not out of the woods yet.'

432

With that, she peeped out of a crack in the material and positioned her bow and arrow as if to strike. 'What're you doing?' I asked, shaking my head. She did not answer me. None of them did. All four of them were doing the same. Arming themselves with bows and arrows that had been hidden under the straw.

'Who's after us?' I called out, as we raced on, the horses thundering us through the night. I crouched down next to Ned, holding onto his sleeping body as the wagon rocked violently from side to side.

'Not many at the moment,' Connor called back over his shoulder. 'Three horses, but we can sort them out when they catch up.'

Sort them out? Dry mouthed I looked at the weapons in their hands. The metal tips of the arrows looked impossibly big and sharp. I didn't want to think about it so I curled up small next to Ned. For a moment, as the wagon jolted him from side to side, his eyes opened and he stared up into my face.

'Ned? Ned! It's okay we're getting out of here!'

'Out of where?' he asked, before giving in and closing his eyes again. I ruffled his hair lovingly.

'You don't even know what's going on,' I muttered. But he must be getting better, I thought. Before I knew it, he was snoring deeply and loudly. I saw Connor looking down at me.

'He'll be out for the count for a while,' he said. 'Mum gave him something for the pain but it kind of knocks you out. We thought it best, under the circumstances.'

'Escaping you mean?' I asked him. 'Why didn't you tell me? Did you know about this all along Connor?'

'Kind of. There's a lot you don't know...'

'Story of my life!' I barked back angrily. He shrugged and looked sorry. 'What about the little girl?' I remembered then. 'Didn't you get her too? What's happened to her?'

Connor shook his head. 'There's a lot to explain...' he started but Tate held up a hand.

'Not now,' he warned him from the flap. 'They're getting closer.' He stood up, his head pushing into the roof of the wagon. Without being asked, Connor stood up too, wrapped one arm around his brother's middle and then held onto the wagon with his other arm. Secured in place by Connor, Tate brought up his bow, positioned the arrow, pulled the arrow back and aimed.

I watched in dumb confusion. What the...?

'Now!' Serena barked, and Tate released the arrow. I heard it go. It whistled through the air and despite the roar of the horses' hooves, I heard the dull thud of its arrival.

'Bullseye!' Connor yelled in triumph, grinning back at me. I was horrified and yet relieved. I opened my mouth to say something, to question them, to ask who was dead, but I couldn't. There were no words. I closed my mouth, held onto Ned and longed for this to be over.

Suddenly there was a loud bang and the horses reacted instantly, rearing up in fear and sending us all flying to the bottom of the wagon. Jonas was knocked off his feet and only stopped himself from flying out of the wagon by clinging to Serena, who was on the floor and holding on for dear life. The horses flew on, whoever was driving them gaining control. Connor grabbed his mother and Tate grabbed Jonas, and for a moment none of them were watching the entrance or aiming their arrows, and that was when the gunman took another shot.

But it was not just one shot. It was a whole volley of them, and the noise was incredible. Like we were all exploding. Like we were all on fire and burning. I covered my head with my arms and threw myself over Ned, cradling his head.

The horses were going crazy now. I guessed they had never heard gunfire before, and neither had I. But I knew this was what it was because the bullets were slamming into the wagon all around me, splintering wood. The horses were weaving from one side to the other and I could hear the guy up front yelling at them desperately.

I thought, this is it. We'll die now. Maybe this is better. We'll die on the run. Like true rebels. Fighting back. But this was not what happened. I watched Connor crawling towards the opening and while he did, his brother seized his ankles and held on tight. Serena had pulled Jonas inside, but the bullets were arriving so thick and fast that it was all they could do to stay alive.

I watched Connor with one eye open, my arms still tightly over my head. I saw him hanging out of the back of the wagon while Tate held onto him. I saw him positioning his bow and arrow. I thought; any minute now, any minute now, the bullets will hit you, the bullets will destroy you, the bullets will tear you apart before our eyes...

I couldn't look. I buried my head. Closed my eyes. Be over, one way or another, just be over! The noise was deafening. The explosion of gunfire. The horses terrified hooves. The wagon bumping and crashing and swinging from side to side. And in all that chaos, Connor Smith raised his simple bow and arrow and fired.

All at once the noise stopped. No more bullets. He looked back at us and grinned. The horses were still spooked, but the instant the noise stopped, they started running smoothly again and the wagon stopped swinging us all about. Tate helped pull his brother further back into the wagon.

'How many left?' Serena asked him.

'Just one,' he said. 'But he's quitting. Look.'

I scooted forward with the rest of them, desperate now to see what it was we had escaped. Feeling safer now that the horses had settled down, I laid flat on my belly and lifted the material to squint out at the world outside.

I saw one horse. One guard. Slowing.

Harold. Staring back at me.

Did that mean Saul was dead?

I dropped the flap and shuffled quickly back to Ned. Saul dead? No, it couldn't be possible. He was just like us really, he was just our age, just stupid and headstrong and trying to impress... I glanced at Connor and Tate, and I was thinking, which one? Which one of you killed him?

I thought I was about to cry for Saul bloody Lancaster. That heartless boy who nearly killed us on the way here. The tears were brimming; my lip was wobbling. What was wrong with me? I opened my mouth to address the silence of the wagon. He was just a kid, I wanted to tell them but the looks on their faces stopped me. They were all staring at Ned.

I looked down at Ned. I saw Ned and I saw what was his

stomach. I saw what was his flesh and bones. I saw the skin smoking. I saw the hole. The explosion. The smell. The blood. The blood running like a river. Running faster than the horses. Running, escaping. His blood was escaping just like he was.

No, Ned.

No.

Hands in my hair. I was one long scream. I was wide eyes, eyes so wide they filled my face and screamed so loud it filled my head, and it exploded my brain and my sanity and no, no, no, please, *please no*!

50: No

She said that to me, didn't she? That there would always be those who said no. And no was all that I could say. Just over and over again while the tears blurred my vision and the screams numbed my ears. Somewhere in the chaos was Serena, with her dark knowing eyes, whipping off her coat and pressing it down onto his stomach. The blood soaked through and the coat was red and her hands were red, and still I was saying it over and over and over, no, no, no, no.

The horses thundered on. The three men held their positions at the back of the wagon and I was dimly aware of more gunshots, more violence, more danger. But I could not care. I cradled his head and I was screaming no, but inside my head there was a dark silent corner where I looked at myself in a mirror and told myself that *I* did this.

I told him about the tree and the dog. I let him know my secrets. I dragged him along. I made him rebel. And now this...but no, no, not Ned, not my Ned, she would save him, surely she would, she would know how, she would save him for me...

I screamed this at her and she kept screaming back at me that she did not have anything else. There was nothing else. This could not be. This could not happen. He was just lying there, still ill, barely conscious, just lying there waiting to be saved.

The blood never stopped. His head in my lap. My arms wrapped around his skull, my face against his cheek, my eye to his eye, my breath waiting for his to kiss me back. But it never came. My eye stared into his eye, and his eyes were rolled back into his head taking him with them, taking him to a place he could not come back from. His body was limp and his mouth hung open and maybe he

438

never knew anything about any of it.

And he died.

51: Burial

I had no idea what happened to me after that. I could not
scream any more, as my throat was stripped raw. I just pressed my
face into his, and held him in my arms and cried. I did this. I did this to
him. Serena was there, watching me silently. The danger was not over.
The bullets rained on. We bumped and jumped and thundered through
the night towards something.

And Ned was gone.

When I woke up, I was facing the floor, my head buried in my
arms. I rolled over and sat up and I saw Ned covered with coats and I
remembered again. I did this. I started to cry, useless, pointless, selfish
tears. Connor sat beside me and tried to touch me but I pulled away.
We all did this. Tate and Jonas sat at the back, bows on their laps, eyes
down. Serena was the only one to speak.

'We're sorry, Lissie. We are so very sorry.'

I couldn't answer her. I wanted to lift the coats and see his face
again but at the same time I knew that I couldn't. Because he had gone.

'We're safe for now,' Serena was saying. 'We got away. But
they'll send more. They always do. We've had to change direction,
because we don't want to lead them to the camp. But we'll be there
soon. I promise.'

'Where is it?' I asked, and my voice came out hoarse and cold.

'West. To the coast. It will take all night. The more distance we
put between them and us, the better.'

'You planned all this,' I meant to put this as a question, but it came out as a statement, and when I looked up and saw their faces, I knew that I was right. Serena nodded.

'This has been planned for a long time, Lissie. Years.'

'There are always people like you,' Connor spoke up then, an awkward look on his face. 'Every Province has them. People who want to get out and live life differently.'

I shook my head at him, tears still flowing freely from my eyes. 'I didn't know I was helping you. *We* didn't know. Helping you do what? What is it all about?'

'It's a long and complicated story,' Serena said with a sigh. 'I think for now it will be best if you get some sleep. You're in shock. You're just a child.'

I glared at her, outraged. 'I'm fourteen years old. I am an adult.'

She shook her head sadly. 'Not in our world you're not. In our world, you are just a child and you have seen too much. Let us take care of you now.'

'Where are you taking me? What happens to me now?'

'You can stay with us,' she said gently, hopefully. 'We're going to one of our meeting points. There is a big camp. A settlement. We can stay there for a while. It will be safe. Aisha will be there by now.'

'She knew? She knew about all of this?'

'Some of it,' Serena replied. 'She told us about you when she found you down by the stream.'

'Was she there by accident? I don't understand any of this!'

'She was hunting,' said Connor. 'But not just for food.'

'What?'

'We drift as close to the Provinces as we can,' Serena explained, sitting back on her heels with her blood-stained hands resting in her lap. 'We can't just forget about the people in them, Lissie. These are our people too. They want to get out and we want to get in and help them.'

I was so confused my head hurt. I wanted to understand all of this, but there was Ned, poor, dear Ned lying under the coats at the side of the wagon...I stifled another round of sobs and clenched my teeth.

'She was looking for someone like me?'

'In a way, yes. Just looking,' shrugged Serena. 'Looking for signs of escape. Struggles. Communication, that sort of thing. People leave notes, you know. Help us. Come for us. It starts with the scavengers usually. They've come across us while searching for resources. They like what they see sometimes. They start to see things differently. As I said, it's a long, long story, but you need to believe us Lissie. She was there looking to help people.'

'And when she saw me there?'

'She told us,' Connor added with a sigh. 'And we knew right away, when she told us you were on the wrong side of the fence. We knew right away that you were one of us.'

'My great grandma told me that too...' I murmured, looking away from him. 'She was one of you.'

'Connor told us about the diary,' Serena said gently. 'She

442

sounds like she was an amazing woman.'

'You lied to me,' I said then, looking at Connor. He frowned.

'When?'

'When you said you stay away from the Provinces...when you said you leave them alone.'

'Look, we don't attack their food convoys,' he said, shrugging his shoulders at me. 'We wouldn't touch that poison anyway!'

'I don't know what to believe,' I said, looking from Connor to Tate, to Serena. 'I saw things...when they took me. There was this screen, and it was alive and moving...I don't know how they did it but they showed me the Old World!'

Serena's head tilted slightly to one side and she nodded. 'The TV Room. It's all propaganda, Lissie. Do you know what that means? They've chopped and sliced up the pictures to make it look how they want it to look. They have this stuff, you see. The power is on for those who need it. Don't you see, Lissie? Don't you see? There are people living in one world, while they exist in a completely different one, and they lie about all of it! The way things are, what happened, *all* of it was planned, Lissie. It was a long time coming and some people predicted it. People like your great-grandmother. But they were ignored or made fun of. And the lies are still being told.'

I couldn't go there now. There just wasn't time. I narrowed my eyes at her. 'Never mind that. The Governor told me you are trying to overthrow them, is that true?'

Connor opened his mouth to respond but his mother answered too quickly. 'No,' she said firmly. 'We have no interest in taking their power from them. They can keep their domes and their food and they can carry on exactly as they are. All we want is to be left alone to live in peace and for the people who feel like us to be allowed free. That's it Lissie. That is what we do. People like you should be able to come and try our way of life if they wish to.'

'But how do you do it?'

'Like we said,' she went on patiently. 'We hunt close to the Provinces. We look for signs that people want out and then if we can we help them. Jonas joined us from your Province a long time ago. His father was one of many not happy with the way things were. He was a scavenger too, you see. Jonas came looking for us as soon as he started work.'

'They said he went crazy,' I heard myself whispering. 'They used to tell us not to go near him. Then he died peacefully in his sleep.'

'He didn't die, he was arrested in the night, much the same way you were,' said Connor, gravely. 'They found out he was in contact with us.'

I looked at Serena. 'How did you end up in Province 1?' I was becoming overwhelmed with exhaustion now. It was like a thick black cloak enveloping me and pressing me down. But I had to know the answers...I had to understand why Ned died...

Serena seemed to shift under my gaze. She looked at her sons and at Jonas. 'We wanted to free Jonas,' she said, 'and to do that we had to get more of us in there.'

'You mean Tate got arrested on purpose?' I almost screamed. My head was lolling now. My eyes were so heavy. I leaned back

444

against the side of the wagon and fought to stay awake.

'Yes,' Tate nodded, speaking for the first time. 'We set it up. They always keep all the prisoners at 1. We knew I'd find Jonas there.'

'But what about you?' I asked, my voice no more than a sigh now. 'Serena. How did you get in there? How did you get to be a guard?'

She looked down for a moment. 'There is so much we need to explain to you, Lissie.'

'Tell me,' I insisted, but I didn't last long enough to hear it.

The next time I woke up, warm sunlight streamed into the back of the wagon and my stomach growled loudly. When I woke up I remembered poor Ned and I started to cry again. I didn't think I could bear it. The pain of it was inside of me and growing bigger, stronger, squeezing my lungs and crushing my chest. I didn't think I could breathe. I didn't think I wanted to breathe. I sat up and pulled up my knees, hugging them to me and turning my head so that I could see him. He was once a person, he was once my best friend, and now he was just a lump under a pile of clothes. I closed my eyes and sobbed.

The others left me alone. We stopped twice to feed and rest the horses and it was on the second stop that Serena and Jonas started to move Ned from the wagon. Instantly I was on my feet, wobbling and weak, outraged and horrified.

'No! What're you doing!'

'We can't go on like this,' Serena explained to me patiently as they gently lifted him down to the ground. 'My darling, it's time to say goodbye.'

I slipped down to the ground on weak legs. 'No.'

'Yes, Lissie,' she responded. 'We can't carry him around like this. It isn't right. We have to lay him to rest.'

'How? We can't just leave him here! What about his parents?'

Jonas and Serena looked at each other awkwardly. 'What do you think they would want Lissie? We can try to do what you think is best.'

Tears in my eyes yet again. Snot hanging from my nose. 'Well they never cared much about him,' I said bitterly, 'so I don't think they would care much either way. But *I* care.'

'Of course you do,' Serena said softly, coming to my side. 'I am so sorry Lissie. It was not meant to be like this...'

'You killed them too,' I said, looking at her coldly. 'You killed two of them. You killed Governor Lancaster's son. He's not going to like that very much.'

She backed away from me, wringing her hands. 'I know that Lissie. It's not what we wanted but we had to get away. We had to save you.'

'But not Ned. Ned didn't get saved.'

'We're going around in circles here,' a voice spoke up, as a man in dark clothes came around from the front of the wagon, where the horses were enjoying their food. I looked him up and down. He must be one of the drivers, I thought. He had a wispy grey beard, not much hair on his head and was smoking a pipe. 'I'm sorry lass, I really am.

446

We're all sorry about your friend. But if you'd stayed where you were they would have tortured you to death. We've got to get moving again as soon as possible.'

'Were you a spy too?' I asked him, my voice small and hard. 'Were you pretending to be a guard?'

He rolled his eyes in slight impatience and nodded back at me. 'Not pretending. I *was* a guard, just like my mother and father before me. Only they'd been told a different story by their ancestors. One that didn't involve keeping nature locked up. Get my drift?' He looked at Serena and lifted and dropped his hands.

'This is Flynn,' she informed me. 'He's just like you, child. He has wanted to escape the Province for many, many years. Today was a huge day for all of us.'

I wanted to say something in reply. I wanted to argue with him and with all of them, but I couldn't because I did not understand any of it. I just shook my head, sat down on the grass and allowed them to get on with it.

In the end, they dug a shallow grave and lifted him into it. While Jonas was hunched over and throwing dirt back on top, Tate and Connor wandered around, picking flowers and leaves. By the time they had finished it looked like a mound of flowers and was quite beautiful. Serena took my hand and eased me down to the ground. She had a collection of leaves and flowers in her hands and as she gently lifted one of my broken, bleeding feet, she told me what they were.

'Yarrow,' she said, plucking a spiky looking leaf from the pile. She broke it into pieces and applied them to my foot. 'Rose petals,' she went on, holding my foot firmly in one hand while she placed the dark red petals on top of the Yarrow. She then used long narrow leaves to wrap around my foot. She did this again and again until my foot was covered in green. 'Plantain,' she sighed, before lowering my foot and picking up the other one. 'Makeshift bandage Lissie. To stop the bleeding and stop the germs getting in. The plantain will alleviate the pain too. Just you wait.'

I just stared as she worked on my second foot. Wrapped up in cool green leaves, the pulsing pain started to relax its hold on me almost at once.

'The Governor has poisonous flowers...' I murmured, and she looked up at me grimly. 'I was allowed to water them for him...Then he used one to kill my great-grandmother.'

Serena shook her head briefly in response. 'Vile. Turning nature against people. Goodness knows what things they come up with in those domes. They twist everything into evil, that's what they do. I am sorry Lissie.'

When she had finished, Connor handed me a bunch of clovers and daisies he had picked and I got up and limped over to the grave with him and Serena just behind me.

'They burn bodies back home,' I said to whoever was listening. 'Turn them to ash.'

'This way he will sink back into the earth,' said Connor. 'There will be new growth.'

'I'm never going to see him again...'

It hurt more than I could imagine. It ripped through me, wave after wave of agonising despair. And thick black guilt. Clinging to my skin and to my soul. I placed my flowers on the grave and started to cry again.

'I'm so sorry Ned...I am so sorry I did this to you...'

52: The Sea

Time and space and distance took me further and further away
from Ned. I slept and woke and remembered and cried. And then did
just that all over again. I felt certain it would destroy me. I did not
speak to the others. I did not feel like I could trust them, and it was a
horrible way to feel. I looked at Connor and thought, you knew all
along. You knew your brother and mother were there. You *wanted* to
be taken. You set this up, you and Aisha. I didn't know what to think
or who to trust. I kept seeing flashes in my head of the images from the
strange screen. Rebels attacking the domes...just like the Governor had
told me. All I knew was that I dragged my best friend into this and
now he was dead. I wished it was me who was dead. I wished the
bullets had hit me and not him. It should be me lying back there in the
ground.

The wagon rumbled on, shaking gently from side to side. I was
lost in a world of my own, a world of confusion and pain. I thought of
my parents and started to weep again. I should have stayed there and
shut my mouth. I should have handed that wretched diary back to the
Governor and let that be the end of it. If only I had! If only I had, Ned
would be alive...We would both be back there, living in our new huts.
Sitting out by the fire night after night, talking and sharing food. It
would have been okay. We could have lived like that. We could have
been happy. Who the hell was I to question it? To want so much more?

All I could do was cry and shake my head and allow the wagon
to take me on. And outside the smells and sounds were changing. I
could smell something I had never smelled before. It invaded my
nostrils, and my hairs all stood on end, reacting to it. I sucked it in,
examining it, questioning it. It seemed to tingle through to my bones...
450

When we finally stopped moving, I felt cold air on my arms and on the nape of my neck. I crawled towards the opening and jumped down to the ground, stretching and yawning. The others were chatting, sounding joyful and relaxed.

'We're here,' Serena said to me, her hair loose now and blowing back out behind her in the wind. 'We made it. We're safe now.'

I didn't answer her, but I wandered slowly away and towards the great vast thing that was shimmering on the horizon...

It was silver and blue and dipping and rolling. It was like the sky, only in motion. And up above these big white winged birds were sailing and squawking and the smell was like nothing in this world.

'You've never seen the sea before?' Tate asked gently, coming up beside me. I shook my head and started to walk towards it. I kept going, walking away from the wagon and from the rebels. I kept walking towards this magical shining thing.

I was dimly aware of eyes watching me. Of people, near and far, and voices murmuring, but I paid no attention, just kept walking forward. At some point the land changed beneath my feet. The ground softened and yielded to my weary tread. The grass became sparser. Warmth slipped up through my toes. Something incredibly soft and warm was smothering my feet, and I was sinking into it as I walked. My knees dipped and gave. I stuck out my arms for balance. I was trembling.

I kept it in my sights. I could hear voices. Children. Dogs barking. I could smell food cooking. But nothing was as great or as wondrous as the expanse of rippling blue that beckoned me forward. I trudged on, hurrying now, going as fast as my battered body could carry me. Tears fell fresh on my cheeks. Ned, I was thinking as I ran towards it, oh Ned, you would have loved it...Oh Ned, you did not get to see it!

I would see it for him. I would be his eyes. I ran on. The stuff under my feet grew colder, wetter, harder. It was compacted. Hard things jabbed the flesh of my soles. I tripped and stumbled and kept running on. The water came for me. It rushed up, frothing at the mouth, rolling and tumbling before withdrawing again, urging me forward, calling me. I fell, got up, ran on. As I ran through the water it splashed up my legs, onto my chest, my face, my hair. I wanted to bathe in it. I wanted to be clean.

I was waist deep when I stopped running. I stood there feeling it rock me. I rolled back on my heels with every wave. I stared down into it, at my splayed fingers like stars, and I waved them about under it and I wiggled my toes and buried them in the strange ground. One by one the green leaves came loose from my feet and floated away on the froth. The water stung my cuts and I held my breath for a moment, accepting the new pain. It smelled salty, fresh, vivid and alive. I felt my body absorbing it, taking the energy back inside. I felt stronger. I felt alive.

Oh, Ned. He would have loved it. We would have run and jumped and pushed each other into it. I stood there for a long time, just staring at it. It went on forever. The sun twinkled on the horizon, the sea shushed and soothed. I thought it was the most beautiful sound I had ever heard. It was sending me to sleep. And suddenly my knees were so weak I could barely stand.

Stumbling, panicking slightly, still crying, I turned around and waded my way back the way I came. I sat down and pulled up my knees, shaking violently. There was someone there behind me. Someone approaching slowly and warily and when they arrived at my side, I glanced down at their bare wet toes and then I looked up.

Aisha.

She smiled the saddest smile. 'I'm so sorry, Lissie,' she said, and I could see she meant it. She sat down slowly as I nodded at her. She tucked her hands into her lap and her bare legs stuck out, her toes digging into the earth.

'The sea,' I said, taking a huge breath. 'You tried to tell me about it.'

'You've never seen the sea,' she said, remembering. 'You've never felt the sand between your toes.'

I plunged my hand into the ground and let it fall through my fingers. 'This stuff?'

'Sand,' she smiled gently. 'I'm so glad you got to see it, Lissie. But I'm so very sorry about Ned. Serena was just telling us. I'm so sorry that happened. Poor, poor Ned.'

'All my fault,' I told her.

'No,' she shook her head adamantly. 'You didn't kill him. *They* did.'

'And Saul died too,' I shrugged. 'He's dead as well. Connor killed him, and another one.'

'It's not right,' she said, her loose hair whipping back behind her as the wind came in off the sea. 'But they did what they had to do, to get Tate and Jonas out of there.'

'But what about the little girl?' I looked her right in the eye and she held my gaze. 'There was a little girl tied to a tree outside the Province. Saul said the rebels leave children like that when they're unwanted. He said they take them in, make them better. Why isn't she here, Aisha? Why didn't Serena rescue that little girl as well as us?'

Aisha breathed out slowly, as if steadying herself, as if trying to decide what words to speak, when she knew so many of them would be useless. 'I don't know,' she said. 'I haven't had a chance to talk to Serena yet. Maybe she didn't know about the little girl?'

'Aisha, I don't understand any of it...I don't know what is right or wrong anymore. I don't know who to believe about anything...I just wish that Ned was here. For that, I regret everything.'

She reached out and patted my shoulder. 'You'll feel differently one day. I promise you. Ned's death was like Lawrence's. A sacrifice. For a bigger cause.'

Tears pricked at my eyes and I shook her hand away. 'Don't say that. It doesn't make it better.'

'I'm sorry, Lissie. I truly am. You're exhausted and confused. You need sleep and food. You must let us care for you now.'

It was only then that I looked behind me, at the people and the lives I had ran blindly past. Up on the grassy banks, there was a camp. Like Serena told me. Makeshift tents and huts were dotted about; thick sticks and shafts of wood tied together with rope and twine, roofs thatched with a type of grass. There were wooden wagons, like the one I had come in on. Horses, grazing with their long tails flicking. Small children ran about, chasing each other. Chickens scuttled between the

454

tents, pecking at the ground. Several fires were burning, and as I lifted my nose I could smell delicious unknown things cooking. My mouth filled with saliva.

'I don't understand what happened,' I said weakly. 'I don't know who I can trust. You came to the river looking for someone, didn't you? You found me by accident, but it was an accident you were looking for.'

Aisha smiled gently and shook her head, so that her hair sailed back over her shoulders again. 'They're cracking down on scavengers,' she said. 'After Jonas betrayed them, and some others. They decided it wasn't worth the risk any more to send people out. They probably didn't bother announcing it or anything, but the scavenger job is over. We had to find other ways to help those that wanted to get out, as well as the ones they've taken from us. Does that make sense?'

'No, not really.'

'Come on,' she said, still smiling that gentle smile, like a big sister looking down on me in amusement. 'There is plenty of time for talk later.' She got up and held out a hand to me. 'One thing at a time, Lissie Turner. Okay? One step at a time. Come and eat with me.'

It was good advice. It was like something Grandma Elizabeth would say. I had no choice anyway, so I took her hand and let her pull me to my feet and lead me slowly back towards the camp. As we went, people stopped and stared. I looked into their faces and they smiled and nodded at me, and their shoulders relaxed, and some waved and some said hello.

Aisha led me through the tents and the dens. Some were tiny;

hastily thrown together. Some seemed more established, more secure, as if they had been there for years, sheltering people like me. As I passed, I peered in. I saw blankets and pillows, discarded shoes, pots and pans, signs of lives. A woman sat outside one of them, a tiny baby feeding at her breast. Two children peeked out of another, dirty cheeked and bright eyed.

Aisha led me through the homes of the rebels and she took me into a large tent which was built under a tree. I ducked under the covering, and saw that it was made from several tall branches which had been tied together at the top. Like a cone. I sort of collapsed once I was inside. I was done in. Could not function a second longer. I crawled under some blankets and slept.

53: The Rebels

I slept for the longest time. I was not aware of much. When I woke, I was groggy, barely with it. Aisha spoon-fed me warm, spicy soup and I went under again. Other times I woke up and Serena was there, wiping my brow, offering me water. Night came and went. Day did the same. I slept so deeply and I dreamed. I dreamed about home, and Grandma and Mum and Dad, and I dreamed about Ned, and Saul and Charlie.

I drifted in and out of consciousness and I heard the noises of the camp. The calls of the mothers to their children. The squeals and the laughter and the scolding and the crying. The hearty bellows of men. The yelps and growls of dogs. I smelled the food, rich and spicy, hearty and fragrant. I smelled the sea. I heard the crackle of fires burning. I heard the songs that they sung around the campfire at night, and the sound of a banjo reminded me so much of my father, that my stomach crunched up in pain, and fresh tears stung my eyes.

When finally, I had slept enough, I crawled out of the tent and sat there, blinking. The thought of Ned came to me instantly, as did the tears. My eyes were never free of them. They were the constant salt in my mouth. My heart ached for him. My chest was stuffed tight with the guilt. I had to take the deepest of breaths to breathe. It was not easy.

It was early morning, and those huge white and grey birds were sailing in and out from the sea, screeching loudly. Beneath that, the constant shushing of the waves. Just to the left of the tent was a clearing, and Serena was there, bending over a pot, stirring something with a large wooden spoon. I watched her for a while and she did not

457

know I was there. She wore long trousers with patches sewn across each knee. Her hair was tied back while she cooked. There was a slab of wood beside her, and a large knife. She picked up the knife, chopped at something I could not see, and then sprinkled it into the pot. Satisfied, she got up, hauled the pot from the ground and hung it on a hook above the fire. On the grass behind her a long stick was stabbed into the ground. From the top of it three white and grey birds were hanging lifelessly by their feet. It was then that she saw me.

A smile crinkled up her eyes, and she wiped her hands down her legs before coming to me and ducking inside the tent. 'Dinner,' she nodded at the birds. 'Tate brought them down just a few minutes ago. He's one of the best shots we have. Takes after his mother.'

I looked away from her, my heart beating fast. I thought back to that terrifying black night, when the gunshots rang out after us, and the arrows soared through the air from the wagon and into the young flesh of two boys I once knew.

'You have questions for me?' she said, crossing her legs and leaning over them to peer at me. 'Now is a good a time as any. You can't let it all eat away at you, child. You must let it all out sooner or later. Anger, fear, confusion. Everything.'

I took a breath and looked back at her. Her dark hair was shot through with wisps of grey. Her eyes stared back into mine, hard and unflinching. 'You were born out here?' I asked. 'Like this?'

'No,' she shook her head at my first question and I was already more confused. 'I was born in Province 4.'

'What?'

'Province 4 has always struggled,' she said this slowly,

carefully, as if picking her words from too many she could use. 'It's further North. Some domes survived close to a place that was once called Manchester in the Old World. Lots of people survived there. I hear the latest count makes it a bigger population than Province 1. Well over a thousand people. But there are less resources. A lot of unhappiness. It's working, but not as well as 5, or 1, for instance.'

'You were not born a rebel?' I asked her, my throat dry and tight.

'Not on the outside,' she corrected me. 'But on the inside, yes. There were constant rebellions up in 4. For a long time, they had a weak leader. Governor Kyle was a good man in many ways. He tried to keep the peace, or so I was told. Tried to negotiate with Central Government. Listened to his people.'

'How did you get out?'

'We left when I was four years old,' she smiled. 'So I don't remember too much about it. But my parents told me stories. A fair few people left 4 over the years, and it was never made that hard for them to go. In the end, Governor Kyle was overthrown and charged with treason himself.'

My eyes grew wide. 'They threw out their own leader?'

'No, the people didn't. Central Government did. Province 4 was letting the whole system down. They needed to tighten things up again, so Kyle was thrown out and a new one brought in. People weren't happy to begin with but he soon worked his charms on them. They were appeased in several ways.'

'What do you mean?'

'They were allowed a second child. They also got the power on. Electricity.'

I stared at her, shaking my head. 'But we've only just been told people can have a second child. When did this happen? And what do you mean, *power?* The oil ran out generations before...'

She raised her eyebrows at me. A look that told me I ought to know better. 'It ran out for *some,* Lissie. Look, just get your head around the fact everything you've been told since you were born is a lie. That's the best advice I can give you. Anyway, we were long gone by then and I spent the rest of my childhood out here. Learning how to live alongside nature.'

I stared back outside. There was plenty of movement within the camp, despite the early hour. I could see figures moving about down on the beach. Small babies were crying to be fed, and mothers were shushing them gently. I scratched my head and rested my chin on my knees.

'It's all so confusing,' I sighed. 'I still don't understand why we all can't go where we want. My people would love it here, Serena. My parents would. Everyone would. They could all live like this, couldn't they?'

She lifted her chin and blinked up at the sky outside the tent. 'It's hard for you to understand,' she said, and yet again I had that feeling that she was picking her words carefully with me. 'The way you were brought up, you were protected from the truth. The truth about human nature even. And especially the truth about how societies work, how governments work. You know nothing of history? Is that right?' I nodded, and she glanced back down at me with a heavy, sorrowful sigh.

460

'There's time for me to teach you,' Serena went on. 'If you want me to. But the gist of it is, Lissie, people, *some* people, like power. They *crave* power. And when these sorts of people get into power, they get even crazier with it. And to a large extent, that's what happened to the Old World. A small handful of people came to own and control all of it. And when it wasn't working the way they wanted it to…' she drifted off for a moment, looking down at her lap where her hands had clasped together. 'They decided to wipe the slate clean and start again. It was nick-named Plan B.'

My mouth dropped open. 'You mean…?'

She smiled tightly. 'My grandparents were there. They passed on the truth to my parents and I've passed it on to my sons. Your Governor, and the rest of them, they tried to bury the truth and anyone who tried to speak it.' She chuckled softly and bumped against me. 'Of course, your Governor would call me crazy. They always make out the ones telling the truth are the crazy ones.'

I closed my mouth and then opened it again to ask a question. But there were too many questions, and they all hurt my head and my heart. How? Who? Why? Sensing my distress, Serena slipped a motherly arm around my shoulders and I could not resist relaxing into it.

'I've spent many years trying to understand it myself,' she said. 'But human nature is a strange and complicated thing. Power ruins. Fear wins. In many ways, people want to be controlled and told what to do. It's comforting for them, when there is so much confusion and uncertainty in life. We just believe there should be a choice. Stay within the Province and be well cared for. Well organised. Or come out here and try your luck. It's not easy out here. If you stay with us, you'll soon find that out, Lissie. You might want to go back!'

She said this with a grin, but it led me directly to my next question. 'Would they let me back, though?'

She looked at me evenly before shrugging slowly. 'I got back,' she said softly. 'Back into 4, and then transferred down to 1 because they needed healers, especially among the guards who deal with so many injuries.'

'That's how you got in there?'

'Yep. Back into 4 wasn't too tough, though they did interrogate me for weeks on end. I had an advantage really. Taken away by my crazy parents as a child! Lived a wild life on the brink of starvation until they died. I said I'd mostly been wandering alone.' Serena shrugged again. 'That's how it happened, Lissie. We wanted to help Jonas, and others like him.'

'So you went there first? And then Tate?'

She opened her mouth and then closed it again. I stared at her expression, trying to work out what I saw. It felt to me like she was buying time, trying to decide what she should and shouldn't say.

'I went first,' she nodded, eventually. 'I've been in there two years. Tate was caught a year ago. There were many whispers, Lissie, in Province 4. Distrust of Central Government. We had word that there were spies in 1 that would help us. Flynn, for instance. It seemed a worthwhile risk to get me and Tate in there and see who we could get out.'

I shook my head. Something was not right. 'That's a lot of risk to get one man out. You had no idea back then that me and Ned would be there. Or even Connor.'

She smiled briefly before lowering her eyes. 'You have a right to be distrustful, Lissie. I know what you saw on that screen. I also know what's been drummed into you since birth. Let's leave it at this, for now.' She looked up then, right into my eyes. 'We had our reasons. A greater plan, you might say. Something your great-grandmother would no doubt understand and approve of. And there is plenty of time to explain it all to you.'

I nodded, falling silent. I was still not sure I could trust her, but I didn't know why. Maybe she was right and it had something to do with those horrible images I had seen. I had still not told anyone the details of it. How could I, when I was unable to understand or process anything about it? I pushed that aside and tried to concentrate on what she had told me. It seemed incredibly risky, I thought, as she heaved herself back to her feet. Going back into a Province she had run from. Risking being arrested, tortured or killed. All to help someone else escape? How did she know they would transfer her to 1? I had never heard of anything like that happening before. I rubbed my eyes and shook my head. She looked back at the pot and then beyond that, with a smile she lifted an arm in a wave.

'Here's Aisha. I'll leave you girls to it. Anything else you want to know Lissie, you come and find me, all right? Promise me?'

I nodded and she nodded back, satisfied for now. With that, she stalked back to her cooking pot and left me there with even more questions than before.

'So what do you think?' Aisha wanted to know. Her hair was tied up tight and she had her bow and arrow over one shoulder. A furry black dog was wriggling around her ankles and she scooped him up and plonked him on my lap. 'Baby,' she said. 'Charlie had some little ones.'

I stared at the little scruff of a creature as it pushed its face into mine, huge brown eyes melting my heart. 'Charlie had children?'

'Yes. You want her? The others are all taken. She needs training up. We need dogs that can help us hunt.'

'I don't know how to do that...'

'I'm going to teach you,' she grinned. 'When you're ready.'

I wrapped my arms around the bundle of fur, and she let out this huge sigh and rested her chin on my arm. 'Aisha, I don't know how long I'm here for...I don't know anything...I don't know what to do.'

She smiled encouragingly. 'It's okay, Lissie. You've been through so much. Just take your time, okay?'

'And then what?'

'Well it's up to you. We won't lock you up or make you stay. You've got all the information now, Lissie. You know the truth finally. You know there is this world where we live, and there is the world you came from.'

I looked down at the little dog. 'Home,' I sighed.

'Do you miss it? You must miss it. And your parents.'

'I keep thinking about them, and Ned's. Will they know anything about what happened? What do you think Aisha? Will anything get back to them? Will they know Ned died? Will they know I got out?'

She shrugged. 'We can't know for sure, but I wouldn't be surprised if something is constructed. You know, another version of what happened. Your Governor told your people Connor attacked their food convoy and was arrested?'

'Yes.'

'So people there are afraid of being attacked. He might tell them you and Ned were taken from their guards. I don't know. What do you think would serve him better?'

I shook my head. 'I have no idea. I don't understand any of it. I don't get why they do what they do and I don't get why anyone had to die... I just don't.'

Aisha pulled one of her arrows free and lay it across her lap. She ran one finger back and forth against the tip. 'Maybe you should stay with us for a while,' she suggested gently. 'Until all your questions are answered. Then you can decide for yourself.'

'Would they ever allow me home again anyway?' I asked her wearily. 'To them I am a traitor. I'd be arrested again surely.'

'Maybe not. You could say we coerced you or forced you. You escaped and want to help them defeat us now you know our evil ways... That's what Serena did...'

'I know,' I said, bleakly, wondering why none of this new information made me feel any better. 'She just told me that story. I had no idea she was born in a Province.'

'Her parents were healers, like your mother is. They need more of them in 1 as it's the biggest and the most violent. That's how she got in to help Jonas.'

465

'What about Tate?' I asked. 'How could she let her own son go in there? Knowing what happens to people in there?'

'All part of a bigger plan,' she said, uneasily, for a moment, not making eye contact with me. 'It's complicated.'

For some reason, I had not expected her to say those words. All I could do was stare. I didn't know exactly why this information shocked me so much, but it did. Except shock was not the right word. It did something to me that I could not explain. My hairs all stood on end and I was tingling all over. I felt the need to shake myself violently. I felt like jumping to my feet and running as fast as I could.

Aisha looked slightly sheepish before putting her arrow back and dusting off her knees. 'So do you want to come hunting with me or not? You can bring that little fur ball. You can both start learning.'

I gulped down my fears, my words, my everything. This was not the time. Right or wrong, I was here. I lay my hand on the little dog and felt her quiver under my skin. I nodded hesitantly.

'Okay.'

We both got to our feet, and, carrying the fur ball, I followed Aisha away from the tent. She led me through the camp, weaving from side to side, responding to hello's and how are you's. People wanted to talk to me, I could see it in their eyes. But I looked down, I looked away. I was not ready for that yet.

'What are you going to call her?' Aisha asked me as we headed away from the camp, wandering barefoot through the trees until the sky was blotted out by the canopy above.

The baby dog was tucked up under one arm. I thought back to

that day that I saw Charlie, scrabbling away at the fence. How he started all this...How I had never seen one before. They were all supposed to be dead, I remembered. Extinct. Wiped out. He was dangerous, in the eyes of my father and the Governor. He had to be destroyed. Poor Charlie. All he did was show me the way...

'I think I'll name her after her dad,' I said, glancing at Aisha, who smiled in reply. 'She can be a Charlie too, can't she?'

'It's a great name. Course she can. Maybe she will be a better hunter than him!'

'You said he wasn't much good...'

'No, not really, but he did try. He was a good friend, and that was enough.'

'Hi Charlie,' I said, tickling her under the chin. 'Do you hear that? You've got to be better at hunting, and you've got to help me too. And I'll look after you, because I didn't look after Charlie...'

'Not your fault,' Aisha said it quickly and firmly. 'You have to start believing that, Lissie. None of it is your fault. Your Grandma gave you a gift and you absolutely did the right thing with it.'

'You mean I started a load of trouble and got my best friend killed?'

'No. You didn't do that. I really hope you can believe that one day.'

'I miss him so much Aisha...' I sighed and wiped my eyes. 'It's horrible living without him.'

'I know,' she said, as we walk on. 'But it won't always be. I

467

promise you.'

We walked on in silence for a while. I gazed around us, at this new world I found myself in. Trees I had never seen before. Birds I had never heard. Furry things with bushy tails that scuttled up the trunks away from us. Aisha took out an arrow and winked at me.

'Dinner is everywhere.'

And she showed me how to tread so silently that it was like we were not there. And she showed me how to stay so still it was as if we did not exist. We became shadows. And she showed me how to spot the things that we could eat. The things that we could pick, and there were so many things. And the clover and the daisies made me think of Ned, and as ever, the tears ran down my cheeks. And they were everywhere, these wild things. They'd escaped the domes, just like us. They'd escaped and started again. Just like the tree of rebels.

I watched Aisha and I learned quickly. And all the time I was thinking about what she said to me. What she said to me about Serena, about going home, about getting back in...

I didn't know if she did it on purpose but nothing would surprise me anymore.

I didn't know if she knew that she had planted a seed...

Coming soon...

Return To The Tree Of Rebels

'My great-grandmother once tried to tell me a story from the Old World...A story about the last people on Earth. It must have been terrifying for them to realise their end days had come, that the last war had destroyed everything...But some survived. They thought they had left evil behind. They thought they lived in Everlasting Peace, and they thought that there were no more guns, and no more war.

But I found out the truth. The evil never left. The evil carried on, and duped the people into believing a lie. They believed that they were safe and provided for, but the truth was, they were living inside a prison. I escaped that prison, but now it is time to go back. Now I must tell them the truth. Now I must start a new war. I must go back to the home I was banished from. To where it all began. I must return to the tree of rebels.'

About The Author

Chantelle Atkins was born and raised in Dorset, England. She still resides there now with her husband, four children and multiple pets. She is addicted to both reading and music, and is on a mission to become as self-sufficient as possible. Her debut Young Adult novel, The Mess Of Me deals with eating disorders, self-harm, fractured families and first love. Her second novel, The Boy With The Thorn In His Side follows the musical journey of a young boy attempting to escape his brutal home life. She is also the author of This Is Nowhere, This Is The Day and has recently released a collection of short stories related to her novels called Bird People and Other Stories.

You can find out more about Chantelle and her books by following her here;

Blog; https://chantelleatkins.com/

Facebook Page; https://www.facebook.com/chantelleatkinswriter/

Twitter; https://twitter.com/Chanatkins

Pinterest; https://uk.pinterest.com/chantelleatkins/

Instagram; https://www.instagram.com/chantelleatkinswriter/

Goodreads; https://www.goodreads.com/author/show/7142038.Chantelle_Atkins

You can also sign up for the author newsletter and receive free short stories, exclusive sneak peeks and free books! http://eepurl.com/bVVbGD

Finally…

Thank you so much for reading this book! Is it cheeky to ask one more thing of you?

Would you consider leaving a review? Reviews are fuel for writers!

If you enjoyed this book, or even if you didn't, please consider leaving an honest review on the site of your choice. Reviews can be short, just a sentence or even one word. Reviews are important as they let the author know what they did right (or wrong!) and they encourage other readers to try the book.

Your help in spreading the word is truly appreciated!

The Tree of Rebels

Bonus Material

Tales From Province 5

We Are Seeds

The chain pulls us on.

Chain link. Linking us all up. Turning us from three people into one moving organism. Or four, if you count the guard who pulls us, hauling his end of the chain up and over his shoulder, like he is pulling a train.

Inevitably, we are made weaker than them. We are feeling the strain.

And so they walk faster, harder, taller, and we are the weight they drag, the baggage they lug, the rebels they own.

Linked, jangling, we stumble on obligingly, like small hurried children tugged on by an impatient and displeased mother.

I lead the way like Mother Duck. Followed by the girl, who is followed by the red-haired boy. Broader, older, I hope to shield them from the sun and from the worst.

The girl, I do not worry so much about. Her legend is now known. We see her as one of our own, as a seed from our tree. Though the wind blew her to different soil, arid and bleak, she inherited strong roots from her elders, and from the past. I see her from the corner of my eye, and her face is straight while her eyes glare murderously. I can only imagine the thinkings going on behind such eyes. Her shoes flap about, ruined by the jagged landscape. She turns her head from side to side quickly, examining her ever changing surroundings.

This makes the excitement tremor in my chest. I think; she has seen nothing yet. She thinks she knows but this is only the beginning. I wonder, can she stand it? My feeling is yes.

But not so much the red-haired boy. Brought down by vicious needless blows when we were removed from the wagon, he has suffered from it since. Grunting, panting, sweating, he is all pale and shiny while his eyes loom huge and fearful. He is small and weak. He

472

scurries behind her and when he can lift his tortured eyes, he gasps in pain and his eyes are only on her.

The chain loops from the manacles around his wrists, to the girls, to mine and onto the guards who hurry us on to deliver us as promised. Clinking, jangling, jostling, sweating under the burning sun, the bright orange eye from above.

Where we were off loaded not far from Province 5, the landscape was barren, dead, a dustbowl of nothingness. Then we were marched on to where the land had replenished itself. Sweet Mother Nature had returned to her child. Soothed and healed, her green fingers reached out as far as the eye could see. Her work was swift, and as we hurried on towards the ruins of cities, we saw her work everywhere. Trees growing through buildings. Flowers dancing in the breeze that blew through the skeletons of rusted vehicles. I heard the girl gasping in wonder behind my shoulders.

The dead dust and bones of the Old World. The graveyard of civilisation. Wrecked and twisted and mangled and confused. Dulled and bleached by the sun, scraped dry by the wind, crawled over and infested by Mother Nature and her rampant, hungry offspring.

It is a wondrous thing, and I take pleasure in her return, in her vengeance. But still, they march us on towards their victory. They still think that they have won. I can see the delight in their young eyes and in the flush of their cheeks. The irony of defeat is lost on them. They cannot see it in the landscape as I can.

And onwards they lead us, back to their leaders.

What will happen there will surprise us, and maybe them. I do not fear them, nor anything else. Like my mother and father taught me, I believe in the cyclical nature of living things. We return to where we started. The soil is always our home. I teach the girl and the boy when I can, when the guards eyes are not on us, but on the monstrous glass domes that rear from the sky line.

I pick weeds the guards do not see or know. I pass them back and we chew and eat, our energy refuelled by the feast Mother Nature has provided. Poking through the broken concrete paths of yesterday. Grass and dandelions and daisies and clover and sorrel.

I see in the young ones faces. They do not know these things in the dried out husk they were born in. They were spoiled there, babied, provided for and lied to. Everything fresh and vibrant in the precious domes, everything controlled and delivered to their grateful, waiting hands. And the land around the domes, silent and waiting. Sullen and impatient. Waiting to start again, waiting to start something.

On we are marched, on we are taken, stolen from the bosom of our loved ones to be delivered as sacrifice, but no matter this. They do not know that we are seeds. They do not know or understand that if they bury us, we will rise again, we will rise in greater numbers, greener and stronger than before. They do not know that our bones will fertilise the land they have imprisoned. That one way or another the cycle of things will go on.

When the domes of Province 1 loom near, they steal our sight and we cannot look away. The red-haired boy suffers now. He lolls and stumbles and the girl slows to allow him to lean upon her. I can see in her face that she fears for his life. I smile gently at them and I want to tell them to not be afraid, to never be afraid of life or nature. For they are simply a part of everything and nothing more, nothing less. Pain will always end.

We trudge and clink and jangle past the shiny bright domes. The blots on the landscape that survived the last war just like all the others. Of course, that was the purpose of them. You can see the sky reflected back at you. You can see the tops of trees and plants. You can see everything curved and shining, lush and full inside of them. They are beautiful and they give and sustain life, yet they are a trap and a lie.

Inside my chest muscles tighten, breath grows short, excitement rises. Past the domes, past the scurrying ants that serve them, onwards to the Great Wall of Province 1. Onwards to face what lies within. I look over my shoulder, see the terror in their young faces, and I have to fight hard not to smile. I wish to tell them that we are all seeds but I fear it would mean nothing to them right now. So we walk on.

And I look forward to what waits within. I look forward to retribution, to justice, to reunion. I look forward to being buried and to growing again.

Jonas The Great

Jonas could have been fifty-five or ninety-five. He was in a state of ruin where age and time no longer mattered. He said he had once had a certificate of birth, but that had caught fire in the Old World. Jonas could not remember exactly how old he was, or what had happened to him.

He stood, every day that they allowed him, in the centre of the square. If you could see him, then you could also smell him. Barefooted, his toe nails clawed and yellowed, he referred to himself as Jonas The Great. He made his stand with an addled mind, but would not bend or yield or fluctuate, until they said enough is enough and shut him down for the night.

His trousers were old denim, short in the leg, naked around the knees, large in the waist and held up with string. His stance was also a dance. He could not stand still. He swayed and dipped, lunged and sighed, but always on the same warm spot. His shirt had one button left which hung on for dear life, just above the belly button that no one wished to glimpse. His chest was on show, two hardened dried nipples on either side of bone and waste. His arms skeletal, his shirt cuffs frayed and fluttering in the wind.

The dust of Province 5 coated his skin, his sparse grey hair and the inside of his mouth. He tasted it there, warning his words away, from the moment he started to dance to the moment they urged him back home. Jonas The Great always laughed when they came for him. He put up no fight and offered no spite. He just laughed and lolled loosely into their grip.

The children of the Province knew he was a relic; like the broken machines, and the books and photos in the museum. Only Jonas was not locked up under glass. Their parents walked around him, as it was not their business to listen to him, or to shut him up. They politely ignored him, and warned their children that they should eat their greens so they wouldn't end up like Jonas in the square.

For the children, Jonas passed letters. They had no time to stand and talk, so he wrote to them instead. He wrote notes and letters and dropped them like confetti. He didn't worry about what happened to the letters, or who read or didn't read them. Some were snatched, burnt, stolen or thrown away, and some blew away on the wind. It didn't matter to Jonas, because he was a tree and the letters were his seeds.

One day a boy named Tobias Green picked up a letter and took it home to read. In the letter Jonas The Great told him that the people from the Old World had let it die because they were in love with money, plastic, and the world wide web.

Tobias imagined a great spider web, made by such a monstrous and gigantic spider that it stretched across the world. Jonas wrote that the web was just as sticky, and that millions upon millions of people became trapped in it, glued to it, unable to break free. Their feet were no longer on the ground or part of it. People, the letter said, lived imaginary lives back then, making imaginary money, to buy imaginary things. These things were mostly made of plastic.

Tobias knew about plastic because he had scavenged some from the ruins. Depending on what you found, you could take it to the museum and swap it for tokens to spend in the stores. Just recently Tobias had found a strange plastic rectangle with lumps and bumps on it. He took it to the museum and they gave him enough tokens to hire one of the town bikes for two whole hours. He hadn't asked them what the strange rectangle was, or had once been.

He had once found a metal box full of colourful bricks. The bricks were dirty, some of them loose, some of them stuck onto other bricks. In the museum, they had taken it seriously from his hands to be washed up. Another day he saw it on display behind glass in the 'Old Toys' section.

Plastic came from oil, the letter told him, *I remember this. They dug it out of the ground and the sea. It damaged the world but people needed the oil for so many things, and plastic was one of them. Plastic for things they wanted.*

Jonas didn't say much, but he wrote things down when he remembered them, when they seemed important to pass on.

I was only a child when I came here, he wrote, *but I can hear my parents telling me why, telling me what happened. And then, like so many others, they died in the dust.*

Jonas was crazy and old and ragged. Nobody paid him any mind. He remembered that was how it always was. People were always too busy, too busy with the day to day, with whatever had them trapped, with whatever had them addicted, with whatever they were in love with, or slaves to. No one listened because they had no need to, not then, not now.

Jonas The Great soon became a problem in the square because he would not stop writing words and throwing them to the wind. He didn't really expect any of his letters to grow roots and plant themselves, but others feared that they would. One day Jonas was gone. The people of Province 5 were told that he had the best death you could hope for. That he died in his sleep, happy and old and smiling. He no longer swayed and swung in the square in the centre of town. He no longer scattered words as people passed. People sighed and missed him and his crazy ways. Then life went on.

The Hunt

She runs, and at first she runs for fun. She runs though the streams of sunlight which light up the dusty ground, breaking it up into bright fragments. She jumps from one piece to another, using the light and the shadows as stepping stones through the forest. She laughs when she runs. She tests out her flight. This fast, this fast, faster, faster...*this fast!* The dried, curled leaves crackle and snap beneath her bare feet.

She stops running when the birds take off, because her father has taught her to pay attention to the birds. First one, then two, then the whole flock, rising up and out of the treetops. She stands still, thinking, listening, sniffing. She turns her face up to the dappled sky just visible through the canopy of leaves and boughs.

Her eyes widen and her mouth opens and her heart stops beating for just a moment., while her feet concentrate on picking up vibrations from the ground. She feels it, the ground thrumming beneath her heels, under her toes. She takes a deep breath and her heart leaps into action, and her right foot lifts off and then lands with a thud, propelling her forward, putting the process into action.

She runs, and now it is not for fun. It is to outrun the noise behind her, and the earth trembling menacingly under her feet. She runs as fast as she can, zipping around trees, leaping over logs, pumping her arms with her small chest thrust forwards, her hair streaming out behind.

The birds are not just taking off now, they are screaming. Circling and flapping and crying out their warning, and she would scream too, except she knows it would slow her down and steal the oxygen from her limbs. She runs from the noise, but it is coming up behind her. Hooves pounding the earth, trampling it down, crushing everything in its path into submission. The hooves are sending a message through vibrations to her as she runs. *We are coming, we will catch you, we are faster than you!*

She runs as fast as she can, and she wishes she had not wandered off from her brother, but he was annoying her so with his determination to hunt rabbits, and not have fun or climb trees, and making her be quiet all the time. She'd just wanted to play. She'd just wanted to run and skip and climb and chatter. And now this. She is running from them.

478

She is running from the dogs, and she can hear their blood thirsty yipping, and she runs in terror and in hope, thought deep down inside she already knows she cannot outrun them. She is not even sure if she is going the right way. Heading back to her brother or running the wrong way?

Her mind turns to hiding, and she remembers what her mother said. Get down, get under, get small, curl up. But there is nowhere she can duck down and curl up, so she looks up at the trees instead, and she thinks, I am such a good climber, I am one of the best, I can do it! She keeps running, now searching the trees for a bough low enough to welcome her.

She finally spots one and races towards it. It is a good one, and the noise is getting closer now, and she can hear the breath snorted through the horses flared nostrils. She throws herself at the low branch with no time to waste, and she is panicked and scrambling and her breath is now ragged and painful in her throat and chest. Her feet kick and flail, her grip will not hold and she falls back, fingernails tearing at the bark as she fights to hold on. She lands on her backside, winded, not blindsided by terror, and a dog has broken ahead of the hunt, a tongue streaming, mouth frothing beast who wants to kill her, who wants to tear her limb from limb, and this time she throws herself back at the tree and begs it to take her, to help her. She digs in with her knees, pushing herself up, and she closes her eyes as the relief spins through her, and she can hear the dog barking and snapping around the bottom of the tree.

She thinks; I did it, I am safe, I am safe, and she starts to stand up, shaking like a leaf, reaching with both arms up to the next branch so she can get higher and hide. It is higher up than she would have liked, but she has to do it, has to stretch, jump and get that grip, and wrap those trembling, jellied legs onto the branch, out of reach. And she takes another breath and tells herself she can do it, as more dogs arrive and circle the tree in a teeth snapping frenzy.

She takes a breath and leaps. And for a moment she is flying, not connected to anything, not the tree or the ground, or the beasts that mean her harm, and then her fingers make blessed contact with the skin of the branch, and then something has her around the middle. And it all happens so quickly, the snaring and the pulling and the falling back down to earth. She is torn down, ripped from the tree and she hits the other branch on her way down, and she can't quite believe that any of this is happening. They told you scary stories, they scared you with myths and warned you not to go off too far on your own. But you never saw anything, you never knew whether it was really true, you never believed that monsters and men in black would want to catch you and take you away.

But it was happening.

She is down on the ground, flat on her back and staring back up at them. They have climbed down from their horses, masks in place as they gather around her. She is so terrified she cannot breathe and her bladder lets go, releasing warmth between her legs which spreads out beneath her. They stare down at her, while the dogs sniff and snuffle and she wonders if she was their intended prey all along, or merely a surprise, a piece of luck.

And then she decides to fight. Like her people told her to do, if this ever happened to her. Fight back, they said, always fight back, never give up, do anything you can and don't stop, ever. So she struggles and she kicks and she hits and pulls and screams and bites. It is a good fight and she wishes that her brother was able to see it, but they are all laughing at her.

'Ferals,' they say sneeringly, as they lift and bound her and throw her onto the back of her horse. The ropes bind her to the animal and the game is over. One of the masked men jumps onto the horse and they all are getting back on, all laughing and cheering and hooting. Her hair falls down, so long it almost drags on the ground and she hopes her brother finds the patch where she let her bladder loose. She hopes he finds her trail and gets back to her family in time.

The man on the horse looks over his shoulder and down at her face, as she turns it up to view him. She can only see his eyes, but both the amusement and the disgust in them is plain to her. She shivers violently and begins to fight again. She knows she has to. It is all she has.

'Keep that up as long as you like,' he growls at her. 'You're not getting out of that. You're coming back with us to learn your lesson. You'll be grateful too. Grateful for a better life.'

'Needs major work that one,' another voice laughs as the horses start

480

to trot back through the forest. 'The young ones are the worst! Bloody wild animals.'

She listens to their words as they take her away from everything she knows. Rehabilitation, they say, education, treatment. She keeps fighting, because she was taught to, because that is all there ever is, and you never know, it might work. She might slip free, she might work the ropes loose, she might do something...

Made in the USA
Columbia, SC
19 July 2017